COMPANY OF GHOSTS

J. KYLE TURNER

Company of Ghosts by J. Kyle Turner ©2025

All rights reserved.

LEGAL DISCLAIMER: No part of this book may be reproduced or transmitted in any form or by any means, electronic or mechanical, including photocopying, recording or by any information storage and retrieval system, without written permission from the author. You may not reprint, resell or distribute the contents of this book without express written permission from the author.

Without limiting the author's exclusive rights, any unauthorized use of this publication to train generative artificial intelligence (AI) technologies is expressly prohibited.

This book is a work of fiction. Any references to historical events, real people, or real places are used fictitiously. Other names, characters, places and events are products of the author's imagination, and any resemblance to actual events, places or persons, living or dead, is entirely coincidental.

First Edition.

Editor: Valerie Gwynn, PenGwynnEditing.com
Design: Liz Mrofka, WhatIf?Publishing.com
Cover Illustration: ©Bruce Brenneise, BruceBrenneise.com

ISBN: 979-8-9994604-0-0

COMPANY OF GHOSTS

PREFACE

I collected secrets as a child. From my perch behind the counter, I could hear every word spoken in my father's little shop, and I repeated all of them. I didn't yet understand that there was such a thing as a private conversation, that it was rude to be interested in the details of a stranger's life.

My father had a very practical solution to the problem. Mind the shop. He repeated the phrase any time I tilted my head toward a whisper or spent too long tidying a display and sent me scurrying off to a far corner to sweep some imaginary dust across the floor. I think he feared I'd grow up to be a gossip. Considering my career as a historian, he might not have been far off. The line between rumor and history is frighteningly thin.

In any case, half the fault lies with him. He had so many secrets of his own, and as the only parent, he had twice the practice at deflecting my curiosity. With so little bread at home, it was only natural that I'd go looking elsewhere for crumbs.

I had a different solution to the problem, of course. As far as I could tell, secrets were only dangerous when you shared them. *Knowing* a secret hurt no one and was immensely satisfying in its own right. I was still too young to have learned that bitter lesson, that knowing a thing could be dangerous, too. Meeting Andza changed all that, and as fate would have it, I was alone in the shop when he came in.

The door swung open one evening, and a rush of cold air swept in. All the display candles along the back wall flickered and guttered out. My father had told me to put the covers on them, and as usual I had forgotten. The back wall of the shop was thrown into dimness, full of thin tendrils of smoke just visible in the light from the street. The door swung closed, and the man in the doorway crossed the floor to stand in front of my father's counter.

"How much for a wax candle?" he asked.

"Six peras," I told him, already drinking him in. He stood somewhere around six feet, maybe less, with close-cropped hair and a thin layer of stubble. Plain clothes, but tidy. Thin in the way that a tightened string is thin, all full of quiet energy.

"Are those unscented?" he asked. "I need a steady light, not a bottle of perfume." He was impatient, I thought, though not with me.

"Eight for the unscented," I told him. Then, catching his expression, "We save on the oils, but the wicks are harder to make."

"Yes, fine. I'll take two."

He paid, and I wrapped his purchase and tied the paper with a length of string. He tapped the side of his thumb against the counter while he waited, and the motion distracted me so much that I had to restart. When I finished, I handed him the package. He turned to leave but then hesitated.

"What's your name, child?" he asked me, one hand still on the counter.

"Jalina."

"Good night, Jalina," he said. And then he left.

Afterward I sat on the little stool behind my father's counter and replayed all the details of the conversation in my head, a habit I've never really grown out of. After half an hour my father returned from his errand and made me relight all the candles that had blown out. We stayed open for another hour and then went upstairs to eat a late supper. Father worked while he ate, whispering to himself about the shop or about money that we didn't have, which left me free to sit quietly and ponder. I thought about the man I'd met and the short conversation we'd had. I decided that I liked him, though I didn't yet know his name.

The next morning there was a knock at our door.

I slept on the very top floor of our house, in a little loft by the window, so I barely heard the noise. My father stirred, then walked downstairs. I waited until I heard voices, then put on the little house slippers we wore in the winter and crept down the ladder to the main floor. From there, I tiptoed past our sleeping cat and leaned over the staircase that led down into the shop.

"—would have been about thirty or forty, not from around here."

It was the constable, talking to my father. About what, I couldn't guess, but I knew it had to be something important. People from other nations might not understand the signif-icance of this. Contrary to popular belief, we *do* have petty saints in Kerra. A large town like Casmhe would have at least one Reader to perform basic acts of divination, but law and long custom prevented them from interfering with matters of state. As state officials, our constables did their work by going door to door.

"I could try to make a list, if you like. We couldn't have had more than twenty or thirty customers yesterday."

"And you recognized them all?" The constable spoke crisply. He likely had other stops to make. "No strangers?"

"None," my father answered.

"Then that's enough. Sorry to bother you." A moment later the door opened again and swung closed.

I heard my father's footsteps approach the stairs, and I rushed to the stove to make some tea so that I'd have an excuse for being up and about. He said nothing when he saw me, only kissed the top of my head and sat on the edge of his mattress.

"Who was downstairs?" I asked.

"An angry customer. He said you'd given him the wrong change."

"No, it wasn't!" I shot back. But then I saw him smiling and realized he'd caught me.

"Sorry."

"A proper father would scold you, but you're making tea, so I suppose I'll have to forgive you."

The kettle reached a boil, so I quieted the flame and poured the water into a small teapot. When it had steeped, I poured two cups and handed one to him. He set it on his nightstand to cool.

"What did he want?"

"Only to ask if I had any little girls who asked too many questions. It's against the law now, you know." A favorite joke of his. He always found it funny. I never did.

"Father!"

"Only joking, little one." He smiled briefly, then frowned. "Lina . . . Did you sell anything yesterday while I was out?"

I felt a sudden urge to lie. My father held so many secrets of his own—secrets I felt I had every right to know. Whenever I asked him about his life before the war, or about my mother's death, he refused to answer. But he expected me to give my secrets away just for the asking?

It was futile, though. He would find out as soon as he checked the ledger. "Two candles," I said. Then, struck with a sudden inspiration, "Warren came to pick some up just before you came back."

Warren was the clerk's assistant. He was two years older than me, born mute after a difficult pregnancy. He'd become a ward of the city after his parents passed and sometimes ran errands. I told the lie smoothly and hoped my father wouldn't notice.

But he was already drinking his tea. "Good," he said, his eyes closed and his nose just over the rim of the cup. "Otherwise, I'd have to chase poor Gellin down the street and tell him my daughter was an accomplice to murder."

Guilt weighs heavily on me. I suppose it does for everyone, but as with other skills, things are easier for those with natural talent and years of practice. At the time I had neither, so I worried constantly.

For a month I believed they would catch him at the border, still carrying the murder weapon. They'd torture a confession out of him and drag him back to Casmhe behind a pair of mules. There would be a trial, and in madness and desperation, he would name me as his accomplice to lessen his own sentence.

I saw the ripples of shock spread through my friends and neighbors in the crowd, heard my mother's desperate wailing (my mother featured constantly in my daydreams, though she died when I was an infant). I saw my father wrap an arm around her and bury his head in shame, and I hated them both for excluding me in their grief.

Later we found out there was no murder weapon. The sole witness, an old woman who lived across from poor Miss Talia, had only thought she'd seen an upraised arm on the strange and fearsome silhouette. The vicious broadsword, the hacked-up body: we had invented these details ourselves. The magistrate had released the report to silence our guesses.

No, the late Miss Talia had not been the subject of any violence. Yes, a strange man had forced his way into her apartment. No, he hadn't stolen anything. By all appearances they had surprised each other, the victim's heart had given out, and the would-be thief had fled the scene.

But rumors are pernicious things. They'll cling to bare rock, if they have to. Besides, we still had the questions of "Who?" and "Why?" to occupy our thoughts. Was he merely a thief, or was there something more to the story? Was he a spurned lover who had tracked her down? An angry brother who had been cheated out of his inheritance? An abandoned son who had come seeking closure? Talia had been mysteriously private, so all theories were possible, and none could be proved or disproved.

In the end, the rumors died down the way most do: simple repetition. The moment someone hears an old version of the tale, the first death knell is sounded. By the end of the week, the coffin is closed, the earth shoveled over, and the marker erected. Two months after her death, everyone seemed to forget that Talia had lived or died.

Except for me, who had helped to kill her.

⁓

I passed these dismal days in the pages of books. No lurid dramas or tales of suspense. My imagination conjured enough of those already. But I couldn't quite rid myself of my interest in people, of their daily lives and habits. I read biographies instead: personal accounts, diaries, letters. All were of famous people, like the Dowager Empress of Ghant or the chief concubine of the Hensian Talarch. I spent more time at the library than I did at my own home and often hid a book or two under the counter to read while I worked. In the space of three months, I learned about the fall of the Red Empire, the northern expeditions of the previous century, and the lives and deaths of a few dozen famous rulers from the past six hundred years.

My father noticed the change in me. "Where has my little bird gone?" he asked one evening. "She used to sit behind the counter, just there, and tilt her head to listen every time someone spoke."

I turned the page of my book but didn't look up. "She must have flown away, Father."

He crossed the room to where I sat and lifted my chin. The candles behind him wavered, but every detail of the room was crystal clear. "And where would you like to fly, my little one?"

I didn't answer. I just sat there staring back at him. I couldn't understand what he meant. I was fourteen years old, and no one had ever asked me that question before.

"I don't know," I said finally. "I suppose I'll learn to run the shop."

Spring came, and with it the promise of warmer weather. I'd made good on my promise to learn my father's business, and so the shelves of our little shop were always stocked, always tidy. I enjoyed the routine of running the shop: so many hours for this task, so many for this one, until the whole day was filled with work that was neither too hard nor too easy.

It brought me closer to my father, too, which was something I didn't properly appreciate at the time. Though we lived in the same house, I'd always considered his world as something apart from mine. But for a season at least, the gap vanished, and I grew closer to him than I ever had before. Which made what came next even more surprising.

We'd closed the shop early after a slow morning, and the two of us sat down at the table together over a plate of cold sandwiches and a pitcher of cider. My father looked at me as he spoke.

"The Reader says the rains have stopped for the season. The road south should be passable within a week or two."

"Are we going somewhere?"

He took a sip of his cider. The rim of the cup hid his expression. "I thought we might take a trip to the town of Sharme. We need to get there early, before enrollment closes, or you'll have to wait until the fall."

I had no idea what to say. I think I stammered something unintelligible.

"I'll be fine in the shop. And anyway, you needn't be gone longer than a year. And you'll be quite safe, I think. Sharme itself is not so much larger than Casmhe."

And in the space of a breath, my father had quieted all my fears, long before I ever gave voice to them. People often say that I have a knack for listening to people, for peeling away their many layers and seeing what lies beneath. If I have any gift at all, it is surely inherited.

"But what about—" I trailed off. Surely there had to be something. "What about all my clothes?" I finished. "What will I wear?" I must have seemed stupid, more flighty girl than somber scholar. But my father laughed.

"Space for them on the wagon, little one. And a few books, too, I should think. Though I can't imagine you'll need them. The Library must have plenty of their own."

I won't bore you with the details. Suffice it to say that I passed my entrance exams and enrolled as a student. I missed my father terribly at first but less and less as the months passed. I loved my classes and got along well with most of my classmates. I spent countless hours in the city itself, wandering Sharme's maze of streets before coming home each night to the little room that I didn't have to share with anyone else.

I chose to study history, with a focus on ancient civilizations. Even now, I can't imagine a less useful way to spend one's life. But that didn't bother me at the time, and anyway, no one in academia will ever dissuade you from wasting your life on something. If anything, I developed a reputation as a model student. For the first time in my life, it was safe to be who I was. My curiosity was a virtue, not a vice.

Best of all, the night of Talia's murder seemed to fade with each passing month. I could remember the details, but there wasn't any weight attached to them. It was as if I'd carried the memory with me to Sharme but left the guilt behind in Casmhe.

Every summer, the teachers at the Library hold assessments, which all students must endure. First-year students need only demonstrate a reasonable amount of progress in their chosen discipline. But for the older students, the second and third years especially, assessments mark a time when you're pushed to pursue a narrower focus.

Once you make that choice, your life changes considerably. Certain areas of the Library become open to you, while others are rarely ever visited again. Your teachers shrink down to two or three veteran scholars, and you and your classmates become so busy that you're reduced to nodding at each other in the hallway over your armful of books.

My assessors were a pair of modest historians, Dran and Liseth, a married couple well into their sixth decade together. They bickered constantly but without any real heat. I enjoyed them both immensely. The classroom where we met occupied half the third floor of the teacher's wing, with fresh breezes and pleasant views at every window. A stack of desks sat in the corner, unused for years but kept against the possibility of a surge in enrollment. A crate of talc pencils beneath the north window gave the air a musty, dry quality. Despite the humble surroundings, I fidgeted beneath the weight of the proceedings.

"You'll need to master your Ghant, of course. Your grasp of the lower forms is faltering at best, and don't think I haven't noticed." This from Dran, who fixed me with a look like a vulture daring the carcass to move. I didn't.

"Once you stop speaking the language like a child," he continued, "you can get into the real texts. Gramme the Blind has a three-volume set that's worth reading. He was an idiot, but he was the only one paying attention when the Hensian Empire started, and no small irony there."

Liseth interrupted him with an irritated gesture, slashing the air in front of her with a liver-spotted hand. "Bah. Reading, reading. Are we scholars or buzzards, circling the same dead things year after year? Where are you from, child?"

"Casmhe," I said. "A small house on the merchant's row, not far from the town center."

"And how long would you say the road is between Casmhe and Sharme?"

I smiled. "Just long enough to reach, I think."

She cackled, a harsh, unpleasant sound. "Good, that's good. The world has plenty of uses for witless girls, and none of them are worth your time." The smile disappeared. "You're not seasoned yet, though, and I won't inflict another naive scholar on the world. Too much room for pretentiousness to creep in, eh?" She shot a pointed look at her husband, who frowned.

"The point is," she continued, "there's a great deal of difference between knowing the lines on a map and walking them. You can't *be* the next Gramme if all you ever do is read about him." She folded her arms, a sure sign she'd chosen a course. "I have an acquaintance named Andza."

Dran snorted. "Ah, yes. Our itinerant scholar."

"Itinerant?" I asked.

"Homeless, if you prefer. Sleeps in a wagon, teaches a course every three or four years. Doles out mountains of assignments and then leaves again before grading any of them." Dran looked thoughtful. "He's either an idiot or a genius, and I've never decided which."

"He may be an idiot," Liseth allowed, "but he pays attention, and no small irony there."

Dran rolled his eyes.

I held back a smile, a study in polite curiosity. "What does he teach?"

Liseth grinned like a fox. "Speaking as a member of the committee that approves his research stipend, he'll teach whatever we damn well want him to. More importantly," she leaned forward, "he's recently requested a pair of research assistants from among the students here. Make sure you're one of them. I'd hate to see the opportunity wasted on someone else."

This led to an argument: how many years I'd fall behind, what books I'd have to bring on a journey, whether I'd bring any books at all, how I could possibly continue my education in the dimly lit common room of a noisy inn. The afternoon light reached in through the window and warmed my shoulders, and the rhythm of their conversation lulled me into a kind of daydream. I fell to musing. *Andza,* I thought. *What a curious name.*

And so my secret guilt came back to haunt me and, with it, the story you now hold in your hands. Interested? I'd be surprised. Even as forewords go, this one is remarkably indulgent. I'll acknowledge the touch, though, if you'll allow me an explanation.

Andza's book summarizes the story I'm about to tell in one neat, efficient sentence.

It reads:

And so I set out from the Library at Sharme with two assistants, seeking the answers to several unanswered questions behind the latest war of succession.

No indulgence there, you'll notice. Every word is carefully chosen, stripped of all emotion and judgment. No comments on the all-too-common melees between Kerra's bloodthirsty princedoms. No names, when the mention of assistants gives all the necessary context. No "hoping" when "seeking" will suffice.

That opening line was Andza to the letter. Spare, unyielding, precise.

And yet, you can almost picture the man behind the prose. A bit too serious, perhaps. Uncommonly driven. The kind of man who would sneak into a home to question a woman about secrets she'd long thought buried. Someone who could remember every detail of the conversation for the rest of his life, constantly arranging them until the full picture emerged. A man who wouldn't hesitate to trade a fortune for a fact, a scar for a whisper. Fearless. Heroic, in his own quiet sort of way.

This book is not written as a counterpoint to Andza's work, but as a complement. To fill in the details that were too unimportant for the original, too insufficient in gravity and meaning. To give names to the people history forgot to include, and to explain, I hope, why we chose to reveal what we did.

Most of all, I've written this book to remind us that there is no comfort in bitter secrets, no grave deep enough to bury the past. It always comes back to haunt us. The only way to escape it is to go looking for it.

PART ONE

The Fifteen-Year Thread

CHAPTER ONE

Sharme sits on the western side of a hill and is the only city I know of that was built for a single hour of the day. The people who live there rise well after dawn. Once awake, they only take short breaks for tea or small plates of food from the countless market stalls that line the streets. They talk while they work, gesturing wildly with their hands, laughing and singing, burning through their energy in one frenzied rush. Then, just before nightfall, they filter back to their squat little houses and sit on their porches to bask in the sunset.

The view is magnificent: a hillside of red roofs descending toward the plains; a row of low clouds on the horizon, lit by the last fires of the day. Visitors to the city are entranced by it, but those who have lived in Sharme their whole lives hardly notice. This is a sacred hour, meant for sitting quietly with your eyes closed and your hands and mind perfectly still. Even the children know better than to peek.

I sat with my friend Elaise on the terrace of a small teahouse. As second-year students, we were familiar with the ritual, but not beholden to it. We knew the best places to spend the evening hour and which places got annoyed at us for talking the whole time.

More importantly, we knew better than to spend our final nights of freedom indoors. It was the first month of autumn and the last week before classes started. In a month, we'd be overwhelmed by assignments that lasted until curfew, but for now we were free to visit the city whenever we liked.

Elaise sighed. "There's a poem about this, I bet."

"About sunsets?" I snorted. "I imagine so."

She waved a hand at me while she sipped her tea. Tea in Sharme is a potent thing, almost gritty with spices. Only the very brave take more than a small sip.

"This feeling, I mean," she continued. "Something in Hensian—"

"Oh, there's definitely a poem about it in Hensian."

"Joy and Sadness on the Eve of a Great Journey," she said with mock sincerity. "*Hela cath muira*—or is it *muiren?*" She gave up. "Ridiculous language, by the way. Have I told you that?"

"No one's making you become a linguist," I pointed out. "I'm sure there are still plenty of grapes in Greymarsh that need tending."

"Hush," she said. "Complaining about it helps." She adjusted the blanket in her lap. "At least the curse words are easy."

"I wonder why that is," I said. "Maybe it's too hard to think through the grammar when you're angry."

"Or it would take so long that you'd get punched halfway through."

We laughed and then settled into a comfortable silence. I'd known Elaise for two years, almost my entire life at the Library. We were both part of a caste of students that came from money, but not too much of it. Her father was a wine merchant, and her older brothers spared her the need to learn the family business. Neither of us knew what we wanted to do after we finished our studies. Some days it seemed like we never would. A surprising number of students never moved out of their rooms.

That owed partly to the Library's curriculum—or lack thereof. Students were free to change focus as many times as they liked and never officially graduated until they'd expressed an intention to. For many, the freedom of choice was its own snare.

"How many classes do we have together this year? Two?"

"One," I corrected, shuffling my blanket across my lap. "I dropped *Ghantish Dialects in Literature*." It meant another year of hearing Dran complain about my honorifics, but I didn't have room in my schedule for it.

"Coward."

I shrugged. "You always say you'll help, but two months into the semester, I'm surrounded by declension charts and you're snarling at everything that moves. Besides, we'll still have Andza's class."

"Mm, our mysterious guest lecturer. Did you ever figure out where he was from?"

I sipped my tea and set it down, shaking my head. "Traste, I assume." When you were from smaller towns, like Elaise and I were, you assumed every stranger came from the capital. "Someone mentioned that he used to be a courier, and I heard someone else mention that he was a soldier, but that's all I know."

In truth, Andza had become somewhat of a celebrity among the students, and the rumors crowded him more thickly than the facts. A soldier, yes, but for which army? And what was his field of study? The title of his class—'History, A Critical Review'—was maddeningly vague. Most of his colleagues advised their charges to avoid wasting their time with his class, which drove enrollment up. The classroom had already changed twice, each time to a larger auditorium.

And then there was the matter of the research assistant post. Liseth had told me, and I'd shared the secret with Elaise. Who else knew? I was a good student, but the competition worried me.

I sighed. "Well, I suppose we'll find out soon."

Night fell and the chill drove us indoors. We finished our teas and left our blankets in a bin at the bottom of the wooden staircase. The owner smiled at us as we left, and we smiled politely back. Outside, a lamplighter started his first round of the night. He tipped his head toward us from atop his short ladder, then turned back to his work. There was no breeze, and the flame caught quickly. Elaise and I turned left and headed up the hill toward home.

The Library itself looked out of place in the city, a transplant that had never fully put down roots. Built by an expatriate from the Greymarsh region, the tall white walls would have looked perfectly at home surrounded by gray fog and attended by herons and cormorants. Compared to the rest of the buildings in Sharme, it looked overly proud, with its narrow towers and stone columns. It even faced the wrong way, with generous eastern windows built to welcome the first hints of sunrise. It had been many things in its lifetime: a winter home, a fortress, a hospital. The books were a recent addition and another mark against its character. No one in Sharme spent a great deal of time reading.

Inside, the halls were already dark, but there were still a few people about. First-year students often asked why the Library wasn't more brightly lit at night. The Library's resident scholars usually saw this as a teaching moment. Once you'd worked out the cost of an hour's reading each night across a hundred and thirty scholars—controlling, of course, for the volume of various candles, the burn speeds of different types of oils and waxes, the light requirements for readers of different ages, and the varying times of sunrise and sunset throughout the year—the answer became obvious. Somewhat more importantly, you learned that wherever professors are concerned, there's no such thing as a harmless question.

I said goodbye to Elaise at the stairway to her dormitory and told her I'd meet her for breakfast in the morning. My room was a private little thing at the end of the hall. I'm fairly certain it was a reformed closet. I liked it, though, eastern facing window and all. I finished getting ready for bed and lay there for a few minutes, daydreaming.

There was always a kind of energy that ran through the halls on the night before a new semester: worried excitement mixed with the bittersweet feeling of a final night of freedom. Further up the hall, laughter broke out and was shushed down. A nightjar in the courtyard started its raspy call, and a chorus of others joined it. Moonlight from the window brushed everything with a cold, clear light. I smiled quietly at the sights and sounds of my second home, then rolled over and went to sleep.

Despite being a place of knowledge, the Library could be awfully disorganized at times. Elaise and I walked to Andza's class early after breakfast to get seats, but apparently no one had told the itinerant professor his classroom had changed, and so we bullied one of the younger students into running around to search for him.

The auditorium was one of our larger ones, and little used. Judging from the confused jumble of items pushed against the wall, it had most recently served as a storage closet. Old wire bed frames from the Library's days as a hospital piled atop one another across the back wall. Dusty suits of decorative armor flanked the tall windows, and the corner opposite the door had been ruthlessly packed with wooden furniture. Rows of mismatched writing desks filled the space between. Some of them had obviously been dragged in from other classrooms.

The other students showed just as much diversity: bright, nervous faces I didn't recognize; older students who passed the time by cracking open books for other courses; a few friends from my other history classes, but a shocking number of students from other disciplines. Most people passed the time by chatting, but a few looked about the room, their faces intent. It took me a moment to realize that they were doing the same thing I was.

"Looks like the secret is out about the research assistant post," I whispered to Elaise. "See Sanca off to the side, sizing up the rest of us? Plus those two in the corner." I nodded toward a group of older boys who had their heads together like Elaise and I did.

Elaise smirked. "Sanca will drop the class in a week. She always overcommits herself. I know for a fact she's in at least two of my classes. Hard ones, too." She looked at the two older students. "The blond boy is smart. I forget his name. And I don't recognize the friend." She did her own survey of the room and pointed out three more I'd missed at first. "Not too many, overall," she said.

"Not too many," I agreed.

So. Simple curiosity had filled the seats, and not forty eager students jostling for a prize. The anxious knot between my shoulders loosened a bit. I supposed it made sense. Of my two advisors, only Liseth thought it was a good idea.

Dran still wasn't convinced. Most of the staff wouldn't be in favor of their charges spending months on the road away from their studies. For that matter, most students would need a bit of convincing. I'd wrestled with the idea myself.

The door opened and everyone stopped talking at once. The younger student we sent to fetch Andza entered quietly and took his seat, plainly relieved. If the professor had been irritated by the morning's confusion, he hadn't taken it out on the boy. A man entered a moment later, back straight, eyes striking. He took in the room with a glance and came to a quiet decision about it, as if the forty unfamiliar faces peering back at him were something he'd seen before and knew he could handle.

Elaise said something beside me that I didn't hear. I'd stopped breathing and was having a hard time starting again.

"Are you all right?" Elaise asked me. She sounded amused, and I realized she'd been talking to me.

"What did you say?" I managed.

"I said he's younger than I thought."

"Oh. I suppose so."

Elaise lifted an eyebrow. "What's gotten into you?"

"Nothing," I answered. "He reminded me of someone for just a moment."

As he stood facing us, I tried to dust off the blurry memory of that night in the shop and fit its edges over the ghost in front of me. He still had the close-cropped hair of a soldier and the brisk, purposeful stride that went with it. He'd lost weight. I remembered him as lean, not wolfish and half starved. Where had he been for the last two years? I'd imagined half a hundred ways our paths might cross again, but even so, the sight of him standing calmly in front of a lectern seemed . . . unreal.

He scanned the faces looking back at him. Did he pause when he looked at me? He nodded once and cleared his throat to speak.

"So. You're here to learn about history. But before we start, let's decide on some terms." He smirked. "Would anyone like to tell me what history is?"

Whatever he'd been doing in the intervening years, this obviously wasn't his first time in a classroom. A neat little trap, one designed to throw us off balance right away. After a few awkward moments, someone took the bait.

"You, in the back." He nodded toward a student, who stood. The rest of us turned to look at him. It was the older of the two boys, the blond one whose name Elaise had forgotten. The corner of his mouth barely resisted curling into a smirk.

"History," he began solemnly, "is what happened."

The rest of the class awarded him with a murmur of laughter. He grinned and offered a mock bow in return. A few people looked at their friends and rolled their eyes. The tension in the classroom eased a bit. For everyone but me, anyway.

The noise died down, but Andza didn't let his smile drop. If anything, it turned more wicked. "Close," he said. "Close enough to start, anyway. But I wonder, did anyone see what happened to the ring I was wearing when I came in?"

That certainly caught us off guard. Several people tried to answer at once.

"What kind of ring was it?"

"What did it look like?"

"*Were* you wearing a ring, Professor?"

He answered these questions, then a few more once we realized that he was willing to give us hints. A simple golden ring, slightly tarnished, with a quarter-inch band. Yes, he'd been wearing one, and no, he hadn't dropped it. Wouldn't we have heard it hit the floor if he did? He turned out his pockets by request. They held a pair of sharpened pencils, a compass, a small knife, and a stale roll wrapped in a napkin, but no ring.

Minutes passed, and the questions grew increasingly outlandish, until finally a young girl at the front of her class raised her hand. "Um, sir? Is this it?"

"Thief!" he yelled in mock surprise. "Return my property at once!" He crossed the room and took the ring from her outstretched hand, sliding it back onto his finger. Then he turned to us. "Witness! This pickpocket tried to rob me!" The poor girl lost half the color in her face before she realized he was joking.

Elaise raised her hand, clearly amused by the game. I willed her to put it back down. I doubted Andza recognized me, but I didn't want to chance it. She spoke anyway, of course. "But Professor, she couldn't have taken it off your hand without you noticing."

"True," he admitted. "Actually, my accomplice placed it on her desk as he passed."

Heads turned. On the far-right side of the classroom, the boy we sent to fetch Andza blushed furiously. A few of his friends laughed in shock, and one boldly claimed to have seen something suspicious. Andza waited for the murmur to die down before he spoke again.

"Consider this. In a room with forty living witnesses, all of whom were present and available for questioning, it took nearly fifteen minutes for a clear story to emerge. How much more difficult to piece together events that happened hundreds of years ago?"

"Well obviously it's *harder*," Sanca insisted, her hand in the air. Judging by her tone, she didn't think much of the example.

"Indeed. Harder still when the truth is dangerous. Fortunate for our poor victim that she was a student in a classroom and not someone I wanted to silence."

Sanca put her hand back down. I felt something cold and heavy settle against my heart.

He continued, the lines of his face suddenly grim. "A clever person, with a clever accomplice, can condemn an innocent person. Or several. Reasons and motives can be conjured out of thin air, evidence can be planted. And by the time the facts emerge, if they ever do, well . . ." He frowned. "A hangman's apology isn't worth very much."

I knew, somehow, that Andza was speaking from experience. This wasn't idle speculation, or even a dramatic attempt at proof by example. He had seen this done, had maybe done it himself.

He started pacing gravely about the room. "I don't mean to claim that history is a fruitless pursuit, or even that a specific account is false. Not without proof, at least. But I hope I've introduced enough doubt that we feel comfortable revising our first definition. History," he paused for effect, "is what we *think* happened."

No one raised a hand to comment. Seizing on his momentum, he continued.

"The aim of this class is to teach you to be suspicious. For that reason, your first assignment will be to choose an event of historical significance and argue that it did not occur. Failing that, you'll offer evidence to support a claim that it did not happen as described. For some of you, I've had a chance to speak with your advisors about your specific fields of study, and so I've prepared more detailed instructions for you. If I call your name, come see me at the front to receive your assignment. If I don't call your name, you're free until your next class."

Nearly everyone in the classroom exchanged looks. A few people mouthed the word *Free?* as if Andza had spoken in another language. Classes at the Library never finished early. They barely finished on time. Andza rummaged behind the lectern and found a small stack of papers, then started calling names. As each student came up, he scribbled something quickly on one of the sheets, folded it, and handed it to them almost without looking.

"Well," Elaise breathed out. "He certainly knows how to make a first impression."

"He does," I agreed, thinking of a different moment.

"I wonder how much of that he planned. Lucky for him that we sent someone to find him, or he'd have had to sneak the ring onto someone's desk himself." Elaise twisted her mouth slightly to the side, the way she always did when she concentrated.

"I don't think it was luck."

"No?"

I shook my head. "Think about it. He's not even reading names off a list right now. What kind of professor memorizes the names of every student in the class but then neglects to find out which classroom they're supposed to be in?"

"An absent-minded one?" Elaise offered.

"Does he strike you as absent-minded?"

Her eyes narrowed. I wondered how she saw him. Did he look dangerous to her? Or was he just another of the many stolid, bookish professors that roamed the halls? "No," she decided. "I don't think he is."

"Me neither. I think he planned it from the start, accomplice and all. But why?"

She raised an eyebrow at me. "Why?"

"I don't know. I'm rambling. I guess I just find it suspicious."

"Well," she said, grinning, "that is the point. Damn. I was

half hoping I'd have an excuse to drop this class, but I think it might actually be . . . *fun*."

I wished I felt the same way, but Andza's appearance was still too much of a shock, and that scene with his ring felt oddly . . . specific. Targeted, even. But was it a warning to keep silent? Or a reminder that I didn't have all the facts?

Actually, when it came to it, I had to admit that I didn't know what happened the night Miss Talia died. The constable had been looking for someone that matched Andza's description, but it wasn't necessarily him. After all, we'd just seen someone framed for theft. Could it have been a mistake? I tried to fit different stories over the man in front of me, but I was still too biased. The image of Andza sneaking through a home, shielded candle in front of him, quietly walking away from a corpse: those were the only ones that resonated.

"Jalina."

The sound of my name nearly made me gasp. I sat rigid for half a second, then stood, shaking. Of course Liseth had spoken to him. He knew my name, maybe even where I was from. I felt my heartbeat in my fingertips as I walked to the front of the room. He was already scribbling something and handed me a folded scrap of paper without looking up. I took it gingerly, turned back toward my desk, and breathed for the first time in several long moments.

He hadn't recognized me. He hadn't recognized me! Relief washed through me. Now I could observe safely, just another face in the crowd. I smiled awkwardly at Elaise and waved, then headed toward the door.

I didn't look at Andza's assignment until I reached my room. A good thing, too. I'd have made a scene in the hallway. My hands started to shake as I read the words.

Why do scented candles cost less than unscented ones?

CHAPTER TWO

Elaise and I sat at the end of a long table, far from the other students scattered around the dining hall. It was early morning, not quite an hour past dawn. I'd decided to tell Elaise everything after a night of fitful sleep, starting with the night Andza came into our shop and ending with the assignment he gave me at the end of class.

My coffee had grown cold while I told the story. I drank it anyway. Nerves tend to sap my appetite, and I needed something to keep me upright.

Elaise held the crumpled paper in front of her, frowning. She flipped it over, looking for some hidden message on the back, then handed it back to me. "But what does it mean?"

"I think it's a warning."

"Against what? Telling people that he bought something from your shop two years ago?"

"Shortly before he murdered someone," I countered.

"Maybe murdered someone."

"Fine. *Maybe* murdered someone," I conceded. As far as I was concerned, maybe-murderers were as frightening as real ones. "Whatever happened that night, he remembers it well enough to remember me. More than that, he wanted me to *know* that he remembers me." I shivered. "Whatever he meant by it, I don't like it."

She eyed me for a long moment, then nodded. "You've had strange hunches before, I suppose, and they usually turn out to be right." Before I could ask what she meant, she continued. "Let's assume that he's not what he seems and that he's warning you to back off. If so, there's an obvious next question. Will you?"

"I . . . don't know. I suppose I should, but . . ." I thought for a moment, then shook my head. "No. I won't make any accusations, but right now he knows more about me than I know about him, and I don't like it."

"I agree," Elaise said. "So what do we do?"

Absent gods, she asked me as if I knew. The heroine in a court romance would have resources to draw on: ladies-in-waiting, a charming suitor, a bodyguard that once served her father. What did I have? A few sets of clothes, some money for food. Books, inks, brushes, pencils.

"We'll check the library," I said. "It's too risky to ask about him, but no one here will find reading suspicious. He was a soldier, so we'll start with the war. Where do you place his accent?"

Sharme and Casmhe sat nearer to Kerra's eastern border and shared more cultural overlap with our neighbors in the Hensian Empire than other regions, including the lilting tones of the Hensian language. Wryn and Greymarsh, far to the west, were dotted with smaller agricultural communities, and each town seemed to choose a random vowel or consonant that its citizens preferred to mumble. Cities in central Kerra —from Lletra, in the north, to Traste, in the south—shared a more uniform accent, with minor regional differences in word choice and turns of phrase. You could generally place a

Kerran within a few miles of their hometown, if you had an ear for that kind of thing.

"Wryn," Elaise answered. "Provincial, but with a bit of an education."

"What do they do in Wryn?" I asked, genuinely unaware. Ask me what caused the civil wars in the last days of the Ghantish Empire, and I can list the crop failures by region. Ask me where the dried figs in my uneaten breakfast came from, and I'd probably have to look it up.

"Horse breeding, mostly," she said. "The southern hills are almost good for wine, but the soil is too thin and hard for anything else."

"If he's educated, he might have started as an officer," I said. "With any luck, he'll be mentioned somewhere." I folded Andza's paper in half and slid it back into the pocket of my skirt, then drank the last of my coffee. "And if not . . ."

"If not," Elaise said firmly, "then we'll have to keep looking."

We didn't actually have a spare moment together for several days. Classes had already started to claim most of our time, and as older students, we had even less freedom to indulge in personal projects. We arranged to meet in one of the private reading rooms on the third floor just before dinner. I arrived first by several minutes, and I spent them wandering through the rows, looking for likely titles.

The Library isn't just a library. It's an institution, a place for learning that encompasses the classrooms, housing, administrative offices, and all the other minutiae that support the hundred scholars that make their home there. For most of us, it meant the building as a whole. For the people of Sharme, the Library meant everything at the top of the hill.

But nestled deep within that structure was the vast, sparsely decorated room that gave the Library its name.

The oldest books predated Kerra itself, written when we were all desperate refugees fleeing the desolation of the western continent twelve centuries ago. Some of the books had survived fires and floods. Most had changed hands a dozen times before finding their way here. Religious texts, mathematical treatises, romantic verse: they filled the shelves from wall to wall. In some places, you had to use a stepladder to reach the stacks of books on top of the shelves.

I picked out three slim volumes and headed to a reading room to wait for Elaise. Autumn air filtered in with its pleasant chill, carrying the scents of the evening meal: cinnamon and cumin, peppers and mint. Cooking in Sharme is a neighborhood affair, with every window in the house thrown open until the aromas mingle in the streets. It's a wonderful town to be hungry in. Passersby are often asked for their opinion on how a dish is coming along. Even the beggars are slightly fat.

Elaise came in and sat down with her own stack of books, and we got to work.

My first book started out well but quickly veered off topic, so I set it aside. The next looked more promising, but the author was unconscionably dull. I persisted and found a few interesting scraps for my effort, but not the scraps I wanted. Soon the light from the window grew dim and my eyes started to hurt. I was nearly ready to quit when Elaise spoke up.

"Hmm. Strange."

I looked up to see her flipping back several pages. "Did you know that Wryn was only involved in the war for about six months?"

"Really?" I frowned. "That's . . . surprising. I always assumed it was the same seven or eight armies the entire time."

"Me too," Elaise said. "Well, I knew Lord Berrach of Greymarsh was defeated early on, but I only know a few of the details."

"I found something, too," I offered. "But it's probably not important. I was trying to find when and where some of the nobles levied troops. According to this, two hundred men from Casmhe joined the king's army in the second year of the war. No names, unfortunately."

To understand how little we knew, it's important to remember that the war of succession started right before Elaise and I were born and ended when we were infants. For us, the distant conflicts of the past were a necessary part of our education, but the war of our own lifetimes was a secret, painful thing that our parents never talked about.

"Did you . . . I mean . . ." I faltered. "Did anyone in your family . . . ?"

Elaise nodded. "Two of my uncles died with Lord Berrach's sons. That's how I know about Greymarsh's defeat."

"Oh," I said. I wondered if my father had been at the battle and, if so, which side he'd fought on. Was Elaise thinking the same thing? I hoped not.

"My mother died during the war," I said. "I . . . don't really ask about it anymore."

"Oh."

The silence grew. Neither of us had the words to fill it. I didn't know how to explain what I felt, the way my mother's absence loomed over so much of my childhood. I was so young when she disappeared that I didn't even have vague memories of her. Just a long list of questions that I couldn't ask without my father growing quiet. It's strange how a person can take so much space in your life even after they leave it.

Elaise must have caught my mood. A few minutes later, she made an excuse about the failing light and started to put her things away. I didn't argue, and we were both quiet as we carried our books back to the shelves.

Aside from the scrap of paper Andza gave me the first day of class, he gave no indication that we'd ever met.

When we passed in the halls, he either ignored me or gave me the casual nod that any professor might give any student. At mealtimes, he sat quietly by himself, or occasionally with a colleague, but I never caught him returning any of the furtive glances Elaise and I cast his way. He called on us in class, but no more or less than anyone else.

Still, I felt his presence.

I started to notice him creeping into the edges of things. It started with my daydreams, those harmless ones where I'm older and have a husband, or a house by the sea, with a writing desk beneath the window. He was never a romantic figure. Some of the professors had an air of worldly aloofness that I found attractive, but never Andza. He was a figure that cast a shadow, something the future Jalina would catch herself thinking about in a quiet moment and feel a chill.

In other ways he became a voice that followed me. It happened most often in class, when the lecturer glossed over an important point or too much information hung on the account of a single eyewitness. *There*, the voice would say, tracing the lines between evidence and conclusion. *Without this thread, the entire story falls apart.* I began to see how tenuous our understanding of our own history was, how murky a primary source could be, how imperfect our own memories were.

Between classes, Elaise and I still met in the library once per week. We still thought the beginning of the war was our best chance to pick up the thread, but we quickly ran out of source material. Too many works focused on the battles themselves, with endless dissection of supply lines, troop movements, and hour-by-hour accounts of the fighting. A few focused on the broader political situation at the time but only mentioned the names of major players. Andza's name never appeared. Nor did my father's.

Other stories fascinated us, though. The worst historians reduce people to a series of events. The best sift through the events to find the people behind them. As we read, names we half knew from stories took form: Kallah Varnin, the peasant farmer who became the king's personal bodyguard before going berserk and killing dozens; Absel, the crown prince who played his murderous uncles against each other in his own bid for the throne. Some days we forgot our purpose entirely and just read sections aloud to one another.

Elaise brought us to our first real break, though entirely by accident.

"I've been thinking," she said one afternoon. The weather had turned from pleasantly cold to bitterly so, and we had started to wear our heavy wool coats indoors. "What if we asked a Reader?"

I closed my book and leaned forward on my elbows, chin resting against my thumbs. It wasn't a terrible idea, but it had its risks. We certainly weren't representatives of the state, like poor old Constable Gellin. But if the answers to the questions we asked touched on anything political, the Reader would be duty bound to report the matter to their nearest chapter-house. And possibly our keepers in the Library. Not exactly subtle.

There were a handful of students from other nations who didn't suffer the same prohibitions as us godless Kerrans. The Free Cities of Jhendi had a very lax attitude about the gods' gifts, and the religious leaders of the Hensian Empire had an understandably broad view of their uses, but we weren't particularly close to any students from Jhendi or the Empire, and anyway, there was still a good chance the news would get out. The Kerran Order of Goodly Works kept a notoriously short list on the proper uses of sainthood.

Part of it owed to our own fractious coalition of miniature kingdoms, only nominally united under a single banner. A religious order that advanced the goals of an unpopular ruler could bring destruction on itself when that ruler's protection ended. But the lion's share of the Order's reluctance traced back to our earliest days. Unlike our neighbors on this new continent, we Kerrans had seen our homeland broken by gods and saints.

"We'd have to be careful what we ask," I said. "And not trust too much in the answer."

Elaise nodded agreement. "I've been thinking about that, too. We should be safe as long as we stick to things that have already happened. And we don't necessarily need anything lurid or shocking, just something to narrow our search."

We spent another week finalizing our questions, and then two days of sleet and rain kept us trapped indoors. We did our best to catch up on our lagging schoolwork, but we kept one eye on the gray, heavy clouds that hung over the city. On the third day, a few wisps of sunlight managed to break through in the morning and looked to hold into the afternoon. Elaise and I exchanged a smile in the hallway. The time had come.

Curfew was at ninth bell, and we left just after the sixth. Our plan was to waste an hour walking along the market row, then warm up at one of the teahouses off the main street. From there, it only took a minute or two to cross the street, head down a narrow staircase, and turn down the alley that led to the humble cottage where Sharme's Reader lived.

Thirty minutes at most to get our answers and another hour to make it back home in time for curfew.

It took a great deal of effort to feign interest in the cheap trinkets for sale outside the gates. For one thing, it was freezing—far colder than we'd expected. When we weren't absently shuffling our feet to stay warm, we had to stop ourselves from moving too quickly toward the next part of our plan. I shivered against the damp, freezing air and did my best to appear interested in the tin necklaces that the merchants kept thrusting at me.

Rain clouds loomed overhead, threatening another miserably wet evening. I would've cursed them, but they drove everyone else in Sharme indoors. We had our own private table at the café, and the warm drinks did a lot to strengthen our spirits, at least temporarily. The wind gusted as we stepped back outside. We saw no one in the streets. Behind us, the owner of the restaurant pulled the door shut and started to close up.

"It should be this way," I said, adjusting my gloves. I crossed the street to a narrow staircase. The archway above it sat crookedly, almost like an accident, as if someone had found an unexpected use for the space between the squat, red-roofed buildings that crowded it on either side. We went down single file, using the cold bricks on either side to keep from slipping.

As I reached the bottom of the narrow stone steps, I leaned my head forward to get a clear view of the street before I stepped onto it. Fortunate for me that I did. I stifled a gasp and pulled back into the shadow of the crumbling archway. Elaise bumped into me, and I held a finger in front of my lips to keep her from asking why I'd stopped.

"Quiet," I warned. "It's him."

Silently, we leaned as far out into the street as we dared.

The lamplighter hadn't made it to this street yet, and the sky had just started to get truly dark. Weak light from the neighboring houses lit the paving stones, but the homes to either side of us had their shutters closed, casting our section of the street into shadow. I remembered a young girl, long ago, in a dimly lit shop, staring. I stared again.

Andza walked calmly down the opposite side of the street. The pools of light fell more regularly on that section of the sidewalk, and each time he crossed one, I saw that same quiet, absorbed expression that I eventually came to recognize as the truest version of him. He didn't scowl, or hum quietly, or huddle against the cold. He simply walked forward, staring at nothing, following some inscrutable procession of thoughts. Then he left the pool of light and was cast into darkness for a time, and became another figure on the street.

I held my breath as he passed us. If he saw us, he gave no sign. But I knew that didn't mean anything.

We sat crouched in that alleyway for several dozen panicked heartbeats. His footsteps faded, and we breathed more easily.

"Where's he going?" Elaise asked. "I didn't realize he knew anyone in the city."

Up ahead, we could just barely make out the Reader's house in the dim light. Still open, but not for long. Beyond it, I saw Andza turn a corner, and I made a decision. "I don't know," I said. "But we're going to find out."

"But the Reader—"

"—will be here tomorrow, and the next day, and all the days after. Andza is here *now*. I want to find out where he's going."

Elaise opened her mouth, then closed it again. She nodded.

We slipped out of the alleyway and onto the street. We stayed on the darker side of the sidewalk until we saw Andza turn the corner up ahead, then hurried to follow. At the intersection of the next street, we leaned around the corner just long enough to see him step through the front door of a small two-story inn.

We stopped to consider our options. We couldn't very well walk in the front door, especially since we didn't know where he was sitting. We could come back later, but would the innkeeper give us information about his boarders? Likely not, and we had nothing to bribe him with. We'd reached a dead end.

"What about that window?" Elaise suggested. She pointed, and I saw a room on the second floor, just above a small toolshed built against the side of the inn.

"We're not exactly dressed for climbing," I pointed out.

"I guess not," she conceded, looking at our damp, heavy coats. "To the Reader's, then?"

I eyed the door a minute longer but couldn't think of a better plan. I nodded, tried not to sound frustrated. "To the Reader's."

We backtracked but somehow got lost and had to spend a few minutes finding our bearings. A light drizzle started to fall, and we slowed to keep from slipping on the paving stones. By the time we made it back to the Reader's house, the gate was shut, the windows dark.

"Maybe she's out of town?" Elaise suggested.

"Could be." Saints didn't exactly post hours. "Or she knew we were coming and didn't feel like answering our questions."

"Can they do that?" Elaise asked.

"Next time we see her, we can ask." I sighed. Two near misses and a wasted evening to show for them. "Come on," I said finally. "Let's get out of the cold."

Freezing and miserable, disappointed and depressed, we trudged home. But the night wasn't done with us yet.

After following the road for several minutes, we came to an intersection with two stone benches and a small green, but not the fountain we expected. We spent another ten minutes finding the right road, but once we found it, we were much farther away from the Library than we expected. The rain started to fall in earnest then, and we picked up speed, running as fast as we could with our arms wrapped around our bodies.

Just then, the ninth bell rang out over the city in its clear, strident voice. Elaise and I exchanged a panicked look. Sweat and drizzle had plastered a few blond wisps of hair against her forehead. I wiped the water out of my own eyes. My throat hurt from the cold air and exercise, but we needed to reach the top of the hill. We sprinted—awkwardly, half tripping—but the bells outpaced us.

The gate stood closed by the time we reached it. We were locked out.

CHAPTER THREE

Nothing blurs the line between a minute and an hour like the sound of rain. We sat in the groundskeeper's office and looked glumly out the window while we waited for the head librarian to appear.

There are no punishments for breaking the rules at the Library, at least not in the traditional sense. Just a shared, unspoken feeling among the professors about whether or not you're taking your studies seriously. If you are, you're allowed to stay. If you aren't, you're asked to leave. Elaise and I were good students in general. Would they kick us out for a single night of broken curfew? Maybe. Probably not. Maybe. The rain fell against the window, and the wind picked up and died down. We did our best not to think about anything and practiced looking miserable and apologetic instead.

Half an hour later we heard the head librarian's slippered feet approach the door, the groundskeeper's heavy boots thudding alongside. The door swung open to admit the two men. The groundskeeper gestured toward us and the head librarian nodded back at him. No one looked at us until the groundskeeper disappeared into the hallway that led to his chambers. As his footsteps faded down the corridor, the head librarian turned toward us.

Dorsen had been the head librarian at Sharme for almost thirty years. Another man or woman might have carried that with a sense of pride, but Dorsen seemed impervious to the kind of status and posturing that plagued other scholars. He wrapped himself in boring: simple clothes, bland expressions, flat tones. He was a thin man with thinning hair and a few vague wrinkles. He seemed completely unsurprised to see us.

"Shall I assume that you've agreed on an excuse by now, or do you need more time? I could always pace the halls a bit."

Elaise and I glanced at each other. Damn! We'd been alone in a room for thirty minutes and hadn't even thought of how to weasel our way out of trouble. What awful spies we were turning out to be.

Dorsen raised a bored eyebrow. "I seem to have caught you unprepared. That's heartening. The routine troublemakers tend to talk your ears off. Elaise and . . . Jalina, I believe?"

We nodded.

"It's been a while since I've read through our students', shall we say, *lapses* in conduct, but I don't recall seeing either of your names. First timers?"

I nodded again, but Elaise's head sank. "I, um . . . knocked over a vase last year? It only broke a little, though. I'd almost finished turning it the other way when someone saw me." Her head sunk a bit lower, cradling a whispered "Sorry."

Dorsen waved this away. "If distraction and clumsiness were crimes, we'd hardly have anyone here. Any other sins to confess? No? Good. I pronounce you both absolved of guilt."

Relief settled into both of us. We'd finally started to relax when Dorsen asked, "What were you doing out so late, anyway?"

A knock on the door spared us from having to think of a lie. Dorsen turned to answer the door, and a note of faint surprise crept into his voice. "Professor! Come to join our little party?"

Elaise and I exchanged worried looks. *Professor?* she mouthed. I shrugged.

The door blocked our view of the visitor, but we recognized Andza's voice from the hallway. "Indeed. I believe you're chastising two of my students?"

"Quite," said Dorsen, ushering Andza inside. He hadn't yet removed his cloak, which was soaked with rain. He looked briefly around the room before letting his eyes settle casually on us. Dorsen waited for him to speak with a kind of bored, patient look.

"The responsibility is mine, I'm afraid," Andza said. "Elaise and Jalina were working on an assignment from today's lesson."

"An assignment?"

"A simple one," Andza said smoothly, "if time-consuming. I merely asked them to study a familiar work in an unfamiliar place and to record the insights that arise from a new perspective. I didn't expect them to walk quite so far abroad, but if they're willing to brave this weather, I can hardly fault their effort."

Elaise and I tried very hard to mask our shock. Andza obviously expected to find us here, which meant he must have seen us in the street earlier. He'd probably even guessed that we'd been spying on him. But why not just come out and say so?

Because, I realized, that would imply there was something worth spying on. Far better to shift the focus to what he was doing inside the classroom than out of it. And he'd trapped us neatly in the process. No way to accuse him of anything without admitting what we were doing, and no evidence to even level against him.

"Ah," Dorsen said. He looked at us. "Did it work?" We nodded. "Good. In that case, have a pleasant evening, everyone."

And with that, he turned and left.

Another wave of relief, though it was short-lived. We were alone with Andza, now, and no closer to guessing his identity or his motives. Would he demand to know what we were really doing in the city? Or would he whisper some vague threat to warn us away?

Neither, it seemed. Instead, he wished us a pleasant evening and walked away, just as Dorsen had.

"What . . . just happened?" I asked, several moments later.

"I don't know," Elaise said. "But I suspect I'll waste a lot of time tonight thinking about it."

"Same," I agreed. "Sleepover?"

"Works for me."

We grabbed a few things from my room and walked up the stairs to Elaise's more populated section of the dormitory. As soon as we'd closed the door, we pushed a heavy bookshelf in front of it, and Elaise locked the latch above the window. No harm in being cautious. We climbed into bed well before the tenth hour, but talked more than we slept, and asked more questions than we answered.

The next week brought more surprises, few of them pleasant.

It started with a new addition to Andza's class—a boy Elaise and I both knew and had plenty of reasons to dislike. I scowled as he swaggered across the room and took a seat at one of the newly emptied desks.

"What's he doing here?"

Elaise grinned evilly. "Ruining your fun, apparently."

Rahad was younger than us by a year, full of the puffed-up bravado that comes from trying to fit a man's confidence into a boy's body. No one knew his background, but it was obvious he came from privilege. He had only been at the Library for a year and was already notorious for missing half his classes. Students had been kicked out for less, rudely packed onto a wagon with a refund for the remainder of whichever semester they'd been unable to finish. The cynical theory for his continued presence was that some refunds are harder to give than others.

"It's not just me. He doesn't pay attention in class, and it's distracting."

"Only if *you're* not paying attention, or how would you notice?"

I glared at her, but she smiled through it. "He draws pictures of people—"

"Pictures of you, you mean."

"—which are completely unrealistic, not to mention cruel—"

"I remember the picture, Jalina."

"—and when he's not doing that, he's—"

"Ladies." Andza's voice stopped us cold. All eyes turned toward us. Rahad grinned at me, and I did my best not to scowl back.

"Sorry, professor," we said in unison.

"Apology accepted," he said. "Though if you're feeling talkative, your energy might be better spent helping your newest classmate get up to speed. Rahad, see that Jalina shares her notes with you after class."

I would've liked to scream but opted for a simmering rage instead. "Of course, professor," I half growled. "Happy to help."

I didn't dare look at Rahad. I already knew the exact shape of that vicious, self-satisfied smirk. I'm not sure I heard a word for the rest of class, even when Elaise tried to whisper jokes to cheer me up. Whatever notes I passed on to Rahad, they were going to be fantastically incomplete.

Summer made a final desperate surge and warmed us for a while. Doves sang in the morning and crickets started their nightly chorus. The weather turned cool again, and our days faded into a steady routine of classes, homework, sleep.

We tried once more to scout the inn where we'd seen Andza, but the innkeeper turned us away as soon as we took our seats in the common room. We soon saw why. Apparently, The Broken Whistle catered to a specific class of working men who wanted an hour of peace between their workplaces and their homes, and a pair of teenage girls had no respectable business being there.

Our idea to meet with a Reader also turned up nothing. Each time we tried to visit, the door stood closed, and a sign in the window turned us away. With each passing failure, I started to feel confident about my earlier theory. Sharme's Reader had seen us coming and didn't want to risk answering our questions.

Rahad trailed us like a shadow. He never asked for notes but took Andza's suggestion as an open invitation to join us whenever he saw us. He divided his attention neatly between pestering me and flirting with Elaise. If I didn't know any better, I'd have thought Andza asked Rahad to join the class just to have someone spy on *us*.

We still met once or twice a week in the reading room above the library. It was the one place Rahad never followed us. We had to sneak into the city to keep from being followed, but the moment we cracked open a book, he disappeared from sight.

Our personal stake in the war had faded from lack of nourishment, but our academic interest in it grew by the day. It was fascinating to read about something so recent, so *fresh*. Maddening, sometimes. The personal accounts differed widely, and very few sources agreed on certain dates. But still fascinating.

"I have a theory," Elaise said one day, all of a sudden.

I recognized that tone. She'd been shirking her coursework and had fallen behind, and now she was caught between an insurmountable pile of work and an unshakable urge to put it off forever. She did it every semester and spent days scowling at everyone she passed until she worked through it.

"Oh?" I asked as neutrally as I could manage. I had to try very hard to keep the corner of my mouth from curling up into a smirk.

"I think you historians just pick a side at the beginning of an argument, and the winner is the one who has the energy to keep talking." She slammed the book on the table. "I could swear I've read about the Battle of the Two Windmills in three different places, and none of them make any sense side by side."

"I'm noticing that, too." I frowned. "I suppose we could skip to the end." We'd been sticking to primary sources and firsthand accounts, trying to follow the thread chronologically. Elaise was right, though. It took decades to settle the arguments and produce truly comprehensive works of a given period. It had been fourteen years since King Sethric assumed the throne. Might someone have taken an early crack at it?

We went back to the shelves and consulted the index at the end of the row. Convention divided the shelves into their own subjects, but no one agreed on how to sort the works themselves. The indices were a form of compromise. The caretaker for a particular section could argue for whatever method they chose, so long as it was readable. Thankfully, the scholar for our section had an eye for practicality, and it didn't take us long to find an account of the war published in the early years of Sethric's reign.

The Kerran Order of Saints and Goodly Works preaches that the gods take no part in the daily struggles of mankind. While they certainly had a hand in creating the world, their attention is directed elsewhere, and the occasional gifts that they bestow are arbitrary and not a result of divine intervention. It's the responsibility of mankind to avoid the temptations of greed and selfishness, and to put those gifts to use for the greater good.

Occasionally, however, something so unlikely, so incredibly serendipitous will happen that you can't help but feel a divine Presence behind your shoulder, pointing the way out for you.

We walked up the narrow staircase to our reading room and opened to the title page of our book. For any account written by the victor, it's important to know who wrote it and to discern what their motives might have been. Our earliest teachers had taught us that, and Andza had hammered it into us over the course of the semester. We scanned the title page for the author's byline, and for a moment we both stopped breathing. There, in simple black ink, we read:

Andza of Wryn
Royal Historian

The next day in class, we saw Andza in a new light. Some different, complicated hue of colors that we hadn't noticed before. Andza hadn't just been a scribe in the king's army, but his personal historian. They'd parted ways since then, at least ostensibly, but how much of the king's hand was still present in Andza's decisions? We still didn't know what he was doing at the Library, or in the little inn in the city, or long ago on that winter night in Casmhe. But we had the hint of a motive now, at least.

"There's something about all this that worries me," Elaise said. The two of us were alone in the courtyard, basking in the weak sunlight. "He's just so *confident*. Between the letter he gave you and the way he handled Dorsen that night we got in trouble . . . What if the reason for his confidence isn't because he thinks he won't get caught, but because it won't matter if he does?"

"I've been thinking along the same lines. Well, sort of. What if . . . well, what if he hasn't done anything wrong at all?" I paused for a second, marshaling my thoughts. A group of first-year students walked by, laughing. I waited to let them pass. "I've been thinking about what he teaches us in class, about all the hidden things that never make it into the histories. Do you ever get the feeling that . . . ?"

"That the war isn't over?" Elaise suggested.

"Exactly. That something is still going on beneath everyone's notice. If he really did work for the king, and if he still does, there might be a reason behind what he's doing."

"Like that Talia was a spy, or he's sneaking off into the city to meet contacts, or to get instructions. But if so, what's he doing here?"

"I don't know," I admitted. "I still haven't puzzled it out." I laughed. "And I thought last semester was difficult."

Elaise snorted. "Yeah, me too. What fools we."

It took a long time to fall asleep that night. My thoughts ran in endless circles. I missed the simple problems of childhood, where all the stories had an ending and the answers to the riddles were always in the next chapter. It struck me as odd that we could guess at a truth and die someday without ever knowing. In light of that, all our searching seemed futile, the mismatched facts and evidence no real substitute for that elusive proof. I rolled over to lay on my side and stared out the window.

Could it be possible that Talia died for a reason? And not just the petty reasons of vengeance or greed, but a real one, one of those mysterious greater goods? From my window I could see the glow of the city lights, though I couldn't see the houses. I'd been able to see Talia's window from my own in Casmhe, and I remembered seeing it the night after she died. Death, to me, is a darkened window in the home of someone you used to know.

CHAPTER FOUR

The last week of term came before we expected it. It finished as it always did, with half-frozen students climbing over mountains of assignments. Elaise's room had been freshly wallpapered with a madwoman's assortment of charts and graphs. I'd gotten off lucky. Dran and Liseth had preemptively given me an extension on all my assignments for their classes. When I asked why, they only said that I'd be busy enough soon.

Andza's class had shrunk noticeably since the start of term and barely held enough students to justify the large auditorium. We'd moved the desks closer together as students dropped out and the room got colder. I sat between Elaise and Sanca, who surprised us all by dropping two other classes instead of this one. The two older boys from the first day sat just in front of me, with Rahad to their right. Beyond the six of us, there were roughly a dozen other students.

On the first day of the final week, Andza showed up almost five minutes late—a rarity for him. We spent the minutes guessing what our final assignment might be. Before we could agree on anything, he opened the door and came in. We grew silent. He didn't keep us waiting long.

"On the third floor of the eastern wing, there's a painting that hangs just across the hall from one of the unused classrooms. Supposedly, it's an original work by Arvas. The brushwork is distinctively his style, and the subject is a favorite of his—a cavalry officer atop his horse, with a low but even light vaguely suggestive of dawn or dusk. Two similar paintings hang in the Royal Museum in Traste, and I've seen a third in the private study of the former Countess of Wryn. The resemblance is striking. Unfortunately, I have compelling evidence to suggest that the painting on the third floor is a fake.

"For your final assignment, I'd like you to prove that this is the case. You may reference any sources you like, and the essay may be of any length, so long as it's persuasive. The students that submit the most convincing arguments will have the opportunity to assist me in a separate project, should they be willing to risk it. All essays are due on the final day of term."

We all took a moment to reflect on *that*. A hand went up in the back of the room. "Can we ask you for help, professor?"

He smiled amiably. "I'm afraid not. My knowledge on the subject is something of a state secret."

Well, well. He hadn't shown this kind of flair for the dramatic since our first day in class. I filed that away to think about later. For now, I was still stuck on 'should they be willing to risk it.'

Another hand in the front. Rahad? Showing interest in a class? This was turning out to be an eventful day.

"What else did Arvas paint?" he asked.

This time Andza's smile turned distinctly wicked. "Excellent question!" He pulled a slip of paper from his pocket and handed it to Rahad. "In anticipation of it, I've reserved an illustrated copy of a few selected works at the library's reference desk. Unfortunately, I only found the one, so the rest of you will have to share with young Rahad."

I could have spit. I had to remind myself that getting angry wouldn't be helpful.

"Can you tell us more about your other project?" Sanca asked. An intense silence followed her question. Apparently, more than a handful of us were curious.

But Andza didn't even tease us this time. "No," he said simply. "Class dismissed."

Elaise and I met in the hallway. "What do you think?" she asked without preamble.

It didn't take long to answer. "I want it," I said. "Two months ago I would've balked at the thought of being on the road alone with him, but I think his story is more complicated than I gave him credit for, and I still want to know what it is. Plus, if it's not just me alone . . ."

She saw right through me, of course. "We'll both go," she said firmly. "Gods know I wouldn't mind some time away from this place, and at this point, I'm as curious as you are." She grinned. "Besides, we're probably each other's biggest competition. With the two of us working together, we're bound to win the spots."

I went to see the painting later that day. Andza hadn't been specific, so I had to wander a bit to find it. The eastern wing of the Library had been abandoned for years. Dust gathered thickly on everything, and the air felt stuffy despite the chill. My breath fogged in front of me as I walked through empty hallways. An echoing whisper led me to the right classroom. A small crowd of students had already gathered around it.

The classroom door opposite the painting had been opened to let in more light, and two people stood to one side of the door. A third sat on the ground in front of them, and I scowled when I saw who it was.

Rahad sat cross-legged on the floor, wearing an expression I'd never seen on him before. It almost reminded me of Andza, that dangerously quiet focus. To his left, a heavy book sat open, the page turned to a miniature illustration of the painting in front of him. To his right, several pieces of paper had been discarded. Another sat in his lap, clipped to a thin piece of drawing board.

"Afternoon, Jalina," he said without looking up.

"Afternoon, Rahad," I said coldly.

As I circled around behind to get a better look at the painting, he clipped a new piece of paper onto the board and started fresh. He dipped a thin brush into a small ink jar, and in a handful of quick, fluid strokes he painted the line of the ridge beneath the horse's feet. Another thirty seconds, and the horse and figure had taken shape. A few quick messy splotches for the sky, and a sudden tearing sound as he pulled the paper away and added it to the pile of discarded sketches he'd already made.

He was duplicating the painting, but I realized after a few minutes that he was switching back and forth: creating his own sketch based on the book and comparing it to the painting in the hallway, then working from the painting and comparing it to the illustration in the book. If there was a difference in the result, I didn't notice it. All the copies were exceptional.

"Why are you doing that?" I asked.

"Jealous? I still have a few portraits of you, if that's what you're here for."

One of the other students laughed but stopped when I

glared at him. I tried to keep the anger out of my voice. "Are you sure?" I asked sweetly. "I wouldn't want you to be lonely. The girls in your portraits are the only ones who smile at you, after all."

He laughed, then went back to drawing.

I watched for a few more minutes and left, discouraged. I hadn't expected competition from Rahad, but he was going after the task with a skill I'd never guessed at and had no way of imitating. I wondered again at his joining Andza's class so late in the term and didn't like the gnawing doubt that accompanied the thought.

When I came back to my room at the end of the day, Rahad had slipped a piece of paper under the door. A crude version of the painting on the third floor, with me on horseback instead of the cavalry officer. The girl in the drawing had my hair—long, dark, and slightly wavy—and the same slight tilt to the eyes that I imagined I inherited from my mother, but the resemblance stopped below the neck. I wore an idiotic smile and little else. I crumpled the picture into a tight ball and wondered, briefly, what it would feel like to break someone's fingers.

I never got the chance to find out. As far as I know, no one else saw Rahad for the rest of the term.

"Okay, let's go over it again."

I sighed. There's a point in every term where my head starts to spin and I feel slightly nauseous at the thought of looking at anything but the inside of a dark room. Elaise and I had reached that point days ago, but dusk still found us slumped over our well-worn table, reading.

"Niran Arvas was born . . ." I began tiredly. The story, though dull from repetition, was actually an interesting one.

The only son of an officer in the Hensian Liberation Army, Arvas fled to the Free Cities of Jhendi after his father's death in that disastrous coup. For six years he lived in the port town of Mara, selling paintings from a small studio apartment with a narrow window overlooking the Azure Plain, the oddly still sea that surrounds the islands. There he met his wife, who died giving birth to their only daughter, Zera.

Struggling to support his daughter with his paintings, he abandoned their home in Mara and traveled northeast to the Hensian border, hoping to sneak by with a false identity and leave Zera with a relative. He was only partially successful. Officials apprehended him at the border, and he spent two years in prison for the crime of conspiracy against the state. Zera spent six months in an orphanage until Arvas' aunt came to claim her. Arvas never saw his daughter again, and for nearly a dozen years after his release from prison, his story becomes almost impossible to follow.

Eventually he settled in a small village near Lletra—about as far north as you can go and still remain in Kerra. He spent the remaining years of his life painting hauntingly empty landscapes of rocks and snow. When he died, he left behind thirty-six unsold paintings. It took three months for news of his death to travel the long road to Hensia, and for his daughter to return along that same road to lay claim to her inheritance. She left with twenty-nine paintings; seven had already been sold.

"Of those seven, four are currently on display in the capital," I continued. "The other three are a bit difficult to track."

Elaise picked up the thread. "Fortunately, two of those are landscapes and don't matter. The last is almost definitely in the Portrait Gallery in Jhendi, and if it's not *there*—"

"—then it was destroyed in the sack of Lletra, which was its last known location," I finished.

That story had taken over forty hours to compile from at least a dozen sources. Elaise and I may very well have been the most knowledgeable living experts on Niran Arvas, unless someone else in the class had surpassed us. That would have been hard to do, though. We'd furiously guarded almost every book on the subject.

I slumped back into my seat. "I don't think I've ever been this exhausted." Between studying for our normal coursework and the extra hours we'd spent on Andza's assignment, neither of us had gotten much sleep.

"I know. And we still haven't even written the thing."

We'd compiled extensive notes and organized them well. Writing the essay would be a pleasant walk compared to researching it. But she was right. We still had at least an hour of work to do before we could go to sleep.

We cleaned up our materials and headed back to our rooms. This was the last night of term, which meant the last night of waving good night to one another before we cloistered ourselves away for the evening. I smiled. After all, it also meant one last night of slumping over a desk trying to rally our flagging spirits to another hour of consciousness. I took a seat at my desk, stretched my back, and reached for my ink jar.

When I lifted it, the paper it had been sitting on unfolded just a bit, enough for me to make out the first words. Andza's first assignment, the one I'd never finished. The ink hadn't faded, and the words looked as clear as the day he'd written them.

Why do scented candles cost less than unscented ones?

A mad thought took shape, a chance to return boldness for boldness. He'd acknowledged the night we'd met, and my reaction had been to whisper, to plan, to stalk. I'd never considered the tactic of acknowledging it myself. Did I dare?

I knew the answer to the question, of course. Both are relatively easy to make: one uses finer oils for a more pleasant smell; the other uses a carefully braided wick for a slower, clearer flame. Neither accounts for the difference in price, though. The truth was something much simpler, something that any shopkeeper could tell you if you asked. The people who bought the unscented candles were, quite simply, willing to pay more for them.

I thought about the essay I had planned to write, with its carefully researched facts and arguments. I held the shape of it clearly in my mind, from its opening line, down through the paragraphs to its irrefutable conclusion. I knew the answer to the question, to both of them, but which was more important? I dipped my freshly clipped pen into its inkwell and wrote beneath Andza's crisp, precise letters:

Because a clear light is worth more.

CHAPTER FIVE

Two caravans set out from Sharme on the last day of term to deliver students home for winter break. Elaise had a longer trip than I did. South until she reached the coast, where the students from Jhendi would board a ship to the Free Cities, then west along a winding coastal road, with a stop in the capital before continuing on to Greymarsh and Wryn on the far western coast. My caravan technically had the longer route, circling north and west until it reached the mountains around Lletra, but Casmhe was its first stop, so I only spent two days on the road.

We arrived at the southern gate in the late afternoon. Nearly everyone else had to continue on the next day, but they'd have stopped in Casmhe even without me. There are only so many inns on the road north. I rode with them until they parked and untied the horses, then waved farewell to everyone and set off for home.

There's something about the last mile of a long journey home. At first you only notice the differences: the sign that's painted a different color, the street corner you don't remember, the sea of unfamiliar faces. As you get closer, the familiar reasserts itself, until you know with a deep certainty that this is the place you left, almost exactly as you left it.

From the inn, I turned left onto the main road that ran east toward the center of town. When I reached the fountain in the middle of the main square, I walked a slow circle around it, and a group of shrieking children ran past me in the other direction, absorbed in their game. From there I turned south again, down the narrow streets that I'd played in as a child. Some of my neighbors had moved away, but the ones that recognized me called out, and we spent several minutes chatting before I could disentangle myself from the conversation.

Finally I reached our little shop on the corner. The lights were on inside, and I saw my father talking with a customer from his usual place behind the counter. I smiled, taking in the scene, and walked in.

"How long are you staying?"

I swallowed my food—spiced bread and lentil stew—and reached for my glass. The shop had been busy all afternoon, and we'd barely had a chance to speak until dinner. "Only a few weeks," I said. "The caravan turns around the day after it stops in Lletra." Sensing his disappointment, I added, "The students there barely get any time at all to visit."

He nodded but didn't look completely satisfied. "And how's your friend? Elaise, wasn't it?"

"Elaise," I confirmed. "She's well. In fact, we're working on a project together." I gave him a *very* abridged summary of the last semester, our class with Andza, and the research assistant positions we were trying for. "It sounds like a good opportunity," I said. "And I think we'll both appreciate the change of scenery."

"He sounds like an interesting man," my father said, somewhat distractedly. He had a habit of looking down while he was lost in thought. Before I could ask what was bothering him, he asked, "Have you thought about what you'll do once you finish?"

I froze, caught by the sudden shift in the conversation. I honestly hadn't given it much thought. My father was paying my tuition for now but obviously couldn't keep doing it forever. I'd considered a staff position at the Library, but the more I thought about it, the less I wanted to stay cooped up in one place. Where else could you work as a historian? Traste would have the best opportunities, as the seat of power in Kerra. But was my father hoping I'd return to Casmhe once I finished?

"The reason I ask is because, well," he paused, considering what—or how much—to tell me. "I'm thinking of closing the shop."

Now it was my turn to hide my disappointment.

"It's been a lot to manage lately, and the winters are getting harder. These old bones need sunlight, I think. I have friends in Jhendi from the war. They're always telling me to come visit, and I think I may finally take them up on it."

I nodded but lifted my glass to my lips to hide my expression. It would hurt to lose my childhood home, but was it really fair to ask him to stay? He had no wife here and only half a daughter. And what if I did move to Traste after I finished my studies?

I tried to read his expression: the slight crease between his eyebrows, which had deepened since I'd last seen him; the hopeful, anxious tilt of his eyes and mouth. When had so much of his hair gone gray? I realized he was trying to read my expression, too, and I knew that he would stay here if I asked him.

"That sounds nice," I said cheerfully. "You'll have to write to me once you get there. Do you know which city you'll be in?"

We steered the conversation to more idle subjects for the rest of dinner: the weather, the news from other parts of the world, stories about the shop or about my schoolwork. Afterward, I helped him clean up the kitchen, and we both got ready for bed. The obvious question didn't occur to me until I'd nearly fallen asleep.

When had my father ever mentioned a friend from the war?

The next few weeks passed in pleasant monotony. Take nearly any day and switch it with another, and I'm not sure it would have made much of a difference. Every morning, I woke up, ate breakfast, and helped in the shop for a few hours. After lunch I went for a walk in town, sometimes for several hours. After the semester I'd had, it felt good to devote half my days to just *moving*.

At first I tried to vary the walks, but eventually I just fell to retracing my steps each day. I made a kind of game out of it, trying to notice things I'd never noticed before, even though I'd walked past them every day. Andza's lessons about paying attention to the things around you had apparently stuck with me. I started to pick out little details I'd taken for granted since childhood, like the way the snow gathered in the gables above the windows, or the curious little illustrations painted on the signs that hung above the shops.

One day I turned a corner and froze in place. The constable was only a few paces ahead of me, and I suppose some latent, guilty part of me still expected to be hauled away and questioned for what had happened years ago. He didn't see me, or anyone else, for that matter. His attention was entirely devoted to the rows of sweet cakes on the display table in front of him. He took a cautious glance around and surreptitiously swept one of them into his pocket. Then he marched away, as stern as unflappable as I'd ever seen him.

I nearly laughed as I ducked back around the corner. Who would have believed our dear old constable was a petty thief! I wondered if anyone else had ever seen him do such a thing. Was it possible that this was his first time, that I had witnessed this single moment of harmless self-indulgence in his long career of public service?

I realized that the things I knew to be true about my hometown were only true for me, and only for the narrow slice of time that I lived there. For each of the tens of thousands of souls who had lived in Casmhe over the centuries, there was a slightly different face of the city that only they had seen. Two hundred years from now, who would know that Federo the blacksmith walked with a limp, or that the stonemason's son had fallen in the fountain once and gotten a cold that lasted nearly a week? For that matter, who would remember me?

The caravan returned too soon, as always. A knock on the door preceded a short, handwritten letter that requested my presence at the inn by the seventh hour the following morning. We closed the shop early to pack and have our final meal together. We sat quietly for most of it, unsure what to say.

My father broke the silence by handing me a package. It was small, about the size of a closed fist, and crudely wrapped in the brown parcel paper we used to wrap small goods. I took it, surprised. Gifts weren't common growing up. I got them once a year on my birthday, and my father never got them at all.

"What is it?" I asked.

"Just a small thing," he said. "It belonged to your mother. Open it."

Just a small thing? A fist-sized diamond would have been less exciting. I opened the paper carefully, resisting the urge to tear into it.

A weight dropped into the palm of my hand, a small hair ornament made of some smooth orange stone. Carnelian? One side of the stone disk had been worked into the shape of a flower, with a pair of bronze pins extending in a slight curve away from the center. I turned it over to look at the back. A small *S* had been carved into the flat side of the disk, for Serine. One of the precious few things I knew about her.

"It's beautiful," I whispered.

"Too beautiful for the box it's been lying in," he agreed. "It seemed wrong to pack it up and take it with me. I bought that for her in Traste, and I've lost count of the times we thought we'd have to sell it." Some memory brought the ghost of a smile to his face. "In any case, she'd have been upset if I kept it to myself, especially when I have a perfectly wonderful daughter to give it to."

I didn't know what to say. My father kept so many things buried that I felt like I'd grown up on tiptoes, trying to step around the things he clearly wanted to leave unsaid. Now, after years of prying, he mentioned my mother? A hundred questions sprang to mind, but I failed to snare a single one.

"I thought you could wear it somewhere nice," he said, the silence growing awkward. "Especially if you're on the road next year. Just make sure to keep it packed up when you're traveling. Don't want to attract bandits. Though I suppose there aren't as many of those since Sethric made himself king."

A chance presented itself, and I took it. "You fought for him during the war, didn't you?"

He nodded. "I wouldn't say we fought *for* him. But yes, the men from Casmhe were called up early, and I was of fighting age. Your mother was pregnant with you, but we didn't know it yet, and so we went with the rest of the young men."

"She went with you?" I asked, shocked. "But I thought—"

"That you were born in Casmhe?" He laughed. "No, little one. Not unless Casmhe is a little roadside tent a few hundred miles from here. The army surgeon made a fuss, but a worried young father is hard to argue with. We don't listen to reason. Anyway, he came around by the end. I think it did him good to tend to someone who wasn't sick or dying." His smile faded, and he looked grim. "But no more war stories tonight, I think. You have an early start tomorrow, and I still need to clean up."

"Let me help," I said, standing and turning toward the sink.

For some reason, it felt very important to hide my reaction. I was shaken, but I'd be fine after a moment, and I didn't want him thinking he'd upset me. So I was born in a tent, was I? That was strange, I supposed, but nothing earth-shattering. More importantly, what was my mother doing in a war camp? I knew that she'd disappeared *during* the war, but the possibilities for tragedy had seemed much smaller when I imagined her safe at home.

We finished cleaning up and got ready for bed. I pressed for more details about my mother, but my father retreated into his usual half answers and deflections. It was hard not to resent his silence, but I had years of practice converting anger into bitter disappointment. I resolved not to do anything that would spoil our last night together. Besides,

I could hardly expect him to undo years of silence in a single evening. I would keep the small treasures he'd given me and not spoil them by hoping for more.

After I got into bed, he surprised me by kissing me on the forehead and wishing me pleasant dreams. He hadn't done that since I was young. I realized that it might be the last time we ever slept in the same home. He must have been feeling sentimental.

I woke up before the sun the next day, and we shared a final cup of tea. My father said his farewells at the door, and I walked alone to the inn. I arrived just in time, climbed sleepily into the back of the rear wagon, and cracked open a book. I wasn't particularly interested in reading, but I wanted to be left alone, and no one bothered me at all once I laid a translation of Gramme's impressively titled *Sunset of the Red Empire* across my lap.

I lost myself in the creak of wagon wheels, the crackle of frozen pine needles, the gentle scratching of pages as they flipped by, unread. Shortly after we left town we topped a small hill, and I could see Casmhe from a distance as it began to stir. From this distance, the chimney smoke looked frozen in place, suspended there by the cold. I could only make out a few of the larger buildings, but even the ones I didn't recognize looked familiar. As the sun rose, we turned to follow the curve of the road, and I watched my home fade slowly from view.

Would it be home again the next time I saw it?

The warm, crackling fireplace of the main hall seemed like an oven after two nights on the road. A damp sleet started to fall as we were unloading the wagons, and we'd all rushed inside to get warm. I took my gloves off, preferring to warm my hands with a mug of hot tea, then circled the room to catch up with friends I hadn't seen in weeks.

Everyone had the same news: their families were well; the weather hadn't caused too much trouble; yes, the other caravan had arrived yesterday; no, they didn't know where Elaise was. Andza had also returned from a mysterious week-long sojourn, though no two guesses were the same about where he'd gone.

I eventually got tired of the crowd and gulped down the rest of my tea. The drivers had finished unloading the luggage and stacking it in the entryway, so I grabbed the small bags I'd taken and carted them up to my room.

When I arrived, I saw two sealed envelopes stuck beneath the bottom of the door. I unlocked the door and pushed it open, dropping my things just past the threshold and bending to pick up the letters. I unsealed the first envelope and pulled out a letter from Elaise, which I tucked under my arm while I fiddled with the second envelope. Inside that one, I found a single piece of folded paper that read:

Meet me in my office as soon as you're back. —Andza

I turned and rushed down the hall, leaving my door open behind me. My heart thudded as I fumbled for Elaise's letter. I skimmed quickly over what she'd written, missing half the words. Several paragraphs about her trip, her family, news from home, another two on some theories she'd drummed up about our mutual investigation. She must have written these on the road; her handwriting looked shaky. I skipped to the end. She finished with a maddeningly vague reference to "interesting news," but before I could read back to see if there was something I'd missed, I arrived at Andza's office.

Still breathing heavily, I knocked on the door. A patient "Come in" sounded from within, and I turned the knob and entered. Andza sat behind his desk, and he smiled at me as I walked in.

"You asked for me?" I said.

"Indeed." He motioned to a chair, and I sat down. "To begin, congratulations on your excellent choice of tactics."

I didn't know how to take the compliment, so I smiled awkwardly and smoothed my dress out over my knees. It was still damp from the rain.

"I suppose that means I was chosen?" I asked.

"Indeed," he confirmed. "I imagine you have questions about it, and I'll answer what I can." His eyes sharpened a bit. "Some answers will need to wait until we're on the road, I'm afraid, and you may never know some parts of the story, but . . . well, as I said, we can wait until we're on the road."

"Can I ask where we're going?"

"West for a while. After that, it's hard to say." He gave me a meaningful look, and I nodded. He knew but felt the need for caution while we were still in the Library. But who would be spying on him in his own office?

"How long will we be gone?"

"Two months at the least, I should say. Probably less than a year."

A year! "That might be, umm, difficult to pack for."

He smiled. "We'll have some funds at our disposal, so don't worry about anything beyond the next few weeks. Anything else for now?"

I still had questions, of course, but I suspected I'd have to wait to get meaningful answers to any of them. I shook my head. "Good," he said, in a clear tone of dismissal. "We'll leave early tomorrow, so the rest of the day is yours. Be outside the front gate an hour past the breakfast bell."

The silence dragged out, and I felt the need to say something before I left. I broke eye contact with him and lowered my voice.

"I was terrified, you know," I whispered. "When you remembered me. I suppose you knew that." I looked back at him. His face had gone carefully blank. "Curiosity won out eventually, or I wouldn't be here, but I was terrified at first. Was I right to be?"

Seconds passed. Finally something relaxed in him. "You were right to be cautious," he said. "But no. You have nothing to fear from me."

Somehow, with quiet certainty, I knew he was telling the truth. What was it Elaise had said about my strange intuition? I hoped it was as reliable as she thought. I stood to leave, but as I reached the door, Andza answered the question I'd forgotten to ask.

"Oh," he said, "and if you see Rahad, tell him to come find me."

Rahad? I almost asked. *But why—oh, no . . .*

I turned and saw Rahad walking toward me. We both froze in place as the realization dawned on us. His vicious, self-satisfied grin was exactly as I remembered it.

CHAPTER SIX

The sun shone clear in the sky all through our first day on the road, easily penetrating the leafless branches above us and warming the ground below. The rain hadn't dried up from the day before, so Rahad and I ate lunch in the back of the wagon while Andza drove and drove. I hoped that the winter storms were done for the season, and that we'd enjoy a nice gradual progression into spring. We were far from the coast, and the weather was much less fickle here. Even our mules seemed to be enjoying the outdoors.

I embarrassed myself at the gate, I'm afraid to say. Elaise came to say goodbye, and it was suddenly all too much. I was worried that Andza's departure might be a big event, but the only witnesses to our sobs were Andza, who ignored us, and Rahad, who grinned. Infuriating.

I buried myself in a book to avoid seeing how they looked at me, but the creaking, bumpy roll of the wagon made reading difficult. A few jaw-rattling minutes later, I took my final look at the city. The early morning sun hadn't quite cleared the hill, and the red roofs looked almost dull compared to the corona of sunlight that surrounded the town. I stared for a while, then turned away.

Half an hour after sunset, Andza pulled the wagon to a stop and climbed down from the driver's seat. Almost before we came to a stop, Rahad stood up and hopped off the back. I looked up from the book I'd been reading, wondering what was wrong. I rubbed my eyes. I'd kept reading long after the light faded. I'd have to be careful about that.

Andza came around to the back and started rummaging around in one of the drawers built into the underside of the wagon. A moment later, he pulled out a few scraps of dry paper and a tinderbox. He took them over to Rahad, who was already busy kicking the brush away from a clearing beneath the boughs of two enormous firs. I closed my book and climbed down to join them. A splinter caught the edge of my skirt, and I took a minute to fumble with the snag, trying not to tear the fabric. If we were going to be on the road for a while, I needed to take good care of my things.

By the time I made my way over to the campsite, Rahad had gathered a few sticks of dry timber and stacked them on a clear patch of dirt. Andza leaned down with his tinderbox, and I stood there awkwardly while he frowned a small fire into existence.

"Anything I can do to help?" I asked.

The two of them exchanged a look. Apparently they hadn't expected me to do anything. Rahad shrugged, and a moment later, Andza asked me to look under the wagon for our bedrolls and some wool blankets. I tried to keep my face neutral. They obviously thought I hadn't spent much time on the road. Compared to Andza, I probably hadn't, but Rahad?

I set the bedrolls down around the edges of the campfire, and Rahad and Andza immediately started to rearrange them. After a moment I understood why, and I felt stupid. I'd set them all side by side, with one end of the bedrolls next to the campfire. Rahad and Andza moved theirs to opposite sides of the fire and turned them sideways, which made sense. That way, everyone would be able to lie down with their backs to the fire. I moved my bedroll to match and tried not to get frustrated with myself.

No one spoke at dinner, and small wonder. Andza could be amiable enough but only if he made a point to be. Otherwise, he brooded like an old oak tree. Rahad would start talking once he felt like getting under my skin, but for now Andza's presence seemed to keep him in check, and I planned on enjoying the silence while I could.

The meal didn't help matters either. Dried meat, dried fruit, and hard biscuits. After my fourth or fifth bite, I understood why I'd only ever eaten those things on little snack plates between pots of tea or coffee. What was the point of food you didn't have to cook if you spent all your extra time chewing?

After dinner, Andza and Rahad finished setting up camp. I watched, deciding that if they wanted my help, they could ask for it. Where did Rahad learn how to do these things, anyway? Based on his mannerisms and his clothes, I'd always assumed he came from money. Even his traveling clothes looked sturdy, new, and well-fitted. But what kind of privileged life taught you to hang a rope between two trees and drape a spare blanket over it to block the wind? Not only that, but his accent was pure Jhendi, and the Free Cities made sailors, not woodsmen.

I tried to do what I'd done to Andza months ago in class, settling characters and stories onto the person in front of me to see what fit. Son of a traveling merchant? Perhaps. He could certainly pass for one in the city, but out in the wilderness, there was a hard edge to his eyes that I'd never noticed before. It looked . . . strangely natural, as if a mask had slipped and he hadn't bothered to put it back on.

A life of hardship then, someone used to hunger or privation. A family fallen on hard times? I tried to imagine the people in his life: a mother, a father, siblings. None of them seemed to match. For some reason, I had trouble imagining Rahad as anyone's brother. Or anyone's son for that matter.

He caught me staring, and I looked away, trying not to blush. I've always been nosy, but when possible, I prefer to be nosy in private.

Rahad turned his back to me, then reached into a bag next to Andza's bedroll and pulled out a small trowel, which he used to pry rocks out of the soft layer of dirt. When he was done, he handed the trowel to Andza, who did the same. They had an oddly comfortable relationship, I noticed. They seemed to work well together without needing to communicate. I tried to imagine them as friends, but even when I put them at a similar age, it didn't fit. No, theirs was a father-son relationship, or an approximation of one. It was easy to picture them together, quietly occupying the same space, traveling from town to town . . .

"So," I said, trying to keep my voice level. "First time traveling together, or have you done it before?"

They paused just long enough to give themselves away. Rahad, to his credit, recovered quickly enough to feign confusion. Andza just smiled.

"When did you figure it out?" he asked.

"Only a few seconds ago," I admitted. "But when? Over the winter break?"

"Longer before that, I'm afraid. I've known Rahad for . . . nearly two years?" He glanced at Rahad for confirmation, but Rahad kept his expression blank. His normal easy confidence had dissolved into something cold and unfamiliar.

"Two *years*? But that means . . ." I faltered, trying to count back. I'd seen Andza for the first time just over two years ago, so he hadn't met Rahad at that point. Did Rahad know about what happened in Casmhe? He couldn't have, unless Andza had told him.

"How much did you—does he . . ." I stopped, then asked the question that actually mattered. "When will you tell us what this is all about? I assume that he," I nodded at Rahad, "knows more than I do. But neither of us know everything, do we?"

Andza looked at me, took a slow breath, and nodded, coming to a decision. He sat down on the end of his bedroll and laid his arms across his knees. He motioned for us to sit across from him, and we did—though not very close to one another. "It'll take too long to tell from the beginning, and we're not quite safe to talk openly," he started. "But I can shed light on a few things."

Not quite safe? We'd left Sharme early in the morning and stayed off the wide track that cut through the plains, heading straight for the woods instead. We'd traveled all day on twisting dirt roads, clogged with roots and overgrown with trees. I hadn't seen another soul since leaving town. Who could possibly bother us out here? I spared a nervous glance for the shadows just beyond the edges of our camp.

"A few years ago," Andza started, "I had some business in Casmhe, where we met." He nodded at me. Rahad looked briefly confused, then understood. His eyes narrowed. So. Andza hadn't told either of us about the other. Interesting.

"From there, I traveled south and booked a ship across the Azure Plain. I spent some time in the Free Cities, which is where I met Rahad. A month later we returned, and Rahad enrolled at the Library. I was his sponsor."

So many blanks in the story. My mind rushed to fill them in. His business in Casmhe had led him to the Free Cities of Jhendi, which had an . . . aggressive stance to interference from other nations. A good place to lay low, provided you kept your business to yourself. And I suppose he'd just plucked Rahad off the street

I glanced at Rahad, remembering the hard eyes and how difficult it had been to picture him surrounded by family. Damn. Maybe he *had* plucked him off the street.

"So, you sponsored his enrollment." I nodded. "That explains a lot, actually."

Rahad arched an eyebrow. "What's that supposed to mean?" he sneered. His arrogant schoolboy persona had started to reappear, but not as naturally as before. It seemed more brittle somehow. A line of defense that had started to crack.

So there was a layer beneath the swaggering adolescent. And it carried knives, apparently. Now that the real Rahad had started to come out into the open, I couldn't resist baiting him.

"Oh, please. You're a terrible student. You miss class, you barely pass any of the tests. If anyone else treated—"

Rahad opened his mouth to say something, but Andza spoke first. "Enough."

My mouth clamped shut at Andza's rebuke. I had an annoying tendency to respond to authority. I was the good student, after all. Andza fixed me in place with a stare, then continued when he felt sure I wouldn't interrupt again.

"Yes," he said. "Rahad has special considerations when it comes to his studies. I won't go into his past. That's for him to share, if he decides to. But seeing as he doesn't have the typical student's background, he's measured against a different standard."

A *lesser* standard, I amended. Silently.

I stole a guilty look at Rahad, irrationally worried that he could read my thoughts, but he wasn't looking at me. He had the set jaw and distant look of someone wrestling with a private shame. Andza may not have said "lesser," but we'd both heard it, and it gnawed at him.

"In any case," Andza went on, oblivious, "he has a handful of skills that might be useful. As do you. As did some of your classmates."

"But why did you tell us there were two spots if you'd already filled one?" I asked, genuinely confused.

Andza shook his head. "Rahad had to fight for his spot, same as you. I'll admit that you both had advantages, but neither of you were guaranteed to win. In fact," he said, motioning toward me, "if things had gone differently, it might have been your friend Elaise sitting there instead of you."

Oh.

The sting of that simple statement left me breathless for a moment. I'd thought being stuck on this trip with Rahad was the worst-case scenario, but I'd nearly been left out of my own story.

"That's a shame," Rahad said, in mock regret. "It would've been nice to have someone pleasant to talk to."

My hands started to shake. I wanted to slap him. If not for the campfire between us, I might have tried it. I made a wild guess instead, flung it at him like a knife.

"Yes, well, at least I can read all my assignments without help."

I guessed too well, apparently. For a second, the facade slipped entirely, and I could see the orphan from Jhendi beneath the face he showed the world—some desperate street-thing, wild with fear and hunger. His hands clenched once, then went rigid at his side. I imagined those hands around my neck and felt something flutter in my throat.

"Enough," Andza cut in again. "And I mean it, unless you'd like me to leave you out here in the cold and make you walk back." He looked back and forth between us, glaring at us in turn. We withered under that quiet anger. "Now, would either of you mind explaining *exactly* what I've signed up for with you two?"

Neither of us answered.

"I'm going to assume, in the absence of any well-articulated explanation, that this is an argument between children. If so, let me be clear. You can waste your own time and energy as much as you like, but not mine. I don't care if you settle your differences or not, but from here out, you will both work together, or you will both be left behind."

I nodded. I assumed Rahad did as well, but I was too busy looking at the ground in front of me to notice.

"Good."

The rest of the night passed under a quiet, heavy tension. Andza broke off his explanations after our spat, and neither of us had the courage to ask him again. Best to let him brood. Rahad and I readied ourselves for sleep and settled into our respective bedrolls. Eventually the darkness enfolded our little, petty silences into its own, and we slept.

CHAPTER SEVEN

Sleeping outside in the middle of winter has a way of altering your perspective. All the thoughts and worries that normally occupy the last few minutes of your day shrink in importance. In their place, you're left with a simple, unyielding truth about the world: winter is cold, and there isn't much you can do about it.

At some point in the night I realized that the campfire was about to go out. I considered the problem with a very real sense of fear. If I slipped out of bed to build the fire back up, I didn't think I'd ever get warm again. But if the fire went out, I wasn't sure I would last the night. I knew those were the only two choices, but I didn't have the courage to choose either one.

Fortunately, Rahad and Andza were still acting under the assumption that I wouldn't be much use around the camp. I heard one of them stir and blessed them silently when I heard a fresh log settle onto the fire and start popping cheerfully.

There's a lesson in that, I suppose. Something in our nature makes us comfortable with misery. We hope that things will get better, but as long as we have enough to survive, we aren't willing to risk what little we have. I remembered a woman who lived down the street from us when I was young. Her husband used to terrorize her, and I never understood why she didn't just run away. I found myself wondering what kept her warm in that awful house.

That's a lie, actually. I didn't wonder about any of that until later. It's hard to think when you're shivering so hard your back hurts.

Morning came to chase away the worst of the chill, but I stayed in bed while Andza and Rahad made a clattering attempt at breakfast. It served them right, I thought, and anyway, I would have only slowed them down. I fully intended to do my equal share of the work, but for now I was happy to let them manage without me. I wasn't mad at them anymore, but I don't think that counted as maturity on my part. It's hard to wake up angry when you're cold. You tend to just wake up cold.

Eventually I found the courage to crawl out of my pile of blankets and hold my hands toward the fire. Andza handed me a little wooden bowl: stewed oats, with little figs and dried almonds mixed in. I burned my tongue on the first bite, then again on the second, before finally just sitting there and enjoying the steam.

"I've been thinking about our problem," Andza said.

I sighed. I'd been thinking about it, too. "I'm sorry," I said. "For the way I acted. It won't happen again."

Rahad looked at me for half a second, then nodded agreement.

"Appreciated," Andza said wryly. "But apologies aren't solutions. I'm hoping that this will be."

Andza reached into his backpack. "This" turned out to be a slim book with a stack of papers on either side of it, all of it loosely wrapped with a piece of twine. Andza handed the book to me, as well as the smaller stack of papers. The larger stack of papers went to Rahad, who turned them over and looked at them dubiously.

"Last night, you asked me what this was all about. I very nearly told you, but I realize now that doing so would've been a mistake. To make sense of all this—what happened and what it means—you need to discover it the way I discovered it. And considering that I've only given each of you part of the story, you'll need to work together to do it." He lifted a spoonful of oats to his lips, but I could have sworn I caught the hint of a smile.

I set my bowl down to look at the book. No title on the spine, so I flipped it open to the first page, then groaned. "It's in *Ghant*?"

"Yes," Andza confirmed. "And a fairly old dialect of it, if I'm not mistaken." This time he smiled openly. "Most of it is unimportant, but there are a few pages that make it worth the effort."

"Let me guess. Telling me which pages would spoil the surprise."

He shrugged. The bastard.

"At least mine's in Kerran," Rahad said, frowning.

I wondered. Kerran was his second spoken language, after Jhendi, but there was a very real chance that it was the first language he learned to read and write in. If so, had he ever gone back and learned to read Jhendi? What an experience that would've been, to go back and learn the other half of a language you'd spoken since birth. An interesting case, but there was no polite way to ask about it.

I set down the book and looked at my stack of papers. "These, too. It looks like an interview. No, two interviews. Firsthand reports of a battle?"

"Same," Rahad confirmed.

"Careful," Andza warned. "Study them a bit on your own

before comparing notes. It's important to draw your own conclusions first. Then, once you've talked about what you've found, you can swap and look for things the other person might have missed."

I nodded. Elaise and I had done a bit of that ourselves.

Rahad had a more cynical interpretation. "In other words, be quiet so you can enjoy your breakfast."

"That, too."

I wish I could say the time passed quickly.

The Empire of Ghant—often referred to as the Red Empire due to its sudden and bloody decline six centuries ago—organized its society around a rigidly maintained caste system. In addition to the usual tools of violence and generational poverty, it enforced this policy of social immobility through the use of language. Each caste had a specific grammatical mode of address for the castes immediately above and below them, but no others. There was literally no way for a laborer to speak to an emperor, even if they happened to be in the same room.

As droughts, crop failures, and civil unrest began to unravel the empire from within, the emperor's officials attempted to purge the religious caste of any saints who weren't explicitly loyal to the emperor. During one such arrest, they found a stack of diaries written by a minor saint named Hensia. Throughout her writings, she addressed the gods using the same informal mode you would use to speak to an equal. Citing this as proof of her heresy, they exiled her and published her writings as evidence of pervasive rot among the religious caste itself.

It had the opposite effect. For the vast majority of the population, this was a revolutionary departure from the system that kept them in poverty and squalor. Dissidents began speaking and writing in this informal mode, now known as Hensian, which grew in size and complexity to handle the needs of a rapidly integrating society. Three years after her exile, Hensia returned as a hero to an empire that now bore her name.

While modern Hensian has its roots in Ghant, and shares a great deal of vocabulary and minor syntactical elements, the two languages couldn't be more different. Reading Hensian is like walking through a market square. There's a vibrancy to it, a busy clamor that celebrates togetherness and exchange. Reading Ghant is like storming a castle. The walls are *meant* to keep you out.

As far as I could tell, Andza's text was nearly eleven centuries old. I wasn't familiar with many of the words, but the tone and subject made me think it was written by a Ghantish cleric to a senior member of his order. It was also the most boring thing I've ever read. When ten minutes of difficult translation yields a sentence like "We bought a box of nails for the fence and also a few planks of lumber," you tend to lose enthusiasm quickly.

By our fourth morning on the road, I'd only finished about ten pages. Two paragraphs into the day's reading, my head started to hurt, so I climbed out the back of the wagon and hopped to the ground. The weather had turned mild after that first miserable night, and I wasn't the only one enjoying the reprieve. I spotted at least two foxes looking for food, and countless birds flitted between the branches of the trees that lined the road. Most were too high to see clearly, but a little robin with an orange chest and a bit of white at its throat landed ahead of me on the road and looked up curiously as I passed it.

Once my headache started to pass—or, more importantly,

once my feet started to hurt—I climbed into the driver's seat next to Andza and took out the little book again. He ignored me, which was fine. I didn't particularly want or need his company, but I needed to sit somewhere besides my usual seat in the back. It was a trick I'd learned long ago. When I sat down and read in the same uncomfortable position all day, I always regretted it. But when I sat in several different uncomfortable positions throughout the day, I could read for weeks.

"Where are we going, anyway?" I asked.

"Barste."

"One of the nicer neighborhoods, I hope."

Barste had a reputation, though it was more accurate to say it had *two* reputations. Some people described it as a center for the arts, the bustling home of a thousand would-be poets, musicians, painters, dancers, and actors. Others described it as a festering midden of violence and corruption, where duelists fought in the street and assassinations were conveniently difficult to prosecute. Both faces of the city tolerated—even appreciated—the other, but everyone generally preferred to stay on their side of the river.

Andza grunted, which filled me with inexpressible hope.

"Barste is what, seven or eight days west of Sharme?"

"If you take the main roads," Andza said, "which we're not. Call it two weeks."

"Which means we'll get there in ten days," I said. "Should we, um . . . should we interpret that as a deadline?"

"If you like."

I translated two more pages before we stopped for lunch. The first held more of the same mind-numbing minutiae, but the second had a passage that sparked my interest.

Apparently one of the local guardsmen had broken the handle of his sword while training, and the village smith was already overwhelmed with requests for tools for the upcoming harvest. The guard had come to the monastery for help, and they'd repaired his broken sword handle for free.

Most small-town monasteries had at least one Fabricant, someone who could seamlessly join lumber or reshape metal tools. They were the most common sort of saint, after Readers, and especially useful in the more remote areas, where you couldn't rely on a local craftsman to do repairs, and the sickle you used to harvest grain in the morning might need to be a hammer that same afternoon.

I'd never heard of a saint helping to fix a weapon, but the tone of the passage had the same dry, informative feel as the rest, which made me think that this wasn't the kind of task that needed special permission—but might have been odd enough to warrant mentioning.

Could it be the passage Andza wanted me to find? I couldn't imagine it being relevant. The saint in the passage had lived a thousand miles from here, and we were separated by an even greater number of years. What importance could a long-dead Ghantish saint have to present-day Kerra?

Lunch was a loaf of bread, halved and then split three ways, along with a few pieces of the same dried fruit that Andza apparently kept sacks of. No one felt particularly talkative today either, so I walked while I chewed. I'd never spent much time in the woods growing up, and winter seemed like a good time to get started. There were no insects, for one thing, and no nettles to brush against your skin. The lack of underbrush meant you could see for a good length in any direction, and the thin canopy made it easy to mark your way by the sun. Still, Andza's warning from the first night made me cautious about walking too far from our camp.

The next few pages of Andza's book didn't yield much, so that afternoon I switched to the stack of papers he'd given me. Halfway through the first page, I realized I'd actually read it before. It was an account of the Battle of the Two Windmills, which Elaise had complained about months ago.

We'd read a few different accounts of the battle, but none of them made much sense side by side, and they didn't really have any details relevant to what we were looking for. Considering they were both useless and inaccurate, we'd moved on from them. And yet, Andza thought they contained something crucial.

I checked the second interview, and yes, I'd read this one, too. I skimmed both of them quickly to refresh myself on the details.

The Battle of the Two Windmills happened in spring and was one of the first minor engagements in the third year of the war. This was the battle where Kallah Varnin had earned his notoriety. Before the battle, he'd been a simple farmer from an unnamed village, conscripted into service. After the fight, he'd been appointed to Sethric's personal guard, a decision that would later prove disastrous. What he'd done *during* the battle, however, was a subject of fierce debate.

Though it was called the Battle of the Two Windmills, most of the fighting took place in the village of Harna. The windmills themselves—one to the north, another to the east—sat a good distance away. Sethric had stationed a small force of twelve inside each windmill to watch the surrounding areas, with instructions to signal the town if anyone approached. Another fifty soldiers were stationed in the village itself, and a dozen of these were senior officers. The main body of Sethric's force had camped some four or five miles to the west, where they . . . I forget, honestly, and it probably wasn't important.

What *did* matter was the mercenary company that attacked from the north. They'd been limping away from a costly fight of their own when their advance scouts spotted the watchtower. They attacked from a nearby tree line at a change in the watch and managed to overwhelm Sethric's force before they could warn the larger contingent in town.

After a few minutes of questioning, they learned that Sethric had set up camp in Harna's town hall, along with half his senior officers. Though Sethric was only a minor warlord at the time, by no means favored to win the crown, this still represented an undeniable opportunity to change their fortunes. They decided to risk an attack and split their forces into three groups: one to begin torching buildings on the southern end of town, one to attack from the north, and another to intercept riders who tried to make it to the main army with news.

It very nearly worked. Sentries within the town saw the smoke from the fires just as a few dozen men charged in from the north. The mercenaries took advantage of the chaos, hitting small groups of defenders, then melting away into side streets whenever they met resistance. Officers fell one by one. Battle lines vanished, and lone soldiers fought in hallways, alleyways, doorways. Sethric himself held the top of a staircase while his archers fired from the windows, desperately targeting any enemy with a torch.

Kallah Varnin was the one who broke them, but few people agree on how he did it. Different reports place him in different parts of the town: leading charges, holding lines, reinforcing pockets of resistance. All describe his frightening stature, the vicious swings of his blade. One account even affords him a valiant, bloody death, backed against the town's central well and hacked to pieces. That one has the feel of a tall tale, though, especially when the writer devoted an entire paragraph to the buckets of blood that had to be drawn up before the well's water ran clear.

Of course, reports also disagreed on whether the fight lasted five minutes or fifty. One poor soul even had the time of day wrong. Plenty of minor details failed to match up. Firsthand accounts are notoriously unreliable, as Andza had demonstrated on our first day in class, and even the sharpest memories dull with time. Despite the frequent use of the phrase, we rarely even remember yesterday as clearly as if it had happened yesterday.

Did it matter that the accounts didn't match up? Or was Andza just belaboring the same point he'd been making since the first day of class?

I decided that I couldn't put off working with Rahad any longer. It was time to compare notes, but I didn't want Andza to overhear our guesses until we were more sure of them, so I waited until he was busy with dinner and Rahad walked off to gather water.

"Hey," I whispered, falling into step beside him.

Rahad lifted an eyebrow. Two inches taller, but you'd think it was two feet with the way he looked down at me. "Why are you whispering?"

"I . . . Never mind." I shifted to a normal voice. "What do you think so far?"

"About what?"

"What do you mean 'what'? What else? Yours are about the same battle, too, aren't they?"

"Oh, that." His eyes snapped forward, focused on nothing. "I'm not ready to talk about it yet."

I was honestly confused. Then I realized. "Oh. If you need help with either of them—"

"I said not yet," he growled. He picked up his pace, and I let him stalk off into the woods without me. I stood there for a long moment after, wondering what I could have done differently. This new Rahad was a stranger to me, with his quick temper and brittle confidence. He couldn't have changed so much in a week. Had he dropped his privileged son act since leaving the Library, or had I crossed a line by finally seeing through it?

Andza hadn't called it a deadline, but I was treating it as one. Every step closer to Barste cost us a grain of sand in the hourglass. Andza had designed our task so that we'd need to work together to figure out the clues, but I'd gotten lucky with the subject matter. Assuming I knew what Rahad's papers said, could I work it out alone? And would it count if I did?

CHAPTER EIGHT

Our seventh day on the road brought us to a village so small that we didn't even see it coming. A long twist in the road skirted around a low hill, and as we rounded it, a row of houses came into view on either side of the dirt lane. It was as if the town had been folded closed and only popped open as we approached. A tiny little hamlet. If it had a name, I never learned it.

Andza tugged on the reins, and our mules ambled dutifully to a stop. I looked around. We weren't next to an inn, or even a proper house. There were a few feet of struggling grass between us and a wooden fence. Behind that, maybe fifty feet from where we'd parked, a little shack stood at the edge of someone's property. I saw smoke from a few chimneys but didn't notice anyone about.

"Why are we stopping?" I asked.

"I need a walk," Andza said, hopping down from the driver's seat and pushing his knuckles against the small of his back. "Pass me my cloak?" He nodded to a bundle tucked underneath the seat. I reached down and handed him the folded cloth. Strange. It wasn't his usual cloak. This one was threadbare and poorly patched. He flung it over his shoulders without comment, and I didn't ask him about it.

"Should we stay here?" I asked. I could have used a walk as well.

"Suit yourself. Just stay within sight of the wagon." Then he turned away, pulled his cloak tighter, and wandered off.

"Where's he going?" Rahad asked, leaning against the side of the driver's bench. I started, which obviously pleased him. I hadn't heard him walk up. The boy could move like a shadow sometimes.

"A *walk*, apparently."

Rahad snorted and went back to his reading. He'd been doing more of that lately, thank goodness. I hadn't broached the subject again since our argument in the woods, but if testing his confidence produced this kind of reaction, then it was worth renewing the bad blood between us. He carried his papers everywhere now, instead of just flipping through them absently at meals.

He'd shown that kind of focus before, with the painting, but it still surprised me. It reminded me of something I'd read about the great cats that prowled the northern mountain ranges between Kerra and Haln. They either looked lazy or hungry, and never anything in between.

I decided to get back to my own assigned reading, the daily maunderings of my frightfully dull junior cleric. I'd been avoiding it in favor of the text I already knew. But if Rahad could plow through a difficult read, so could I.

The next few paragraphs didn't yield much. Short, spare little sentences that could have been copied from earlier pages. I breezed through them. Then I turned the page, and my breath caught.

I sat up, reading the passage twice to be sure. Fortunately, the writer hadn't described the events with any turns of phrase that could have gotten twisted with time. *Demri has been killed for his involvement in an assault.* There was no mistaking the meaning. Once a language finds a word for "kill" it tends to use it for a while.

It took a fair bit of backtracking to find out who Demri was. He was the Fabricant who repaired the guard's sword using the same kind of minor miracle that Fabricants perform daily, practically everywhere. After he finished, one of the young boys at the monastery delivered the sword to the guard, who must have died (I counted the days) practically the same day. I didn't recognize the word he used—brigand, probably, or maybe cutpurse. Either way, the thief claimed the weapon along with its owner's life and fled into the night.

He was apprehended two days later after a failed attempt at a robbery. In going through his effects, the constable found the sword, which bore Demri's mark along the hilt. A miracle, a physical representation of the gods' touch upon the earth . . . and it had been used for theft and murder.

I couldn't find any mention of what happened to the thief, but it must have been cruel. Whatever punishment the guard deserved for his negligence was surely being weighed in a higher court. The boy who carried the sword earned three lashes for his kindness. As for Demri, the account is silent.

A quick skim of the remaining pages didn't turn up anything interesting, so this had to be what Andza was looking for. What it meant, I didn't know. I had another piece of the puzzle, though, and our deadline still loomed. I went to find Rahad.

I found him a short distance away. He'd found a clear patch of dirt and was scribbling something in it with the back of a pencil. He frowned when I walked up, annoyed that I might bother him, but I didn't need to. I could see what he'd done for myself. He'd drawn a map of Harna! There were lines for the roads, and little squares and rectangles marked the main buildings. He'd drawn the village green at the far end, and . . .

"Just ignore me," I said, crouching beside him. I'd forgotten my own news in the excitement. "Actually, wait. That's the main street there, right? And the town hall to the north?"

He sighed, then pointed. "That's north." He tapped three of the little rectangles with a stick. "Inn. Courthouse. Town hall." He motioned to the other side of the street. "These are houses, but I don't know how many there were, so I just made them all the same size."

"Got it. Okay, now ignore me."

I circled around to one side. This made everything so much easier. Even the sight lines were perfect. I realized now why it would have been hard to see the market stalls from the second floor of the inn, and why they couldn't have gotten away with one lookout, or even two. You'd need at least three to cover all the nearby streets. I reached over and added a small circle, just inside the southern corner of the inn.

"What are you doing?"

"There was a guard posted here. One of Sethric's men. I'm sure one of the reports is from him. He talks about watching the southern road into town."

Rahad frowned but added two little circles of his own.

"It still doesn't make sense," he sighed.

"No," I agreed. "But I don't think it's supposed to."

"It isn't?"

"Did you pay attention once in class?" I caught his glare and checked my tone. "Sorry. But we went over this kind of thing. A lot. Firsthand accounts are unreliable, and the stories often disagree."

"So why is he having us go over it again?"

Because you obviously weren't paying attention the first time? I kept that one to myself, at least. Progress.

"Because this one's different somehow, and I might have a clue as to why." I filled him in on what I'd just read.

"And they killed him for it?"

"Yes."

He shook his head. "Madness."

"Unfair at the very least, but that's been the rule there since . . . well, since before they called it the Hensian Empire. We're not much better in Kerra, to be honest." I thought for a moment. "What do they do with saints who break the law in Jhendi?"

"The same thing they do for anyone else," he said, as if I'd asked a stupid question. Maybe I had. "Thieves get fined, then branded, then lose a hand. Murderers get executed. Our saints aren't really powerful enough to do anything serious, but even if they did, the Crane would probably handle it himself."

The White Crane. Jhendi's local deity, and a bit of an oddity. "Does he . . . 'handle things' often?" Another suspicious look for what I suspected was another stupid question. "Kerran, remember?" I reminded him. "Absent gods, all of that."

"Not often," he said, "but sometimes. I met him once. He gave me a picture of a horse, but it was really bad, so I threw it away." He snickered. "He drew all the legs in front, the way really little children do."

I needed a minute to recover from that. Truth be told, I probably needed a *year* to recover from that but didn't have that much time to spare. "Sorry, I just want to make sure I understand. You *met a god?* You actually met him? And you're sure it was him?"

"Yes," he said. He didn't sound defensive. He just sounded . . . certain. As if I'd asked him whether the sky was up.

"And he gave you a drawing? Do you think that's wh—"

"Why I draw so well?" he finished for me. "No. I'm good because I practice, the same way you get good at anything else."

"Fair enough." I thought for a moment. "Speaking of drawing," I began. I wasn't even sure where I was going but went ahead with my question anyway. "What did you write for your final essay?"

He gave me a guarded look, but when he couldn't find a knife hidden in the question, he answered it. "Not much," he admitted. "I said that it didn't look like a painting. It looked like a painting of a painting."

"Wait, really? How can you tell?"

"A hundred little ways," he said. He really did have an annoying tendency to brag. "When you're painting something for the first time," he continued, "you work differently. You have to figure out everything as you go. If it's a portrait, the subject is easy, but where do you want them to stand? How do you want them to stand? What are they doing, and how do they fit into the scene around them? It's . . . messy sometimes, filling in details as you think of them, trying to paint over decisions you made earlier.

"I probably made twenty or thirty copies before I realized the pattern. The person who made the forgery was talented. Very . . . precise. But they painted it in a way that you could only paint if you already knew all the answers." He shrugged. "I can't explain it any better than that."

"So nothing about the history of the painting, or the artist, or anything like that?"

"No." He frowned at me. "History isn't . . . my strongest subject."

Rahad admitting he wasn't good at something? I hid a smile. "Well, it's definitely mine, but I didn't write about any of that either. Elaise did, and she wasn't picked."

I paused. In order to reveal what I'd written, I would have to tell Rahad about the night I'd met Andza. I resigned myself to it and spent a few minutes giving the barest possible overview of what Elaise and I had been doing the previous semester.

"Okay," he said slowly. "So neither of us wrote a history essay for our history class, and we both got picked. Which means that Andza's looking for . . . people who break the rules?"

"Not quite," I said. "Well, maybe. He already told us that he's looking for people with specific skills or talents, and those obviously don't include lots of reading. I'm good at recognizing faces and keeping secrets. And he knows I'm willing to take risks," I added, remembering that he'd caught us spying on him. "You're good at observing, picking out details that aren't what they appear to be. Not just in a figurative sense, either—in a literal, visual sense."

"That's true," he said. He looked at me for half a second, then nodded. "And I'm good at keeping secrets, too."

"That's right," I agreed. "Until a few days ago, I wouldn't have guessed that you knew Andza at all. The question is, whose secrets are we trying to ferret out?"

He frowned, tapping his pencil absently against the dirt. "I don't know. But if you're right, and the battle isn't supposed to make sense, then . . . someone at the battle was either mistaken or lying, or . . . or I don't know. But what does that have to do with a painting?"

"Or a Ghantish saint from a thousand years ago."

"Okay, three things. The painting that doesn't look like a painting, the battle that doesn't make sense, and the saint who was killed for being a saint." He frowned. "I can't tell if this is a riddle or a bad joke."

I snorted. "It has that feel, doesn't it? Anyway, I keep coming back to that story about the saint, and I can't figure out why Andza picked it as an example. It's too old to have any bearing on current events, unless . . . unless that's why he picked it? Maybe it isn't meant to tie in with anything that's happening now. Maybe it's just meant to point us in the right direction?"

"You think a saint was involved? Isn't that . . . a very, very bad thing here?"

I nodded. The chill that tightened my shoulder blades had nothing to do with winter. "The Order formed at the beginning of our long exile. Some people claim that they started earlier, when the saints of Old Kerra started to grow too powerful and too interested in politics. If someone from the Order went against their own teachings and supported a contender for the throne . . . yes, it would be very, very bad."

"But what would happen, exactly? Would they be killed for it? Some people might consider that worth it." Not him, his tone implied, but some people.

I shook my head. "We sunk our homeland into the ocean, Rahad. Entire kingdoms drowned, and half the people who survived ended up dying in the crossing to this continent. Most of our laws—practically our entire written history—can be traced back to people who thought the world had ended. Kerrans might have a reputation for being godless, bloodthirsty warmongers, but there are lines even we wouldn't cross. For a lot of people, seeing the Order get involved in a war would be a sign that those times were coming again. I . . . don't even like to consider it, to be honest."

"But it's not impossible," he argued. "And it would fit with the clues."

I took a slow breath, then nodded. "Okay. Let's assume that. But how? A few Readers in the ranks would make any spy network obsolete, but if King Sethric's army had Readers working for them, they wouldn't have been caught unawares like that. Fabricants can make tools or weapons faster than a blacksmith, and Architects can tear down a house even faster than they can build one, but I've never heard of anything like that, in this or any other battle."

We fell silent. Neither of us could figure out the last piece of the puzzle, but we could feel its edges beneath our fingertips.

"Do you know much about Hensian saints?" I asked.

"Not much," he admitted, "but why do you ask? They obviously weren't involved."

"Why not?"

He gave me a blank look. "Seriously?"

"From now on, Rahad, just assume I don't know anything about how gods or saints or miracles work in other nations," I said. "I barely know how they work here. I've met two Readers in my life, but only if you count the same one twice. This isn't something Kerrans talk about. We've spent twelve centuries *not* talking about it."

"Okay," he said. "But I'm not a monk. I've never explained this stuff before."

"Start with the basics," I suggested.

He rolled his eyes. "In the beginning, the eldest gods created the world and the heavens. But they were either tired or it killed them or something because no one worships them anymore. The traces of what they did settled into the earth, and occasionally someone is born with a stronger trace of that first miracle." He counted off on his fingers. "We all understand matter because that's what the world is made of, but Fabricants can move it around. Same for Readers. Everyone understands the difference between the past, future, and present, but Readers can ignore the rules sometimes and look at tomorrow as if it's happening now.

Architects can change the way objects interact with each other. You really didn't know any of this?"

"Be a good person, and don't ask how miracles work," I said. "That's basically the entire Kerran religious tradition. Oh, and we're allowed to pray, but we're not supposed to expect anyone to answer."

"That's the saddest thing I've ever heard."

"Does anyone answer when you pray?" I countered.

"Just the once."

Under normal circumstances, that would've brought an end to the conversation, but I still had questions to ask. "So what's different about saints from Jhendi or the Hensian Empire?"

"The everyday saints get their gifts from the eldest gods, who existed everywhere," he explained. "If a saint gets their gifts from a local god, those gifts only work in the nation where that god is revered. If they leave, the gifts stop working."

I took a minute to puzzle through the implications. "That doesn't leave many options for our saint theory."

"Not many," he agreed.

Andza came back a few minutes later and placed a small bundle in the back of the cart before he took his seat at the front. I gave it a glance as we climbed into the back of the wagon. Some bread, a few small citrus fruits, and a dusty bottle of dark liquid. I didn't ask him about it, and neither did Rahad. We had too much to think about and didn't speak a word until night fell and the mundane tasks of making camp made it necessary. Even then, we kept all talk to a minimum and turned in early.

Sleep eventually overcame my buzzing thoughts, but it certainly took its time about it.

CHAPTER NINE

Andza explained the cloak and bundle at breakfast. Before passing through the town, he'd gone door to door in shabby clothes, begging for scraps. Better to give them the story you wanted than the one they made up, he said. The stories people made up were always more interesting. Rahad, as his mute son, thought the guise was amusing. I didn't really appreciate my role as his worthless, pregnant daughter, but I suppose I have always been a bit of a prude.

Winter made its last stand, with six nights of bitter cold before the temperate air from the southern coast dulled its edge. The weather could be fickle this late in the season, but a few of the trees had decided to risk it, so we rode under the green buds of early spring and woke to birds searching our campsite for last year's twigs. Rahad and I found a few moments every day to compare theories and suggest ideas. Our relationship was better than it had been at the Library, but I still wouldn't have called us friends. We made no attempts at small talk.

Eventually the tree line thinned out onto the open plain that led to Barste, and we saw the glint of sunlight against the river that would lead us to the city. We'd already seen two or three families on the road. Soon we would see a flood. Andza, aware that our last chances at privacy were dwindling, stopped early in the day and found us a dry place to sit far from the road. We made a pot of tea and spent several moments considering each other over the rims of our cups. I looked at Rahad, and he nodded back at me.

"We have a guess."

Andza nodded, unsurprised. "Tell me."

"Based on the evidence," I began, "we believe that King Sethric had outside help in the war to secure his throne."

The barest shadow of an expression crossed Andza's face. Pride? Or amusement? Gathering my confidence, I continued.

"It took us a while to figure it out because we had to admit the impossible first. The identities of those responsible . . ." I trailed off. "They hardly bear thinking about, and anyway, it's probably dangerous to name them out loud. Isn't it?"

This time he actually smiled, an amused little smirk that gave away nothing concrete. So be it. We only had one guess anyway, so I kept on.

"If so, then it would be difficult to prove exactly how they helped, but we know what it would look like. Spies that gather information too well, especially from places they couldn't have been. Defensive structures that get built too quickly or hold too well. Quartermasters that always have the supplies they need. I've heard accounts of the king that say he has the gods' own luck on the battlefield. His enemies used to curse him for it."

"They say it less now," Andza said, his tone neutral. They said it less? Or there were less of them alive to say it? It came to the same thing in the end, I supposed.

"In any case, those might explain the overall success of a campaign, but none of them explain the Battle of the Two Windmills. Sethric was caught by surprise on so many fronts that he could have hardly been less informed. Soldiers fought in whichever buildings they were trapped in, wielding whatever they had to hand. None of the accounts fell in with our theory, unless . . ."

I took a breath and looked at Rahad for confirmation. This was pure speculation, and on the thinnest evidence. But we both believed it. He met my eyes and nodded in support.

"Unless we were looking for the wrong gifts. Your other clue gave us what we needed."

"My other clue?" Andza lifted an eyebrow. He seemed to have genuinely forgotten.

"The final assignment. The painting on the third floor? I wasn't chosen for my answer to the essay, but Rahad was, and it wasn't for his brilliant historical insight. No offense," I added quickly. He waved the comment off.

I bit my lip, unsure how to phrase what came next. "It's . . . important that Rahad can see forgeries, isn't it? Edges that don't line up, colors and shadows that aren't where they should be. Because if Rahad were at the battle, there's a chance he'd have been able to see the things that really happened. Or spot the things that didn't."

A long silence followed, with nothing to fill it. It was too early in the season for insects, and there were no people in sight. Not even the wind stirred. Andza gave away nothing, his eyes closed as he sipped his tea. I felt a hole widen in my stomach. We'd gotten it wrong, and now we were going home . . .

"Good," he finally said. "Better than I'd hoped, in fact. Well done."

I let out the breath I'd been holding, and I saw Rahad's shoulders relax. "Wrong in some crucial ways, of course," Andza continued. "The Order itself wasn't involved. In truth, they're more upset about the matter than anyone. And Sethric himself didn't know until much later."

"Who, then?"

"Saints, most certainly. The Order calls them Ghosts, though they don't call themselves that. There are a few dozen at least, acting under their own discretion and for their own reasons."

"That's heresy." I knew I sounded ridiculous but couldn't stop the words before I said them. I'd never considered myself devout, but the Kerran religious tradition is a fairly simple one. Unless you've been told otherwise, it's none of your business. Easy to learn, easy to follow, and everyone stays out of trouble.

"True," Andza allowed. "Fortunately for those involved, they have a handy way of escaping detection."

"What else can they do?" I asked.

"They work the same way as other saints," Andza explained, "but where a Fabricant shifts matter around, a Ghost works with light and sound. They can make people see or hear things that aren't there, and can disguise nearly anything they touch, including themselves. A few can even disappear from sight, which is probably how they earned their name, once the Order learned about them."

"I've never heard of a saint like that," I said. It was true that certain gifts waxed and waned over time, but new ones almost never appeared without precedent.

"Neither have I," Andza said. "But I never claimed to know everything."

"So what are we supposed to do about it?" Rahad asked. He'd been watching the exchange for several minutes without saying anything. Now he seemed impatient, anxious to know what came next.

"You mentioned the painting as a clue," Andza explained, "and I suppose it is. But it's significant for another reason. Weren't you curious how I knew it was a fake?"

"I assumed you knew some source that mentioned the real story and hid the Library's copy before you gave us the assignment."

"Oh, hmm. That would've been clever. But no. The truth is much simpler." He sipped his tea. "I burned the real one ages ago."

"*You* burned it?" I asked, shocked. "Where?"

He smiled, but it had a bitter cast to it. "Tactical retreat. I fought for Wryn at the start of the war. Did you know that?"

I shook my head. "I knew you were from Wryn, but only that you fought for Sethric in the end. But then, so did almost everybody."

"True. Well, as I said, I fought under Wryn's banners, and those didn't fly for very long. The Countess had plenty of wealth but never quite managed to convert the little bronze men on the peras into veterans on the field. One retreat after another, we burned our riches before the enemy could take them and lost all our treasures along with the war."

"So who painted the fake?" Rahad asked.

"No idea, but it doesn't matter. The point is that in all your research, you never found proof of what happened. I might be the only living soul who has the story, but I've never written it down, and no one else has ever cared enough to ask. Once we forget, no one else will ever know.

"A hundred years from now, it might be significant that a group of heretic saints helped the king win his crown. It might not matter. Either way, the parties involved will have had a century to silence witnesses, alter evidence, or think up elaborate explanations for why a thing happened—or couldn't have happened."

"Write it down while it's happening," I quoted. The historian's call to action. "That's what you mean, isn't it?"

"Exactly that."

"Who else knows?" Rahad asked.

"The king, and it's safe to assume he trusted a few of his officers at the time. He tends to use those close to him to cover his blind spots, which might be his one true mark of genius. Higher ranking members of the Order would know, but probably not all of them."

"So why trust us with the secret?" I asked.

"Several reasons. First, because while my arguments are very convincing to me, I have no idea how they will sway others. I had to know whether someone else could follow the trail and come to the same place."

"You could have picked anyone for that," Rahad said, flatly. "Why us?"

Andza met his eyes for a long moment before answering. "Because you both trusted me first."

After we finished our tea, Andza walked a short distance away, just out of earshot, and waved Rahad over. I hadn't quite started to process what it all meant. For the most part, I was enjoying the warmer weather and the sense of relief at having solved the puzzle. A few minutes later, Rahad took my place on the sunny hillside, and I walked over to stand next to Andza.

"What are you feeling?" he asked. A strange question, coming from him. Certainly not the one I expected.

"Relieved," I answered honestly. "A bit frightened, or maybe just anxious. Confused. Curious." I shook my head.

"Too many things to list."

"I can help with the confusion, at least. You're entitled to a few answers at this point."

"As easy as that?" I asked.

"Just so. This may be your best chance for a while."

"When you came to the Library, you could have easily ignored me or pretended you didn't know who I was. But you didn't. You showed your hand right away. Why?"

He grinned, the way he always did when he thought someone was being clever. It might have been the only honest expression he used, aside from the neutral-grim one he carried everywhere.

"I gave you that first assignment because I was curious how you'd respond when something knocked you off balance. Everyone has a face they present to the world. Yours is the quiet, hardworking, inquisitive student, which is one version of the truth. Rahad's is the spoiled son of a rich family, which isn't truth but speaks to something he believes to be true: wealth is power. Or, at the very least, safety.

"Crack that outermost shell, and you can see the other truths that lie beneath it. Call Rahad on his bluff, and he reaches for a knife. That's literal, by the way."

Somehow, that didn't surprise me.

"You, on the other hand," he said, turning toward me and giving me a hard look. "You play the spymaster, which I didn't expect. Tell me, how long before you told your friend that you knew me?"

"The next morning, at breakfast."

"Anyone else?"

"No." I frowned. "I didn't think it would do any good. And besides, there was no way to tell it all without implicating myself in Talia's . . . I'm not sure what, exactly. They say you murdered her, or someone matching your description. Back then, I was sure you did it. Another one of your misdirections?"

"One of many," he said. "Did Elaise tell anyone else that you know of?"

"No one," I said confidently. "Why? Afraid of loose ends?"

"Constantly. But not that one. More interested in your judgment."

I gave it another moment of serious thought, but I felt sure. "No, Elaise didn't tell anyone. And I don't think she ever will." *Unless I don't come back,* I realized. She would risk it then, and maybe even try to pick up the thread herself.

"Maybe not," he said. "But I wouldn't have risked it. You did, and you were right. It's been a long time since I've trusted others. I worry sometimes that I may be losing the knack for it."

"Covering your blind spots?"

"Just so."

Off in the distance, some miles away, I saw the dim outline of our next destination against the morning sun. Small groups of people trundled toward it, so far away that I couldn't make out any details except whether they were on horse or afoot. A mix of both, as far as I could tell. I watched them move along the road while I thought of my next question.

"You said there were dozens of these saints. How many have you met?"

"Seventeen. A few died before I could speak with them, and others have likely hidden themselves too well."

"Died how?"

"The specifics don't matter," he said, though his voice sounded grim. What manner of death could frighten a soldier? "The better question is why, and I think you know the answer."

Indeed. I could think of a few *very* powerful people who wouldn't be comfortable with a secret like that walking around.

"And Talia was one of them?"

"Yes."

"So she helped fake her own murder?"

"It would be more accurate to say that I helped her, but yes. I made a few small contributions. A broken door handle, some half-opened drawers, a bit of mess around the room. Things she could have done herself, given the time. The body might have been difficult, but we were lucky there. Some nameless wretch who'd died of the cold. If she recognized him, she didn't say."

"There were witnesses that saw you."

"I know." He smiled. "She played two of them herself. Small work, compared to what some of them can do."

"And so she told you what she knew, and you helped her escape from others who may have found her instead."

I hadn't phrased it as a question, but since he didn't contradict the statement, I took that as confirmation. So he was saving them. Noble, but I'd gotten the feeling that he'd killed in the past, and I still believed it. A former soldier might be hard-hearted enough to appreciate the windfall of a convenient corpse. Would he have made his own if he hadn't found one? For all Andza's talk about trust, I found myself growing more paranoid by the moment.

"Last question, and then we can go. What are you still looking for? Surely seventeen confessions are enough to make a case."

"With regard to facts and events, yes, I have what I need. But there's something missing in all the stories they tell me. They're willing, if hesitant, to tell me what they did, and when, and where. But none of them have told me why. Why Sethric? Why this one contender above all the others? Why help him win and then disappear back into obscurity? When I have that," he said, "I'll be done."

"And if you never find it?"

His answer was a long time in coming. "Then I never find it."

We camped outside the city that night. We'd only been two weeks on the road, but I'd gotten used to the dark, and the light from the city kept me awake. After speaking to the two of us separately, Andza brought us together to give us our instructions for Barste. Strange to do it that way, but perhaps it was for the best. Andza must have known that Rahad and I would each have questions that we didn't want to ask in front of the other. I wondered if the three of us would ever trust each other completely, and how many secrets we'd be carrying with us until then.

I sat up on my bedroll and rolled my shoulders. I may have gotten used to the dark, but I didn't think I'd ever get used to sleeping on the ground. I had to roll over every five minutes until I fell asleep, and once an hour after that. The others never seemed to have the same trouble, but as a former soldier and probably-an-orphan, they would have had more practice. Some skills just weren't worth what it took to learn them.

Somewhere in the city below, another saint waited for us. Andza seemed confident he could find them, but then, he had done this kind of thing before. I had no clue where to start or how to help.

"You should try to get some sleep."

I flinched at the sudden sound. Shadows, the both of them. "Sorry. I was thinking."

"What about?" I heard Andza shift a few logs around our fire and then stand up to walk toward me.

"About what's happened," I said as he settled onto the

ground a few feet away. "About what's next. It's strange how much has changed. For fifteen years, this thread ran down the very street where I grew up. I walked past it every day without knowing. Now I've picked it up, and I don't know what to expect anymore."

"I remember feeling the same way."

I didn't turn to look at him. I couldn't have seen much in the darkness anyway, but I thought he sounded sad. With all his talk about facts and evidence, he'd carefully avoided telling us how his story had gotten tangled with theirs. I wondered who he'd lost during the war, and what kind of person he'd been back then.

"Who was she really?" I asked. No need to clarify who I meant.

He seemed to hesitate. At least, it was a long moment before an answer came back in the darkness. "She wouldn't thank me for telling you. Even now, with a years-long head start, that name could be the key to finding her again." Another pause, and then five words that stopped my heart.

"Serine. Her name was Serine."

I was confused at first. How did Andza know my mother's name, and what did it have to do with Miss Talia? But even as I denied the coincidence, an image started to take shape in my mind. Of a mother who lived in fear, close enough to see but forever out of sight. Of a father who never remarried, who never spoke of what had come before, and who made plans to move to Jhendi as soon as I was old enough to leave home. I saw the two great mysteries of my life settle into place and traced the line where the edges met.

I was glad of the darkness, then. I can't imagine what expressions must have crossed my face. Shock gave way to sudden anger, followed by a sense of betrayal that cut so deeply I thought it might kill me. Fifteen years, and not a single word in passing. Fifteen years of lies, and now a stranger dropped the truth into my lap. My mother lived, and both my parents had conspired to keep the truth from me. But why? What had I done that made me so unworthy of their trust?

One thing was certain. Andza had chosen well when he picked me. This went beyond the dry pages of history or the political ramifications of the Order's shameful heresy. This mattered to *me*. To uncover this secret, I would pull dead men from their graves. I would follow this thread if it unraveled the whole world.

PART TWO

The House of the Falling Curtain

I've put this off for as long as I could. Some of you will be upset with me, but there's no avoiding it. There are other threads to weave in, stories that I wasn't there to witness. Many of you will claim that I'm overstepping myself. Perhaps you're right. I've taken as much care as I can to stick to known events, but conjecture has filled in many of the gaps. I don't apologize for it. Besides, my own firsthand account—written decades after the fact—is hardly infallible.

And besides, history is only what we *think* happened.

CHAPTER TEN

Ferrec half expected the floor to be cold when her feet touched it. It was bare stone, after all, and the air had a chill to it. This far north, the chill would last until late spring, and even then it would leave a good month of sullen rain in its wake. The kings in Lletra had built their castles well, though, with heavy curtains on the windows and pipes to carry hot water through the floors. The warmth under her feet reminded her that she was Governor Ferrec now, not Lieutenant Ferrec. That she lived in a palace and not a garrison. All her decisions were mundane these days. Almost boring. The thought warmed her more than any fireplace.

She frowned at the harsh light coming through the windows, then felt around for her slippers with her feet. She found one easily enough but had to search for the other under her bed on hands and knees. Her servants would have been scandalized if they'd seen her in such a position, and she wondered, with a kind of malicious glee, whether or not she could time it just right one morning. Little satisfaction to be had if she did. They'd probably just end up sending someone half an hour early to put her slippers on for her.

Ferrec sighed. If battles were all about the ebb and flow of retreats and advances, politics were all about *compromises*. It was hard not to keep a running tally of hers: most of them were in her own chambers. A feather bed with a massive, hand-carved headboard and pointlessly sheer curtains. Bookshelves of polished wood filled with someone else's books. Wardrobes and closets packed with clothes she never wore. Ornate gilded tables whose only real purpose, as far as she could tell, was to keep you from crossing the room too quickly. All this to maintain an appearance of wealth and status befitting her position, as if being paraded around like a show horse was the most important thing she could do in a day.

Still, she supposed it was better than the alternative.

A small silver bell sat on her nightstand. She rang it once. In five minutes, one of the kitchen girls would come bustling in with her morning tea, the first in a daily procession of servants, functionaries, and bureaucrats. There were days when she enjoyed the routine of it. And there were days when she had to remind herself that she'd chosen this . . . retirement.

A sudden knock at the door surprised her.

"Come in," she said, with a bit of the old steel in her voice. No, not steel. Weariness? Maybe just age at this point. Not that she'd ever spoken in lilting tones, even as a child. She pulled on her robe and settled into the straight-backed chair that faced the door.

A heartbeat later, her head servant walked into the room, back straight as a fencepost. Niklas Harran wasn't a tall man, but he walked with the kind of bearing that suggested his ancestors had invented the word and firmly expected him to live up to it. He crossed the room quickly, bowed, and set a small platter on the table in front of her. Then he stepped back, obviously waiting for further instructions.

So. Out with the routine today. She wondered why, then caught sight of a little square of paper on the tray.

Someone had tucked an envelope just beneath the little plate of biscuits she always ignored. She picked it up and slid her nail along the wax seal to break it, not caring where the little crumbs of red fell. Three paragraphs of ornate calligraphy: a long list of honors and titles followed by meaningless pleasantries. The sentences at the bottom were written in a neater hand. Ferrec read these several times before folding the paper closed and setting it back onto the tray.

"The king," she said, voice hollow, "is coming for a visit."

"That's . . . wonderful news, Governor. Did he say when?"

Ferrec caught the anxious tone of the question. As the head of her household staff, Niklas was every bit as competent as she could hope. But even a skilled carpenter needed a foundation to build on. "Two months," she answered, and saw some of the tension fall away from his posture. Still a drawn bowstring, but not one threatening to snap.

"I have no doubt we'll be ready for His Majesty by then," he said. "Perhaps you would like to start by getting dressed, Governor?"

Ferrec looked down at her robe, which had fallen open to reveal her rumpled pajamas. Of all her bitter compromises, being dressed by someone else irked her the most. Doubly so on a day like today, when every open mouth in the palace would soon be full of gossip about the king's visit. "Jaeri can help," she said, seizing on a sudden inspiration. "She'll be up early for archery lessons today. Send her in when you find her, please."

Niklas frowned but said nothing. Ferrec knew she shouldn't use him so. A man of Niklas' station had more important uses for his time than chasing children around the castle. On the other hand, it would do him good to step outside of his accustomed role every now and then. Besides, Jaeri was the only one who actually liked the little plates of biscuits.

"What do you think it means, Niklas?"

"His Majesty didn't say?"

Ferrec picked up the letter and held it out to him. He hesitated a moment before taking it. Ferrec was unsure whether or not it would be a breach of one of his countless unwritten protocols. She never could keep track of all of them. Once he had it in hand, he read it quickly, his eyes darting across the lines as efficiently as he did everything else. Then he refolded the letter and handed it back to her.

"It seems simple enough on the face of it. If there's a hidden message somewhere, I confess that I don't see it. But then, you know His Majesty better than I do."

"Better than most," Ferrec admitted. "But I don't see any hidden messages either. Still, I find it hard to believe that he's going to spend a month on the road just to visit an old friend. I'm not *that* likable."

"It's been a long while since I've written to my friends in the capital. I can ask if they have any news, if you like. Some of them even—" he paused, then seemed to remember himself. "Well, you never know who might overhear something interesting."

Ferrec waved a hand. "Don't bother, unless you like chasing shadows. He was good at misdirection twenty years ago. Better than anyone else on the field, or he wouldn't have gotten where he is. I can't imagine what fifteen years in Traste has done to him. We'll find out when he gets here, and not a moment sooner. Anything else?"

The confidence was easier to feign than to feel. Sethric worried her, but when the leaders buckled, the whole line fell. She tried to assume the bored, just-another-day posture that she'd used in front of her sergeants.

"Half a million things, Governor, but thankfully not all at once," Niklas said, confidently. Or was he feigning as well? She supposed he had his own troops to inspire. "I'll need to take a look at our larder," he continued, "and it's been too long since we've gone through the closed rooms. I have no idea what state some of them are in, but I should be able to get a general picture by this afternoon. If you'll excuse me, Governor."

He bowed once, then turned smoothly on his heel and left the way he'd come in. Ferrec read the letter twice more after he left, then tossed it into the wastebasket beside her bed. She'd find out what it meant soon and would plan for as many possibilities as she could in the meantime.

Jaeri floated into the room soon after, all infectious energy. At twelve, she wasn't the oldest of the children Ferrec had taken in, but she'd been one of the first. She was at that perfect age where she still believed anything was possible, if just slightly out of reach. Constantly in motion, her hands always seemed to be reaching for some new task. She tidied the room, talking while Ferrec made herself ready.

Six of her arrows had landed in the smallest ring today, she announced happily, and the last had been at twenty paces. She'd had to adjust for the wind, but she knew it would hit as soon as she'd let go of the string. Even the Captain had said he'd have a use for her on the wall one day, and Ferrec had to stifle the flutter of terror that clawed its way up her shoulders at the thought of Jaeri on Lletra's walls.

Anxious to change the subject, she asked after Jaeri's other studies, and the girl went on without slowing. Geography was her favorite. Languages were mostly boring, but one of the Hensian soldiers promised to teach her a drinking song if she could recite twenty sentences in the past tense. Arithmetic was her trickiest subject. Fascinating when it worked, frustrating when it didn't.

Pride might have been the right word for someone else, but Ferrec wouldn't lay claim to it. You couldn't take credit for an orphan's upbringing when you'd made them an orphan in the first place. Responsibility fit better, partly because it cut both ways.

"Is the king nice?"

The sudden question shocked Ferrec into answering directly. "No."

Jaeri took a moment to orient her worldview around this new information. "Are kings and queens usually nice?"

"Rarely," Ferrec admitted. "Most rulers are conquerors first, and people tend to remember what worked for them in the past. But 'not nice' isn't the same as evil. King Sethric is . . ." She faltered, as always, over the title she'd helped him earn. "He's fair where others are cruel, and quick to offer help to those who need it. He recognizes the value in other people, even those who have wronged him, and he has no patience for vengeance or bitter grudges. If there's anything evil about him, it's his selflessness. Most people shy away from hard decisions to spare themselves the pain of having a conscience."

Ferrec wondered if she'd said too much, but Jaeri looked thoughtful, not puzzled. "Is that why you're just a governor and not a queen?"

This child is much too old for her age. "Just so," Ferrec answered.

After that, they both moved a little more quietly. Jaeri was aware that her curiosity had crossed a line, but Ferrec wasn't in the habit of admonishing anyone for asking questions, and certainly not a child.

As a result of their diminished conversation, the two of them quickly ran out of things to do, and Jaeri excused herself. All the castle's children were given free rein after their chores were done, and some of them took it as a personal challenge to finish all their work by noon. The young girl made an effort at decorum, though, and waited until she was past the threshold of the door before she dashed down the hallway.

Ferrec followed at a more solemn pace. She was sure that Sethric wouldn't march on Lletra again. Putting down the rebellion twelve years ago had been a powerful example when they needed one, but the situation was different now. He wasn't a newly established conqueror, fresh from the field of battle, enemies plotting in secret behind every raised cup. He was a king now, with years of peace and prosperity behind him. Conflict would harm his image more than help it.

She turned down a hallway at random, letting her feet wander while her thoughts followed their own tortuous threads. Parts of her mind that she hadn't used in a long time were starting to wake up. Slowly at first, like a bear coming down from the mountains after winter.

Was he after an alliance of some kind? Ferrec was the last of his lieutenants, and they'd shared an ironclad mutual trust, but they hadn't spoken in years. Besides, what could she offer? Declarations of support, promises of aid. Small help, when any troops she could send would arrive weeks after anyone needed them.

Ferrec walked through a doorway and was surprised to feel the sun on her face. The clatter of wooden swords reached her ears, and she looked around in confusion. Why was she in the practice yard? A dozen men stopped in the middle of a drill to look at her, and the training sergeant bellowed a string of blistering curses at them, smacking shields that had lowered with his cudgel. One shield flew out of the poor soldier's grip, skidding across the courtyard stones. Ferrec grimaced in sympathy. Bad enough to lower your shield without thinking, but to forget you were even holding one? Her own sergeant would have peeled the skin off her feet.

Across the yard, she saw her captain of the guard exit the barracks and start walking toward her. Byren had been her friend for years, though perhaps friend was the wrong word. But what else fit that strange blend of trusted subordinate and occasional confidant? That sense of trust buoyed her spirits even now. She felt calmer as he approached.

"Something on your mind, Governor?"

Oh, yes. We're under siege, with no spies in the field. Strangely, the thought settled her mind. This was familiar ground, at least. "I'd like to inspect the gates today, Captain. Perhaps a few sections of the outer wall if we have time."

"If you're curious about the repairs—"

She raised a hand to forestall him. "Your progress reports are very detailed, Byren, but it's been too long since I've seen them with my own eyes, and I'm tired of sifting through paperwork. Humor me, will you?"

"Of course, Governor."

Dozens of possibilities to plan for. She'd see to the walls first.

CHAPTER ELEVEN

The heavy stone of the main archway slid into place with hardly a whisper. It weighed just over six hundred pounds, but the two men who guided it home didn't show the least sign of strain. To them, it might have felt like lifting an extraordinarily large box of feathers. Bulky, perhaps, but not difficult.

Twenty paces away, a boy of fourteen stood with both hands outstretched. He wore the same clothes as the men on the scaffolding: a long wool tunic with a slender leather belt and an old pair of cloth shoes. His clothes were clean, if a little large for his frame. They had probably belonged to someone else before him. That was the way of things in the more remote places of worship. You wore the clothes you were given until they became dusting rags, then inherited your next set of castoffs. Nothing set the boy apart from the others, except perhaps a bit of subconscious reverence from his fellows. He was, after all, performing a miracle.

One of his outstretched hands pointed toward the archway, the other to a nearby stack of wooden pallets. The wooden slats lay perpendicular to one another, the heavy boards crisscrossed and reinforced with iron springs. The whole contraption creaked under an invisible weight, compressing the springs several inches as they absorbed the strain. The boy could have directed the displaced force into anything else—the ground, or even some of the other stones—but this gave them a chance to study the effects firsthand. Two of the scribes circled the creaking wood, taking measurements and talking to each other.

Jurald smiled. Even as a senior cleric of the Order, he was forbidden from preaching the unknowable will of the gods. In the Order's view, the duty of any devout Kerran was to leave them to their mysterious plans, trusting that strength of character and upright moral behavior would serve their divine ends. There was no prohibition against interpreting the signs for himself, though, and to him the message had never been clearer.

Rebuild.

Fifteen years ago, the Order could have traveled the width and breadth of the realm without finding more than a handful of saints with this particular gift. Now it seemed they discovered another dozen every year, many born during the worst years of the fighting. With a bit of training, an Architect and a team of craftsmen could build a house in a matter of hours. Jurald had heard stories of entire neighborhoods being rebuilt in weeks, of survivors who returned to the homes they'd abandoned to find new houses on the old foundations.

One of the scribes next to the pallet waved a hand to catch Jurald's attention. Jurald motioned for the boy to stop, and the invisible weight eased. Now that they had their measurements, they could compare them to the numbers that had just arrived from Traste. So far the variations had been minor between Architects. As with most things, skill and confidence carried more weight than any sort of inborn talent. There were a handful of souls who never quite achieved the finesse needed for delicate work, but even they had their uses. The Order did not waste the gifts it was given.

Jurald pushed himself to standing, ignoring the cracks and pops in his knees. They rarely hurt anymore, and he couldn't bring himself to begrudge them when they did. He'd put them through hell for years, and if they wanted to complain while they worked, they'd earned the right.

One of the village stonemasons approached him with a roll of paper tucked under her arm. He put on a smile. He'd had a growing number of these conversations over the years, starting with the slim metal chain that marked him as a senior member of the Order. Most people simply thought it polite to have a conversation with him before asking his blessing, though a rare few actually wanted his advice. He spent the next few minutes politely implying that, as the expert, she could do whatever she liked to the building, and he happily agreed to pass her prayers on to the gods.

The boy approached him next. This conversation, at least, Jurald felt qualified to handle.

"You did well."

"The gods did well," the boy said dutifully. "I'm honored that they've chosen to work through me."

"And yet, if you hadn't gotten out of bed this morning, they'd have felt quite useless, I think. Maybe they're the ones who should feel honored." The boy gaped, and Jurald couldn't help but grin back. "Peace. I only mean to say that it's not impious to take joy in useful work."

The boy closed his mouth and managed a bow before shuffling away. Jurald knew he should set a better example, but he'd spent too many years being grim and solemn. Now that he was older, a streak of his boyhood mischief had started to resurface, and he was happy to see it.

The morning's task done, Jurald left and started the long climb up to the monastery itself. The seclusion of the main living area was meant to facilitate quiet contemplation, but it made these in-between areas necessary. The farmers and crafters who made their living in the foothills would walk or ride the low mountain trails for miles to receive blessings, and the brothers and sisters of the monastery would walk just as far down the mountains to meet them.

Over time, these meeting places became small communities in their own right, halfway between chapterhouse and trading post. The building they'd worked on today would become an inn, a place for families to rest when they couldn't make the journey here and back in a single day.

They had a much smaller house for the brothers and sisters, two adjoining rooms with barely enough space for a pallet and a washbowl in each. If a third person came down during the day, they'd have to choose between the long trip back or sleeping outside. There was a time when he'd found the mountain air bracing, the walks invigorating. Now he wondered how many years it would be before someone found him beside the path, a single fist clutching his galloping heart.

Still, there were worse places to die. Jurald reflected on a few of them as he walked.

Up ahead, a dark figure struggled against the rising slope, wool cloak wind-wrapped around slumped shoulders. Jurald didn't bother quickening his pace. Whoever walked ahead of him on the trail, they clearly weren't used to the thin air or the cold. He remembered his first months in the mountains, when he practically lost his breath sweeping the floor. After a few minutes of easy walking, he pulled even with the stranger.

"Pleasant day for a stroll," Jurald remarked.

The man's face whipped around in surprise. A pale face with a thin nose in the center, red from the cold. Brown eyes and hair, both so dark they were nearly black. He had the look of someone from Greymarsh, and his accent confirmed it when he spoke. "If you say so, stranger." He didn't take his hands from his cloak and kept trudging forward through the cold.

"If you're bound for the village of Whitethrush, I'm afraid you've missed it by about half a day. There's nothing along this road but a flock of doddering old crows."

The stranger turned again and finally noticed the chain around Jurald's neck. He dipped forward in a quick bow. "My mistake. Forgiveness, umm . . . ?"

"Jurald. And you are?"

"Kirain of . . . Greymarsh, I suppose, though I haven't lived there since I was eight. Lately from the capital."

"That's a long way to walk. What brings you to the edge of the world, Kirain of Greymarsh, lately of Traste?"

The stranger moved his cloak to the side just enough to reveal a handful of letters. "Messages for the village of Whitethrush, as you said. And one for the Prior of White-thrush Monastery."

"You've found one of us, at least. May I?" Jurald reached for the bundle and Kirain handed it over. As his hand touched the letter at the bottom of the stack, a clear chime sounded. The stranger didn't react, but then, no one but Jurald would have heard it. This message was meant for him and no other.

Did his hand tremble when he took the letter? He hoped not. But if so, who could blame him? It was cold in the mountains, and he was a frail, stupid old man, always hoping in vain that his past would forget he existed.

"Do you travel down to the village often, Prior?" Jurald heard the hopeful note in Kirain's voice.

Jurald brought his spinning thoughts to heel. "About once a week, but others go more often. If you have other business to attend to, I can make sure these are delivered."

"Truly? That's a real blessing, Prior, as good as the gods ever gave. Thank you."

"Happy to help. Stop by the construction site on your way through, and ask one of the monks there for something warm to drink on your way."

"I'll do that, Prior. Thanks again."

Jurald walked further along the road. There was a place along the path where the road narrowed to hardly more than a trail, winding its way between the rocks. In the shadow of the massive stones of the mountain, he broke the seal on the letter that bore his name.

Encrypted, of course. The illusion that originally concealed the message had faded at his touch, but some doors needed more than one lock. Jurald knew the key, however. A few minutes of work lay the original message bare.

Found the trail again, at long last. No longer alone, not sure if the other two are what they seem. Bound for Barste, expect to make contact with someone there. Bless me in this work. We are almost done now.

Years ago, when Kyrede's words had been careful and measured, Jurald had been impressed with the man. He'd seemed quiet and determined. Focused, but not fanatical. Had fifteen years of hunting his fellow Ghosts changed him? Or just worn away the outer layers to uncover what he'd always carried beneath the surface? Either way, he seemed less steady now. Brittle and sharp, like a blade too long at the wheel.

Jurald read the letter again but could barely make sense of it. Insanity was its own kind of cipher, he supposed. Barste was clear enough, but who were "the other two"? Damn this impossible task, and damn the ones who had set it before him. Necessary or not, Kyrede wouldn't move a step without the Order's blessing, and none of his superiors could handle the man. Which meant that it fell to Jurald to loose this arrow.

Because that's what this letter was. Kyrede needed permission to kill in the name of the greater good. But how could you build something new atop a foundation of secrecy and murder?

The walk back to the monastery was a lonely one, with nothing but howling wind and long-buried thoughts to keep him company. Back in his room, he burned the letter in his fireplace, stirring the ashes until nothing remained. When the dark cloud of his mood lifted enough for him to think clearly, Jurald walked to the stables.

The sister on duty gave him a curious look when he entered but didn't ask any questions when he asked her to saddle a horse. While she walked the beast around the yard to warm it up and check its gait, Jurald went to the kitchens and gathered what provisions he could. He'd begged his way across the kingdom years ago and didn't care to relive the experience. Laden with supplies, he scrawled a vague note and left it on his table before heading back outside. By sunset, he was down in the foothills, outpacing the wind.

Jurald knew he'd never be able to convince his superiors to call off the hunt. The sins the Ghosts had committed placed them beyond redemption, but there was a danger in letting the past eclipse the future. This quest to eradicate them may have started as a means to ensure their silence, but Kyrede's success in rooting them out had changed it. There had been nothing holy about this work for years. Only a personal quest for vengeance, with a madman at the heart of it.

On either side of his path, grass and twigs bent flat to the earth as he displaced the force of his own weight in the saddle. To his mount, he and all his supplies together might have weighed as much as a feather. The horse leaned forward, reveling in its own speed, and Jurald shared its thrill. It felt good to finally be moving toward a destination, to take a direct hand in events for the first time in years.

The trail would end in Barste, he decided. After that, they could rebuild.

Rebuild, and pray for it to last.

CHAPTER TWELVE

The cheery warmth of our inn's common room should have been a relief after two weeks of cold, but I was too distracted to enjoy it. A few words from Andza had transformed my quiet childhood in Casmhe into something foreign and surreal. An impossible tangle of moments, with no guideposts linking one memory to another.

Andza outlined the plan before we entered the city—what little there was of it. The trouble was that Talia—no, *Serine*—had given him a name to work with, but it was almost ten years out of date and would have been dangerous to use in the open. In other words, worse than useless.

He'd been in this situation before, though, and knew how to handle it.

The first step involved establishing a purpose in town, and Andza had already done most of that work before we arrived. His credentials as a living historian opened doors to Barste's preening upper class, and Rahad and I could answer most direct questions honestly. We were his assistants, and our part-time jobs in the city would help pay for expenses while we were here.

Rahad's skills merited work as a portrait artist. I was more of a challenge. I'd been granted an interview at a local school, but I had yet to meet the headmaster and was still nervous about making an impression.

"Remember, you're not looking for figureheads," he said, eyes on the nearest table. The inn's other patrons ignored us, huddled around their own conversations. "The people we're looking for never step into the shoes of the truly powerful. You're looking for their assistants, their administrators, possibly their bodyguards. People who live in the shadows that more brightly lit figures cast."

We nodded, as we'd done the last several times he'd told us this. He'd been repeating himself a lot since we arrived in Barste. Someone who didn't know him well might have called him absent-minded, but I recognized that aura of focused awareness from the day he walked into our shop. Not someone who was lost in his thoughts, but fully alive in them, with all the impatient energy of a banked fire.

If he repeated something, then it was likely worth hearing more than once.

I tried to emulate what I saw in him, to pick up those pieces of his personality and lay them over my own. I would need every bit of his cleverness to work out who we were looking for. I would need his caution, too, in order to avoid exposing our task. Most of all, though, I needed his distrust. I'd already decided not to tell our little group about my connection to Talia, which meant that I'd also be looking for parts of my own story—and deciding which of those parts to share.

And there's the little matter of staying alive, I thought, remembering the city's reputation. Just a little thing, hardly worth mentioning. The kind of thing you might forget if you were careless.

The front doors of the Withered Rose had been ornately carved a century ago, but standing before them, I couldn't guess what the pictures were supposed to be. Time and weather had done most of the work. Even the vandals' additions to the delicate murals looked faded and shallow. The effect made the door less of an entryway and more of a relic, some worn-down plaque that marked the building's claim to a forgotten time. Which was probably the point.

I knocked, and nothing happened. Hardly surprising. A school is like any other place of business. If you have business there, you just walk in. But I felt justified in being cautious. To hear Andza tell it, Barste's ruling class added significance to every little thing, and barging into a room without announcing myself had all the makings of a serious social misstep.

After I felt sure that no one was coming to answer the door, I turned the handle and walked in. I immediately saw why no one had heard me. This outer door led into a large courtyard, and the nearest building sat at the other end of it, sixty paces away. Two cobblestone walkways branched off to follow the outer edge of the courtyard, while a third ran straight ahead. Nothing grew between the walkways but grass.

The statue in the center of the courtyard was clearly meant to be the centerpiece, the only exception to the calm austerity of its pristine surroundings. The scene depicted a rose bush in full flower, carved from stone. A faceless gardener stood next to it, examining a plucked rose. I followed the shadow of his hand and saw a ring of stone markers set into the ground.

At first, I couldn't make sense of the layout of the stones. The ring stopped as it approached the walkway on either side, but judging from the position of the shadow at this hour, the missing part of the ring would have marked the hours when the sun was down. A sundial. I realized that the entire orientation of the school had been built with that in mind, and that casual display of wealth and influence carried more weight than gold or gems could have matched.

It also made me a bit more confident in my wardrobe. I'd considered wearing my mother's hairpiece today, some small bit of jewelry to show that I wasn't just a poor girl from a small town. After seeing the neglected front door and the understated garden, I knew that what I looked like didn't matter—only what I said.

The headmaster's office sat just behind the main reception area, a spacious room with a curved wooden desk at the far end. Bookshelves lined each wall, and I scanned the titles with open curiosity. Mathematics, astronomy, politics, natural sciences, with as many works of fiction scattered between. They weren't organized by any system I could discern. It had the look of a well-loved collection. Only its owner could make sense of the chaos.

I accepted the servant's offer of tea and settled into one of the two leather chairs in front of the desk. A window behind the headmaster's chair opened into a private garden, and a skylight above the desk filled the room with natural light. Both windows were barred, and I suspected the desk drawers had locks on them. Unlike the haphazard shelves of books, everything on the desk was neatly arranged. Some fastidious servant, I guessed, imposing their own will on the mess.

Tea arrived with the headmaster, a middle-aged man with a receding hairline and a sour expression. Based on his simple clothes and sturdy build, I'd have placed him as a common laborer. He took a teacup from the tray with a calloused hand and motioned for me to do the same.

"So you're looking for a position here at the school."

"Yes, sir."

"Qualifications?"

"Two years of study at the Library in Sharme. Mostly history and foreign languages, a bit of literature. I also have a letter of recommendation from one of the professors there."

He waved this away, uninterested. "You're familiar with the Forsten rebellion, I assume."

Not the type to waste time. "I assume you mean the first one? The second one ended within a few hours. Most people barely mention it at all. The first, however—"

"Stop. I'm sure you're capable of reciting facts. I have books that can do that. My question for you is, what does it have to do with me?"

"I . . . don't know?" I faltered. "Sorry, but I don't know anything about you."

"Tough. You won't know anything about the students you're teaching, but you'll still be expected to hold their interest."

He leaned back in his chair and took a sip of tea. He'd taken the wind from my sails, and he knew it. I felt a stir of panic but managed to push it back before it overwhelmed me. I would *not* be sent away. If this door closed, and Andza was right about this school, it might take us months to find another way in. I was our best hope for following this lead.

It was true that I didn't know anything about the headmaster, but I could guess. His clothes were clean but practical, and the loose cut of the fabric didn't do much to hide the size of his arms and shoulders. I cast him in a few different roles before deciding on some kind of dock worker. Barste did most of its trading on the river, and I had an easier time imagining him unloading crates than sitting behind a desk.

Calloused knuckles and a crooked pinky confirmed him as a brawler rather than a duelist, but that sharp gaze wouldn't square with the image of an unschooled street tough. No, he was far too intelligent for that . . . But he might have *started* there. An intelligent man with a simple job, which led to more and more responsibility as he proved himself capable.

What else could his superiors have trusted him with? Handling accounts, resolving disputes. Perhaps even smuggling sensitive goods? Those roles fit him seamlessly, but I had a hard time imagining the journey from savvy enforcer to private school headmaster.

"How many of the students here have ties to nobility?"

"Nearly all."

Aha. Talk about impressing the right people. But how far under their thumb was he? I had a difficult time imagining the hardened soul in front of me as a grateful lapdog. I decided to gamble. "Most people talk about the Forsten rebellion as a failed revolution. The peasants rise up, they're put down, everyone goes on with their day."

"And how do you talk about it?"

"The first rebellion cost thousands of lives, but it also brought sweeping changes to tenant farming, which was basically inherited indentured labor. The second rebellion, a famous failure, happened the same year they closed the doors of the last debtor's prison. By the time the Accords went into effect, people didn't even have to rebel anymore."

"So you're saying the rebellions were actually successful?"

"I'm saying that someone saw a pattern and realized one would be. Barste had passed the point where things could continue the way they had been. People weren't satisfied and were willing to do something about it. Acknowledging that saved both sides a few thousand lives, not to mention a few centuries of time." I decided to steal a line from Andza's class.

"The point of studying history is being able to realize when it's happening to you."

"True," he said. He fixed me with a hard stare. "Of course, it would be easy to take the opposite lesson. Tighten your grip on power, no matter the cost. That's a winning strategy nine times out of ten."

"And catastrophic for everyone when it doesn't work." Time to play my hand. "Besides, why bother covering that perspective here? I suspect they learn enough of that at home."

It was a gamble, and it all depended on how the headmaster saw his superiors. If he was here to follow orders and make sure his students fell into the roles their parents had planned for them, I was out. But if he was here for a different reason . . .

He extended his hand. I shook it, relief washing over me.

"Welcome to the Rose."

"I don't think I can teach at the Withered Rose anymore," I told Andza later that night.

He lifted an eyebrow, waited.

"They have me teaching the youngest class!" I wailed. "All I do is wipe noses and break up fights. I barely have a chance to talk to the other teachers, let alone the headmaster." My room occupied a forgotten corner of the school, several minutes' walk from the teacher's room and an impossible distance from the headmaster's study. "Unless we think Miss Talia's friend is posing as a six-year-old, we're wasting our time."

"First of all," Andza said flatly, "I would never waste *our* time. At worst, I'm wasting yours, and that's a risk I'm willing to take. If you think you have a better use for *your* time, feel free to suggest it, but you'll forgive me if I don't hand control of my life's work over to someone who loses her patience on the first day."

I wilted.

"Time is the one currency we have to spend," he continued, his tone softer. "The truth is, we do waste most of it because we can't possibly guess how we're supposed to spend it. But I've been at this a long time, and you can trust me when I say that we need eyes at the Withered Rose."

"Well then, do you at least have any teaching advice?"

"Bring extra handkerchiefs," he suggested, without a speck of humor. Then, as an afterthought, "And I wouldn't recommend wearing jewelry. Children have a tendency to grab anything they can reach."

"Thanks," I said, "But I'd figured that last one out for myself."

If I ever had any desire to become a mother, I lost it during the next few weeks. Every day was worse than the last. I caught two colds in ten days; I learned to dread every sneeze and sniffle. I went to sleep with aching feet every night and woke up with the remains of yesterday's headache.

Worst of all, Andza and Rahad came home every night looking cheerful and refreshed. I had no idea where either of them spent their days, but I'd have bet both my swollen feet that it didn't involve *children*.

Near the end of my first month, I stumbled into the teacher's room to collapse into a desk I hadn't seen in days. The wooden chair back dug into my shoulder blades, but I didn't care. Anything to avoid supporting my own weight for a minute.

I sighed and heard my sigh echoed from a desk across the room.

When I opened my eyes, I saw another teacher grinning at me. He looked almost as tired as I felt. I smiled back at him, dimly aware that I should take the opportunity to get to know him, that I'd taken this job for the sole purpose of getting to know the other teachers.

But the air in the room had that perfect winter chill, and the sunlight felt warm on my back, and I had a hard time thinking about anything else.

CHAPTER THIRTEEN

"Your lines are getting worse," Rahad pointed out.

I'd been sketching unconsciously, no longer making any real effort at the impossible task of learning to draw. I looked over the section I'd just finished. The left side of my candlestick meandered off course, getting thicker and thinner at random intervals. I held it up to compare, but the brass candlestick on the table between us did not, unfortunately, have matching deformities. "Last week you said my line work was horrible."

"Well, now you're worse than horrible. What are these supposed to be?" He pointed to a cluster of rough ovals that were meant to be blobs of wax but looked more like frog eggs.

"A mistake?" I offered.

"I'll say."

The inn had cleared out after the lunch hour, and the two of us were both off for the day. I'd hoped to spend the time learning more about the city. Our innkeeper had a penchant for gossip, provided Andza wasn't around to correct him on his history. Half of what he said was hearsay, but the local viewpoint made it invaluable.

Unfortunately, Andza still held to the as-yet-untested theory that Rahad's skill at spotting forgeries would help him spot illusions in the wild. As soon as we'd announced we were heading downstairs for a late lunch, he shouted "Lessons!" over his shoulder and went back to his notes. My only consolation was that Rahad hated history lessons as much as I hated drawing.

"Time's up, by the way."

"No fair," he complained. "You weren't even trying."

"I drew the candlestick! I'm just not good at it."

"You drew *a* candlestick. But not the one in front of you."

The waitress came by to refill our drinks, and I used it as an excuse not to ask Rahad what he meant. It always ended the same way, with some maddening half explanation that made no sense unless you already knew what he was talking about. The more I spent time with him, the clearer it became that we had very different minds.

"Either way," I said, closing my sketchbook. "Time's up."

He sighed. "What are we learning today, then? Droughts and floods through the ages? Or do you have another list of boats that sank a thousand years ago?"

When we'd first started, Rahad had a tendency to be . . . unkind as a teacher. The old petty rivalry had surfaced, with all its former heat. The first few lessons had been pure vengeance, but after we'd stopped flinging barbs at each other, I'd intended to use the "boats" as a kind of olive branch.

The library at the Withered Rose filled two rooms. Nothing approaching the wealth of knowledge in Sharme, but Sharme didn't hold all the books in the world, and the Rose had acquired a number of private collections through the centuries. One unassuming tome had been copied at least twice from the original, and even its dusty pages were frail with age. It held a handful of personal accounts about the crossing from the old world, with a section at the back for ship names and passenger lists. I found them absolutely engrossing. Rahad, unfortunately, did not.

"Nothing so dull, I hope. Actually, I was hoping to talk more about the city."

Suspicion. "What do you want to know?"

I wasn't clever enough to circle around what I wanted, so I tried to make my tone conversational and went straight to the heart of it. "Well, how's work, for one thing? You only ever talk about it with Andza."

"It's fine," he said, closing his own sketchbook. He'd tilted it away from me when we started drawing, but I caught the top edge of the page as he folded it closed. A snowy canopy that gave way to clouds, with the top of a building in the distance. No doubt drawn from memory, the monster.

"It must be nice doing something you enjoy so much."

"It's fine," he repeated.

Why was he being so defensive? I took a sip of my drink and tried to make the next question sound casual. "Where does he have you working, anyway?" So far he and Andza had been light on specifics.

I expected him to change the subject or say something vague. Maybe even lie outright. His sudden, defiant glare took me by complete surprise.

"What? What did I say?"

"Too much, as usual," he snarled. Then he gathered his things and escaped upstairs without another word.

What exactly did Andza have him doing? One thing was clear. I wasn't the only one in our little group keeping secrets.

When we weren't busy with work or lessons, Andza had us take lots of walks. Sometimes we had a specific goal in mind, but we wandered more often than not. One of his many precautions against unfriendly eyes, apparently. Moving about the city in twos and threes, we spent entire days covering a daunting amount of ground. Anyone trying to guess our purpose would have needed to spend a lot of time and energy chasing false leads.

On one occasion, the three of us had gone out shopping. I forget what we needed. Pencils, paper, candles, lamp oil. Food, possibly. Andza and Rahad got irritable if they didn't know where their next six meals were coming from.

We'd gone to one of the daylight markets, named less for its operating hours and more for the type of trouble you could expect. Barste classified petty theft, drunken brawls, and a dozen other minor crimes as "daylight crimes." In other words, things the average citizen might get up to on a normal day.

I'd fallen behind the group to browse a shop that sold little wooden figurines. The shopkeeper was polite but guessed that I didn't have any money to spend and wasn't far off. We dressed plainly at the Library, and the last month hadn't done my wardrobe any favors. Should I be looking for new clothes? I thought about my stack of unassuming wool dresses back at the inn and decided that I probably should.

A sudden noise cut through the normal din of the market. I heard the crash of something being knocked over. Raised voices spread outward in a ring as the shock reached the crowd. People pressed around me suddenly, backing away from something I couldn't see. I looked for Andza and Rahad but lost them in the swarm of people.

Panicking, I started pushing forward in the direction I'd seen them last. The crowd pulled back, and I shouldered past a pair of people backing away from something up ahead. I stumbled and straightened to find myself in an empty circle ringed with people. Two men occupied the center. Neither looked at me.

I can picture the scene clearly now, but at the time fear had me in its grip. Everything moved in a fog of too-sharp details that I couldn't work into a full picture. The man to my left was a few years older than me, maybe a hair taller. He held a long knife in his left hand. Was he injured? He was shaking droplets of something dark from his fingers and had a spreading stain across his shirt.

The man facing him was older and a bit taller, but unarmed. His neck and shoulders were stooped with fear, but he had a grim, stubborn look on his face. They stood over the wreckage of a wooden table, plates and food scattered in a careless arc at their feet. I had the stupid urge to ask them what they were doing.

A hand grabbed my wrist and pulled hard enough to turn me half around. I tried to pull away from it on instinct, but the stranger's grip tightened, and I yelped in pain and surprise. After a momentary struggle, I realized I recognized him.

"I know you," I said. He worked at the Rose, one of the teachers who got contracted out as a private tutor. I reached for a name but couldn't find one.

"You do," he agreed, loosening his grip. "Jalina, right?"

His name drifted across the fog. I reached for it. "Aian," I said. "From the Rose." I looked around but still couldn't make sense of anything. "What's going on?"

"If I had to guess," he said, "one of those men is getting ready to die, and the other's offering to help him along."

"Someone should do something!"

"Someone should," he agreed. "But not you. And certainly not me."

I'd never seen real violence before, and I didn't particularly want to. I turned to look anyway, the bones in my neck guided by some grim, irresistible curiosity. I saw the pitiful, ineffectual swing from the unarmed man. Then a flash of steel and a grunting exhale as his killer's fist guided a blade deep into his gut.

He fell to the ground. Why stand? He was dead and knew it, and no one dies on their feet. He steadied himself with one hand while the other felt around for his wound. Not to stop the bleeding—the dueling blades they use in Barste are as long as your forearm; they can reach your heart through your stomach. He felt for it, I think, to confirm that it was real, to know for sure that he was dying and only had a few moments to make his peace with it.

I don't know if he managed to or not. He died on a crowded street, curled around himself, quiet. I couldn't see his face.

Aian saw me safely back to the others, and we cut our shopping trip early. After half an hour of nervous shaking —and a dozen worried glances between Andza and Rahad when they thought I wouldn't notice—I steeled myself enough to walk downstairs to the common room for dinner.

A warm meal and an early night seemed like the perfect cure for my nerves, but the scene in the marketplace had thrown a pall over everything. The low mahogany timbers of the ceiling, which had once seemed cozy and private, felt too crowded, and every shifting log in the generous fireplace sent up a crash of sparks that made me flinch. I ordered a thin vegetable soup, not trusting my stomach to handle much else, and sat quietly while I ate.

Our innkeeper noticed my somber mood. "What's the matter with her?" he asked Andza.

"Duel in the Flower Market today," Andza answered.

"It's been a bad winter," the innkeeper said. He spoke as if cold weather and public stabbings were the same thing: forces outside your control, better or worse from year to year. "The families aren't usually this active until the Long Night."

Andza grunted but didn't respond. Rahad took the bait. "What's the Long Night?"

The innkeeper grinned and tried to share a look with Andza, but Andza either didn't notice or didn't care to participate. Unfazed, the smile slid smoothly over to Rahad. "It's an old custom," he began. "Almost as old as the city itself. People in Barste have longer memories than most, at least for things worth remembering."

He had a rich voice, if a quiet one. I think he would have struggled to hold an audience on any street corner, or even the whole of his own common room, but it reached the three of us easily enough. A campfire voice, meant for close gatherings on dark nights. I felt my ears prick up and saw Rahad lean in.

"The Long Night is the one night of the year when the families put away their knives and cudgels and meet each other out in the open. Sunset to sunrise, on the shortest night of the year. Any longer and they wouldn't be able to stand each other."

"So why do it at all?" Rahad asked.

"Some say it started as a peace offering. A chance to mourn and bury your dead. Others say it was a bribe from the city guard, who gave up trying to enforce the law and agreed to turn a blind eye to certain matters on the condition that they get one sorry holiday a year to spend with their own families.

"But if you ask me, it's a matter of pride. Any animal can fight over a yard of territory, but only a thinking man can rein in his instincts. Keeping a handle on their tempers adds a sense of dignity to the drama, if you catch my meaning." He shrugged. "The reasons have been lost to time, but the custom remains."

"Wine imports," Andza muttered. The innkeeper frowned at him.

"What do they do instead?" Rahad asked.

"They do what any sorry soul would do when separated from their one true love. They drink."

"That's it?"

"It is and it isn't, like anything else to do with the families. Everything is a performance for them, and the duels don't stop just because the normal weapons are put aside. They raise glasses to their enemies' health instead, and their enemies are honor bound to respond. Mostly it's the young duelists who suffer, accepting the toast on their patron's behalf. The way they stumble through the streets afterward, I'd bet even money they prefer getting stabbed."

"Wine imports," Andza muttered again. This time the innkeeper shot him a sour look.

"But no one dies?" I asked. "Through poison or drunkenness or some other accident?"

"It happens, but not unless someone's willing to risk great offense. Which means," he leaned in meaningfully, "that if you truly want someone dead, and the Long Night is approaching, it's best to get your knives in while you can."

"Interesting fellow," Rahad said once we returned to our room.

The partition between my bed and the rest of the room was a welcome change from our previous arrangement, but the thin wooden divider only afforded one kind of privacy. There was no missing Andza's derisive snort.

"Interesting, I'll grant him. But he's as blind dumb as anyone else in this city. The Long Night started almost exactly two hundred years ago, for very practical reasons."

"I believe you mentioned wine imports," I said. I finished buttoning my woolen pajamas up to the neck and walked around the divider to sit across from them. As always, they gave me a look of pure confusion, as if I'd been up to gods-knew-what on my side of the room, and they were trying very hard not to guess. It was a strange sort of problem. On the road, I'd been uncomfortable about my lack of privacy, and now they were uncomfortable with me having it. "Some money-making scheme, I assume?"

"A conspiracy between two families. One family has a well-known financial tie to a vineyard and offers to throw a massive party to celebrate their good harvest. Another family spreads rumors that half the vines have failed, and they cast the party as an attempt to disguise the first family's catastrophic misfortune. The rest of the families buy up all the other wine in the area, knowing they can resell it to the host later once the shortage drives up the price."

"Only there was no shortage."

"No. Not near Barste, anyway. While the other families here were buying up all the local wine, the first two used the funds to purchase future wine shares from all the surrounding areas. Since there *was* a shortage in Greymarsh that year, they bought the futures for a steal. For the next three years, they were the only two families capable of importing wine and charged accordingly. In the meantime, the original party became a recurring tradition and spent the next two centuries evolving into what it is now."

"Seems like a lot of trouble for a temporary victory." Rahad frowned. "That's like sticking a knife in someone, but not deep enough to actually hurt them, and then letting them walk away. Except it's a dozen people instead of one, and they all know where you live."

"You're not wrong. It *is* ridiculous, but those are the rules to their absurd game. Barste is a city haunted by itself. When our ancestors fled the old world," he nodded at me, "the noble families who settled here clung to the one remaining vestige of their identities, which was their enmity for one another. That's the beginning and the end of the history of Barste, with the occasional twist and turn to account for personal acts of greed or ambition. If this city's bizarre customs start to make sense to you, consider it a mark against your sanity."

CHAPTER FOURTEEN

Spring came early to Barste, and my charges at the Withered Rose found other uses for their energy. We had class outside most days, and the students took the larger space as a kind of challenge. They wanted to prove to the world that they were older now, more powerful and more capable than they'd been last year.

Mostly this meant a lot of screaming. Children, in my limited experience, shriek at every unexpected thing, whether in fear or delight. I became an expert at telling the difference, which meant that I could conduct class from the edges rather than the center, trusting the softness of the ground to keep them from any real harm.

I saw Aian more often, or perhaps I just felt more comfortable approaching him since he'd rescued me in the market. Everyone else in the teacher's room seemed very impressed with his heroics. I blushed every time he told the story, though he was kind enough to paint me as a hapless bystander instead of the terrified idiot I'd actually been.

"I wanted to thank you, by the way. I don't know if I ever actually said so."

It was late morning, and the two of us were the only ones in the teacher's room. The younger students ate lunch earlier, so I had an hour free before afternoon classes. Aian's workday typically started in the afternoon and went until late evening, so our breaks occasionally overlapped.

"Not at all," Aian said. "Though I don't think you were ever in any real danger. I doubt either of them even noticed." He grinned at me, and I smiled back. I'd wasted a pleasant half hour daydreaming about his smile, but he was at least twenty years older than me, judging by the gray in his hair, and obviously uninterested. I kept my daydreams to myself.

"Well, thank you anyway."

He motioned to a stack of books on my desk. I'd raided the school's library again, and as usual I'd taken more books than I possibly had time for. "That seems like an ambitious curriculum," he joked.

"Just a few books for a friend," I explained. "And maybe one or two for myself."

He looked over the titles I'd collected so far. One stuck out: a biography of the king's early years, before his unlikely rise to power. "And here I thought your subject was ancient history."

"It is," I agreed. "But I realized that I never get to read biographies about anyone who's still alive. I'm curious if they read differently when the subject is still able to argue with the author."

That wasn't quite true, but I wasn't about to tell Aian the real reason. I had a hunch that Sethric's past might contain hints about who the illusionists were (I felt strange calling them Ghosts when they didn't call themselves that). More importantly, it might offer an answer to Andza's question, some explanation for why they picked Sethric above any other contender.

But most of all, I hoped to find my mother's name in the pages somewhere.

Come to think of it, was my mother to blame for my field of study? Was I only interested in the details of other people's lives because I had so many unanswered questions about my own? Had I chosen ancient history because it was safer, easier to hold at a distance? How much of my personality had been decided by someone I'd never even properly met? I shelved those questions for later and tried to focus on the conversation at hand.

"I suppose it depends on the ruler," Aian said, trying his best to look thoughtful, though a grin still lurked at the corner of his mouth. "And how likely they are to execute people who disagree with them."

"Or reward those who agree," I pointed out.

"What do you think of the king?" he asked suddenly. I don't think I'd ever seen a more carefully blank expression on a person's face.

"He doesn't have much to do with me," I answered honestly. "Which is probably what most people want in a ruler."

"True," he acknowledged. "But humor me. You've read about more historical figures than anyone I know, except maybe Headmaster Griffe. You must have some idea how he compares."

"He isn't as bloodthirsty as his predecessors," I said, "or as vindictive. Most seem to use the crown as an opportunity to punish their enemies or secure power for their friends. He appoints both to prominent positions and expects them to do the work that comes with their new titles."

"He did invade Lletra three years after his coronation," Aian said, voice still carefully neutral. "Some would call that bloodthirsty."

"To be fair, they did rebel. And Governor Ferrec hasn't exactly been a despot since she took over."

"Ah, so you're anti-rebellion now. Are you sure you're not from Barste?" His characteristic smile had returned. Just conversation now, no more careful questions.

"Certain." I had a sudden suspicion but wasn't quite sure how to voice it. "Where are you from, by the way? I don't think you've ever said."

"North of here. I'd call it a village, but I'm not sure it even merits the name."

"Do you ever visit?"

"No." He sighed. "Not that there's much left to see. But even if there was, I'm not sure I would go back." He smiled again, but it seemed forced. "Too boring, you see. Even the people who lived there got tired of it a long time ago."

A peal of bells from the inner courtyard announced the start of afternoon classes, and Aian looked toward them. "Ah, but I'm late for an appointment. Enjoy your reading, Jalina." He turned and left.

I watched him go, frowning. There were layers to Aian that I hadn't looked for or expected, but that was true for most people. Could these be important? I put it out of my thoughts for now, hurrying to my own classroom. Some part of my mind had already started working on the puzzle. Sooner or later the pieces would click into place.

"I have a suspect," I announced, to very little effect. The door swung closed behind me, and I realized that I'd announced my discovery to anyone who might have been in the hallway. Not that the people inside the room acted like it was anything worth mentioning.

"About time," Rahad said. "I've found three."

I ignored him, a sure sign of my immense maturity.

"Who?" Andza asked without looking up. The piles of paper on his desk would have slowly devoured him if he didn't burn more than half of them in the fireplace each night.

"His name is Aian. He's a tutor at the Withered Rose, but since the students' parents are all determined to give their child an advantage over the others, he gets contracted out to individual houses for weeks at a time." I pulled off my shoes and crossed the room to my side of the divider, tossing my shawl onto a chair as I passed.

"Granted, he can't always pick the house he's attached to, but he has easy access to a number of important families. And he seems interested in the king, and how he's perceived, but doesn't want to share his own thoughts. I got the feeling he was looking for . . . I'm not sure. Justification?"

"Plenty of people talk about Kerra's king," Rahad pointed out.

"You weren't there to hear him." I pulled on my slippers before walking back out to the common area. "He wasn't gossiping. He was looking for my opinion and being very careful about sharing his own. Do you know of any villages north of here?" I asked Andza.

"How far north? There are dozens of smaller towns between Barste and Lletra."

"He didn't say, but it might not be important. Just something I found odd."

Andza pursed his lips. "It's hard to say without more clues, but you're right. Odd is what we're looking for. I'll add him to the list. Any luck with the headmaster?"

"None," I said, my tone apologetic. I hadn't seen Headmaster Griffe at all since our first interview and didn't have any ideas on how to get closer to him. "What do we do when we find the person we're looking for?" I asked.

"We don't do anything," Andza said. "You come to me, and I figure out the best way to approach them. Remember, we can't disguise ourselves as well as they can. If we scare them off, we'll never get close again."

"Thanks for the reminder," I said dryly. "But I meant after that. Let's say they tell us everything we want to know, and you finally get your answers. Who do we tell? How do we tell them? I assume we aren't just going to run around shouting the truth in the streets."

"I'll handle that when the time comes. You just worry about finding more suspects." He turned back toward his stacks, a scowl of concentration already tugging at his eyebrows. "Oh, before I forget," he added. "Rahad showed me your candlestick. Lessons again after dinner. An hour for each of you."

I shared a look with Rahad. He looked as unhappy as I did, which served him right. I sighed. Maybe if I ate slowly enough, we could delay lessons until after sunset. Andza always complained that we were using too many of his candles, even though he went through two a night.

Food had already been brought up to the room, so I lifted the cover off my tray and sat down to eat. Chicken stew, with rice and wild mushrooms. The broth had more salt than flavor, but the mushrooms had an earthy, peppery taste to them. I tore off a hunk of bread and soaked it in the broth while I chewed.

So Rahad had found three suspects, and now I'd found Aian. Four people, plus however many Andza had identified. And one of them knew my mother, an immensely frustrating thought for a number of reasons. The knowing made me desperate, but I knew so little about her that the little scraps of her story I had weren't helpful at all.

Worst of all was the thought that I had to share this quest, that someone else might find some link to her before I did. How much could I learn without revealing my own secrets? How much could I accomplish on my own, risking nothing? Difficult questions. I turned them over and over again while my food went cold.

The youngest of three children, Sethric of Easthome was the only one to survive to adulthood. His mother and sister both died in his eleventh year, taken by the same fever. His older brother suffered a riding injury the following summer, which left him paralyzed below the neck. He survived another two years before malnutrition and lack of exercise—and a barely concealed struggle with alcoholism—eventually claimed his life. His father soon remarried and retired to an estate in the country, leaving a sixteen-year-old child to manage this recently diminished household alone.

If it's true that we are most shaped by our childhoods, which lessons did Kerra's future king carry with him out of this tragic upbringing? Which ghosts spoke to him most in those empty halls?

"Pardon me, miss?"

I closed my book and looked up at the stranger that had wandered into the teacher's room. There were no rules against visitors to the school, exactly, but most people stopped at the entryway and waited for someone to come to them. He must have walked past the assistant's desk without noticing and gotten lost in the corridors.

"Good morning," I said brightly, setting my book on my desk and standing to walk over. "How can I help?"

He smiled back at me, wrinkles forming at the corners of his eyes. He might have been fifty years old, definitely less than sixty, with thinning hair and a build that ran more to fat than muscle. Based on his clothes, I wondered if he was a grandparent to one of the students—prosperous enough to have passed his wealth onto his children, but without much left over for himself. It was strange how quickly the city had shifted my thoughts concerning a person's wealth and influence.

"I'm new to town and looking for an old friend. I was told he works here."

"What's his name?"

"I knew him as Haime," the old man said, frowning, "but there's a chance he's changed it. It's a bit of a sensitive matter. I was hoping to speak to him alone if I saw him."

"I see. I'm sorry, but I don't know anyone named Haime. You could check with Headmaster Griffe. He's been here since the school opened. If your friend worked here at any point, I'm sure he would remember."

"I'll do that," he said. He looked at me a moment longer, weighing his words before speaking. "Forgive me, but have you been here very long? You can't be much older than my granddaughter."

"Only a few months," I admitted. "I studied at Sharme before this and expressed interest in being a lecturer one day. My instructors thought it best to test the waters before I made a career of something I hated, so here I am." The practiced lie came smoothly after so much repetition.

"And you're here alone? I don't mean to pry, but Barste is a dangerous city, or so I've heard."

"It can be," I agreed, "but it has a few charms to balance out its faults." Songbirds had been chirping outside the open window all morning, and the scent of flowers filled the halls.

"And no, I'm not here alone. One of my professors came with me, as well as another student in my class."

"You must trust them a great deal, to travel so far with them."

"I do," I said confidently. *With my safety, at least. Just not with my secrets.*

"Ah. Well, as long as you're in good hands." Strangely, he seemed saddened by my conviction, rather than relieved. Perhaps he thought I was too young or too gullible to place my trust in the right people. I wondered if his granddaughter had made a similar mistake.

The silence lingered until it became awkward. He ended it by thanking me for my time and wishing me a pleasant day. On his way out the door, he paused to ask if there were any good inns that I could recommend for a long-term stay. I mentioned a few neighborhoods without giving any hint to which one I stayed in. He sensed my evasion, I think, and didn't pry. Then he left, presumably to seek out the headmaster.

A curious meeting, I thought as I returned to my desk and my book. It reminded me of the night I met Andza. The two had similar personalities, as if the conversation we were having only served as a brief interruption to some larger thought that occupied their attention. They'd both appeared suddenly, when I was alone, and they both left a space behind themselves in the room after they'd gone. The only difference, I realized, was that this stranger hadn't bothered to ask my name.

CHAPTER FIFTEEN

Ferrec's palace had a receiving room, but she'd never had much use for it.

She'd always prided herself on her ability to delegate, to trust other people to do the work she'd appointed them to do. While her predecessor might have enjoyed holding court and hearing petitions for an hour every day, she had an army of judges, ministers, advisors, and other bureaucrats that were more than capable of doing the work people expected her to do. Half of leadership, she'd decided long ago, was in getting the right people to talk to each other—or preventing the wrong people from doing the same.

It had taken a long time for people to get used to the arrangement. The children adapted to it first, having no prior bias, and when she didn't lose patience with them, the rest of the palace had followed suit. Anyone who wanted to approach her with a question could do so; she was easy to find. On the rare occasion she actually was the best person to handle the problem, she handled it.

Best of all, she never had to sit in this awful chair, pretending not to squirm while people bowed and kneeled and begged her for things. That had been nauseating, the few times she'd allowed it to happen. She'd spent years running away from this room and everything it meant.

And yet it had only taken an afternoon to undo all that progress. The king's visit had become a kind of talisman. People could win an argument simply by waving it around. Of course they would welcome King Sethric with a parade. Anything less was unthinkable, a disgrace. And there certainly *would* be a smaller, more regal reception in the receiving room afterward. Why had they stopped using the receiving room in the first place? No one could seem to remember. And as for Governor Ferrec's wardrobe . . .

She sighed. She'd have to fight for it all over again, and she wasn't sure she could win this time. She had less energy than she used to, less patience for the long campaign. And a shrinking list of allies, for that matter. She'd probably die in this chair now, no doubt dressed in something *appropriate*.

How very like Sethric, she frowned, to show up out of nowhere and change everything.

The heavy oak doors at the far end of the room opened with a crash of trumpets. Ferrec winced. She remembered a time when they'd stayed up until sunrise stuffing fabric into saddlebags and between armor segments so their heavy cavalry could crest a hill without announcing the fact for miles. Kings, apparently, were not meant to move about unremarked.

The musicians ended in perfect unison, the silence bright and sudden in the wake of so much noise. Everyone craned their necks to get a better look at the door. They looked dazzled, expectant. A pair of halberdiers in gleaming breastplates stepped aside, and in walked the king.

Time had been kind to him. Ferrec had worried about not recognizing him, about trying to resurrect some sense of familiarity with a stranger that carried her friend's name and nothing else. But it was still him. A few new wrinkles framed his face without marring it. His eyes—bright blue, like the sky—took in the room with the same confidence they always had. If he'd added a few extra pounds since they'd last met, or carried a bit more gray on his scalp, well, he could probably say the same of her.

She felt ridiculous all over again. Forget how he looked. Was *she* recognizable anywhere except atop a horse or hunched over some dimly lit map? She imagined him looking around the room, confused, trying to figure out which of these overdressed, soft-handed, walking sachets was supposed to be her. What she wouldn't give to have this meeting in a tent somewhere, preferably over a bowl of stew.

Their eyes met. He nodded once, briefly, and that was enough.

He strode forward—that limp was new—and the musicians lifted their instruments to their lips. A quieter song this time, a bouncy parade march. She knew what was expected of her here. As he reached the halfway point of the room, she stood, prepared to bow the instant he stopped in front of her. Though it was her palace, he still ruled—a custom they'd taken care to reinforce early on. Once she bowed, she'd hold for three heartbeats, unless he told her to stand. Most people rounded down to two heartbeats, or even one. Minor breaches like that hadn't seemed worth the trouble to enforce.

The king reached his mark at the bottom of the steps, but kept climbing. The whispers grew as he climbed the three short steps to her dais. She could practically hear the sweat break out on Niklas Harran's neck. Half an hour into the king's visit and things had already gone wrong somehow. She decided to take matters into her own hands, but before she could bow, the king snapped a crisp military salute: a fist over his heart, one officer to another. The room held its breath.

Ferrec almost cackled. All that work to honor him as a king. They'd forgotten he was a soldier first.

She returned the salute. The whisper of a smile touched the left corner of his mouth, and they dropped their arms to their sides. She felt the tension ease out of those around her but couldn't let go of her own. She knew that look: eyes steady, but something held in reserve. Eleven years without contact, and now he came to her with a plan. What battles were left to fight? She suspected she'd find out soon.

The rest of the ceremony went well. No missteps, or at least none that could be laid at her feet. No one got overly drunk on the wine or made any inappropriate remarks. No one collapsed over a plate of poisoned food or challenged anyone else to a duel. A successful state visit, if a boring one, for anyone who kept score on such things.

And if the king seemed a little tired, or a little reserved, well, who could blame him? He was getting older, after all, and had just spent a month on the road, and no doubt had other matters on his mind.

"So what's all this about?"

The seven of them stood atop the southeast tower, which gave an impressive view of the plains below. Her retinue consisted of: Niklas, her chief servant; Byren, her captain of the guard; Hilim, her court scribe and personal secretary; Elda, her lady in waiting. Sethric brought no one except his bodyguard, Swordmaster Yara, who Ferrec knew by reputation but had never met. The slim woman hovered a pace and a half away, graceful and calm, sure of her own skill.

"I have a proposal for you to consider."

Elda gasped, raising a hand to her mouth. Byren and Niklas shifted uneasily. Even Hilim stared in badly concealed wonder.

"Oh, hush, all of you. He's not here to ask me to marry him."

The king turned to face her: tall, broad-shouldered, regal. He wore a long coat now, and no crown. He looked . . . himself again, the way she remembered him. What was that look on his face? Amusement? Shame? *Oh, absent gods.*

"Well, actually . . ."

Ferrec had been stabbed twice before. The first time, a spearhead found a space in the shield wall and buried itself in her right shoulder. That had been a fiery pain, instant and all-consuming. The second time had been a sword, wielded by one of those reckless young fools too stupid and blood-thirsty to realize his line had overextended. The tip had slipped past the scales of her armor and stopped squarely in her hip bone. That one had been worse, like the left half of her body collapsing in on itself.

This felt like the second time. "What?"

"I'm old, Ferrec." He explained clearly, patiently. He always explained things clearly and patiently. "My rule will come to an end, and it's time for me to start thinking about the world that comes after me."

"And what am I supposed to do about that? Produce an heir? I'm *forty-five*, you idiot!"

Sethric smiled patiently at the horrified onlookers. Only his bodyguard had the wherewithal to return his smile with an open grin. The rest looked as if they'd been stabbed them-selves. "Leave us for a moment?"

Niklas, Hilim, and Elda scurried away as if chased. Yara stayed, and Byren hesitated. He'd be no match for her even in an unfair fight, but if the king had a bodyguard, then so would the governor. He planted his feet and settled into a parade rest. Yara winked at him.

"How much have you been paying attention to what's going on in Traste?" Sethric asked her.

"I moved as far away from the capital as I could eleven years ago. What do you think?"

He nodded. "Thought as much. Let's walk."

Yara took the lead by about ten paces, which left Byren the rear guard. She and Sethric walked quietly between them, shoulders inches apart. The wind might have been enough to carry away their conversation, but they kept their voices low anyway.

Ferrec asked the first question that came to her. "Who? I can't think of anyone strong enough to make a play."

"Oh, our old enemies are quiet. They wouldn't dare voice their complaints aloud. Their sons and daughters talk enough for both generations. No doubt they've been raised to believe their inheritances are half of what they should be, and a quarter of what they deserve. But they don't worry me much either. Opportunists, the lot of them. They won't act until someone else acts first."

"Who then?"

Sethric gave her a heavy look, then nodded toward his bodyguard. "Yara knows."

Ferrec slowed, then stopped walking altogether. That could only mean one thing. She turned to face her guard.

"Captain Byren. Wait here, please." Byren frowned, glancing at the swordmaster, but couldn't defy a direct order. He saluted, then stood sentry along the wall as if he were just another guard.

They walked another twenty paces before Sethric spoke again. "You remember the night Kallah Varnin attacked us."

It wasn't a question. No one who lived through that night could forget it. On a normal day, Kallah Varnin had the strength and skill of any two men in the king's army.

Desperation seemed to deepen both reserves. That night he'd been death incarnate, a howling, elemental thing of steel and blood. It had taken twelve arrows to send him over the wall and into the river below.

"In fairness, he thought you killed his wife."

"I didn't. Obviously. But it did get me thinking. With the war over and our . . . allies no longer needed, what would happen to them? Would they stay to see what they had built, or would they return to their own lives, scattered about the realm? So I had them followed."

"And?"

"And Kallah was right. Someone *has* been killing them. Not me, and no one acting under my orders, but at least a dozen of the Ghosts are dead."

"But why?"

"I'm more worried about the threat it represents. Whoever's responsible for the murders knows who our allies were and what they did. By killing everyone else involved, they'll have a monopoly on the truth of what happened. If they keep it to themselves, if they also want peace to continue, the realm goes on as it is now. Kerra enjoys a few generations of peace. But if they decide they aren't happy with how things are, that weapon could tear down everything we've built."

They walked in silence for a while.

Ferrec spoke first. "So what do we do about it?"

Byren found her some time later. He settled his cloak onto her shoulders without asking, but the chill she felt had nothing to do with the cold. She gripped the stone crenellation to keep her hand from shaking. Bastard. She'd forgotten this fear.

"Forgive me for saying so, Governor, but you don't look like a woman who's about to be happily married."

She laughed. "No, I suppose not."

"But you agreed?" he guessed. "To the king's proposal?"

"I did."

He didn't ask. It wasn't his place to ask, but for some reason Ferrec wanted desperately to be understood. To give her reasons to someone else, if only so she could hear them out loud for herself. But how could she make him understand? Easily, she realized. She'd just have to break his heart.

"Do you know why we attacked Lletra eleven years ago?"

He shifted uncomfortably, her dutiful captain of the guard. Wrestling with the words he wanted to say, choosing instead the words he was allowed to say. "To put down the rebellion."

She sighed. Was explaining this worth it? Even considering what the knowledge would do to him? Worth it or not, she'd never led her soldiers blindly into battle, and she didn't intend to start now. "Yes. To put down the rebellion. But here's the real question. Why did Lletra rebel in the first place?"

He didn't have an answer for that. Not one he felt comfortable voicing, anyway. She filled the silence he left for her.

"Think about it. A newly crowned king, surrounded by former enemies. All of them wounded, certainly, but a few strong enough to challenge him if they're smart about picking their moment. And they were smart, or they wouldn't have made it as far as they did. Those first few months . . . We spent our nights in the king's own bedchambers, all of his lieutenants, trying to guess which of a dozen directions the first threat might come from."

She shook her head, remembering the feeling of constant exhaustion. "All this, mind you, while a bunch of soldiers were trying to wrap their heads around the bureaucracy of ruling, most of which had to be built on top of the old bureaucracy.

"So we cheated. We picked someone from the middle of the list and lured them into making a play. We needed someone who was a competent commander, but not a tactical genius. That narrowed it down a bit, but not much. We also needed someone with a respectable standing army, but no reserves, and little hope for reinforcements. Cut the remainder in half, and you're looking at two or three likely choices."

Ferrec held up three fingers. "Greymarsh was the first," she said, "but we worried about what a prolonged fight could do to the farmland there. A vineyard can take nearly ten years to get back on its feet, and we didn't like the thought of starting our first year by ruining one of our major exports." She put a finger down.

"Next we considered a coup from within Traste itself, but we gave it up as too risky. For one, everyone has spies in the capital. There are too many threads to keep track of, too many players at work. Not to mention the story that would tell. An uprising in the king's own city would tell the world that the king couldn't manage a few square miles in his own backyard, let alone a kingdom." She put another finger down.

"That left Lletra. Far enough to the north that most people think of it as somewhere else, if they think of it at all. A few good exports, but nothing irreplaceable. The natural barrier to the north makes it easier to close the city in, and Lletra made too many enemies with its neighbors early in the war to hope for their aid."

He didn't say anything. She didn't expect him to. She went on.

"We got lucky with the nephew. If we hadn't been looking for an excuse, we could've played it down as a drunken tirade.

All sins forgiven when the hangover starts. But to make *those* threats in front of *those* witnesses. That gave us what we needed. A chance to make an example of someone, to pull Lletra into a war, and to silence dissent for a few years and get this kingdom back on its feet."

Byren stood as if facing the gallows: spine straight, face grim, eyes . . . distant. She sighed. Maybe it had been too much.

"Even so, I wouldn't call him evil. Evil is selfish. It's a decision to put your needs above someone else's, and he never does that. He's cruel, certainly. But he always does the math himself. And when there's a kingdom at peace on one end of the scales, nothing can shift that weight." She sighed. "And that's why I'm trapped, you see? Because he'll convince me that it's for the greater good, and I know he'll be right."

"With all due respect, Governor, if the greater good involves . . . whatever that expression on your face is, you should've pushed the king over the side of the wall."

She arched an eyebrow. "That's treason, captain."

He shrugged. "Hang me. And while you're looking for the rope, maybe you can put in a good word for a few of my nieces. I'm sure one of them would like to be a queen."

She laughed. Soldiers were the only people with any decent sense of humor. "I'm sure they're lovely, but I'm afraid lovely doesn't cut it." She tapped a finger against the wall, thinking. "No, Sethric was always going to marry for practical reasons. I just didn't realize I made such a practical choice."

CHAPTER SIXTEEN

L ife at the Rose finally settled into something approaching a routine. As much as it pained me to admit, being a teacher was harder than being a student, but I still found a few chances every week to continue my investigation. Aian came to the teacher's room less and less as his contract work took over, but I talked to the other teachers every day and even managed two brief interactions with Headmaster Griffe.

From these, I learned a bit more about Barste's political landscape: which families were on the rise, which were perilously close to a fall. The trouble with Barste, I came to realize, is that *everyone* knew about everyone else's business. Andza had instructed us to look for people who had connections to those in power, but nearly everyone I spoke to fit that description. Our mules at the inn probably overheard enough gossip to qualify.

I didn't press Rahad about his work after our first argument, and he didn't seem interested in anything I was doing, so we rarely spoke. I wouldn't have heard him at all if not for our vague reports to Andza, which we both preferred to handle without the other present. Lessons were a hateful affair. Each of us endured the other's corrections in frosty silence.

Andza brought more and more work home every night. So far we'd learned very little, but he didn't seem bothered by our lack of progress. After all, he'd been on this quest for half his life and had only found seventeen people—the last one over two years ago. A few months weighed very little against fifteen years of work.

The door to our room opened and Rahad came shuffling in. Odd. I'd left work early after my final class ended, but Rahad didn't usually return until late afternoon. Andza said as much from the little writing desk he'd set up in the corner.

"You're back early."

Rahad ignored him, stumbled toward his bed. Had he been drinking? He clutched his stomach as if nauseous. He had a glazed, wandering look, eyes searching around the room at random. They eventually settled on the window next to me, and he opened his mouth to speak. Then his cloak fell open, and I saw the spreading pool of blood just above his hip.

As soon as Rahad collapsed onto the bed, shouting erupted in the hallway. I recognized the innkeeper's voice, but not the person making the scene. A man, but not one I recognized. He spoke with a booming voice. This was someone who expected obedience and was outraged that a soft-spoken peasant should get in his way.

Andza opened the door calmly.

"Where is he?" the voice thundered. I moved between the bed and the door, pulling the blanket over Rahad's crumpled body as I passed. Andza stood opposite a massive figure in the doorway. The stranger might have been half a foot taller than him, and easily double his weight, but Andza held his ground. He also held a small knife behind his back, his grip on the handle firm but relaxed. When had he grabbed that?

"Can I help you?"

Eyes narrowed, the stranger took Andza in: his clothes, his build, his meek posture. I saw the calculations running behind that look as he tried to guess Andza's social rank—or at least his affiliates' reach. He must have come up wanting.

"You can help yourself by standing aside, stranger. Unless you'd like to bleed on the little eunuch's behalf."

He loomed forward, but I didn't see any change in Andza's posture. Nor did the grip on his hidden knife change by a hair.

"This is my room," Andza explained patiently, "and the boy is under my care. You might be able to claim insult, but this isn't the time or place to demand a touch. Unless your honor is worth so little that you can satisfy it by dragging a wounded, unarmed boy out of bed and stabbing him to death in a hallway."

The muscles in my stomach tensed so hard that I started to shake. Andza had no status here. None of us did. This man could kill him where he stood and claim any insult in defense. As kindly as the innkeeper had treated us, I didn't think this stranger was overly worried about his testimony.

Which made it all the more surprising when he backed down.

"No, you're right," he growled. "This isn't the time or the place. Thank you, stranger, for reminding me of the proper way of things. I sincerely hope to repay the favor."

They exchanged curt bows, and the nobleman walked away stiffly. Andza closed the door as soon as he was out of sight.

I realized I'd been holding my breath and let it all out at once. "That could have gone a lot worse. He looked ready to snap."

Andza shrugged. "I wasn't terribly worried."

"What? How could you not be worried?" I felt like my heart wouldn't stop racing until I went to sleep tomorrow night.

"Most people need permission to kill someone," he answered, turning to face me. He set the knife onto his writing desk. "For soldiers, it's usually enough that your captain gave the order. You can put the moral implications on their shoulders and tell yourself that you're just fighting to protect your line. It makes it easier. Even the lowest criminals have to talk themselves into killing for the first time. They manufacture some need that justifies the act, and even if we don't agree with their line of thought, it's worth noting that the most vicious murderers still need a reason to kill. They have to give *themselves* permission first."

I nodded, but mostly because that's what you do when an insane person is talking to you.

"The so-called upper class in Barste," he continued, crossing the room to where Rahad lay bleeding, "has a complicated system of honor and insults and revenge to goad themselves into killing each other in the streets. They'll try to maneuver you into the system, but if you don't participate, if you don't give them permission to duel you, they have to give themselves permission to murder you. And I didn't think our friend was a murderer."

I thought of Andza's bored, flat voice, the ease at which he'd held himself, his comfortable grip on the knife. No, our friend might not have been a killer. But I think he recognized one when he saw one.

Andza pulled the blanket away gently, and I came over to look. I expected Rahad to be unconscious, but his eyes were wide open, and his mouth had a grim set to it. His right hand clutched . . . not his stomach, but a knife. The sheets beneath him were dark with blood.

At Andza's direction, Rahad rolled over and lifted his shirt. A shallow cut went from hip to rib on the right side of his stomach. Nothing life threatening, but running through the streets had clearly worsened it.

"What happened?" I asked. "Who was that?"

"One of the Meadowlark's clients, if I had to guess."

I'd heard that name before but only in whispers. People spoke of such places in Barste, but rarely around me. I realized now why Andza had been so secretive about where Rahad was going, and why Rahad had been so defensive when I asked.

"You got him a job in a *brothel?*"

"Several. The more respectable places can afford portraits of their . . . well, merchandise. And since most of their customers are well connected, it made sense to have eyes there."

"I assume he's only drawing pictures of their faces," I said dryly. Then again, I'd seen some of Rahad's *artwork* back at the Library. I resisted the urge to pull him out of bed and stab him again.

"Assume whatever you like. I'm more interested in what he was doing instead of painting. But I suppose he needs a doctor first."

"I'm fine," Rahad said, managing to sit up. "I can do the stitches myself."

"You've already made one poor choice today," Andza said. "Let's not risk a second. Jalina, sit with him until I return. If anyone comes to the room while I'm out—"

A sudden knock on the door caught us by surprise.

Andza sighed. "May as well get this out of the way."

I didn't recognize the woman at the door, but Andza

didn't seem to need a knife during this conversation, so I relaxed a bit. Rahad had squirmed halfway across the bed in search of something to press against his wound, making a mess in the process. I handed him a clean pillowcase and told him to lie still, then set about boiling some water. Andza and our new visitor moved into the hallway. I couldn't hear their whispers over the simmering flame.

"That was the Meadowlark's owner," Andza said, closing the door. Then, to Rahad, "You're fired, by the way."

"What did she want?" I asked.

"A full refund of the girl's contract. A thousand silver crowns."

I nearly choked. Our little shop had never earned that much in a *month*. It seemed fantastically expensive, but I suppose the girl being sold probably didn't see it that way. "You didn't agree to pay it, did you?"

"No. I offered to pay for a full investigation instead."

"Let me guess. The magistrate, had they bothered to investigate, would have found the girl's contract wasn't as exclusive as her madam had advertised."

"Undoubtedly."

"Clever."

Andza shrugged. "I have my moments." He checked Rahad's wound again, then went off to fetch a doctor.

I sat there awkwardly, unsure what to do. After a few minutes of fidgeting, I realized, with blessed relief, that I didn't actually have to do anything. The stress of the evening had overwhelmed my already anxious mind, and for once, I was happy to let the world carry on without my worrying about it.

"I wasn't . . . with her," Rahad said from his sad post across the room. "If that's what you're thinking, I mean."

Why bother to tell me? I hardly had a good opinion

of him to start with, and that hadn't dented his self-esteem one whit as far as I could tell. It seemed important to him, though, and it's easy to be kind to people who are worse off than you.

"I believe you," I said. Then I sat with him until Andza returned.

The full story came out after an hour of relentless questioning. I thought I wanted to hear it, but by the end, Rahad was so miserable and embarrassed that I wished I could have spared him the shame of my being there.

It started innocently enough. The sad orphan girl strikes up a conversation with the quiet artist who's there to paint her. It isn't long before they realize that they enjoy each other's company, and they start looking for more excuses to see one another. Always something believable: a smudge of ink on the last portrait or a new dress that looks much nicer than the old one. Soon they're making plans for a life after this one, when things are different and the world's an easier place to live.

As far as I could tell, Rahad hadn't been dishonest with her. He seemed to mean all that he'd said and had even been helping her save money. It had all the elements of romance and longing and scandal you want in a good love story. And if the hero of the piece was a little foolish and naive at times, that was to his credit. People like their heroes to be a little foolish.

As he spoke, I found myself wondering about Rahad's life before the Library. I'd missed something in my first estimation of him, when I thought him a spoiled child, but I wasn't sure my second impression hit much closer to the mark. He claimed to have met a god, but I'd never given thought to what kind of prayers that god might have appeared in answer to. Were there things in his past that still haunted him? Regrets that might prompt him to take stupid risks for a girl he barely knew?

I sincerely hoped Rahad wasn't a nicer person than I'd suspected. I'd gotten used to quarreling with him.

"I have a question," I said, after it had all come out. "Why were the two of you so secretive about everything?" I knew the answer of course, but I wanted to make them say it out loud.

They shared a look that I'd come to hate. "We thought it might lead to . . . awkward conversations," Andza finally managed.

"Please. I read *Song of the Moon* a year before we met. I could probably *run* a brothel." That wasn't true, but I felt the need to overcorrect whatever impression they had of me. "Besides, what if all this had happened while you were away? I wouldn't have had any idea what was going on."

"Fair point," Andza admitted. "And I apologize. Keeping information from you was a mistake. I won't do it again."

I may have taken a moment to revel in *that* little victory but tried not to let it show. "So what now?"

"Now we wait for Rahad to heal and for some other scandal to capture everyone's attention. Probably a week or two at the most."

"And in the meantime?"

"We do what we've been doing. It may not look like it from day to day, but we're making progress. In the past three months alone, we've made connections with a few hundred people. At least. None of the major players in Barste, but again, that's not who we're after. We're looking for someone who has access to someone in power." He looked at each of us in turn. "It's very likely we've already met the person we're looking for."

"Here's hoping they don't try to stab me, too," Rahad mumbled from his stack of cushions. He'd been given very strict orders not to move until his stitches had healed, and he looked ridiculous amid a small mountain of pillows.

"That's up to you," Andza said, more than a little grumpy. "But I wouldn't rule it out. Speaking of," he said, turning and fixing me with a curious expression, "how are you with a knife?"

CHAPTER SEVENTEEN

With Rahad stuck in bed, I spent more time in the city than before. Despite my experience so far, I had to admit that Barste deserved its reputation as a city for artists. As the weather grew warmer, musicians lined every street, and actors performed plays in every square. The window boxes along the river nearly overflowed with flowers, their petals falling to drift quietly atop the water's surface.

In the evenings, people spread blankets on any patch of grass they could find. They sat in loud groups or quiet pairs, all their blankets carelessly overlapped, as if everyone in the city had been invited to one continuous party. Even members of rival houses nodded cordially as they passed one another.

It was exhilarating to think that any of these countless strangers could be the person we were looking for. Exhilarating, but also frustrating. We had no way of knowing how close we were to an answer. What if we'd already met them? What if we'd given ourselves away weeks ago, and they'd fled the city rather than risk discovery?

My father once told me I looked like my mother, but I had no way to know if that was true. I didn't even have a picture of her to compare against my own reflection. What if her friend in Barste recognized me? Would they approach me? Or would they keep their distance?

I didn't see any repeats of my earlier foray into the markets. Sudden, violent duels seemed to be the exception rather than the rule in Barste, at least on the streets I frequented. I had a knife at my belt, which Andza had begun teaching me to use, but it didn't make me feel much safer. It didn't help that I kept dropping it during practice or flinching in shock every time I actually landed a proper hit against the thick band of cushions he'd tied around my bedpost.

"I don't see how this is helpful," I told him after a particularly depressing practice session. "My grip on the handle hardly matters if I'm too frightened to draw the knife in the first place. I start to shake just thinking about it."

He looked at me for a long moment, mouth set, eyes thoughtful. "There's a practical demonstration I once found useful, if you're up for it."

"What is it?" I asked nervously.

Instead of responding, he reached toward me, placing a hand against my throat.

"Very f—" I coughed as his thumb pressed against my windpipe. Wild, indignant fear rose up to replace the air I wasn't getting. I slapped him, hard. He loosened his grip.

"Bastard!" I coughed again. "What the hell was that?"

"A killing blow, if you'd been holding anything heavier than a book." He rubbed his jaw. "Or at least enough to make me reconsider grabbing you in the first place."

I saw the skin start to darken on his face, a hazy handprint that ended two inches above the vein in his neck. A blade there would have . . . I had the sudden urge to vomit but set my jaw against it. I focused on breathing, on calming myself by getting air back into my lungs.

"The only difference between a veteran and a new recruit," Andza said flatly, "is that the veteran isn't ashamed of feeling afraid. Fear can help you, once you get used to it. Do you know why shields are so effective?"

"That feels like a trick question."

"It is, in a way. They're effective because people have a tendency to raise their arms when they're frightened. It doesn't have to be taught. You're born knowing how to do it. Teaching someone how to use a shield properly is just a matter of building on that natural instinct. Setting your feet more effectively, turning your body with the blow, training your eyes to look toward the next swing instead of away from it. You can learn the basics in an afternoon because your fear already knows half of what you need."

"I froze like a scared rabbit when that man was killed. When is that ever useful?"

"Rarely," Andza admitted, "but that's an easy problem to fix. Practice walking."

"Walking?"

He nodded, all seriousness. "Whenever you think about that scene in the street, take a short breath, then walk forward. Just a step or two, and always start with the same foot. Focus on the intent at first, make it something that connects your mind to your body. Eventually it becomes automatic, and you won't have to think about it."

"What if moving would get me killed?"

"Then don't move."

Compared to that, Rahad's drawing lessons were a relief. With spring in the air, neither of us had the motivation to rekindle our feud, and the simple act of sketching lines made for a quiet, restorative hour at the end of a long day of teaching. I borrowed books from the Rose's library that I thought would interest him, and he read them without comment or complaint.

I wished Elaise could see us now and wondered what she was up to. I had no idea when I would see her again, and little chance of sending her word in the meantime. I hoped she'd found another friend to spend time with while I was away, but I couldn't help feeling sad at the thought of her enjoying the sunset with a stranger.

Another month passed, and with it, the mood of the city changed.

We'd heard about the Long Night weeks ago, but as few people had mentioned it since, I assumed its importance was overblown, its participants limited to some echelon of society that I would never cross.

I was wrong.

Andza came home late one night, which was a rarity in itself. He seemed to make his own schedule and would come and go at odd hours but almost never missed the evening meal. Rahad and I ate in silence, glancing between each other and the door. We'd just started to worry when it swung open and Andza strode through, tense with that tightly coiled energy that meant he was close on the trail of something.

"We may have made a breakthrough," he started, before fixing me with an unreadable stare. "You need to go shopping for some new clothes, by the way."

I gaped. Rahad snickered.

"For what?" I asked, irritated. He did realize I didn't teach class in bedroom slippers and a faded old shawl, didn't he?

"For the Long Night," he said. "I just found out that one of the organizers was my officer at Seventree. I think I can get us an invitation."

"Fancy," Rahad remarked. "I wonder what the dress code will be," he added. Purely for my benefit, I was sure.

"Whatever it is, I'm sure I'll be fine," I snapped. "But why are we going?"

"*We* are going," Andza explained, "because the most powerful figures in the city will be in attendance, and you can bet that the person we're looking for has already gotten an invitation."

"And they might do something at the party to reveal themselves," I said, finally catching up. "But won't we stick out?"

"We won't be the only gatecrashers. If anything, being unimportant will help us. We can observe everyone else without being noticed ourselves."

"Unless we show up in our pajamas."

"Shut up, Rahad. Where is this party?"

"The venue is called the House of the Falling Curtain. It's one of the older buildings in Barste and has a history attached to it. Acquiring it was somewhat of a social coup among the people who care about that sort of thing."

"What kind of history?"

"The players were notorious for never actually finishing a show," Andza explained. "They'd veer off script and start insulting people in the audience until someone powerful decided they'd crossed a line. Men with cudgels would rush the stage, the curtain would fall, and everyone would stumble laughing into the street. Then they'd meet back the following night and do it all again."

"Why did it close?" Rahad asked.

"The novelty wore off, I suppose. No joke is funny the third time."

"Unless it's about my clothes," I muttered.

We spent the rest of the night discussing plans: what we should look for at the party and how we would signal each other once we'd found it; whether we'd show up together or separately; who we would talk to; what we would talk about. We talked until Rahad and I got caught up in Andza's excitement. Only three weeks to go, and then perhaps our search would pay off. I remember falling asleep that night with the thought still buzzing in my head. Three more weeks to wait for answers I'd dreamed of for half my life.

Of course, as a handsome young lord, fresh from the field of victory, the king had his pick of friends and suitors. There were certainly plenty who wished to ally themselves with the new court, or at least close the chapter on some bitter memory from the war. A few even happened to have a son or daughter around the right age. They arrived at the capital in packs, only to be turned away, one after another. Some have speculated that he hoped for a foreigner, someone who would be willing to ratify Kerra's borders, or at least a portion of them. The truth, however—

"What's that?" Andza asked from over my shoulder.

With less than a week to go until the Long Night, classes at the Rose had been canceled, so I had time to spare in the afternoon. Reading had always been a favorite pastime, and the chair next to the window offered a splendid combination of warm spring weather and bright sunlight.

"I'm not sure," I confessed. "I picked it up on a whim but haven't really come across anything useful. Just some light reading, I guess." I showed him the cover. His eyes scanned the title, then the author's name. He scoffed.

"Familiar name?" I asked. "I hadn't heard of her before."

"I knew her. We both lived in Traste after the war. I

suppose we were contemporaries, but I never got along with her. Too many obvious political ambitions, too little substance. She'd print any rumor if she thought she could turn it to some advantage. I wouldn't waste my time."

"Rumors can be useful if enough of them point to the same thing."

"All rumors point to the same thing. People with too much free time and not enough attention."

I shrugged. "Sounds like a pleasant way to pass the time to me. Did it ever work?"

Now he was frowning. When had I gotten so comfortable with goading him? "Did what ever work?"

"Her 'political ambition.' Did she flatter some noble into marrying her and giving away their fortune?"

"She did," Andza admitted. "But she died of the flu a few years after she married, so who can say whether she had time to enjoy it."

The door to our room opened, and Rahad swaggered in. His brush with death hadn't done much to dim his confidence. I think he was already looking forward to showing off the scar someday. It didn't help that his scandal had made him famous. People were practically begging to have their portrait done by the romantic young fool from Jhendi. He was even more well placed than he'd been at the Meadowlark, to say nothing of the amount of money he was bringing in.

"Good, you're back," Andza said, as soon as the door closed. "There's something I want to show both of you."

Rahad and I exchanged a brief look before crossing to stand at either side of the room's one tiny writing desk. We'd never been allowed to get close to the perilous stacks of paper that Andza surrounded himself with each evening. Not because of the secrets they held, though there were certainly enough of those to inspire caution. We'd been carefully instructed to touch nothing, to avoid letting so much as a breath disrupt the careful placement of every sheaf. The tone in his voice had been warning enough to keep us away.

"What is it?" I asked.

"It's our investigation so far." He handed me a sheet of paper from the top of the stack.

I scanned the list. Dozens of names I recognized and more than a few I didn't. Aian's name appeared near the bottom, but we'd added four more since.

"What are those symbols next to the names?" Rahad asked.

"House affiliations," I answered. "Don't you see? There's the wood thrush from Cantel's crest and the wagon wheel from House Kuri. Is there another—never mind, I see it."

I moved to the next stack of papers. Little of interest there, at least to me. Houses had footnotes estimating their perceived wealth, actual wealth, income, solubility, and half a dozen other financial indicators I didn't understand. Another list held a summary of contracts, costs, dates completed, and the names of any executors or administrators that served as points of contact. Any name that appeared more than twice was circled and cross-checked against our first list.

"The numbers next to the names. That's how long they've been in Barste, isn't it?" Rahad asked.

"Years of service, or my best guess. Add a year at most for them to establish a presence here. We're looking for someone who's been here between eight and ten years, which rules out about two-thirds of the first list."

"This . . . is incredible," I breathed. I couldn't help but notice the crisp, dark seven next to Aian's name.

"Incredibly boring," Rahad added.

"That, too," I agreed. "How did you ever get access to this much information?"

"House Trevis occupies a strange position in Barste. They have very few holdings outside the city, none of the lavish estates or scenic vineyards you'd expect. They lost much of their wealth over a few generations of bad decisions and couldn't afford to spend time or resources on anything that didn't bring in twice what they spent."

"Most of their income flows from their relationships to trade guilds, which doesn't help their status. Everyone thinks of them as barely above middle class, forced to build and repair the kinds of palatial mansions they can't afford to live in themselves. I suggested this," Andza motioned toward the desk, "as a possible solution."

"Oh, I see," Rahad said, finally showing some interest. "If you were able to get all this information from scribing at one of their construction companies, then House Trevis must have its hooks in deeper than anyone suspected."

"Exactly. Six months from now, most of this will get published under the name of a disgruntled employee, ostensibly getting even after a sour business deal. At which point House Trevis won't just be charging for the skill of their laborers but also for their *discretion*."

"And we'll be gone, with any luck." I shook my head, wondering. "Absent gods. They paid you to do what you already planned on doing."

"You'll recall," Andza said dryly, "that I have some experience with this."

"Noted. So now that we have this, how do we use it?"

"The next step relies on Rahad." Then, turning toward him, "We'll need to get portraits of as many suspects as possible. We only have a few days to learn their faces. If you get any more requests for portraits in the next week, prioritize the houses on this list and try to make a rough sketch that you can take back here with you."

"That shouldn't be necessary," Rahad said. "As long as I see them once, I can remember what they look like."

Show-off. "What can I do?" I asked, eager to be of some use, annoyed at how eager I sounded.

"I want you focused on the night of the party. In the meantime, you can help me sort through what we have so far. Perhaps you'll recognize some details from when you lived in Casmhe."

Unlikely, but I didn't say so. I'd spoken to "Miss Talia" four or five times in my life. Once I realized who she really was, I'd hauled those conversations from the depths and searched them again for any drop of significance. No, Andza's task was fruitless. But at least it would occupy my thoughts.

One more week. I went back to my reading and willed the time to pass.

CHAPTER EIGHTEEN

The gates of Lletra didn't pretend to be anything they weren't. Kyrede respected that. So much of his life had been devoted to misdirection and deceit that it was refreshing to see something present a single, unapologetic face to the world. There was no artistry to the stonework, nothing imposing or dignified or symbolic. A wall, nothing more. It would do its best.

People filled the street that led into the city, shuffling forward in a buzzing mass of humanity. He waited patiently, never giving in to panic or frustration, even when the weight of the crowd pushed his elbows into his ribs or carried him in a direction his feet never intended to go. He'd been on this road for half his life. A few more hours wouldn't hurt.

He'd been surprised by the crowds of people, but then, a great deal had surprised him in the past few months.

First the prior's appearance in Barste. Kyrede hadn't spoken to the man in years except through letters. He'd fallen to Jurald's feet in supplication when he recognized him. It had been so long since he'd been blessed in person, since he'd had any contact with anyone from the Order, anyone who knew who he was or what he'd devoted his life to. He was dimly aware that he'd lost something in that lack of contact. People weren't meant to be alone for so long.

Instead, Jurald had commanded him to call off the hunt. His work was over, his long mission finished. Other men and women would handle the rest. Words that filled him with disappointment at first. Only later did he realize that they'd also freed him.

The second surprise had been the news he heard on the road south. The false king's caravan had passed the same way, headed north, not a week earlier. No one knew the reason, but Kyrede couldn't dismiss the coincidence. Sethric had left his seat of power for the first time in a decade, just a few weeks before Jurald's visit, and now their paths had crossed. It was a sin to interpret the will of the gods, to ascribe some divine pattern to chance and coincidence. And yet . . .

He left the village, headed north.

Since then, everything had worked out in his favor. Every inn he'd stopped at had a stable he could sleep in, every farmhouse a hayloft. When he begged for alms in the street, passersby filled his cup in minutes and gave him what he needed to continue his journey. Even the setbacks proved fortuitous: wrong turns led to shortcuts, broken axles diverted him to swifter river crossings. And now he stood at the gates of Lletra, a few miles from the false king, free to follow his own will for the first time in years.

A shadow fell across him as the crowd carried him into the city. He passed through it and out into the light.

He found work laying cobblestones. He had no experience, but he could listen to directions well enough, and the work kept his hands busy but his mind and ears unoccupied. He learned about the false king's arrival, Governor Ferrec's acceptance of his marriage proposal, the hopeful mood of the people. And he learned a thousand other things about the city: which merchants were honest, which employers were fair, which inns watered down their drinks. He spent an entire week just listening to conversations in the street, shaping his lips quietly around accents and unfamiliar turns of phrase.

At the end of the week, he collected his wages. He didn't bother telling his employer that he wouldn't be back the following week to finish the work. Men disappeared from jobs all the time, and Kyrede didn't plan on wearing this face for long.

The gambling house in the South Quarter didn't provide much in the way of luxury. The rooms were spare, but the owner kept them decently clean, and the food and drinks were cheap but edible. It boasted a regular but undiscerning clientele: soldiers, mostly, and a few day laborers—men and women who wanted a bit of fun but very little trouble.

Just as night fell and the guard shift at the palace changed, a group of six men wandered in. They headed for their usual table but soon changed their minds. Where their regular dealer normally stood, a dour, unfamiliar face scowled at them, and the smell of cheap cologne nearly knocked them over. They chose a new table instead, closer to the kitchen, and asked the dealer to set up a game of Ramps.

As far as their usual dealer knew, the six men never walked in at all.

Almost as soon as the men sat down, Kyrede began his work. Subtle things at first: a dimming of the lights and sounds from other tables that made them feel set apart, isolated, an island of six in the vast ocean.

As the night went on, he grew bolder. Waitresses that had spurned them for years winked as they turned away. For the first time in years, all six men came in ahead of the house and spent lavishly on food and drink to celebrate their luck. The house didn't play with loaded dice, but Kyrede had other ways of shifting fate.

The next night, when the men came in, they sat at their new favorite table.

It wasn't that Kyrede hated the false king. It was hard to hate someone who'd delivered you from hell. That feeling of gratitude had settled somewhere deep within him and attached to the core of who he was, like a new vine grafted to the old rootstock. The fruits it bore were charity and compassion, of a strength and potency he knew that he could never have cultivated in himself. These things were what led him to the Order in the first place, full to bursting with the desire to follow the example he'd been shown, to return what kindnesses he'd been given.

His sainthood had been secondary to that calling. A minor embellishment to the soul, some lingering touch of the divine to remind him that he hadn't just been delivered from that cave. He'd been *called forth*. Whenever his strength or his determination failed, his gift was there to remind him of what he'd survived. He relied on it for that, used it as a source of light on his darkest days.

But the others . . .

The others had used it to conquer.

He'd reasoned with them, but they were resolute. When the Order demanded their lives to ensure their silence, he did his work obediently. The rage didn't come until later, when his superiors warned him away from the man who'd orchestrated their sins, who had poisoned his own soul in the process of suborning others'. Even that rage had diminished over the years, until all that remained was a sense of something wrong in the world, with one man at the heart of it.

So no, he didn't hate the false king.

But he came close to it.

The soldiers parted ways with good cheer, and Kyrede chose to follow the one who turned left away from the main road. Norin, he thought, but it was hard to tell in the darkness. It didn't matter too much which one he picked. They all had similar builds, and he knew their voices and faces equally well. It was more important to manage this part without being discovered, and that was easier when you weren't desperate for a particular face.

As always, he prayed that he would fail. The zeal he'd shown in his youth was a sin, he'd come to realize. There would never be some message from the gods, no clarion voice in his mind telling him that he was doing the right thing. Not unless he constructed one himself, deceived himself into thinking that divine will guided his hands. And so he prayed that he would one day miss, be caught, be killed. He prayed for the gods to stop him and took their inaction as a sign that he hadn't strayed too far from their purpose.

As always, his prayers went unanswered.

The knife slid in easily and the soldier fell to the ground. The wretched, choking sound the soldier made didn't move past the circle of quiet Kyrede had created around them. A look of recognition passed through the man's eyes—it was Norin, after all—then confusion, then emptiness.

Kyrede dragged the corpse into a nearby alleyway and set to work. Minor changes to the face and skin, layers of illusion thinner than a hair that nevertheless made the man unrecognizable. When he was satisfied, he exchanged clothes with the corpse, said a small prayer for the deliverance of both their souls, and left.

He had a room at the inn but didn't return to it. That room belonged to someone else now. His new room was a bunk on the top floor of the fourth street guard house, next to Pell and Whit. If he hurried, he could make the nightly card game, but he slowed his pace instead. He took the long way back, soaking in the warm weather, trying to get used to walking with these feet, to seeing with these eyes.

From his spot on the wall, Kyrede could see most of the city.

He could see the gate he'd passed under less than a month ago, still busy with foot traffic. From there, he traced the path to the intersection where he'd laid cobblestones and on to the inn where he lived while he worked at the gambling house. He still went there most nights, but as a customer now. When he walked back to his bunk at the guardhouse after a night of gambling, he passed the alleyway where they found that man's corpse a week and a half ago. As far as he knew, no one had identified the man yet. As far as he *knew*, no one ever would.

Not a bad start, all things considered. Other men might consider it slow progress to walk two miles in four weeks, but Kyrede had been at this a long time. If there was one thing he'd learned in the last fifteen years, it was patience.

CHAPTER NINETEEN

The House of the Falling Curtain stood at least thirty feet taller than its neighbors. White stone columns supported a grand entryway that had been decorated for the occasion. Colored glass nestled among the garlands, reflecting the light from the torches below. Already people milled about outside, ignoring the open doors in hopes of making a grander entrance once the party had started and there were enough people inside to properly take notice.

"No drinking under any circumstances," Andza warned as we approached the doors, invitations in hand. "I'd avoid it if I could, but some fool will push a glass into my hand, and I won't be able to argue, so I need the two of you to stay sharp."

"I can promise not to drink any *more*," Rahad joked. He'd been in a fey mood all evening. He even smiled through Andza's glare.

"What's wrong with you?" I whispered to Rahad. "You've been acting strangely all day."

"Something on my mind."

"Something other than this?"

He shrugged. "What can I say? I'm a complex person."

We reached the top of the stairs, where Andza presented

our invitations to the usher. I held my breath but had nothing to fear. The man waved us in almost immediately. The room beyond opened into a large lobby. The lights had been dimmed to the warm glow of banked embers, deepening the reds and blues of the room to garnet and indigo. Long tapestries hung from floor to ceiling, each woven as a single scene in a story that wrapped around the room entire.

Three staircases led to the upper seating areas. More ushers guarded the double doors to the auditorium below. I understood now why we'd been waved through so quickly. We hadn't been admitted to the party yet, just the party's entrance.

Rahad broke away first and swaggered toward one of the staircases. He'd have a clear view of the auditorium from up there. Andza made for one of the tapestries. He made a show of following the story around the room, but I could see where he'd end up in a few minutes. The swordmaster Tavim Daine leaned against a wall six panels down, talking to an escort. He'd been on our list for a while but rarely left the grounds of House Kuri.

I walked the opposite direction, pretending to be captivated by the decorations while I searched the crowd for familiar faces. Irritating as he might be, I had to admit that Rahad's sketches were flawless. Within minutes I found another suspect.

Keia Murava had been a dressmaker in Barste for nearly twenty years, so she wasn't high on our list of suspects. Even if the real Keia had met with some accident, no illusion could serve as a substitute for skill. An easy mark to rule out, though, and a good chance for me to practice.

I saw a table filled with trays of food across the room but took the long way around, passing within arm's length of Miss Murava as I walked. The food, we'd been told, was among the safest in Barste. The hosts of this year's party staked their honor on both its safety and quality. Inspectors from multiple houses had signed off on each stage of its preparation, with armed guards to enforce their right to question anyone they found suspicious. I decided on a small platter of roasted vegetables on slender wooden sticks, and the server bowed as he handed them to me.

I took the same route on my way back, passing again within reach of Miss Murava. This time a hand settled on my forearm, and I turned to face its owner.

"Your dress is marvelous, young lady." Her voice was soft, predatory. Her eyes nearly glittered as she spoke.

I looked down, my blush completely unfeigned. It *was* a marvelous dress. I'd been given a budget, and I told the dressmakers they could do whatever they liked with it. The only thing I'd given them as inspiration was my mother's hair ornament, the finest piece of jewelry I owned.

It was also my secret weapon. To a casual observer, I'd chosen it to match the deep orange hues of my dress, but I hoped at least one person at the party would recognize it for something else.

"Thank you, miss. But I can't take credit for it. I'm barely good at wearing fine clothes, let alone picking them out."

Her eyebrows climbed a fraction of an inch in surprise, and I caught the double meaning in what I'd said. Whoops.

"Beauty *and* modesty," she said. "A rare enough combination. What's your name?"

"Jalina, miss."

"A pleasure to meet you, Jalina," she replied. No need to give her own name. I was the stranger at the party, not her. "Do find me if you ever need help with your . . . wardrobe, in future."

I told her I would and thanked her again for the compliment.

Feeling slightly heady, I picked a less crowded section of the room and walked toward it. I'd made my first contact and, as far as I could tell, had come away with exactly what I needed without saying anything completely disastrous. I wanted a quiet moment to celebrate my success and to let the feeling of excitement pass before I tried again.

"Find anyone yet?" a voice asked at my shoulder.

I'd gotten used to Rahad appearing with no warning and managed not to flinch this time. "Just one so far, but I think she was flirting with me. Or I was flirting with her, and she went along with it. Hard to tell."

"Well, don't ask me for advice. You're the one who's read *Song of the Moon*."

"Funny. Truly. Are they putting you on stage later?"

He responded to the jab with a distracted smirk, eyes roaming around the room without settling on anything.

"What's your problem tonight?" I asked. "You look like you're waiting for someone."

"What? No. I'm just keeping an eye out for trouble."

He almost didn't sound guilty.

Almost.

"Uh-huh. And is this trouble in any way related to the *tremendously important* job we're supposed to be doing?"

"Tangentially." He shrugged.

"What do you mean, 'tangentially'?"

"Touching on a single point, but otherwise completely unrelated." Seeing my surprised expression, he added, "What? I went to the same school as you, remember?"

Before I could think of something else to say, Rahad's eyes narrowed. "Damn. Trouble."

"What?" I whispered, following his line of sight. A tall man strode through the crowd, eyes intent but unsteady on his feet. The other attendees parted before him. Anyone not intimidated by his rank still had to contend with his size, and he stood half a head taller than anyone here. I remembered the way he had dwarfed Andza at the inn, shoulders nearly touching the doorframe on either side.

"Boy!" he barked at Rahad. Heads turned toward us, drawn by the excitement.

"Get lost," Rahad whispered. "I can find you later."

"I'll find Andza."

Rahad made some indecipherable motion with his hand, but I didn't have a chance to ask him what it meant. I sank into the crowd just as he leaned forward in a bow too deep to be anything but mocking. "Apologies, my lord. I didn't recognize you at first."

It was the wrong thing to say. I heard the gasp from the crowd, the stillness that followed like a held breath. Pretending not to recognize a rival was a good way to start a duel in the best of times. Whatever else was on his mind, Rahad should have known better than to antagonize someone like that in front of a crowd.

I had a feeling that the Long Night's injunction against violence was about to be tested. I started pushing people out of the way, gently at first, then slightly harder when a light touch didn't work. I earned a few glares, but for the most part, people were happy to step into a space closer to the front.

Tavim Daine still lounged against the wall where I'd seen him earlier, arms crossed but perfectly at ease, engaged in conversation with his date. Andza would've had a chance to speak with him by now and must have moved on to another suspect. I searched desperately around the room. My eyes landed on a familiar face, but not one I expected to see. Aian. He noticed me before I could look away.

"Jalina!"

I tried to pretend I hadn't heard him, but no luck. He started pushing through the crowd toward me, with only slightly less difficulty than I'd managed, squeezing past people and offering apologies to anyone he bumped into. He called my name again, and I turned to him and smiled politely.

"I didn't realize you'd be here tonight," he said. Coming from someone else, it could've been a slight (I didn't realize *you* would be *here*), but he sounded genuine. "Are you meeting friends?"

"I came with people," I answered. "I'm actually looking for them now."

"I think you've mentioned them before. Also from Sharme, right?"

"More or less."

"Ah."

The silence dragged on, and I didn't see a way out of it. I considered leaving Rahad to deal with his own problems, but the thought of him stumbling into the room covered in blood stopped me short.

"I should really—"

"Are you—"

A loud crash interrupted the both of us. It came from where I left Rahad and sounded like someone had stumbled into a table—or been thrown into one. The laughter that followed ruled out a serious fight, though. As the crowd broke apart, I saw Rahad and his erstwhile enemy laughing together, arms around one another's shoulders, both of them soaked head to toe in wine. Well. One problem solved, at least.

"Looks like Lord Caithe is right on schedule," Aian said. "At least he's consistent, I suppose. Makes his own enemies, drinks his own toasts, and always passes out by midnight. I wonder who his friend is."

"Some idiot, I'm sure. What were you saying before?"

A thoughtful look crossed his features, some tidbit that needed to be weighed, sorted, and filed away for later. Why did he care who Lord Caithe made friends with?

"Nothing important." He turned back to me. "So. You're dressed . . . nicer than usual."

I raised an eyebrow. "Ouch. Unless you're flirting, and if you are, don't. We both know you're too old for me. Not that that stops some people."

He laughed and raised his hands in mock surrender. "I won't ask. I only mean to say that I didn't recognize you at first." His eyes flicked toward my hairpiece. "And look, you even found some jewelry."

I laughed. "Now you're just being mean. I wear jewelry all the time. At least when there aren't any children around."

"It looks nice. It reminds me of something my friend used to wear. Did you buy it recently?"

"An heirloom, actually. It belonged to my mother."

"Ah."

The silence dragged on again, but I had nowhere to be and hadn't seen any other suspects yet. This was as good a place to watch the room as any other. "How about you?" I asked. "Are you here with friends as well?"

"Me? No, I'm here alone. I usually just pick a secluded spot and watch the proceedings. Supposedly there's a terrace on the second floor that overlooks the gardens. Maybe I'll get lucky and find someone to blackmail. It would be nice to retire early."

"Or end up at the bottom of a river," I pointed out.

"You know, it's strange. The drunker I get, the less I worry about things like that."

"Inexplicable."

"I've always found it so." He smiled. "Anyway, I'll let you get back to your friends. Have a pleasant evening, Jalina."

"You, too," I said. "Enjoy your terrace."

He'd already turned to leave but waved a goodbye over his shoulder to acknowledge the comment. A nearby woman with a dark red dress and a pretty smile stopped her conversation with a friend to lean toward me and whisper, "You do know he was inviting you somewhere private, don't you?"

"I highly doubt it."

"Suit yourself." She gave Aian an appraising look and laughed. "Maybe I'll meet up with him for you."

I shrugged. "If you like."

Andza had made considerable progress by the time I found him again. Four more suspects: one worth considering and three others ruled out. I gave him my update: just one, Keia Murava, but at least I was doing better than Rahad.

He nodded as I spoke, no doubt updating his own internal lists. I wondered how many of those he'd accumulated over the years. "I saw your friend earlier, by the way," he said. "From the Withered Rose. Aian? Have you had a chance to talk to him yet?"

Damn. Thanks to Rahad, I'd completely forgotten that Aian was on our list. I'd even been the one to argue for him. I replayed our conversation in our head and felt the blood drain from my hands and face. Two details stood out. Apart, they meant nothing, but together, they remade the world.

It reminds me of something my friend used to wear.

You do know he was inviting you somewhere private, don't you?

"Not yet," I lied. My mouth felt dry, my tongue wooden. "I'll track him down next."

"Be quick," Andza said. "I think we're about done here."

"I will."

It took ten minutes to find the gardens, and another five to find the staircase that led to the terrace above them. I rehearsed what I would say but changed my mind at every turn. There were too many things to cover, too many years to fill in. In the end, I decided to ask about my mother. I didn't begrudge Andza his story, but I wanted my own first.

The hallway that led to the terrace had a hushed quality. Open doors on either side led to small closets filled with props, costumes, and old set pieces. The upper half of the walls held irregular bits of wood and fabric to dampen the sound. If the terrace had ever been used as a set, this hallway would've been where the performers prepared. I saw curtains at the far end, half drawn. Two people stood on the platform beyond them, their heads close together.

I waited. One of the figures split off and walked toward me. The woman in the red dress, the one who'd said she would handle Aian for me. She winked at me as she passed.

"He's all yours. Apparently. Break his heart for me?"

"I'll do my best."

I waited at the curtain until the sound of her footsteps disappeared behind me. Aian hadn't seen me yet. I took a moment to gather my courage, to prepare what I would say. *You knew my mother.* Four simple words and, beyond them, answers to questions I'd never had the chance to ask.

I heard a small sound from the shadows behind Aian and froze. I couldn't have told you what it was. The scrape of a shoe against the stone, maybe, or a rustle of clothing. Aian turned toward it, and . . .

. . . and crumpled. I don't know how else to describe it. One minute he was standing there, leaning calmly against the rail with a thoughtful look on his face. Then a sound like tree branches breaking under the weight of frozen snow. He fell to his knees, legs ruined, clothes already soaked with gore. I heard a whimpering sound, and then his chest and face collapsed under the same unseen force.

He fell forward, dead. An empty thing, a wet sound against the stone.

CHAPTER TWENTY

The shock saved me. My heart forgot how to beat for a moment. My lungs forgot how to pull in air. I stood there, still as a mouse, until someone stepped out of the opposite archway and onto the terrace.

He would've looked friendly if I'd met him on the street. A kindly old man dressed in simple clothes. A little shorter than average height, a bit fat. He wore a dark gray cloak that hid the lower half of his face, but I could still see his eyes. Those eyes were what broke the illusion. He stared down at Aian's body for half a moment, frowning slightly in disappointment. Like he saw a mess in front of him, not a person.

He glanced toward the upper balcony, and I saw his profile clearly in the light from the window. I recognized him at once: the mysterious visitor at the school, the one who didn't want to leave a message. He must have been tracking Aian for weeks, and there could be no question as to why. Only an Architect could kill like that, with a crushing weight that needed no hand to wield it.

But why was he still there, if he'd done what he came here to do?

He's waiting, I realized. *He needs to wait here until someone finds the body, and then he needs to make sure they come to the correct conclusions.* How long would that take? A few minutes at most. How much of a head start would that give me, and more importantly, what could I do with it? Whatever it was, it would have to be enough.

Fear had taken hold of me, but Andza's trick for moving through it worked wonders. A slow, shaky breath, and I picked my left foot up off the ground. The right followed, and I found myself moving back down the hallway and through the party, trying not to give in to terror, resisting the urge to run screaming through the crowd.

I made it outside, the open air of the city a relief despite the heat and humidity. I wanted nothing more than to stop and breathe for a moment until the nausea subsided, but I couldn't waste the precious few seconds I had. There was no way to know if Aian's killer could see me from the terrace, so I tried to blend in with the people walking near me. No time for a proper disguise, but I pulled out my mother's hair piece and stashed it in the pocket of my dress. Just a young woman with shoulder length brown hair. I could've been coming from or going to any of a hundred parties in the city tonight.

While I walked, I tried to reason through what had just happened. Whoever killed Aian knew who he was and knew him well enough to know where he'd be tonight. They would have seen me at the party, probably even recognized me from the school, but I was just a colleague. It made sense for Aian to approach me at a party. The real question was whether or not they'd seen me follow him up the stairs.

I decided not to go straight back to the inn. The safety of a locked door didn't outweigh the danger of being found alone. Andza and Rahad would eventually notice my absence from the party and come looking for me. Until then, I wanted to keep moving, and I had an idea of where I needed to go.

I turned a corner, and the street ahead of me opened into a grand plaza. Two more blocks until the side street that led to the Withered Rose. I didn't even know if the gate would be unlocked at this hour, but it was the only connection I had to Aian, my only chance for some clue to who he was or what he knew.

Oh, gods. Aian. I'd barely known him, but I could still picture his face. I'd never see that grin again or laugh at his jokes in the hallway. Worse, I'd never learn the secret he wanted to share, never discover that link to my own past. Was it selfish to mourn that more than a person's life? I hated to admit it, but it was true.

A pair of boys my age broke away from the fountain as I passed, but the taller one put a hand on his friend's arm when I looked toward them. They didn't follow. A few seconds later I realized why. I'd drawn my knife without realizing it. Hardly an inconspicuous way to walk the streets, but if it saved me from unwanted attention, so be it. I kept it in my hand until I reached the front doors of the Rose.

The street in front of the school was empty, but I still walked quietly toward the door, afraid that my footsteps might draw someone to a window. I tried the handle. Locked, of course. Old as the doors were, I had no hope of breaking them down, and I didn't think the vines along the wall were strong enough to support my weight.

I looked around. No conveniently placed ladders, no trellis to a neighboring balcony. I wasn't going to make it inside; I wasn't going to find any clues about who Aian really was. There was a very real chance that I wasn't going to survive the night.

I leaned my head against the door. Every sermon I've ever heard has some notion of placing your faith in the gods.

Trusting in their unknowable purpose. But why should they care about our problems? We'd left them behind when we fled our homeland. We didn't even bring their names with us.

Some bleak, desperate part of me wondered if they didn't see us the way we saw them. Vague, unknowable things who couldn't hear them across the distance that separated us. A horrible thought, that the gods might be placing their faith in us.

Then let's help each other. Please let me find a way in. Please let me find . . . something. Anything.

I twisted the handle again, more out of frustration than hope. I heard a click, frighteningly loud in the silence, and felt the handle turn. I pushed the door inward, disbelieving. It swung open without so much as a creak.

The darkness of the courtyard waited just ahead of me. I stared into it. It couldn't be. It absolutely, definitively *could not be.* Just imagining that it *might* be true invited the deepest kind of heresy I knew.

Then again, if we were keeping track of heretics this evening, one had just killed my friend in cold blood. Besides, if the door really had opened in response to a prayer, the gods could hardly damn me for accepting what they themselves had given me. I wondered if my mother saw it the same way, all those years ago.

The door hung open, waiting. I stepped through it and into the shadows beyond.

I sprinted through the courtyard, trusting my feet more than my eyes to navigate the dimly lit walkway. The interior door was locked as well, but I knew that a window around the side had a broken latch. Even so, it had only been built to open easily from the inside. It took several tries to force it open.

Darkness made the familiar hallways seem strange and threatening. I bumped into everything, then waited in the heavy silence, interpreting every sound as an approaching threat. What an awful inconvenience, this fear. Some hysterical part of me wanted to giggle at the thought. It was harder to keep control than I would've liked.

Aian's desk sat in the far corner of the teachers' office, along the back row, right next to the windows that overlooked the river. A thin sliver of moonlight rested on the windowsills, a line of watchtowers in the dark. I made for them, hardly breathing.

There were no locks on the drawers, but I worried about the sound, so I started with the cluster of papers on top of the desk. One at a time, I lifted a scrap of paper to the weak light and scanned it for something important. Any scrap of a message that could tell me who Aian really was or what he knew. Then I placed it back exactly as I'd found it and moved on to the next.

Why bother? The thought came before I could stop it. *It's not like he'll ever notice that someone's been through his desk.* The words on the page grew cloudy for a moment. I wiped my eyes and kept looking.

The bottom drawer slid open without a sound, but I still had no idea what I was looking for. My hand closed around the corner of a notebook, and I pulled it free. As I did, I heard something clatter in the hallway outside the teacher's room.

Don't move. Don't move. Don't move. Moving will get you killed, so don't move.

Minutes crept by without another sound. I knew I couldn't go back the way I came and couldn't risk searching for anything else. The window behind me stood open. We often left it that way to catch the breezes off the river. How far of a drop was it? Twenty feet? For the thousandth time this evening, I scraped for some reserve of courage I wasn't sure I had. Notebook pressed tightly against my chest, I jumped.

I heard the window shatter behind me, frame and all. I plunged into the brackish water, chased by slivers of wood and glass. Before I knew which way was up, the water carried me away from the Rose and around a curve. I knew how to swim, but I'd never practiced being thrown around by rushing water and didn't seem to have a natural talent for it. I finally managed to get my head above the waterline and the rest of me underneath it and swam toward a low stone dock. A slimy length of rope trailed from one of the ties into the water, and I used it to haul myself out.

The heat fell out of my body in a rush, with a feeling like icy needles on my scalp and arms. My legs gave out, my stomach heaved, and an impossible amount of water poured out of me. A ragged breath followed, a desperate, horrible sound I'd never heard a living person make. Then the cycle started again. I lay there for an eternity, retching water and gasping for air, watching with a detached sense of wonder as my body tried to save itself.

Quiet. Street noises above me, distant and unimportant. The world came back into focus. The buildings around me looked unfamiliar, dark and towering. I had no idea where I was, where to go. Up the stairs, at least, and out onto the street. Any street. I'd figure it out from there.

My dress weighed a thousand pounds, and my hair sat in a vicious tangle around my face, but I could see well enough, so I didn't bother to fix it. I still had my knife in my left hand, my hard-won prize clutched against my right side. If I looked dangerous before, I looked positively feral now.

My luck still ran true. I emerged on a street I recognized,

and even better, I was only a few minutes from the inn. I ran, not caring if anyone noticed. I saw no point in trying to be inconspicuous and had everything to gain from moving quickly. Two minutes later, I slammed the door of our room behind me, still soaking wet.

I staggered over to my wardrobe, pried my dress away from my arms and legs, and pulled on something dry. Then I crawled back to the fireplace and managed to light it on the first try. The gods were feeling uncharacteristically generous with their miracles today.

That done, I picked up the notebook I'd taken from Aian's desk. The jacket was made of leather, and I'd been clutching it close to me when I went under, but the pages looked soaked, the edges blurred with running ink. I didn't have the courage to open it yet and see whether or not it was ruined. Some other Jalina would have to deal with that heartbreak.

When I turned it over to set it on the dining table, the light from the fireplace reflected off a small piece of gold lettering in the corner of the front cover. No, not lettering. A symbol, like a maker's mark: a circle slashed by two parallel lines. It didn't resemble any house symbols I knew, but it did look familiar. I let out a sharp, sudden cry when I realized what it was.

I dug my mother's hair piece out of my pocket. The shapes matched perfectly.

Two thoughts entered my mind at the same time, both with frightening force and clarity. The first: I had found something that mattered. Whatever Barste ended up costing us, we'd have something to show for it.

The second: I would have to show Andza, and when I did, I wouldn't be able to hide my connection to the woman he knew as Serine.

What to do? Someone would find Aian's body soon, if they hadn't already, and Rahad and Andza would notice my absence. I didn't have much time to think before they came back. A part of me wanted to tell the whole story, to lessen the weight I'd been carrying quietly for months. But I felt another, stronger part of me close its fist around that prize. I couldn't imagine the words I would use, couldn't even imagine myself looking for them.

In the end, I decided that Andza could have Aian's secrets. All the pages between the covers would go to him, but not the mark on the cover. Was I being selfish? Absolutely. But they were my secrets first, and I felt I had a right to them. Besides, I told myself, my mother hadn't trusted him with the symbol either.

I folded the cover away from the rest of the notebook and held the corner of it over the fire until it blackened. Even as it disappeared, I bargained with myself. I would tell them later, somewhere else, a better time. The final trace of gold disappeared. I sat and waited until Andza and Rahad returned.

Even though I expected them, even though I recognized their footsteps coming up the stairs, I still flinched when I heard the handle turn. They entered the room like thieves and didn't relax until they saw me sitting by the fireplace. Rahad closed the door behind them.

"We saw you leave the party. What happened?"

"Aian. I was right. I approached him at the party," I lied, "but someone killed him before I could speak to him." I gave a brief description of what I'd seen. I tried to spare myself from reliving the worst parts of it, but Andza pressed me for details. When I got to the part where Aian's killer appeared, he made me go over every aspect of the man's appearance.

"Someone from the Order," Andza guessed. "But not the person I would've expected."

"I didn't think . . ."

"That they'd be willing to kill to keep this secret?" Andza asked sharply. "Compare a few deaths against the number of lives they'd save by preventing another war." I didn't realize until later that Andza had already done that math and decided it was worth it.

"What do we do now?" Rahad asked.

"We prepare to leave. Immediately. Gather everything you need. There's only one way out of the city at this hour, and we have to hope it's not being watched."

"There's something I need to do first. I'll meet you at the north gate."

"Rahad!" Andza shouted after him, but the younger man had already sped out of the door.

I threw clothes into my suitcase at random. The journal and hairpiece went somewhere in the middle of the pile. I'd tell Andza about one or both of them later, assuming we all made it out of the city. Anything that didn't fit into our suitcases went into a separate sack, which Andza filled with a few loose bricks from the fireplace and tied off with a bit of rope. He disappeared with this while I kept packing and came back a few minutes later empty-handed.

With the room emptied, we went downstairs to settle our bill. Andza paid for another week in advance but said we wouldn't need any more meals in the common room. The innkeeper postdated our departure for six days out, thanked us for our patronage, and wished us safe travels with an affably blank expression. No telling how well that would cover our trail, but it was done quickly enough.

We didn't speak at all during the half hour it took our wagon to roll through the twisted back alleys that led to the north gate. Andza sat hooded in the driver's seat, and I sat behind in the covered section of the wagon, waiting for the sound of broken bones and splintered wood to come crashing down around me. Our mules either missed our somber moods or didn't care. They trotted happily, excited for the exercise no matter the hour.

We came to a stop, and I stole a peek out of the back of the wagon. No kindly old men lurking in any shadows I could see. A woman stood on her balcony enjoying the night breeze but gave us a passing glance and went back to her thoughts. How close did an Architect have to be to perform their tricks? The answer had never mattered before tonight.

While Andza stopped to have a word with the guard, Rahad materialized from a shadowy corner across the square and hopped into the back of the wagon.

"Where have you been?" I asked.

"Taking care of something."

"Oh, your tangent. And did you? Take care of it?"

He said nothing, but the barest glance toward a corner of the square betrayed him. A girl, roughly my age. She looked . . . I would've said pretty, but her delicate features had no softness to them. She looked determined. She wore a dark brown cloak that hid most of her clothing and stood like she already had an idea of where she'd place the knife if it came to that. She spared one last look toward our wagon, mouthed a silent thank you, and lifted her hood.

So, Rahad had uncaged his Meadowlark. Maybe we would all get away from Barste with something to show for it.

As the wagon started moving again, I decided to risk one more prayer tonight and sent the girl away with whatever blessings the gods could spare. I hoped that she would find something better, wherever she was going.

PART THREE

The Ghost in the Castle

CHAPTER TWENTY-ONE

"Just you today, little one?"

Jaeri tried not to bristle, though it was the second time she'd been asked that today.

The first had been just after sunrise, when she'd shown up alone in the servants' quarters to ask what her chores for the day would be. Well, not alone. The entire serving staff had been there. But she wasn't exactly a servant.

She'd been given a home in the governor's palace, rather than a living. The same was true of her brothers and sisters, the ragtag collection of nearly two dozen orphans that Governor Ferrec had adopted in her first few years here. None of them *had* to do chores, but the older ones—the ones who could dimly remember having parents and losing them—had set the tone, and Jaeri and the others had followed it for years.

They would wake up in the morning, make their way down to Niklas Harran's office next to the silver room, and push past one another to claim a spot on the signup sheet. Most helped with the cooking and cleaning. There was *always* cooking and cleaning to do. But a few of the older children got special tasks, like helping with accounts or working alongside one of the palace tradesmen. Jaeri liked those jobs the best and often got up early twice a week to make sure she had a chance at getting them.

Of course, that had all changed with the king's arrival. Fewer and fewer of her "siblings" showed up every day until this morning, when Jaeri stood alone outside Niklas Harran's office, staring at an empty space on the wall where the signup sheet should have been.

"Yes, ma'am. Just me today."

Normally, there would be at least five or six others here with her in Aulde's makeshift classroom, either sprawled on the cushions scattered across the floor or seated at the dusty furniture that had been dragged in a century ago. Today, it was just Jaeri.

"So. What are we learning about today?"

That was how Aulde started every class. She'd been teaching history and cartography in this room for as long as anyone could remember. She also taught languages sometimes, but Jaeri stopped coming to those lessons once she realized she could learn words from the soldiers that Aulde refused to teach her. And though she didn't always know much about things that had happened in the last seventy years ("Unless it's older than me, little one, it isn't history yet"), she told wonderful stories about the ancient world and knew how to describe faraway places in ways that lifted them out of the lines on a map and made them real.

Jaeri hated to waste the opportunity. She rarely got a chance to decide, on her own, what the lesson would be. Most days there were shouting matches, and compromises, and at least two boring stories for every interesting one. But she'd caught the mood of the palace, and there were other things on her mind than ancient history.

"Can I ask a question?"

"Always, little one."

"When the governor marries King Sethric, she'll be a queen, right?"

Aulde rolled her head side to side, lips pursed, like she was collecting thoughts from an attic and couldn't remember where she'd put them. "It's more complicated than that. She might be a queen, or she might be a queen-consort, or even just a consort. She and the king have to decide what her status will be and what powers and responsibilities she'll have."

Jaeri chewed on that for a moment. "So if she's a queen, she can do things like make laws or command the army if the king is sick or away. But a queen-consort wouldn't be able to do those things." Jaeri had an idea what "just a consort" meant but didn't ask about that one aloud. She was old enough to know that there were things she had to pretend not to know.

"Precisely."

"And what about us? If I'm adopted, and Governor Ferrec becomes a queen-consort, does that mean I'm a princess?"

For that matter, how many princes and princesses would there be? Would Kerra get twenty new heirs to the throne overnight?

"I suspect," Aulde said carefully, "that's one of the things the king and the governor are discussing. Is that what you want to be, little one? A princess?"

Jaeri had never considered the question before. She didn't particularly want to be a princess—not when she could be a blacksmith, or a carpenter, or a stonemason. Or a soldier, maybe, or a hunter. Even a scholar like Aulde must have more fun than a princess.

"I guess it depends," she answered honestly.

Aulde looked amused. "Oh? On what?"

"On what my powers and responsibilities will be."

There was a look that Jaeri had come to recognize. She'd

seen it on dozens of faces over the years: when she struck her first target at the archery range, or solved a difficult problem in class, or convinced one of the new hounds to fetch a training dummy for the first time. That mixture of surprise and delight that meant you'd exceeded someone's expectations, that you were ready for something more challenging.

Jaeri loved that look. Aulde wore it now, her wrinkled face beaming with approval.

"Well said. Of course, you don't have to be the natural, firstborn heir to make history. In fact . . ."

From there, the lesson ran its normal course, though Aulde had to make do with a much smaller audience than usual. She chose a princess from the old Ghantish empire, one who had been exiled as an infant and returned to rule an empire in chaos. After a boring—though mercifully brief— lecture on the situation in Ghant, Jaeri had the chance to choose what the princess should do next.

Normally, this started a shouting match, as everyone in the class had a different idea about what to do. Flin always wanted to raise an army and march on something, and whenever the class followed his advice, they usually ended up getting executed. Rissa mostly just tried to win over powerful allies, which either worked incredibly well or backfired catastrophically.

Today, Jaeri got to make all the decisions, but that also meant every misstep was her own fault. The first time through, she tried to accuse her uncle, the current regent, of treason, but she just ended up exiled again. On her second attempt, she managed to win over two generals and the labor minister and set up a new capital about fifteen miles from the first. She made one terrible decision after another during the siege, though, and ended up having to surrender her armies.

The last attempt seemed like it was off to a good start.

She convinced one of her sympathetic generals to assassinate the regent, which put her on the throne within weeks. But without winning over the ministers in advance, she was woefully unprepared to actually rule the empire she'd won. She had to watch, powerless, as her rivals divided up bits of the empire for themselves.

At the end, Aulde revealed what the princess had actually done. It took nearly six years to win over enough support from the various factions, during which she'd lost a husband, two children, and countless friends to accidents, assassinations, and betrayals. But she managed to depose her uncle the year she turned twenty-three and served as regent in her own right for another seventeen years, when her son took the throne.

Jaeri was a bit disappointed that she'd done so poorly. Being a princess was apparently much harder than it looked. But she'd learned a lot in the attempt. Bold, decisive action was all well and good when it worked. But when it didn't, there was something to be said for patience, determination, and a refusal to give into despair.

Besides, she'd also left the class with something she'd never had before: a very clear idea of exactly the kind of princess she was going to be.

CHAPTER TWENTY-TWO

Andza set a magnificent pace. No need to ask where we were headed. Away, and quickly. If he had a plan beyond that, he didn't share it with me.

We sold our wagon in the first town we came to, and Andza used the money to stable our mules—indefinitely, as far as I knew. Our winter clothes made up most of our luggage, having come with us from Sharme, so getting rid of those lightened our packs considerably. Tents and extra blankets were exchanged for light provisions and camp utensils. When we left the road and set off overland, I only had three things in my pack beyond the bare essentials: my mother's hair ornament, the biography of King Sethric I'd taken from the Rose's library, and Aian's notebook.

I made good use of the silence that fell over us. I knew that Andza would pull me aside for another round of questions, and soon. Would it be possible to keep anything from him when he did? Doubtful.

I'd already glanced through Aian's notebook in secret but hadn't found anything of value in it. If something important lurked between the appointment reminders, lesson plans, and random sketches, Andza had the best chance of figuring it out. But giving it to him meant revealing my detour to the Rose, which I'd left out in the first telling. And once he knew I'd hidden one thing from him, I'd never have his trust again.

Unless I came clean about everything.

So I thought of excuses. I prepared explanations, rather than lies. Reasons why I'd acted the way I did, why I'd kept things from the two of them, why I wasn't a horribly selfish person who'd jeopardized everything and gotten someone killed in the process.

It didn't help. It's hard when your excuses don't even sound good to you.

I've mentioned before that I struggle with guilt. After a few days of waiting for the axe to fall, I realized that confessing might actually be less painful in the long run.

We set up camp that night in a field well off the road. It must have been farmland at some point, though I didn't see any lights or buildings in the distance. Just a few low stone walls that divided the expanse into rugged squares. Andza and Rahad sat across from the bare patch of ground where we'd have built a fire, if we dared. I took the seat they left for me, but not the dried provisions they offered. My stomach felt the size of a plum.

"There's something you both need to know."

Rahad looked curious. Andza didn't. He'd been waiting for this.

I set the notebook on the ground between us. "This belonged to Aian. On the way back from the party, I stole it from his desk in the Withered Rose. The man who killed him caught up with me there, but I got away. This is all I managed to take, but I think it's important."

"It looks . . . damaged," Rahad said, picking it up.

"Partly from the river," I explained. "And partly because I burned off the symbol in the corner of the front cover."

"Why?" Andza asked calmly.

"Because it looked like this." I handed him the second object I'd pulled out of my pack, the hair ornament I'd worn to the party. He looked it over curiously, pausing for a moment to make out the design on the back.

"The *S* stands for Serine," I said. "My father told me it belonged to my mother."

Rahad blinked in confusion. So Andza hadn't shared that detail with him.

"How long have you known?" Andza asked. I had no idea what to make of that quiet, even tone.

"The night before we came to Barste, when you told me Miss Talia's real name."

"She didn't tell me she had a daughter," Andza said. He looked directly at me when he spoke. "If I knew then, I would have told you."

And I believed him. Because he'd told me that he trusted me and never gave me any indication that he didn't. And didn't that just twist the knife?

"She kept secrets, I guess." I shrugged. "Must be a family thing."

I tried to smile at my own bad joke, but my face twisted the wrong way, and the next thing I knew I was sobbing. In trying to keep one part of the story for myself, I'd ruined our last chance at following the trail and had gotten Aian killed in the process. Worst of all, I had nowhere to lay the blame except my own selfishness.

"I'm sorry," I mumbled, after I stopped crying.

"What's done is done." Andza gave the hair ornament back to me and picked up the notebook. "With any luck, we'll still have something to show for it. It was brave of you to retrieve it."

I wiped my nose on my sleeve rather than answering.

I'd prepared myself for anger. I didn't know what to do with forgiveness.

"In any case, there's little we can do about it now. Eat some food, get some sleep. We have a lot of ground to cover tomorrow."

The unexpected kindness unknotted my stomach, but the first bite of food did little to reawaken my appetite. I woke up the next day, starving and tired, but thoughts of dried food and fitful sleep still seemed unappealing. I was ready to walk, though. There are times in your life when you need distance more than you need anything else.

It's said that the king is loyal to his allies and merciful to his enemies. While this is undoubtedly true of the first two years of his reign, some of his oldest friends would object to this characterization if they were still alive to do so.

After Sethric took over management of his family's estates, he had little time for the intrigues and power struggles of his predecessor's court. Instead, he made friends with his peers, far flung minor lords at the edge of the kingdom, with small estates and little influence.

Hinnes and Braies of Lletra, cousins and close friends, first met the king during these years. The three became fast friends, often spending entire seasons in one another's company: summering at Hinnes' hunting lodge near Puhrsa or spending the winter at Sethric's home near the coast.

Their friendship turned sour by the start of the war, though few can say why. There are rumors of a falling out between them, but shockingly few details. So few, in fact, that it seems foolish to ascribe Sethric's betrayal to anything but cold calculation. Though many love the king now, no one would disagree that his murder of Hinnes and Braies did a great deal to bolster his forces early on—not to mention removing two potential rivals from the field.

Andza tossed Aian's notebook back to me. I set aside my biography and picked it up.

"Useless, I'm afraid."

I nodded. "I guess it was too much to hope that he'd leave some hint lying around in a book in his unlocked desk drawer."

"There's a very good chance he did," Andza said. "But we don't have the keys to make sense of it." Seeing my confused expression, he explained.

"They can ward their belongings with an illusion to make them appear to be something else. Changing the form is difficult. A book that *looks* like a hammer still *feels* like a book, but there are other uses. Mostly they use it as a kind of . . . divine cryptography. The recipient would know some key to unravel the illusion, but anyone who didn't know the trick would see a false message. Considering the symbol on the cover, that book was probably meant for Serine."

"So not entirely useless." I sighed. "We just need to bring Aian back to life. Or track down the woman who's spent my entire life hiding from me." Both seemed equally unlikely to me.

"Keep it close, if you like," Andza said. "If you don't think you'll have need of it, I recommend hiding it or destroying it. Either way, it's up to you." He sounded as if he truly didn't care.

I nodded again, then flipped through the pages a final time. I felt nothing as I did. No stir of hope that I'd one day find answers hidden somewhere within. I couldn't even pretend to feel grief over Aian when I held it. Whatever sorrow I felt over our half friendship had run out in . . . less than a week? I didn't need another reminder of my failures, my selfishness, my indifference. My pack was heavy enough already.

I buried the notebook at the base of a stone wall four days north of Barste. We continued on.

The town of Miller's Bend sat halfway between Barste and Lletra. When I summoned a mental map of the kingdom, I couldn't imagine covering that distance in twelve days. Then again, we'd been walking almost twelve hours a day in a straight line over low hills, only stopping to eat or sleep. My feet, at least, had no trouble believing we'd walked over two hundred miles.

Our room in the tavern barely warranted the name. Four narrow cots in a room that must have been a pantry at some point. There were shelves built into the walls, and no wash-stand unless we walked down the hallway to use the one in the kitchen. It seemed like a palace after twelve fearful nights under the stars.

"So what's the plan now?" Rahad asked. I no longer had to imagine the half-starved street urchin he'd been once. Between the exercise and the limited provisions, I could see his cheekbones clearly beneath his eyes. I didn't have a mirror to check my own appearance and wasn't sure I wanted one.

"First, we make sure we aren't being followed. Rahad, you'll need to ask around. Whoever's chasing us has seen Jalina, and it's a safe bet he knows who I am, so you're our best chance. If you're willing."

"But Rahad doesn't even know what the man looks like," I pointed out.

We thought for a minute.

"Could you draw him?" Rahad asked.

"I . . . could try?" I offered. After the disaster in Barste, I was willing to try nearly anything they asked of me.

We found a pencil and a few scraps of paper. I made a rough attempt at his face, and Rahad asked me about some of the details. The nose was thinner than I'd drawn it, the eyes further apart, not quite as deep set. He fixed a few lines based on my suggestions and passed the paper back to me. By the time we got to the third sheet of paper, we had something I thought would work.

"I'll see what I can find out," Rahad said, and he left.

"If we are being followed . . ." I trailed off, not sure how to continue. What chance did we have against the way Aian had been killed? Against someone who could kill us quickly and painfully from any window or alleyway we passed by?

"Then we run, and we keep running. Eventually we'll make our way back to Sharme. You'll be safe there. Just stay indoors as much as you can, and try to avoid walking under any balconies."

"But why . . . ? Oh, I see." Aian's killer must have been tracking him for weeks to know he'd be at that specific party on the Long Night. But he needed to wait until there was an opportunity to make it look like an accident, like Aian had fallen or been pushed from a great height. An Architect couldn't just flatten someone on the street. Not without committing open heresy and accepting the consequences that entailed for both themself and the Order. He'd risked it when we were alone, but I wouldn't be alone once I got back to the crowded dormitories of the Library. It wasn't much, but it was something.

"You mentioned before that it was someone from the Order, but not the person you were expecting. Who *were* you expecting?"

"His name is Kyrede. He's a saint like the rest of them but with very . . . strong opinions about how their powers should have been used."

"As in, not at all."

"Exactly."

Someone walked past our room in the hallway, and we waited for the steps to grow distant before we spoke again.

"How do you know so much about him?" I whispered.

Andza's eyes grew cold for a minute. I shuddered to imagine the kind of memory that could put that look on a soldier's face.

"For the first few years, I only found his victims. I knew that someone was following the same trail I was, someone who took their transgressions . . . personally. The first time I actually found one alive, they gave me the name. Apparently they knew him from childhood."

"Wait. Do they *all* know him from childhood? Does that mean they all grew up together?"

"I don't know," Andza admitted. "The conversation usually goes the same way. I warn them that the Order is after them and that I'm their best chance at having their story told. They thank me for the warning, answer what few questions they're willing to answer, and we part ways."

"So you don't . . . you don't even know if . . ." I felt my throat tighten.

He met my eyes, unblinking. "No," he said, his voice as cold as I'd ever heard it. "I don't. I gave her the same warning I gave the rest of them, which put her on equal footing with her pursuers. But I don't know if she's alive. I don't know if any of them are still alive."

I couldn't respond. I was having trouble breathing.

"You have to understand, Jalina. It isn't the *people* I'm trying to save."

Was that a twinge of guilt in his voice? For all I knew, the Order had just been following Andza around for the past fifteen years, content to let him collect his stories as long as he led them to the next heretic. If so, he'd probably guessed the same thing and considered the trade worth it. He'd made an all-or-nothing bet that he would be able to get away with his prize at the end of the trail and had already wagered dozens of lives on the chance that he *might* be able to tell this story.

I realized now why Andza had allowed Rahad and me to join him, why he was so concerned about getting us back to safety. Whatever moral compass he had left pointed to the final round of this deadly game. By bringing in two other people at the very end, he'd tripled his chances of one of us getting away with the truth.

All it had cost him was a trail of corpses, one that stretched back years and passed within twenty feet of my house. And I'd helped him do it. I no longer felt guilty about keeping things from him in Barste. Not after this.

He watched impassively as my thoughts raced. He saw the leaps I made, the conclusions I came to, and didn't contradict them. I saw the moment, the exact *moment*, when he realized that I'd taken some measure of his soul and found it wanting. That perfect comprehension hung between us, silent and heavy. I looked away first.

"I hope they find you," I whispered. It wasn't true, but I didn't care. Anything to hurt him, to lay some curse against him, however pathetic. "I hope they find you, and I hope you die in pain." I couldn't even meet his eyes to see whether or not my words had any effect.

He didn't answer for a long time. "Get some sleep, Jalina," he said finally. Whatever trace of guilt I'd imagined in his voice had vanished. "I'll wake you once Rahad is back."

CHAPTER TWENTY-THREE

The men and women of the Hartwood Brigade might also object to King Sethric's claim as Kerra's "merciful" king. Though they were certainly little more than common bandits, their crimes were no worse than those of their peers and a good deal less horrific than some of their forebears. Their executions, on the other hand . . .

Again, cold reason is the likeliest explanation here. Early examples like the Hartwood Brigade gave Sethric's fledgling government an opportunity to project power and security after years of chaos. It also gave the roving mercenary companies an incentive to disband and pursue more useful occupations.

"—lina, wake up."

I stirred awake, mumbling something incoherent. I'd fallen asleep with Sethric's biography open across my lap and woke up from half-remembered dreams of bandit kings and grim-faced executioners. I expected to see my father hovering over me. He was the only one who ever called me Lina. I must have overslept while he was busy with the shop.

But this wasn't my bedroom in Casmhe. It was too small, the walls too bare. And it was Andza, not my father, who sat disapprovingly on the pallet across from me. I remembered the last thing I'd said to him, and regretted it, but didn't know how to take it back.

Rahad had come back. There were no windows in the room to gauge the hour of the day based on the light, so I couldn't say for sure how long he'd been gone. The pain in my neck suggested at least an hour. I rolled my head a few times as he came in and closed the door, wincing as I did so.

"Right," Rahad said. "Two things. First, there's been a lot of foot traffic on the road north in the past few days. I started asking around to see if anyone's been causing trouble and mentioned that we ran into some unpleasantness on our way here. The innkeeper recognized the description Jalina gave me and said our man came through here yesterday. Stayed in a small room upstairs, didn't talk to anyone. He just sat there in the common room and stared at people. Seems like he left this morning, a few hours before we got here."

I felt a sense of panic rising in my chest but pushed through it. When in doubt, move. "How did he find us?" I asked.

"If he beat us here, then I don't think he followed our trail," Andza said. "He knows we left through the north gate. He's probably been checking towns along the way. We've avoided most of them by going overland, but there was always a chance we'd cross paths eventually. Did the innkeeper mention anything about the Order?"

"No," Rahad said.

"So he's traveling in disguise," Andza said. "And keeping his task to himself. Both of those work to our favor. What else?"

"This one's less important," Rahad said, "but it's all anyone is talking about, so I thought I'd mention it. Did you know King Sethric is getting married?"

"I knew he was traveling to Lletra," Andza said, "but I

hadn't heard the reason why. I assumed he was checking on the outer provinces. It's been a while since he left the capital."

"Who's he marrying?" I asked and immediately blushed. Faced with the possibility of violent death, I still couldn't help being interested in the latest gossip. In my defense, a royal wedding usually counts as a historically significant event.

"The governor in Lletra. I didn't catch the name."

"Hmm. That could be trouble," Andza said. "Ferrec was one of his lieutenants during the war. Tough as nails and twice as sharp. Not someone I'd want to spend my golden years with, but you'd be hard pressed to find a better ally in a fight. He must expect trouble of some kind."

"Another war?" I asked.

He thought for another moment, then shook his head. "I'm not as connected as I used to be, but if someone is planning a war, they're keeping it awfully quiet. Usually there's a buildup. General discontent, not-so-subtle troop movements, months of public posturing. We haven't had any of that." He shrugged. "Or he's about to die and wants to set some last-minute plans in motion. Either way, I'm not sure it affects us right now, and there's nothing we could do about it anyway."

That last comment confused me. "So does that mean there's something we *can* do about being followed by a murderous saint?" Last I checked, our only plan was to run away, and that hadn't helped much. Unless he meant to turn us southeast and start making our way back to Sharme. I tried not to count the miles. At least we were past the hottest part of the summer.

"Perhaps," Andza said. "But I'll need some time to think. Be ready to leave at nightfall, just in case."

Rahad and I looked at our meager possessions, then at each other. What exactly did we need to pack? But Andza was already lost in thought, not to be disturbed. I shrugged and went back to my nap. I tried not to think about my aching feet.

We ate dinner early, almost an hour before sunset. Roast chicken and grilled squash on a thin layer of some wheat porridge I didn't know the name of. It was bland compared to what we'd eaten in Barste. Whoever made it must have saved a fortune on salt and spices. But after twelve days and nights on the road, and more of the same ahead of us, I took two servings and scraped every speck off the plate.

When we shouldered our packs and stepped outside the inn to meet Andza, he surprised us with saddled horses: a placid, cream-colored pony for me and a gray for Rahad. I was comfortable around horses but only had a little experience riding one, so it took several tries to get into the saddle, even with help. Rahad mounted his quickly, though he looked every bit as awkward in the saddle as I did. Andza led the way on a tall, smoky black stallion, and we left Miller's Bend with the sun just above the horizon.

"Why are we headed north?" I asked. "I thought we were trying to get back to the Library."

"The road forks east up ahead," Andza answered without turning back. "I want to make some distance on the road during the night and cut across the smaller trails south."

I nodded, mostly to myself, then stifled a yawn. I'd managed a few hours of sleep in the room, but not enough to recover, and certainly not enough to ride all night. Fortunately, my horse seemed well-rested and eager to walk, so I relaxed my grip on the reins and let my eyes drift in and out of focus.

Not long after we left town, the shadows deepened around us as the sun set, turning the vivid greens of late summer to a crowded, menacing black. No one spoke. The lush undergrowth just off the road looked wild and forbidding, and the branches above us weaved together so thoroughly that the canopy felt solid, like the roof of a vast, unending tunnel.

Hours passed. We saw at least three camps, mostly small groups of six or seven. The sights and smells of a friendly campfire almost overwhelmed me, but we ignored their invitations with nothing more than a wave and kept on our way.

More trees. More road. More silence. Even the crickets seemed to be asleep. Exhaustion stopped being something I felt inside me. It was its own force, external, conspiring with the oppressive gloom and the gentle rocking of the horse beneath me. I fell asleep half a dozen times, then jolted awake, only to fall asleep again.

Just as I gave up hope of stopping to rest before daybreak, Andza pulled to a stop beneath some vast tree, unrecognizable in the darkness.

"Jalina, you're going to wait here for a few minutes while Rahad and I scout ahead. Try to get some sleep before you fall out of the saddle."

I nodded sleepily and slid off my horse. By the time I slipped my pack off my shoulders and leaned against the tree, they had already ridden out of sight.

As much as I wanted—needed—a few minutes of sleep, I was too tired to actually get any. I sat there, mind buzzing, maddeningly aware of every root and pebble beneath me. How had Andza managed to find the most horribly uncomfortable patch of dirt in the entire kingdom? And in the dark, no less.

Other thoughts ran across the surface of my exhausted mind, niggling things that I hadn't had the chance to pull apart yet. For one thing, who was this new person from the Order? He clearly knew about Aian if he was looking for him at the Withered Rose. He must have known about me as well, considering the time he spent talking to me.

I replayed the conversation we'd had in the teacher's room, and he clearly knew more about me than I did about him. But he spoke like someone who didn't have the full picture yet, like he was hoping our conversation would snap some piece of the puzzle into place.

He must have been trying to guess how much I knew. That's the only thing that made sense. The Order had been following Andza closely enough to report that Rahad and I were traveling with him, but they needed to know if we were involved or just innocent decoys.

Considering that he tried to kill me a few weeks later, I must have done something to tip the scales. But what?

Until the Long Night, I hadn't known Aian was our target, so I couldn't have done anything incriminating before that. And I was fairly certain he hadn't overheard our conversation there. I'd been paying close attention to faces all night. I would have recognized his. Nor could he have seen me walking toward the terrace. He was already hidden in shadow, dozens of feet away by the time I arrived. He had no way to know I was there, unless . . .

Architects could shift forces around. Could they *sense* them, the way a fish senses currents in the water?

If so, he'd have known that someone was standing there when he used his gift to kill Aian. Someone who ran away from the scene and out into the street without alerting anyone. He followed me at a distance, well hidden, trusting that he'd be able to track me even if he lost sight of me. When

I made it to the Withered Rose, he must have guessed that I could lead him to something important, and—this realization jolted me fully awake—*broke* the lock on the door so that I could get in.

But why try to kill me? Why not Andza, or Rahad? For that matter, why try to kill me then? Why not just follow me back to the inn and get all three of us?

Because the Order had already sanctioned killing the illusionists to keep this secret, but they hadn't sanctioned killing *us*.

That was the other half of the coin, the reason they'd left Andza alive to follow his trail all these years. He'd been leading them to the illusionists, certainly, but they must have had some other plan for dealing with him when it was time. Some threat or bribe or plea that this new saint had been sent to deliver. In killing Aian, he'd been trying to close off the trail, but I'd forced his hand by finding something "important" in Aian's desk.

The Architect hadn't shattered the window by accident. He'd been trying to stop me from jumping through it. So he could talk to me.

Despite my frantic heartbeat, I felt suddenly relieved. If we were found, here or at the Library, we'd have a chance to talk. To explain. To get away with our lives, if nothing else. Maybe we'd be cloistered away in some distant monastery in the mountains, bearers of a secret we could never share. Perhaps we could even manage some kind of arrangement. I could write to my father, to Elaise, to my friends at the Library. I could tell them that I'd devoted my life to translating religious texts or writing biographies. It didn't sound like a terrible fate. Not far, in fact, from the kind of life that many scholars led.

In any case, it must surely be better than the way Aian had died.

I felt the weight of dread lift from my neck and shoulders, to be replaced by a warm, dozy weariness. I leaned against the tree, calm for the first time in days, happy to drift into sleep until Andza and Rahad returned.

Less than a minute later, I sprang to my feet and looked around desperately for my horse. She was a short distance away, one eye half open, annoyed at the sudden noise. I managed to claw my way into the saddle on the third try, though my foot twisted awkwardly in the stirrups and my pack nearly overbalanced me. I urged my horse into a run before I'd even settled into the saddle.

Because while I'd been pulling at one thread, some other part of my mind had been pulling at a different one. I understood now why we'd traveled all night—not south but *north*, in the same direction as the person who was chasing us. I knew why we'd ditched our wagon and why Andza and Rahad had gone ahead: two men on horseback, in the dark, when our pursuer expected three of us. After all these years, Andza finally saw a chance to slip the net completely and get away with his prize.

He just needed to kill a saint first.

I couldn't have been more than a few minutes behind them, but the road ahead of me remained stubbornly empty. I hadn't heard them galloping. They needed stealth more than speed for what they planned. But there was also no way to know how far ahead the saint was. He'd left half a day before us, by Rahad's estimate, so it was reasonable to assume he'd make camp on the way to the next town. Andza must've made a rough guess based on the distance he'd covered since leaving Barste and counted the miles since we left town. But how well had he guessed?

A few minutes later, I slowed my horse to a walk. Another thought crossed my mind. What if Andza never intended to come back for me at all? What if he meant to cut his losses, to turn east with Rahad and leave me to fend for myself, hoping that the saint would find me and waste time dealing with me? I tried to tell myself that it couldn't be true, that the stress and lack of sleep made my thoughts run darker than they should. It almost worked.

I heard a cry some distance ahead, then another. The night swallowed both of them a moment later. Everything held still in the wake of that sound, silent and attentive. I could hear my horse breathing beneath me. As far as I could tell, she and I were the only living things for miles.

Two shapes resolved in the moonlight ahead of me. I held my breath. Both were afoot, stumbling in the road. I slid off my horse and ran forward to meet them. Thick, black blood covered the lower half of Andza's face. His eyes had swollen shut, and the bridge of his nose looked twisted, half sunken into his face. His breath came in wet, ragged coughs, and each one sent another spurt of blood over his lips and chin.

Rahad supported him, breathing heavily with the effort. "What happened?" I asked.

"We caught up to your Architect," he managed, gasping between sentences. "Managed to surprise him while he was making camp, but the fight turned nasty. Both horses dead. We need to get off the road."

I nodded and took Andza's other arm. We managed to carry him a few dozen yards into the undergrowth and settle him against the stump of a fallen tree, where we collapsed to either side of him. I was too tired to ask Rahad anything else and much too tired to worry about what would happen next.

I was on the ground, and that was enough. I could feel the sleep that had eluded me for days finally settling over me. I remembered nothing else until morning.

CHAPTER TWENTY-FOUR

Andza swayed in the saddle as we crested another hill but kept his seat. It seemed at times that a light breeze would be enough to topple him, but even with his eyes closed and several hours of steady blood loss, he was a better horseman than either of us. And a good thing, too. Carrying him over this terrain made a terrific amount of noise and was exhausting besides.

"Which way?" Rahad asked.

That question was easier to answer this morning. North and east, away from the road. Picking a path had been as simple as finding a game trail or dried out creek bed we could follow for a while. But *away* would only work as a destination for so long, and with Andza out of commission, we were in desperate need of a *toward*.

"That way?" I suggested. I pointed vaguely to the left, where the ground ran flat for a while in the shade between two hills. If nothing else, it would keep Andza from falling out of his saddle.

Rahad nodded and led the way. He might defer to my directions in order to avoid the responsibility of choosing, but he had much more experience in the woods. Twice already he'd spotted trouble before we came to it. The first had been a snake. Not poisonous, Rahad thought, but enough to scare our horse if she'd seen it. The second had been a rabbit snare, a clear sign that we were on someone's trapline. We changed course quickly. We both agreed that we needed to avoid running into people for as long as we could.

By this time, someone must have found the saint's campsite. *Jurald*, I reminded myself. Prior of Whitethrush Monastery, according to the requisition slip he carried, a little scrap of paper that served as a receipt for his horse and some basic supplies, requested almost two months ago. The horse had bolted into the woods, and most of the supplies were too heavy to carry, but they'd searched him quickly for anything that would identify the man. That was when he'd struck—bleeding from half a dozen stab wounds—as Andza leaned over him to search his pockets.

It was hard to imagine what people would make of the scene when they found it. A stranger no one recognized, stabbed to death in his camp by bandits that took no valuables and left two dead horses behind. Horses which bore no external wounds but had died of massive internal bleeding nonetheless. Two sets of footprints, headed south, with a trail of blood still clear in the dirt. Tracks that led into the woods—north and east, away from the road.

"Which way?" Rahad asked a few minutes later.

I sighed. That question was easier this morning.

We found the shack just before sunset and decided to camp instead of pushing on. Whatever distance we managed to cover in the hour before nightfall wouldn't make much difference, and Andza needed to rest. His bleeding had finally stopped, but he pushed away any food we offered him and made a whimpering noise as he drank. Between his blood loss and the heat of the day, dehydration was as likely to kill him now as anything else.

"Lean him against the corner," Rahad said, once we managed to get him safely out of the saddle. I nodded, and together we helped Andza stumble through the door and onto the dirt floor. We tried our best to brace him between two walls, his upper half elevated and his neck supported by a few loosely rolled shirts. Even that made me feel light-headed. I took a moment to catch my breath and checked Andza's wounds in the meantime.

They looked the same as they had this morning but more swollen. Was his breathing steadier? If nothing else, he'd stopped making that horrid whistling sound whenever he exhaled. That must count for something.

"Okay. What now?" I asked, straightening. Rahad motioned toward the exit, and I followed him back outside.

Rahad led us a short distance away, just out of earshot. "As rough as he looks now, I think he's going to make it. But we still need a plan. I think we should make our way back to the road, try to find a village or a farm or something."

"Risky," I said, "but I agree. I don't think any of us can take much more of this. What do we say if someone asks about Jurald?"

"We could say we were attacked by the same people? And we ran into the woods for safety but got lost."

"Andza certainly looks the part," I agreed. I looked down at my clothes. "We all do, really. Do you think he was lying about the road turning east? I feel like we should've come across it by now."

Rahad shook his head. "We've been traveling east more than north. I think if we turned north here, we'd be able to find it tomorrow."

"I guess we just need to keep going and hope for the best."

Rahad didn't answer, but he looked about as optimistic as I felt. He just stood there, frowning, letting the silence drag on.

"What?"

"What do we do if he doesn't make it?"

I hope they find you, and I hope you die in pain.

"I don't know," I answered honestly. "But we'll figure something out."

We stood there for another few minutes, watching the failing light. This far north, the heat left the air as soon as the sun went down, but the chill was a blessed relief after walking all day. I folded my arms against the cold but didn't go back inside, happy to just stand still for a while. I saw a pine marten scramble down its tree and watch us cautiously for a few minutes before deciding we weren't a threat. A plump, gray bird with a reddish crown and orange wingtips hopped between the branches of a juniper, gorging on berries. Somewhere in the distance an owl hooted. Everything else held still.

"We should check on Andza," Rahad said.

Back inside the shack, the space between the warped boards gave us plenty of light to see by. We set out our bedrolls on the dirt floor and ate a quiet dinner. Rahad went to refill our water bottles from a stream we'd passed earlier, and I stayed with Andza. His swelling had finally started to go down, but his eyes still didn't open very far. They searched frantically around the cabin but didn't rest on anything.

He mumbled something I couldn't hear.

"What?" I asked. "What do you need?" I leaned close, my cheek almost touching his.

"Please tell me," he whispered, "that it's very dark in here."

I looked around. We were well past sunset, but not so far

that I had trouble seeing. I could make out the shapes of the boards on the far wall, if not the grain of the wood. If Andza couldn't even see that much . . .

"Pitch black," I lied. "Try to get some rest."

We found the road just before noon the next day and turned west after a short argument. Yes, it took us further from the Library, but it also took us closer to Lletra and the denser concentration of villages along the main road. We hadn't found one yet, but a thin line of smoke in the distance gave us hope for a warm meal sometime in the next hour.

Andza slumped in his saddle. Despite being able to eat and drink this morning, he looked worse than he had yesterday. He'd been able to make out dim shapes and colors once the sun came up but couldn't focus on anything and said that trying to made him nauseous.

I suspected his semi-blindness was permanent but didn't say so out loud. Jurald had been strong enough to crush a man in seconds and skilled enough to break the lock at the Withered Rose. He might not have been permitted to kill Andza, even in self-defense, but you didn't have to kill someone to make them . . . irrelevant.

Did I feel sorry for him? Yes and no. How many people had he saved in his single-minded quest for the truth? How many had he condemned? Even he hadn't tried to keep count. It felt fitting that he'd been the victim of his own decisions for once, but it also felt cruel to wish that on a person.

"Houses," Rahad said.

Andza looked up reflexively, but couldn't have seen anything, and slumped forward in his saddle a moment later. I followed Rahad's gaze and saw two houses close together, a fair distance from the road. A barn stood just past them, and sheep dotted the hills beyond. Probably a family farm, with two or more generations living side by side.

"Wait here," I said. "I'll see what I can get."

We'd already decided to let me handle the talking. We needed to look pitiful, not desperate, and the lean rations and bad sleep made Andza and Rahad look dangerous, even without Andza's obvious injury. I just looked frail and half starved but hopefully well short of feral.

Halfway up the path, I heard a dog start barking to announce my presence. So much for a polite knock on the door. Someone in the house yelled for it to quiet down, and a moment later the front door opened. A woman in her thirties with light blond hair and a tanned face walked out, one hand up to keep the sun out of her eyes. I waved, but she didn't wave back.

I stopped thirty feet away from the house and waited for her to come meet me. Partly to give her space and partly because I wanted a running start if her dog got loose. When she saw that I wasn't going to get any closer, she walked down the footpath to meet me.

"Sorry to bother you," I began, "but we were attacked on the road south of here a few days ago, and my uncle was injured. That's him on the horse over there, with my cousin. Would you happen to have anything to eat? We don't need much, I promise."

She gave me a cynical look. I didn't try to exaggerate how tired or desperate I looked. I doubted I needed to, and dishonesty would probably hurt more than it helped. She nodded. Apparently I'd passed her assessment.

"I heard about some trouble on the road south. Haven't had bandits in these parts for years. Where are you headed?"

"Puhrsa," I lied, summoning the name from Sethric's biography. It was the only town I knew of this far north.

"We're trying to get back home."

It was the wrong thing to say. Her eyes narrowed, immediately suspicious, and I swallowed. She didn't press me on it, though.

"Whatever you say," she said with a shrug. "Wait here. I'll grab you something from the kitchen."

I waited, trying to remember everything I knew about the village of Puhrsa. All I could recall was that there was a hunting lodge nearby where King Sethric used to spend time with his friends, friends that he'd betrayed at the start of the war. The village must have been abandoned soon after. Anyone in the area would've been able to catch me in that lie.

Come to think of it, hadn't Aian said that he was from a village north of Barste? A village that he never bothered to visit because there wasn't much left to see there.

According to Andza, at least a few of the illusionists knew each other from childhood, and I'd wondered if they all grew up together. Now we stood within spitting distance of a village that matched Aian's description, one where the inhabitants would have had plenty of opportunities to run across the future king. So many coincidences, all pointed in the same direction.

The woman came back out with a cloth-wrapped bundle and handed it to me. It felt warm and heavy and smelled like freshly baked bread.

"Thank you, truly. Could I, um . . . ask another question? We ran into the woods during the night and got turned around. Could you please tell us if we're heading the right way? The right way to Puhrsa, I mean."

She hadn't pressed me on the lie before, but I knew I was stretching my luck. I held my breath.

"There's a trail that turns north about five miles west of here," she said. "Puhrsa's about an hour in that direction.

What's left of it, anyway." She frowned, picking her next words carefully. "I don't know your story, but wherever you're trying to go, there are safer places to spend the night. If you're in some kind of trouble, you can stay here a night or two. Just you. Your uncle and his boy can fend for themselves, injured or not."

She said it begrudgingly, but that only made the kindness of her offer that much greater. I thought about saints, and miracles, and whether we use either of those words the way we should.

"Thank you for the offer, but I'm safe with them, I promise. We're just . . . thank you."

She nodded, still disbelieving, and turned to go back inside. I walked back down the path with my bundle. I lifted the corner of the cloth to peek inside: six crisp apples, a dozen honey cakes, and three palm-sized squares of dried ham. Almost a day's worth of food, compared to how we'd been eating.

We set up a little picnic in the grass south of the road, far enough away that we couldn't be seen from the house. I passed out the honey cakes first, and we started to eat.

"Andza, do you know where Puhrsa is?"

"The name's familiar," Andza said, "but no. Why do you ask?"

"I said we were trying to make it back home, and she seemed to believe me until I said that's where we were from."

"Probably abandoned," Andza said. "What made you think of it?"

"It was in my book, that one about King Sethric's first few years as king. He used to come here when he was young." I bit my lip nervously but tried to sound firm. "I think we should go see it. It's only a few hours northwest of here."

"That's half a day out of our way," Rahad pointed out.

"In the direction we're trying to avoid. Why do you want to go there?"

"It's a hunch," I admitted, "but Aian was a hunch, too. How many suspects did you two find in Barste? Twenty? Thirty? I found one. The right one. Even if I ruined everything by following it."

The two of them chewed thoughtfully. Even though one of them was blind, they still managed to share a look. Andza shrugged. "We don't have anywhere else to be, and we're out of immediate danger. Lead the way."

The trail was just where the woman said it would be, though it was so overgrown that we had trouble finding it at first. Only the slight depressions from old wagon wheels gave us any indication that we were on the right path. We turned to follow them. The trees were thinner here, mostly pine, as if the forest had only recently started to cover old pastures. After about an hour, the trail rose to top a small hill. We reached the top and looked down over the village of Puhrsa.

Or what was left of it.

Abandoned houses lined either side of the main road, their roofs sagging from years of neglect. A wild tangle of weeds marked what used to be the village green, and I could make out a few stone walls here and there. In its prime, it might have been home for a few hundred people, but if so, they'd all left years ago.

Another dead end. Aian had been the first, killed before I could learn anything from him. Then his notebook, which might have held answers, if it weren't impossible to decipher. Now this.

I described the view for Andza's benefit. I didn't even try to keep the disappointment out of my voice.

"We could camp here, at least," Andza suggested.

"No," I said. "It's fine. Let's just go home."

I turned to leave and heard Andza follow me on horseback. Rahad didn't move.

"Absent gods," he said. When had he started cursing like a Kerran? "Andza, you were right."

"What do you mean?" I asked. "Right about what?"

"All the drawing lessons," Rahad said. "Me being able to see through the illusions." He pointed to the abandoned houses. "I don't think this is Puhrsa, or at least not all of it." He swung his arm to the right, taking in the field of goldenrod next to it. "But *that* might be."

CHAPTER TWENTY-FIVE

We made our way through the waist-high grass, stopping every few minutes for Rahad to stare at a piece of the landscape before waving for us to continue. We had to abandon our horse almost immediately, after it refused to walk through a tangle of brambles that Rahad assured us didn't actually exist. Even I stepped through it slowly, waiting for the thorns to snag against my clothes or bury into my legs. Andza had the best of it, having fewer senses to deceive.

"How can you tell what's real," I asked, "and what isn't?"

"It's hard," Rahad admitted. "The closer I am to something, the harder it is to tell. You have to crouch down so that you can see multiple pieces at once, like the foreground and background of a painting. Then you switch focus between the two a few times. Here, try it with this."

I crouched down beside an abandoned cart, overgrown with weeds. We hadn't seen it until we were right on top of it. From a distance, it only appeared as a clear spot in the grass. I reached out a hand to touch it.

"No cheating," Rahad said. "Now, imagine this cart is the foreground of a painting, and that tree over there is the background. Switch focus a few times, and try to find a new detail every time."

I looked at the cart first and tried to pick out the pattern of the wood grain. Then I switched to the tree, a black walnut about fifty paces away. The second time I looked at the cart, I spotted the line of rusted iron nails that affixed the side boards to the body. The tree had a few leaves that had started to turn orange-red for fall. The cart had a few badly warped boards. The tree . . . was just a tree.

"The tree is fake," I said. "And the cart is real?"

"Nope," Rahad said. To prove it, he tapped his knuckles against the top of the side board. His hand met something solid, with a wooden *thunk* to match. Then he reached his hand through the wood just beneath it. His arm disappeared up to the elbow. "Wooden fence," he said, grinning.

"I don't understand. The cart looked so much clearer."

"Exactly," he said. "Remember when you kept drawing the wrong candlestick? You have to train your eye to spot the details that your mind glosses over. That's true of most real things, but with these illusions, the details are somehow clearer. Whoever did this, they draw better than real life."

I felt around for the edges of the fence, then helped Andza step through. The illusion remained. I couldn't see my legs below the knees. I took a few more steps and was back in perfectly normal grass.

"What's the point of these?" I asked.

"To slow our approach," Andza said without hesitation.

That made us pause. "Do you think someone's waiting for us at the center of all this?"

"It's likely," Andza said. I couldn't tell whether he sounded afraid or optimistic.

"How much further?" I asked Rahad.

"Hard to say," he answered. "We should be—"

Rahad's voice cut off as he tripped and fell *into* the ground. I heard several loud thumps and a muttered curse. I froze. "Rahad! What happened?"

"Stairs," he said. "There are three steps, starting a few feet in front of you. Stick to the left side."

I took Andza's hand, then used a toe to feel for the edges of the staircase. The ground looked like any other patch of ground and even sounded like bare grass when I tapped it with the toe of my boot. But it felt like wood. I counted three steps down, and as I took the final step, I passed some sort of threshold, as if entering the eye of a storm.

The first thing I saw was Rahad, standing up and brushing the dirt from his clothes. He'd narrowly missed falling into an open bear trap, which Andza and I had avoided by sticking to the left side of the stairs.

Looking up, I saw a single-story farmhouse with a wooden porch and a stone chimney. It had been painted green a long time ago, with white shutters, but time and weather had worn away both colors, tinging them with dull gray. The shutters had been thrown open to welcome the cool air, and the door hung slightly open. I heard someone approach from within the house, their footsteps clear and heavy.

The door opened, and a man walked out. He looked old, roughly my father's age, but the similarities stopped there. It wasn't just that he was taller, or wider, or more muscular. It was like he'd been crafted on a different scale—a giant in the shape of a man. He held a long-handled shovel with the same ease I'd have held a fork. The porch overhang shaded his features, so that he spoke from behind a thin veil of shadow.

"Visitors," he rumbled. "Haven't had any visitors in a long time." His grip on the shovel tightened slightly. "Haven't wanted any in a long time either."

Andza stepped forward, passing between me and Rahad.

"Hello, Kallah," he said simply.

"Kallah?" I asked, confused. "Kallah *Varnin*? The king's bodyguard? I thought he died."

"He didn't," came another voice off to my left.

I turned, and for a moment, I didn't notice the woman standing there. My eyes were fixed on the crossbow she held, and the single iron bolt that sat ready in its groove. The deadly iron tip wavered between the three of us. I moved my hands slowly to the side, palms out, to show that I didn't have a weapon. Rahad did the same.

"Reia," Andza said. "I thought it must be you, though I wouldn't have believed it if someone else told me. Everyone thinks you're dead, you know. Both of you. But I suppose you planned it that way. How's your knee?"

"Hurts all winter." She circled around slowly, her crossbow still pointed between the three of us, until she was at the foot of the stairs. She looked Andza up and down, grimacing at the mass of swelling and bruises around his eyes. "I recognize you. The scribe, right? What happened to your face?"

"My luck finally caught up with me," Andza said. He spoke with the same quiet calm he'd used in Barste.

"Must have been chasing you for a while," she said. "You look like death."

Her eyes flicked toward me: once, quickly, and then again. I stepped forward slowly, overcome with the most curious sensation.

It reminded me of a day almost two years ago, when I'd waited outside Elaise's class to ask if she wanted to have lunch. Another girl had walked out first—same height, same blond hair—and there was a dizzy, confusing moment where my brain tried to map Elaise's familiar features onto a stranger's face.

That's how it felt to look at Reia. She had brown eyes, like mine, with the same slight tilt at the corners. Her hair was a bit lighter than mine. Dark brown, rather than nearly black, but with the same wavy curls on the left side—the ones that refused to stay tied back because I wrote with my right hand and fidgeted with my left. Not quite the same nose, not quite the same chin. It wasn't my face, but it was close.

"You, on the other hand," she said, slowly lowering the crossbow. "*You* look exactly like your mother."

We made an unlikely cabal, the five of us gathered around Reia's kitchen table to discuss secrets that threatened the fate of the kingdom. Considering what was at stake, it felt like we should be seated in a grand council chamber or cloistered away in an underground command bunker somewhere. Not sipping herbal tea from chipped mugs while chickens pecked in the dirt outside. There weren't even enough chairs for all of us.

Andza led the introductions and kept them brief. He introduced Rahad and me as research assistants, Reia as an illusionist who disappeared from the capital years ago, and Kallah as Reia's husband and a former member of the king's personal guard. We each nodded in turn as our names were called, and Kallah even gave a little wave from where he stood leaning against the wall.

"Pleased to meet you all," Reia said, though she hardly sounded as if she meant it. "But what are you doing on my farm?"

"I'd as soon ask why you feel the need to farm in such . . . secrecy," Andza countered.

I felt a twinge of pain just behind both ears, a sure sign of a coming headache. Had we really traveled so far and risked so much for this meeting, only to tease the answers out of one another piecemeal?

"Enough," I said, interrupting. I was too tired and too stressed to care whether or not I sounded rude. "You two might like to sit up all night trading crumbs with one another, but I don't have the patience for it. If we're going to talk, then let's talk."

"Fair enough," Reia said. "You can start."

Well. I'd stepped neatly into that. But if it gave me a chance to set the tone, then so be it.

"Fine," I said. "But I hardly know where to begin."

It took almost an hour to tell it all, skipping around and then backtracking to fill in details I'd forgotten to mention. I started with Andza's sudden appearance in my father's shop, and the guilt I carried over being involved in Talia's "death." Our second meeting at the Library, and the semester where Elaise and I worked to become his research assistants.

I told them everything that I'd held back in Barste, from finding out my mother's name to meeting Aian in secret on the Long Night. I left out the scandal at the Meadowlark and Jurald's murder. Rahad and Andza could tell those parts themselves. I ended with the decision to come to Puhrsa, based on nothing more than a hunch and a few brief mentions of the place.

I don't know that I finished talking so much as stopped. I'd simply hit a point where I ran out of things to tell. The silence stretched out in front of us. Reia was the first to break it.

"You said Serine was your mother. I believe it, based on your face alone, but what proof did you have?"

"Just a feeling at first," I said. "It explained . . . a few things about my childhood that I didn't think were important at the time. But I suppose I didn't know for sure until I saw the symbol on Aian's notebook and realized it looked like her hairpiece."

"Can I see it?"

I dug it out of my pack and handed it to her.

"This was hers," she confirmed. "And you're about the right age. I wasn't there when you were born, but I was the fourth to hold you." She held up four fingers and counted them off. "The field surgeon, your father, your mother, me." She smiled at the memory, the first sign of warmth she'd shown us. "Serine is my older sister. Pleased to meet you, Jalina."

This time, she actually sounded as if she meant it.

Rahad went next. I already knew most of what he told us, but there were a few places where I'd guessed wrong. Not an orphan, but close enough. His father left when he was young, and his mother didn't stay sober often enough to deserve the word. Andza had found him painting charcoal portraits on the streets in Jhendi and saw his potential even then. He sponsored his admission to the Library, and even tutored him in secret occasionally, which solved the mystery of who Andza had been sneaking out to visit those nights we tried to follow him. He even included his brush with Barste's dangerous upper class, though when the story got to Jurald's murder, he stumbled over his words and fell silent.

"So this one saved you, and now you owe him a debt?" Reia asked. Rahad bristled, but Reia forestalled him. "I'm not judging you. I've done much worse, for much the same reason."

But Rahad shook his head. "Any debt I owed him is paid," he said, more forcefully than I expected. Even Andza seemed surprised by the edge in the younger man's voice. "He saved me from hell, true, and he's saved my life more than once. But I've saved his, too, and I've killed for him. That puts us even. Anything I do now, I do for my own reasons."

That earned a thoughtful look from Reia and a nod of approval from her husband. Andza's expression was impossible to read. He'd depended on Rahad's support for so long that its sudden withdrawal must come as a shock. I pitied him for that, but I hated him, too. For years, he'd treated people as pieces on a board, to be moved in whatever way advanced his goals. What right did he have to be surprised when the pieces started behaving like people again?

"I suppose I'm next," Andza said. Rather than speaking, he stood and made his way over to the door where we'd left our packs. Kallah straightened, instantly suspicious, but Andza didn't reach for anything dangerous. Instead, he turned his pack inside out and dumped the contents onto the floor. With his pack emptied, he carried it back to the table and sat down, then pulled a small tool from one of his pockets and handed it to me.

"It's a seam ripper," he explained. "There are two seams reinforcing the bottom of the pack. You want the blue one."

Confused, I set to work. Everyone else leaned forward to watch. After a few minutes of clumsy work—I've never claimed to be a competent seamstress—the bit of leather across the bottom pulled away to reveal a padded interior section. Between the mats of wool, there was a small book. I lifted it out and set it on the table.

"My story starts and ends with this book," Andza explained. "It holds everything I've been able to gather on the Ghosts and their involvement in the war. Names, places, significant events. Confessions, when I was able to get them."

Reia lifted it and opened to a random page. "What cipher is this?"

"There are a series of designs along the inside cover. Starting at the top right and working your way clockwise, each symbol corresponds to a syllable of the third stanza of a

Hensian prayer. 'Alone atop the cliffs, you sent a host of birds to comfort me.'"

"'And made a song of all my sorrows,'" I finished. That was a popular one for beginners because the full stanza contained at least one of every character. "So it's in Hensian?"

"The cipher uses Hensian phonemes, but spoken aloud, it would sound like Jhendi. You'd have to translate it back to Kerran."

My head swam at the amount of effort that would entail. "That's why you wanted Elaise," I reasoned. "Though even a linguist would need hours and hours to get through it."

"Unless someone destroyed it right here and now," Reia said dryly. I flinched, but Andza didn't.

"True," he said. "There are two other copies, of course, but there's a chance that you could find them before anyone knew I was dead. But the choice to destroy it isn't yours to make. Neither is it my right to publish it. The book belongs to these two."

No one spoke for the space of a long breath. Outside, a lone cricket began to herald the setting sun. Rahad and I looked to each other first and found surprise in each other's faces. Andza hadn't shared this with either of us until this moment.

"I don't understand," I said simply.

"Me neither," Rahad added. "Why would it belong to me? I'm not even Kerran."

"Do you plan on going back to Jhendi?" Andza asked.

Rahad's expression turned cold. "Not in this life."

"Then this is your home, and whatever happens to it, happens to you, just as it happens to Jalina." Andza looked toward Kallah, leaning against his wall, then back to Reia, seated in front of him. "We built this world, the three of us, but it isn't ours to do with what we please. Revealing what happened would expose a few individuals to retribution—individuals that are, for the most part, scattered, forewarned, and adept at hiding themselves. More importantly, knowledge of the king's involvement could very well cause a civil war. If it does, it won't be the three of us doing the fighting.

"On the other hand, hiding the truth of what happened denies the next generation a crucial part of their history. They deserve a chance at knowing, but only if they're willing to accept the consequences. The choice lies with them."

So that's what Andza meant when he said that his story started and ended with the book. He was going to drop the consequences in our laps and walk away. As usual, I wasn't sure how to feel about the man I'd been traveling with for the last seven months. Giving us a say in our own future was, in many ways, an unimaginable sacrifice on his part. If we decided to do nothing with the book, we would make waste of his life's work, and all the trials that he'd gone through to create it—not to mention the sacrifices of those who risked everything in their willingness to tell their story. But if publishing the book did cause another war, could we accept that burden?

I realized now why he'd come back to the Library. It wasn't because he needed help. He needed to find people who could understand the story he was trying to tell and then make them appreciate the stakes of telling it. He'd brought Rahad and me into the thick of it, exposed us to death and danger, all to prepare us for this moment. It was an act of both incredible kindness and incredible cruelty.

As before, Reia was the first to fill the silence. "Well, whatever we decide to do with it," she said, setting the book back on the table, "it can wait until after dinner."

I sat with Andza at the table while Rahad helped Reia in the kitchen. I'd offered to help as well, but she shooed me away, saying that one set of extra hands was more than enough. Kallah excused himself to finish whatever chore we'd interrupted, and I heard the sound of his shovel against the earth a few moments later.

"You lied earlier, you know," I said.

"In what way?"

"You said that your story started with your book, but that's obviously not true. You didn't just appear out of thin air fifteen years ago and start following this thread. Is there a chapter on you somewhere within those pages?"

"I'm the author," he said, with a look of disapproval, "not the subject. The more present I am in the book, the more people will make assumptions about my biases."

"So?" I argued. "Every author has biases. Knowing where a story came from is half as important as the story itself. You told us as much. In fact," I said, gaining confidence, "consider it a trade. You want me to decide what to do with your book? Fine. I want to hear the foreword. Besides," I added, trying to recall the words he'd used months ago, "I might be the only person who cares enough to ask."

All the noise in the house came to a stop. Reia and Rahad stood quietly in front of the counter, not even pretending to chop vegetables anymore. The steady rhythm of Kallah's shovel in the backyard ceased. Every living thing seemed to be holding its breath.

CHAPTER TWENTY-SIX

At first I thought he would refuse again. He'd been alone on this quest for so long, wrapped in layers of his own cynicism and suspicion. He'd admitted as much himself. But then he nodded—just once, softly, as if to himself—and opened his mouth to speak.

I suspected something early on, I think. Though maybe that's just the confidence of someone who already knows the answer to the riddle and so thinks it must have always been easy. There were things I shelved, though. Questions that had no answers, that I set in the back of my mind for unraveling later. Eventually I thought they must all be connected, and in time that set me onto the path that led me here.

I rode courier perhaps a dozen times for the Countess of Wryn before I switched sides. I used to boast that I was born to be a courier. Too highborn for the infantry, with a landed father and no younger siblings, but too light for the massive cavalry steeds and the heavy lances that came with them. I could ride a fair distance, and quickly, and knew enough of horses to push one to the edge of endurance without ruining it.

Most of all I was a layabout and felt perfectly suited to spending the war riding hard from one safe haven to another, trusting my wits and my father's likely ransom to keep me from any real danger.

One day I set out with a satchel full of messages bound for Havar. Havar was twenty miles from our post in Hevlen, with a mostly straight forest road and no enemies within twice that distance. The weather was pleasant, as I recall. I rode alone, as I always did, and felt no danger in doing so.

Two miles outside the gate I passed a field of goldenrod on my right. I would've sworn that I smelled it before I saw it, the crisp sweet smell a pleasant surprise so late in the summer. I'd ridden the path before without noticing it, but that's an easy enough thing to do. You tend to miss the things you aren't looking for, and I always had one eye on my horse and the other on the nearest patch of dense underbrush.

I slowed my horse to a walk to take in the sight. The clouds that day were sparse, and the wind blew gently across that green-gold sea. For years I kept it as a pleasant memory, a sign that even in dark times, there were still bright things to see if we took the time to look. After about a mile, the field stopped abruptly at a line of trees, and I edged my horse into a canter, my spirit refreshed.

There were no messages in Hevlen for the return trip, so I took my time coming back. When I was just a few miles from Havar, my horse started to limp, which surprised me: good horse, flat road, new shoes. Still, you don't do well as a courier by ignoring your beast, so I stopped for a moment to let it browse aimlessly in the grass.

After I dismounted, I set my pack on the ground and leaned against a tree to rest. Wryn might be a poor land, but its weather is nothing short of divine. The last month of summer is full of promises, a long procession of cool gray breezes, carrying the smell of hay and harvest. I closed my eyes and nodded off for what felt like fifteen minutes.

I woke again to fading light.

Late afternoon had snuck up on me, and I cursed, reaching for my pack. Any commander worth their rank is unlikely to take the disappearance of a messenger lightly, and woe be unto those who are found daydreaming in a field when they should have arrived an hour prior. A lame horse might have excused me, but of course the bastard had recovered and was trotting impatiently around the edges of the field. I whistled for him and mounted when he circled back around to me.

The canopy blocked the horizon, so I smelled the smoke before I saw the thin black scar of it against the sky. I galloped the last two miles and left my mount gasping for breath at the ruined gate. Fire still danced along the beams, and the corpse that lay sprawled over the watch post looked as if he were trying to put out the flames.

The camp itself was even worse. There was no place for the eye to rest. Fire and butchery in every direction: men and women I'd laughed with, diced with, cursed with. They lay in heaps here and there between smoldering buildings. A horse whinnied desperately against its post, though the fire was nowhere near it. I walked over to it in a daze, and I did my best to calm it. It was the only living thing in sight.

I rode as quickly as I could for Hevlen. Desperation and horror churned like twin seas, questions breaking the surface only rarely. Which direction had the attack come from? Who had done it, and when had it happened? While I was sleeping? If I'd come back sooner, could I have sounded the alarm? Ridden for help?

One question, at least, was answered for me as I rode. I rounded a corner a few miles from camp, and I saw a field open up along the right side of the road. Footprints snaked in and out of the battered grass, enough for twenty or thirty infantry. I saw no hoofprints. The grasses that remained were short, perhaps knee high. Tall enough for a few scattered men to hide in, maybe, but certainly not more than a dozen. They must have been hidden deeper in the woods and then passed through shortly after I came this way the first time. That would've given them hours to finish their work in Havar, while one witless courier delivered useless information to the commander in Hevlen.

But if that were true, then why hadn't I seen the field on the way back?

There's a tendency for the mind to omit the inconvenient. Show a man two things that can't possibly make sense together, and he will ignore one of them. Show him three, and he'll ignore them all, and you as well. I hadn't yet developed the skill to arrange the pieces before me, to consider all of them equally without regard to continuity or likelihood.

And so I chalked it up to haste, and inattentiveness, and the poor idiocy of a young soldier. And I didn't piece it together until years later. After all, that field of goldenrod was a pleasant memory on an otherwise black day. That battered field of plain grass, that lash of guilt that I carried with me for years . . . How could they possibly be the same field?

A handful of costly defeats in the following weeks took Wryn out of contention for the throne. I was captured in the last of these and spared on the condition that I pay a ransom of two hundred silver crowns and declare fealty to Lord Berrach of Greymarsh, a man I had never met. A surly quartermaster had been given the practical task of collecting both oaths and ransoms, and as I kissed Lord Berrach's signet ring in his absence, I wondered at how stupid I had been to leave home. Half a dozen minor officers to my left and right no doubt wondered the same. They'd executed those too poor to pay the ransom earlier in the afternoon.

I served under Lord Berrach for less than six months, before the winter frost had truly started to thaw. In that short time, he fought six battles and won them all. Then his sons were killed at the taking of Resthaven, and he left for his own lands the same night that he heard the news. The lights of his army on the march, trailing out like a cloak over the hills behind him, was the saddest thing I'd ever seen. One week later, I celebrated my twenty-first birthday in the cavernous great hall of that abandoned castle.

Those of us left behind numbered one hundred and seventeen, and the able-bodied among us took it upon ourselves to form a company of fighting men, with our wounded brethren to receive a share of our pay in exchange for performing the mundane duties of a camp of soldiers on the march. We styled ourselves the Free Company and lost every battle we ever flew under those accursed banners.

We elected a man named Cariza as our captain: a career soldier, the bastard son of a bastard son, raised in the stables of the Hensian court. He joked that he knew six languages: three for men, one for women, and two for horses. I'm not convinced he was lying. He negotiated our contracts in Kerran, but he spoke Hensian when he drank and Halnish when he sang. He played the harp as well as any court bard and seemed to have a knack for nursing half-starved mutts back to health.

It was Cariza who urged us to sign on with the crown prince just before the battle of Seventree. We were war-weary then, and sick of chancing it on any up-and-comer that shook a purse in front of our faces. We wanted a sure thing, and if the old king's own son hadn't shown any promise in the first year of the war, he'd learned quickly enough. Another year, maybe two, and we'd all be begging him for boons: land, or a household, or freedom from one debt or another. A sure thing, it seemed. What fools we.

We reached the castle at Seventree roughly a month before it fell. Of the six thousand men encamped there, less than a fourth were mercenaries. Of those, we might have been the fourth or fifth largest company. There were ninety of us, and we felt like strangers in a crowded room. We were late-comers, after all, and also I had never seen so many soldiers in one place.

Part of our contract necessitated turning over our own provisions to the castle's larder. The prince expected a siege before long, though he wasn't yet sure who would be doing the besieging. There were two armies on the plains. One was led by his uncle, a force of fifteen thousand men who were mostly veterans of his father's forces. The other force numbered nine thousand, led by an up-and-coming warlord named Sethric.

Whoever won would push for the castle at Seventree, hoping to winter there. If the prince lasted until then and waited out the siege, he'd be in the game for another year, with one of his enemies gone and the other demoralized by a fruitless campaign.

It was hard not to be optimistic. No soldier likes to look up from the bottom of a guarded wall, given the choice, and we'd just signed a three-month contract that put us on the ramparts for once. We knew where we were going to sleep that night and every night thereafter. The rations were light but reasonable. Every man knew where his bed was.

A few of us grumbled. It's an easy habit to fall into, especially when you've been on a run of bad luck. And soldiers have a curious knack for turning into amateur historians. Draw up a battle plan with a clear advantage to one side, and someone with a battered sword and too many scars will tell you how Captain This or General That lost a battle in just such a situation. But there was never any real heat in it. The weather was turning colder, but it was cold everywhere, and none of us would've switched places with a soldier outside the gates.

The fourth day after we moved in, we heard the news that Sethric's much smaller force had defeated the prince's uncle on the plains. It was a rout, a collection of all the worst calamities that can befoul a well-planned expedition. An outrider who had seen the battle reported the details.

A cavalry charge over marshy ground that the outrider would have sworn was dry. Nearly a thousand down in the first few minutes, as the treacherous earth snapped horse legs and tossed riders to painful, thundering deaths. Panicked, mixed signals from a dozen officers that sent the infantry into confusion as the more disciplined group steadily chipped away at their numbers. A horn that sounded retreat while the officers rode forward to bolster their lines, then back again as their men broke around them. Nine thousand dead in the course of two hours, with barely a tenth of that number in exchange.

We listened to the tale in silence, repeated it in whispers to those who hadn't yet heard. Soldiers are by nature a superstitious lot, and their moods are blacker than most. The tale spread through the camp on the teeth of winter. Those few who dared to joke about our fortunes were paid in grim looks and muttered curses. In desperation, the officers doubled each man's ration of ale to improve morale, and we held our drinks close to our chests and thought bitter thoughts.

A week later we saw the lights of Sethric's camp outside the walls. Cariza took the initiative to piss over the edge of the ramparts in their direction and laughed when a gust of wind seemed to carry it onward. He'd been in his cups for the better part of the day, and the entire display lasted nearly two minutes. By the end of it we were all cheering him on and nearly roared with applause as he turned to take a bow.

And just like that, the black mood that had smothered us began to lift. Somehow it reminded us of how high our walls were, of the many comrades we had close at hand. We laughed against the night, against the distant campfires, and it felt good to do it. If there's one thing a soldier believes, it's that the god of death appreciates a good laugh.

Andza fumbled for his cup and lifted it to his lips. He drank deeply, and when he finished, Rahad came over to refill it. I walked around the room to trim the wicks on the candles, which had started to throw mad shadows across the walls. The dim light reminded me of the night I'd met Andza. I'd imagined, even then, that his presence had drawn me into something dark and mysterious, something that would expose me to death and danger and leave me forever changed.

Strange, I thought, that insight and ignorance often seemed to come as a set.

⸙

The assault came that night, and it was the single most tiring battle I've ever fought. The walls had been built sixty feet high, and we had enough men to put two soldiers each in three-foot intervals, with a spearman between them and a pair of archers at the rear. These crews could be rotated out every hour or filled at need from the reserves if a man should fall.

We knew that Sethric couldn't afford to test us. He outnumbered us, especially with the addition of the mercenary companies he'd hired on since his unlikely rout in the marsh. But he didn't have the manpower to grind us away week by week, and he needed a quick victory if he wanted to winter at Seventree. He threw everything he had at us that first night, hoping to catch a bit of luck and willing to sacrifice a few thousand men for a chance at it.

⸙

"He almost tipped his hand there, I think," Andza noted. "Another few tricks and he'd have spoiled it."

"What do you mean?" Rahad asked.

"Attacking at night," I said suddenly. "That's it, isn't it?" Rahad looked at me, but Andza didn't interrupt, so I continued.

"I remember reading an account that described the king as a brilliant tactician, but an inconsistent one. Bensen, I think. Anyway, it makes sense in context. Sethric would have had to worry about exposing his advantage on a clear day in an open field. But at night, he would be able to play all sorts of tricks."

Andza nodded. "Arrows that outnumber the archers firing them, campfires that stretch for miles in the distance, even when the scouts report that there can't possibly be half that many. Screams of pain from either side of you that make you think you must be taking horrible losses, hour after hour.

"There's a terrible desperation you live in when you think you're about to lose a battle. Every minute that passed felt like a miracle, as if we'd somehow thwarted a death we knew we'd deserved. Living through a night like that, it's easy to understand why officers don't fight on the front lines if they can help it. Six hours into a fight, most soldiers would surrender a castle for a warm meal and a quiet night's sleep."

"So you lost the battle at Seventree and joined Sethric's army," I said.

"Yes. During the battle, the crown prince was assassinated by two of his advisers, and someone sounded the surrender. I never found out who."

"By his advisors?" I asked. "Or someone who looked like his advisers?"

Andza shook his head. "That one, as far as I can tell, Sethric won in the usual way, with bribes and promises and coercion. But that's another tale."

It's almost universally true that there are more things to do after a battle than during one. The entire chain of command had to be reorganized, promotions doled out, ranks refilled. Some of the prince's most ardent supporters were either imprisoned or set free on ransom. The more pliable officers found a home in Sethric's new army, where they were promptly set to finding food and shelter and pay for thousands of men. The wounded had to be cared for, supplies had to be counted and recounted. When it comes to supplying an army, people tend to remember the food, the weapons, the boot leather. But the veteran quartermasters are the ones who order extra paper.

I'd suffered a broken leg in the battle, which meant that I was spared the worst of the physical labor. But I'd learned long ago that it wasn't a good idea to be a useless mouth in an army—especially a defeated one, and especially with winter already crowding in close around the fire. Being raised on an estate, I could read quickly and had a fairly legible hand, so I spent the next three months shivering behind a desk.

For the most part, I copied pages and pages of mundane reports, the kind of tedious minutiae that might be interesting to a spymaster but deathly boring to everyone else. The actual letters of note were written by trusted scribes, but one project proved to be more interesting than I expected.

In close quarters like that, illness and disease can decimate an army in weeks. The ground had already started to freeze in places, which meant that finding a clean place to dispose of the dead was . . . somewhat urgent. Sappers brought back daily survey reports of soft ground for digging, water supplies to be avoided, newly built roads that could support the heavy, iron-rimmed wheels of the corpse wagons.

These were copied and passed on to the captains of each company, who organized the work details and sent back progress reports to their commanders, which then had to be reconciled with sanitation reports from the medical corps and estimates of losses from each of the reformed battalions. All of these had to be summarized, copied, and distributed to the twenty-odd advisors, secretaries, and generals who made up the actual decision-making body of the army.

Which meant that for three weeks, one of my main jobs was to count the bodies.

The numbers, as you might expect, rarely added up. One report on our losses might say that we'd lost close to two thousand men, almost a third of our number. If so, then the burials should have taken months. It's possible to bury two thousand men in three weeks, if you have the manpower to do it. But anyone who read over the lists of slain, injured, or otherwise occupied would have insisted that we didn't.

Not only that, but the squad leaders

all reported that their teams were making good progress, and anyone who took a walk around the city could see that they were right. After little more than a week, the bulk of the work was done. Many of the teams reported having little to do.

Then the quartermaster's assistant would drop off a stack of requisitions to feed and clothe six thousand men. Even assuming that our losses were light and that Sethric had picked up a few companies of turncoats after his previous victory, the number was outrageous. I thought to point out the obvious mistake, but some instinct cautioned me to observe and to keep my observations close.

And so I kept a separate journal, one that may have gotten me hanged if it had ever been found. I watched the numbers grow and fall to suit one another until all the differences were erased, accounted for only in my private reckoning. I kept note of which scribes looked at their reports curiously and which ones copied them with carefully blank expressions. I thought of the camp in Havar, and the field of goldenrod, and of soldiers that appeared and disappeared like mist.

I woke one morning with a clear idea of what would happen next. I knew now that Sethric would win the war, that the battles yet to come would fall his way as easily as the ones that had come before. And if, at the time, they looked to be stunning upsets or hard-fought victories, it would only be because they were designed to appear that way. Yes, Sethric would be king, and very few people would know how it had been done.

Over the next two weeks, I tossed my hidden journal into the fireplace one page at a time, memorizing as much as I could, repeating the words to myself silently at meals. I started a new project in my spare time, compiling notes and written histories from the early days of Sethric's unlikely campaign. I had full chapters on each battle, with maps sketched largely by imagination and filled in with whatever tall tales I could gather from the other soldiers.

I noted the battles in a kind of cipher. Any paragraph where I thought the Ghosts had played a part would begin with a certain set of letters, and any paragraph where I was sure they didn't would begin with words of a certain length. Even so, I was constantly worried that I might get caught, that someone who knew the significance of what I was writing would find out and hang me for it.

One day I returned to my tent to find my company commander rifling through my things. I say rifling, but in fairness, it was his job to inspect the men under his command, to enforce the proper conduct and ensure that discipline didn't lapse just because he wasn't watching. He'd only picked up my journal out of curiosity, but my heart thudded to see him hold it.

"Yours, I presume?" he asked, expression blank. "A bit of extra work when you can't sleep, perhaps?"

I started to sweat, despite the cold. I was painfully aware of my hands, my face, the set of my shoulders. What did people look like when they lied?

I fell back on military discipline and snapped to attention. "Yes, sir."

A small smirk touched his face, was smoothed away. "And is this a new hobby of yours, or have you been writing about the future king since before you were under his command?"

I stammered a response. "Well, I suppose . . . I mean, it's history, isn't it sir? I may as well write it down while it's happening. Sir."

This time the smirk stayed. "Ah, I see. A learned man." He set the book back on my pillow. "In that case, I'll leave you to it."

I stepped aside to let him leave, more than a little confused. Had I been caught, or was I safe? I knew that my commander was one of Sethric's original officers, but was he in on the secret I had discovered? Had he broken my weak attempt at a cipher in the minutes he'd been alone with it? I had no doubt that a spymaster would be able to and hated myself for my own stupidity.

The next day, when I came back to my tent, I saw that someone had placed a small writing table inside it, along with two candles and an extra bottle of ink. I couldn't understand the significance of it. It wasn't until years later that I realized I had quoted Gramme.

"Funny," Andza said, his expression grim, "that we both ended up blind in the end."

CHAPTER TWENTY-SEVEN

After dinner we dragged our chairs onto the porch and sat together. Reia and her husband took one side of the porch, with Reia closest to the door. Andza and I took the other side, and Rahad sat on the wooden steps, elbows atop his knees. The coolness of the evening air had deepened until we could see our breath fog the air in front of us. Any colder and we would all start to shiver, but the house seemed crowded with five, especially after so many nights spent camping.

"If you found your way here," Reia began, "you must know some part of the story already."

"Only a little," I said. "But I know it has something to do with the king, something that happened here a long time ago. He used to come here often, didn't he?"

"To the village? No. He and his friends mostly kept to themselves, but they passed through the area often enough. If we saw them at all, it was on the main road."

"His friends." I thought back, remembering their names. "Hinnes and Braies. He betrayed them during the war, but no one seems to know why."

"That's the first lie we helped tell," Reia said, nodding.

"The truth is that they tried to betray him, and we killed them both before the trap sprung." She hesitated. "But to understand why we did it . . ." she trailed off. "This part is harder to talk about."

None of us prodded. We just sat with her, quietly, until she found the strength to continue.

"Long before any history book thought to mention Puhrsa, we were attacked by a group of brigands. There were only thirty of them, but thirty men with weapons can do nearly anything they want to a hundred men without. They took food and valuables in the first attack and killed a few people who ran to raise the alarm. When they realized no one was coming to help us, they came back. The second time," she said, voice wooden, "the second time, they took people."

"They marched us to a cave about twelve miles east of here. There were children in the group, and wounded, and it was well after sunset, so the woods were dark. I remember it taking all night to get there. If anyone fell behind for any reason, they killed that person and the person next to them in line. We tried our best to help each other, but . . ." Another pained look crossed her face, and her husband rested a hand on her knee to comfort her. Rahad gave Kallah an odd look, but said nothing.

"I remember our mayor leaning on me as we walked," Reia continued. "He'd been stabbed in the leg, and all I could think was that he was going to get us both killed. I kept waiting for some hint that he was about to fall. If he did, I knew I would push him away so that someone else got killed instead of me."

Reia paused again. We waited. Some silences aren't meant to be filled.

"I can't tell you everything that happened in that cave. I was younger than you are now, and I've spent decades trying not to think about it. But the worst part was realizing that no one was coming to help. We were able to hold out hope for a day or two, but after that . . ."

"How long?" I asked. I couldn't *not* ask.

"Two weeks, give or take. Long enough for a young lord none of us had ever met to ride around the countryside gathering reinforcements."

"Sethric," Andza guessed, "but not Hinnes or Braies?"

"No."

I gasped so loudly it almost sounded like a hiss. "That's horrendous."

"You'd be surprised how many people think of loyalty as a one-way street," Andza said. "Then again," he added thoughtfully, "after Barste, maybe you wouldn't be. So. The local lords were either unable or unwilling to help in a time of need, but were perfectly happy to levy troops from the same village once the war started."

"Just so," Reia said. "At first, we used our powers to hide from the fighting. But when we learned they were luring Sethric into a trap, we turned the tables on them and folded their troops into Sethric's larger army."

"Why would they betray him?" I asked. "It's not like he did anything wrong."

"He saw them at their worst," Andza explained, "and proved that he was better than them. Men will do nearly anything to erase that shame." Andza paused, then added, "I have a few questions. First, did any adults in the cave gain the same abilities? Or any children in the village?"

"Not that I ever knew," Reia said. "Serine was the oldest, at fourteen. There were one or two older children, but they died."

"And none of you had these abilities before, but you all had them after?"

"Yes."

"How is that significant?" I asked.

"Theologically speaking, it changes nearly everything we believe. Most of the time, saints are born so far apart and realize their abilities at such disparate ages that it almost feels random. I've never heard of a single event making someone a saint, no matter how profound. To change an entire group of people and then place them in the path of someone who has an opportunity to make use of them, feels . . . a bit heavy-handed, considering how absent our gods usually are."

"You might see it that way," Reia interrupted, "but we didn't. Whatever else we gained, I don't remember divine clarity or purpose coming as part of the set. If the gods exist at all, they keep their thoughts to themselves. We did what we did for our own reasons, and no one else's."

So much for the idea of praying for guidance. When a living saint tells you not to bother, it's hard to nurse hope that the answers will just come to you out of a clear sky.

"Last question," Andza said, "and then we can get some sleep. Everyone else I've talked to is willing to tell me what they did, and when. You're the first to ever explain why. What changed?"

"If someone had told you, would you have put it in your book?"

"Yes," Andza answered without hesitating. "It would've probably been the first chapter."

Reia nodded. "I think that's your answer. Explaining yourself is always a matter of asking for justification. 'This happened to me, so what I did makes sense.' But saying that I had a right to choose how the world should turn out because of something that happened to me as a child, and if you're not satisfied with it, too bad? Who would want to put their personal tragedy on a scale like that, to be weighed against everyone else's for the rest of history. It's hard enough talking to you three about it."

"And are you satisfied?" I asked. "With how the world turned out?"

She didn't answer right away, only looked somewhere off into the darkness and sighed. Kallah patted her knee, and she covered his hand with hers. "Yes," she said after a while. "Yes, I think so."

I thought it would take forever to fall asleep, but I must have drifted off as soon as my head touched the pillow. I woke as soon as the early morning sun touched my face, feeling rested after a night of easy, uninterrupted sleep. Normally, it takes me half an hour to stir from bed, but my stomach growled almost as soon as I opened my eyes. I'd been on half sleep and half rations for so long that my body was starting to demand its due. Anxiety would have to wait its turn for once.

Nobody else was in the kitchen when I walked in, so I set the kettle on the stove and started searching through cabinets for tea. I found a tin canister of what smelled like roasted chicory, and a cast iron teapot that looked like it might hold enough water for two or three cups. We'd washed our mugs from the night before, so I set them in a line across the counter and waited for the water to come to a boil.

"Morning," Reia said from behind me. "Been a long time since someone else started the tea."

"I'm used to making it for my father," I said, smiling. "In the winter, he won't even open his eyes until he's had something hot to drink."

The kettle started to whistle, so I poured the water and sat down to wait while the tea steeped.

"Have you decided what you'll do?"

"Not yet," I said. "I honestly haven't thought about it at all. I think I was too tired to take it on. I might still be."

"Hmm."

It wasn't exactly an invitation to keep talking, but if I had to think about it, I might as well do my thinking out loud. And I was making the tea, after all. "On the one hand," I started, "we have to think about everything that might happen if we publish it. Civil war, the king dethroned, the Order abolished, all of it. But what about everything that happened before? The people who died? Aian and Jurald, your friends, your hus—" I stopped cold.

But when I looked at Reia, she didn't look upset. A sad smile, but a distant one: the mark of an old hurt. "When did you figure it out?"

"I think we all did, in our own ways. Andza didn't press for his story, which is unlike him. And Rahad kept looking at him oddly all night."

"And you?"

"When I was looking for the tea this morning. The top shelves don't have anything in them but dust."

She nodded. "Six years ago, I found him out in the yard, dead from a heart attack. I cried for the rest of the day. I cried while digging his grave, while covering him over, while gathering flowers for his marker. I cried falling asleep. I cried waking up. Then I walked out of our bedroom and into the kitchen, and he was just . . . there. I could see him, hear him, smell him. But when I reached out to touch him, I didn't feel a thing. That was like losing him all over again. I started tying a piece of string around my ring finger so I wouldn't forget again, no matter what I saw."

"So he's just . . . always around? Whether you want him there or not?"

"Are the three of you any different?" she asked pointedly. "You say you've never met your mother, but she's a character in all your stories, including the one you told last night. I can guarantee you Andza remembers the name of every friend he lost in the war, no matter which side he was on at the time. And if you think that girl in Barste didn't remind Rahad of someone, you're a fool."

"But this is—"

"Insane? Pathetic? If you can think of a word I haven't already called myself, I'll eat that kettle. But no matter how many times I tell myself he's gone, some part of me refuses to believe it. Some advice, child?"

I nodded. "Please."

"We all live in the company of ghosts. Love them, miss them, remember them. But don't worry about them too much. They get their say, whether we like it or not." She stood. "Tea's ready, I think."

They get their say, whether we like it or not. I could attest to that. How many stupid choices had I made in the last month for the sake of a woman who had *chosen* not to be a part of my life yet still managed to sit in on every decision? Forget about my mother for a moment. What did I want from this?

"Thank you," I said. "I think that helps."

The others walked into the kitchen almost as soon as Reia started cooking—all three of them, though no one looked at Kallah directly. None of us felt like revisiting anything we'd talked about last night, and since that conversation encompassed the lion's share of our depressing stories, we had a surprisingly cheerful breakfast.

Andza surprised us by asking Reia if she wouldn't mind him staying for a while. He was still injured, after all, and could only hold Rahad and me back. Reia agreed, which was less of a surprise. If there were only going to be two people living in the house, they may as well both exist.

"You should know," he warned, "that my being here might put you in danger. Jalina guessed the truth of it a few days ago. There's a very good chance the Order will follow me here."

"They've known where to find me since I left Traste," she said. "And they know what it would cost to take me away from my home. I don't plan on leaving here alive, whatever happens."

When it came time to leave, Reia cleared a path through the illusions surrounding her house and saw us to the edge of them. We said our goodbyes, and Andza spent a few moments with each of us to share the last of his secrets: the locations of the two remaining books and the names of half a dozen publishers he thought we could trust. We parted ways, waving at each other until the barrier closed around them and hid them from sight.

It took a quarter of an hour for Rahad to find our horse. She'd wandered into the town to sleep in an abandoned stable rather than face the woods alone. Rahad climbed into the saddle and helped me up behind him. An hour later we found ourselves on the same road where we'd begged for food. It was still well before noon.

"So where to?" he asked.

"West to the main road," I said. "Then north to Lletra."

"Not the Library?" he asked. One of the other books was hidden in the stacks there, and two of the publishers he named lived in Sharme.

"Not yet," I said. Then I explained what I'd figured out during breakfast: a way to preserve Andza's story, shift the Order's attention away from us, and prevent a civil war all at once.

"Risky, but you'd know him better than I do."

"I've never met the king. But I know people who have, and they all trusted him. Besides," I said, smiling, "he just got married, right? The least we can do is bring him a gift."

CHAPTER TWENTY-EIGHT

strand of hair fell into Jaeri's eyes, but she couldn't afford to push it away. She'd made that mistake earlier, and it had nearly earned her a blade across the throat. Well, not really a blade, but it would've counted as a death if she hadn't ducked in time, and she'd already died once today. The lesson always stopped after her third death, even if they'd only been practicing for a minute or two.

Swordmaster Yara lowered her sword until the tip rested just above the hallway carpet. Jaeri had fallen for this trick more than once. That open guard might look like an invitation, but it was unbelievable how quickly it became a trap. Every time Jaeri stepped into it, she died. This time, she lifted her sword into a high guard, still circling to the left.

"Good, but watch your feet. You have too much weight on your back leg."

Jaeri frowned but shifted slightly. She'd been learning footwork from soldiers in the practice yard for years. She even followed along during some of their drills, though she used a much lighter practice blade. She was still too small for the halberds that some of the foot soldiers carried, but sometimes Borre would show her how to place her feet to brace against a charge or pull a man from horseback.

Your feet and eyes were the most important parts of fighting because they were likely to do the wrong thing unless you taught them better. Once you had your feet and eyes figured out, your hands could do almost anything you asked them to.

It had been years since anyone corrected her on her stances, but Swordmaster Yara seemed to find a mistake every thirty seconds. Of course, none of the soldiers moved quite like the king's bodyguard. The woman shifted from stance to stance like a dragonfly skimming above the water.

Yara abandoned the open guard suddenly, lashing out twice in quick succession. Jaeri blocked both strikes and managed a clumsy counterattack. Clumsy was better than nothing, as long as it didn't put her too far off balance. Whenever she stopped countering, the swordmaster would press the attack until Jaeri couldn't possibly keep up. She called it "dying practice," and said that if Jaeri wanted room to breathe during a fight, she needed to earn it.

Jaeri tried a lunge and nearly lost a hand in the exchange that followed. She earned another two steps to the left, though, which put the swordmaster much closer to the bright patch of light on the wall behind her. If she could manage that again, Yara would be distracted by the light coming in through the window, and Jaeri might have a chance to land a hit.

The swordmaster smiled and lowered her guard. Then she stepped into the light and closed her eyes.

Jaeri swung wildly, an upward slash that would've cut her opponent from hip to neck. But Yara stepped gracefully to the side, and by the time Jaeri recovered from the awkward swing, Yara's knuckles rested against her stomach. If she'd been holding a real sword, most of it would be poking out of Jaeri's back.

"That's two."

Jaeri sighed. "You knew I was trying to blind you."

Yara shrugged, and even that looked casually graceful. "It might've worked on someone else."

The door to the study opened, and Governor—no, *Queen*—Ferrec poked her head out into the hallway. It had only been a day since the wedding, and Jaeri still hadn't gotten used to everyone's new titles yet. The queen must have been expecting to see someone else because she narrowed her eyes at the two of them when she saw them standing there. "What are you two doing out here?"

Jaeri held her sword behind her back, which was plainly ridiculous. They'd only been pretending to hold swords. Jaeri knew better than to fight an actual duel in the hallway. "Um, dueling?"

Yara nodded, all seriousness. "It's true. I was about to win again."

"You were not," Jaeri argued.

The swordmaster extended an arm and casually stabbed Jaeri in the heart. "You dropped your guard before the duel was over," she explained. "Easy mistake, though I doubt you'll make it again."

Jaeri frowned. No, she most certainly would not. She saluted with her pretend weapon, and the swordmaster returned the salute solemnly.

"Well, have either of you seen Niklas?" the queen asked. "We need him for something."

"I'll go find him," Jaeri volunteered. She needed to talk to the head servant herself. It had been weeks since she'd had a chance to help any of the secretaries with their ledgers, and Niklas still wasn't putting up the signup sheet outside his office. The odds were obviously against her becoming a legendary swordmaster. She at least needed to learn the proper way to run a palace.

As she jogged through the halls, she saw Captain Byren round the corner ahead of her. She slowed to a walk. The captain of the guard was normally nice, if a little grumpy, but when he was in a bad mood, he would sometimes forget that you weren't one of his new recruits. Today he looked as though he were marching to the gallows to have a talk with the hangman.

Jaeri thought she knew why. She'd heard about the trouble in the South Quarter. Two murders in the same neighborhood, and no suspects in either case. Lletra wasn't so safe that a pair of murders would turn the city on its head, but a member of the city watch had disappeared soon after, and most people expected a third body to turn up any day now.

With the king and queen in the palace—not to mention about twenty new princes and princesses to guard—the captain barely had enough men to keep his own house in order. He definitely couldn't spare to send anyone into the city to help with the investigation.

Jaeri nodded at the captain as she passed, but her thoughts had already turned inward. She remembered a day, years ago, when Niklas Harran had shown her the costs that went into feeding and housing all the servants who lived in the palace. There'd been a separate line for her brothers and sisters, and her mind was quick enough to divide that number by twenty and come to a neat, round figure that belonged to her. The monthly expense that went into maintaining Jaeri: everything she wore, ate, drank, used, or threw away.

She'd spent years trying to match that number, telling herself that if she worked hard enough, or fought well enough, or learned everything her tutors could teach her, she could somehow match the casual charity that Governor Ferrec had shown the day she walked into an orphanage, pointed to a little girl barely old enough to stand, and said, "This one."

She didn't resent that debt. She *burned* against it, as if she could somehow consume it the way fire tore through a house. And now, just as she was starting to pull even, she'd become a *princess*. Some useless creature that needed more food, more clothes, more things. There were guards in the palace who couldn't go out looking for murderers in *her* city because they needed to stand outside her door. Servants who had to work extra hours because she wasn't supposed to lift a finger to do anything for herself.

And what did she do for them? Of all the countless things she wanted to be when she grew up, Jaeri thought she could handle being anything except a burden.

She didn't even wait to round the corner before she started running again. There were too many things to do, too many people who needed her to be something more than who she was right now.

Even if they didn't know her name yet.

"Did you know that your daughter is out there dueling your bodyguard?"

The king—her new husband, she corrected herself—cocked his head as if to listen. So far he hadn't acted any differently toward her, aside from an annoying habit of asking her what she thought of something after he'd ordered one of her servants to see it done. There was a time when he'd asked her advice *before* giving orders, but apparently the years beneath the crown had changed him. He shrugged. "Well, at least they're being quiet about it."

"Oh, they're not using swords," Ferrec said. "They're *pretending.*"

"How do you pretend to have a duel?" Sethric asked.

Ferrec rolled her eyes, then settled into a high guard, invisible broadsword held just high enough so that the "handle" didn't block her view.

"Ah," he said. "Less likely to kill each other that way, I guess."

"If you think your bodyguard has a chance of being killed by a twelve-year-old girl," Ferrec said wryly, "you need a new bodyguard."

Ferrec took the chair behind her desk and rubbed her eyes. They'd been at this all morning, sorting through layer after layer of laws, decrees, missives, and edicts. Anything to find some loophole, some precedent for what they were trying to do. That was the real reason Sethric needed her. Not just as a strategist, but as a wife. Someone who could question his decisions, point out the flaws in his tactics, and, most importantly, spend hours alone with him without arousing suspicion.

Someone who could help him give away the kingdom before anyone else realized he was doing it.

"Do you really think this will work?"

Ferrec blinked in surprise, then gave her husband a flat look. "Why are you asking me? It's your plan."

"I'm asking you because it's my plan. If it didn't make sense to me, I wouldn't have come all the way up here to ask you to help. I assumed you thought the idea had merit, or you wouldn't have married me, but now that you're neck deep in the trenches, what do you think?"

"The timing will be tricky," she said honestly, "but timing always is. I don't think anyone will fight you on the ministry appointments. Soldiers might argue against a promotion, because they know better than anyone how quickly that extra rope becomes a noose, but bureaucrats rarely have that kind of foresight. The real trick will be convincing them you're still trying to hold on to power, even as you give it away piece-meal."

At the moment, only three people in the entire kingdom held the title of minister, but between the two of them, they'd conjured another six positions out of midair, plus a dizzying array of deputy ministers, councilors, secretaries, and undersecretaries. The plan was to slowly appoint members of influential families in different layers of each ministry in the hopes of diffusing any one person's influence.

In theory, each of these appointments would diminish the power of the crown itself, lowering the stakes for anyone who wanted to squabble over the throne after Sethric vacated it. History held countless examples of kings and queens who tried to secure their legacy by amassing and consolidating power. As far as Ferrec knew, this was the first time someone had tried to start a legacy by giving it away.

"We've faked retreats before," Sethric assured her. "We just need one person to chase us, and the rest will follow."

"A scandal might help," she suggested. "Nothing disastrous, but something to suggest you're no longer fit for the job."

He grinned. A rare sight, even in private. He looked about twenty years younger when he did it. "You mean like walking away from the court with no warning and traveling for two months to marry an old sweetheart and adopt her twenty illegitimate children?"

"For a start," she chuckled. "But if you call me your sweetheart in public, people are going to know you're bluffing."

"Suit yourself," he said, still grinning. "Which one was it, by the way?"

"Which one what?"

Sethric smirked and held an invisible sword in front of him.

"Ah. Jaeri. You know her. The tall one with the dark blond hair."

"Oh. Right," he said dryly. "The one with dark blond hair who showed up to the adoption ceremony an hour before everyone else to read the documents herself. I seem to recall an argument about the word 'co-petitioner.' Is she always so . . . enthusiastic?"

Ferrec nodded. Jaeri had always been an odd child. Frighteningly energetic, like a fire in search of something to burn. Since becoming a princess—she'd been very curious about what *exactly* that would entail—it was like someone had poured oil on the blaze.

A month ago, she would've spent her afternoon in the practice yard with the soldiers, or doing her homework in one of the common areas, but she'd never been quite so . . . underfoot. Now there was no escaping the girl. Everywhere Ferrec went, Jaeri was either already there or had just left to chase down some new project.

"More or less," Ferrec said.

"It's a shame she doesn't want the job," Sethric mused.

"No," Ferrec said firmly. "Nonnegotiable."

"I wasn't—all right, maybe I was. But I wasn't serious. Just . . . letting my imagination run for a moment. We'll stick with the original plan. Promise."

Ferrec tried to put her ruffled feathers back in order, but it was hard. The trouble was, Sethric was right. Jaeri probably would have made a good leader in another life. The children she'd taken in were very different from one another, but she could think of something to recommend each of them, whether it was intelligence, or charisma, or a strong work ethic. A few, like Jaeri, seemed to have extra helpings of all three. Most of all, they were resilient, and a leader needed to be resilient above all else. "Sorry. I just don't like to think of them as pieces on a board."

"Is that how I think of them?" Sethric asked. "As pieces on a board?" He managed to keep his tone from turning defensive, but Ferrec heard it that way anyway.

"Don't you? I wasn't aware kings could afford to think any other way. You least of all."

She hadn't meant to say that last part out loud and flinched once she realized she'd done so. It was true, even if she'd never spoken it before. It wasn't that Sethric didn't care about people. He counted his dead the same as anyone, and better than most. If he could win with fewer losses, he always took that fork in the road. But when he couldn't win any other way, when sacrifice was a necessary part of victory?

He sacrificed. And his soul never seemed the heavier for it.

"You're right, of course. I know what my kingdom was built on. I've seen the foundations of it. And if it took another twenty deaths, or twenty thousand, to shore up those walls, I'd spend them." Even that admission came easily. He knew his flaws and had made peace with them long ago.

"But I know that you wouldn't make the same choice. I've seen where you go after a fight, especially when the fighting happens where people live. Those children are yours, even if none of them are." He shrugged. "I also know that I can't do this without you. The simple truth is that I need you more than I need them."

The king's words—she couldn't think of him as her husband, or even her friend, after that speech—didn't comfort her much. Especially not delivered in that even, dispassionate tone. And if she stopped being useful, what then? Why was she even in this situation? What could have possessed him to travel all this way, to risk everything, for *her*?

Because he always covers his blind spots, she realized. He knew the world he wanted to build, the lines he wanted it built along. But he also knew that he couldn't build it without someone who cared about the people who would live in that future, someone who thought of people as precious and irreplaceable. It wasn't her mind that made her necessary but her heart. She was there to love so that he didn't have to.

"So long as you remember that," she said coldly.

They went back to work.

Yara lay quietly in her bed, extending her senses as far as they would go.

As a child, she used to love finding a quiet place to sit and listen. She'd grown up in a castle like this one, though on a much lower floor than she occupied now, and there were always people coming and going. The door of the servant's entrance opened so frequently they might as well have taken it off its hinges. There were deliveries all throughout the day, servants walking to and from town on errands, and people who preferred to take their meals outside no matter the weather. She'd been quite small as a child, so it was easy to find a cozy place to hide where she could avoid her chores and listen to the world turn around her.

The older she got, the more Yara realized that she could sense things she wasn't supposed to. It was one thing to recognize someone by their face, or the sound of their voice, or the perfume they wore. But to recognize the weight of someone's feet against the floor without hearing them, or to know, without opening the door, how many people were in the room on the other side of it . . .

She listened to those senses now. All the normal ones and the extra sense she kept secret from everyone else, layering each one on top of the others until she had a clear picture of the rooms around her. She felt people settle into their beds, toss uncomfortably, and eventually find the slow, easy rhythms of sleep.

Then she stood.

She stalked toward the door on bare feet, making no sound at all. She'd always been light on her feet, and it had been over a decade since she earned the right to call herself a swordmaster. Using her gifts for stealth was hardly necessary, but she did it just to be sure, dispersing her weight to the stones in the walls, making herself so light that she almost floated. The door creaked as she opened it—not much she could do about that—but no one stirred at the sound. She eased the door closed behind her and checked her sword in its scabbard.

It was time to go hunting.

She started by pacing back and forth in the hallway, never getting more than twenty paces away from the royal chambers. She knew that her quarry wouldn't risk approaching with her so close by, but it gave her a chance to extend her mental map of the area. A few of the children had been moved to this floor, but they were sound asleep as well.

Well, all of the children except one. She paused near Jaeri's room for a few seconds to figure out what on earth the girl was doing in there but couldn't stay in one place for long without looking suspicious. She moved on.

Now that she had a clearer picture of this floor, she started widening her patrol, going as far as the end of each hallway before doubling back. Occasionally, she exchanged a wary nod with a sleepy-looking guard, but none of them were the person she was looking for.

She'd almost given up for the night when she decided to do something risky. Heart pounding, she took the stairwell at the western end of the hallway, then crossed the upper floor at a sprint before coming back down the opposite stairwell at the eastern end. From there, she ducked into a small alcove, where she couldn't be seen by anyone coming down the hallway.

She waited.

There. Someone at the far end of the corridor, close to the curving stairwell that led to the great hall, just at the edge of her perception. A man, she thought, or at least someone taller and heavier than her. The way he stood with one foot out ahead of him, she would've been able to see him leaning around the corner. She had to fight the urge to peer out and look for him. Knowing that she wouldn't see anything somehow made that harder.

Instead, she forced herself to stay calm. Whoever it was, if he made a dash for the royal chambers, she felt confident she could beat him in a foot race. But if he got much closer . . .

He took a step. Just one, slow and cautious, then another. Forty-five paces away now, but he was in no rush. He advanced, then waited, never committing his weight. She recognized that pattern. She'd seen it a thousand times in duels, that game of inches where each fighter tried to figure out the other's reach.

There could only be one explanation. The king's Ghost had finally come back to haunt him.

She thought she might be able to catch him on foot. It would be interesting to fight someone she couldn't see. Her trick with Jaeri earlier had been easy. Even before she sensed the girl's shifting weight, she could've guessed what she would try. Much more difficult to manage against a skilled opponent, and if she lost . . .

No, they wouldn't cross blades tonight. But there was still one thing she could achieve.

She stepped out of the alcove and paced back and forth along the hallway, outwardly unconcerned, a bored guard on patrol. She gave no sign that she sensed him until her route took her within thirty paces, and then she looked straight at him.

This close, she could feel him flinch. She smiled and saluted the empty hallway. So he was testing her, was he? Fine. Let him think he knew her limits. Let him know that she wasn't afraid.

She went back to her pacing, back and forth, never more than a dozen paces from the king's bedchamber. On the outside, she projected as much confidence as she could muster. But she didn't relax until she felt him leave and didn't sleep well that night or the night after.

Kyrede wore his own face for the first time in years.

It was strange how liberating that felt. Two nights ago he'd have felt exposed, every passing glance a knife at his throat, even if no one could have possibly recognized him. Living in the shadows, every interaction carried some small risk of danger. But he was just a man now, like any other. What did he and the stranger have to fear in one another? Still, he kept his shortsword close as he walked along the main road through Lletra, its exposed handle disguised as the head of a carpenter's hammer. There were some habits he would keep for the rest of his life.

From Lletra, he planned to strike east and return to Whitethrush before the first heavy snow of the year. That was where he'd originally planned to go after Barste, and Jurald would have been expecting him months ago. There would be repercussions for his detour to Lletra, especially once he confessed his reason for it, but he was willing to do whatever penance the prior set for him. Besides, no man willing to devote his life to the Order was ever turned away, and Kyrede had already devoted more life than most.

He kept to the main thoroughfare as he walked, trying to break the habit of slinking through back alleys. This early in the morning, he shared the street with a few other souls: bakers pulling their first loaves from the oven; lamplighters carrying their ladders from streetlight to streetlight; drunks stumbling home from the night before and watchmen eyeing them carefully. He saw a few guards that he recognized but didn't feel any urge to wave. They were someone else's friends, not his.

Would he have friends now? *That* was hard to fathom. Surely he'd lost the right, maybe even the ability. Another thing sacrificed in the quest they'd given him, the one he'd happily accepted.

The one he'd almost finished.

His hands shook with the fury of it, the way "almost" lingered on his tongue without even speaking the word. He mastered himself. He was done with that now.

For how else could he interpret the sudden appearance of another saint? One who stood at the king's side, capable of miracles that acted as a perfect counter to his own. He had prayed for failure, and his prayers had been answered. And if they were answered right here, right now, at the very end, who was he to question?

That feeling surged again, was quieted.

The south gate loomed up ahead of him suddenly, the same one he'd walked under weeks ago and admired for its lack of pretension. This time he read something different in the stone, some reminder that he was the one retreating from the city. He ignored the feeling and focused his vision on the road beyond the gate, focused on putting one foot in front of the other. Two guards stood at the gate, wearing the chain shirts and leather tabards of the watch. They stared at him as he passed but said nothing.

And then he was free, with the past behind him and the road ahead.

Early autumn dressed the trees in red and gold. The canopy that arched over the road had too few leaves to block the sun, which lit the dirt road a warm shade of orange. The air felt cold, but not freezing. It would get colder before he reached the mountains. He felt lighter, calmer. He even nodded to a few people as he passed: a woman leading a mule; a young man and woman walking together, eyes suspicious; a farmer driving his wagon. A few even returned his gesture with a wave.

Not the two youths, though. They'd lowered their chins and hurried on, anxious to make the city. Fine by him. Their business was their own. But why did they look so familiar?

The sun warmed his face as it rose, and he pushed all other thoughts aside. The warmth of the sun, the food in his pack, the miles of gentle road ahead of him. Those were his only concerns now. What did he care if a pair of strangers looked familiar? But he did care, and he couldn't figure out why.

A few miles later, Kyrede stopped. He remembered them now. The two students from Sharme, the ones who followed the scholar Andza to Barste. What were they doing here? They'd looked haggard and half starved, too scrawny for the packs they carried.

Kyrede hadn't seen the third anywhere, which meant that Jurald must have finally done something about him.

That would explain why the other two had fallen on hard times. But why hadn't they gone straight home afterward?

Because they weren't running away from anything, he realized. Not with those eyes, the ones that said they'd walked twenty miles through the night and would walk another twenty before they stopped to rest. No, they weren't running away. They were walking *toward* Lletra, and Kyrede knew what they wanted to find there.

The false king.

He tried to tell himself that it was no concern of his. He'd been called off this hunt: once by a fellow saint, then once more by the clearest message he'd heard from the gods in years. He tried to quell that rising feeling in his chest, but this time, *this* time, something broke. Something solid and familiar but too old to name. He couldn't have said whether it was something he'd carried for the past fifteen years or something he'd leaned against for strength, but when it crumbled, rage rushed in to fill the space it left.

He turned around.

"Forget something?" the guard asked when he reached the gate almost an hour later.

Kyrede looked up, ready with the lie—and realized that if they recognized him, he was still wearing his own face.

Panic. He should've come back in disguise, walked through the gate unremarked. Now there were two witnesses that saw him leaving and coming back. He had to play this carefully, avoid giving them anything memorable to latch onto.

But they were already taking notice, reaching for their swords, fear and confusion evident on their faces.

Kyrede held his hands up, palms forward to show that they were empty. To his left and right, two other Kyredes did the same thing. Before he could make sense of that, the one on his right leapt forward, his knife hidden until the hilt materialized in the first guard's eye socket. The Kyrede to his left circled that direction, eyes on the second guard, who was still struggling to free his sword.

What was going on?

"Please, wait—" Kyrede said, confused. "I didn't mean ..."

His vision blurred, then resolved to a point three feet ahead of where he'd stood, his knife buried in the second guard's throat. He let go of his knife, and the guard fell back. But how? He hadn't moved since—

He looked back to where he'd been standing and saw himself still standing there, hands up. "Please, wait—" the illusory Kyrede begged. "I didn't mean ..."

The illusion disappeared.

Kyrede looked around. He was alone on the street, but that didn't mean there were no witnesses. They could have seen him and run away. He quickly veiled himself and checked a few alleys but saw no one. Maybe he'd been fortunate, but he doubted it. He didn't drop the veil until he'd gained a few streets' distance and ducked into a tavern wearing a face he hadn't worn in years. Three other men joined him at the table, which surprised him. Then he realized that the other three men were ghosts, and that surprised him even more.

"What do I do?" he whispered once the others took their seats.

"Turn yourself in," the man on his left suggested. Kyrede recognized him, an old miller with a scar on the back of his left hand, dead for six years. "You've killed too many, and you've a taste for it now. No one can stop you but yourself."

"Stupid," said a voice to his right. The voice and the face both belonged to a silversmith from Traste. "No one can stop you because no one's meant to. You have a job to finish."

Kyrede looked to the third man, who wore Jurald's face. When he spoke, it was with Kyrede's own voice. "What do you want to do?" he asked.

His vision blurred again. He sat in the miller's chair now, watching the exchange between Kyrede and the man from the Order. "I don't know," they said at the same time. "I don't know what's happening."

Another blur. "Do both," he said, with the silversmith's voice. "There are four of us. Who's to say we can't all try something different, and may the best man win?" The other three nodded. That made sense. But who would try each plan, and how would they know whether the others had succeeded or failed?

It took another hour to figure out the details: an entire hour, with the tavern's regulars crowding in at different tables to avoid the man talking to himself in the corner, nursing a drink that no one saw him order, whispering to ghosts that no one else could see.

CHAPTER TWENTY-NINE

We reached Lletra after two full days of walking. We'd sold our horse in the first village we reached, knowing full well that the royal wedding would have raised prices on everything. A farmer charged us a silver crown for space in his hayloft, where Rahad and I slept back-to-back for warmth atop a musty old blanket that smelled vaguely of horse.

After all we'd been through together, I trusted Rahad completely, but only as a friend and traveling companion. I'd never thought of pursuing anything romantic with him. Still, the heat emanating from his back made me painfully aware that I was alone and unsupervised with a boy my own age. I suspect that if either of us had reached toward the other in the night, we would have found a willing partner for a variety of activities, no matter what the blanket smelled like. But he kept his hands to himself, and so did I. We set out early the next morning—as friends, and nothing more.

As we walked, I tried to remember some time in my life when I wasn't hungry or exhausted, but all those memories felt like they belonged to someone else. Had I ever really sat in the Library's great hall on a summer day, nibbling pastries and worrying about some meaningless assignment? I couldn't reconcile the idea of me, now, with the person I'd been a year ago. The lines just didn't match up. When was the last time I curled up somewhere quiet and read a book?

Well, yesterday morning. But that hardly counted.

Andza's cipher might not have been very elegant, but it held its own. Knowing the key didn't lessen the tedious, mind-numbing work of unraveling it. After an hour and a half of work, I'd ended up with just over a page, even with Rahad helping with the translation from Jhendi.

Fortunately, Andza wasn't a very flowery writer. Every paragraph opened the door to a new and deeply dangerous line of thought. Assuming the remaining chapters delivered what the first page promised, his book had a very real chance of causing the civil war he suspected. Or preventing one, if we got it into the right hands.

A pair of guards nodded at us as we entered Lletra's south gate. I smiled back, just happy to be off the road. The roads hadn't been very safe for us, all things considered.

"I don't want to ask again," Rahad said, "because you got mad last time. But . . ."

"Where to?" I finished for him. I hadn't gotten mad, exactly, but I was tired of being the one to decide every time, and I had explained—very patiently, I thought—that I'd never been this far north either.

"Food, first of all," I decided. Or my stomach decided, and I agreed. "I don't care what it is, as long as it's hot. Then somewhere we can get clean. They won't let us within a mile of the king looking like this."

Lletra's main street ran south to north, lined with one- and two-story buildings made of pale gray stone. Off to the west, the governor's palace loomed over the rest of the city, backlit by the rising sun. The closer we got to that side of the city, the better, but it would be hard to find rooms we could afford—or any rooms at all.

We followed the main street until we hit the palace road, then turned east away from the walled inner city. Shops had only just opened their doors, but there were already crowds of people walking in and out. Almost every window had a space carved out for little mementos of the royal wedding: bits of fabric embroidered with the new queen's sigil, toy swords with red and gold paint, drawings and carvings of the royal family. The first time I saw the set of twenty children, I thought it must be a mistake, but more than one shop was selling them, and a few had even painted theirs in different bands of color for each child.

We stopped at a street vendor for two bowls of stew, thick with onions and potatoes and bits of stringy beef. Rahad ran across the street to a bakery and came back with two heels of bread, slightly stale but still delicious once we soaked them in broth. We returned our bowls and turned back the way we came, looking for a place to stay.

After an hour of fruitless searching, we stopped in a laundress' shop and handed over all the clothes we had in our packs. If we couldn't find rooms anywhere, we could at least try to look presentable, if only to stop the innkeepers from turning us away before we'd opened our mouths. The woman behind the counter separated our clothes into piles and gave us each a numbered wooden token, then recommended a few cheap cafés where we could sit for two or three hours without spending too much money. We thanked her and headed toward the door to leave.

Rahad made it to the door first, but since I was still fussing with one of the buckles on my pack, he opened it for me and stepped aside to let me through—right as a blond woman with an armful of tablecloths tried to force the door open with her hip. With no door to bump into, she overbalanced and fell into the shop, crashing into me and knocking me to the ground.

I landed hard, right on my tailbone, and felt my teeth knock together. When I opened my eyes, I saw a pair of legs in front of me, their owner's body hidden behind an impressive mound of white cloth. I looked up at the woman's face, and with a shock, I realized that I recognized her.

"Elaise!"

She looked down at me over the pile of tablecloths. "Jalina? Jalina! Absent gods, you look awful. What are you doing here?"

"Ouch," I said, standing up off the ground. "Also, *ouch*."

"Sorry," she said. "This is just the last place I expected to see you. Hi, Rahad," she said, noticing him. "You're looking well."

"Likewise," he said. She blushed.

So I looked awful, but Rahad looked well? Delightful. At least that explained why Elaise never seemed to lose patience with Rahad as quickly as I did. I was suddenly very relieved that I'd kept my hands to myself in the hayloft.

"We're here to visit an old friend," I said, with a meaningful look. "You remember Sanca." Too many people were watching us after we'd collided. I didn't dare risk explaining anything here, even in a whisper. Fortunately, Elaise caught the hint.

"Oh, right. I forgot you missed the wedding. How's her husband?"

"Fatter," I said. "But still handsome enough." That earned a smirk from our eavesdroppers. "What are you doing in Lletra?" I asked, stepping a little further off to the side of the room. She followed me, still carrying her pile of laundry.

"Oh, the entire family is here. Parents, uncles, brothers,

cousins. My eldest brother happened across the king's caravan as it left the capital, and he figured that wherever he was going, he would need something to drink when he got there. We must have spent a fortune on couriers to redirect deliveries up to Lletra, but it's been worth it."

"But why aren't you at the Library?"

She shrugged. "I took the semester off. It wasn't the same without the two of you there."

"Without the—never mind. Where are you staying, and more importantly, do you have some extra room? We'd be happy with a bare floor at this point."

Elaise grinned. "I think I can do a bit better than that."

The proprietor exchanged another wooden token for Elaise's pile and asked if she wanted them delivered to an inn I didn't recognize the name of. Elaise said that would be fine and even told the owner to add our totals to the family's account. Rahad and I looked at each other and shrugged. We could hardly pretend we were too proud to accept charity when we were begging for space on a floor two minutes ago.

Elaise led us out the door and out onto the road. Instead of turning east, toward the market quarter, she turned west toward the palace.

"How far is it?" I asked.

"Close enough," she said mysteriously.

Ten minutes later, we passed under the gates that led to the inner city. The houses grew taller and moved further back from the road, with towering shrubs rising out of pristine lawns and bits of creeping ivy along the outer walls. More and more often, we saw well-dressed guards standing by entryways, who glared at us with suspicion whenever we got a pace too close.

"Um, Elaise?"

"Yes?"

"Is your family staying *in* the palace?"

She laughed. "Not quite, but close. Here we are on the right."

The house she pointed to looked out of place amongst its neighbors. Where the other mansions tried to look like dignified country estates, this one looked more like a grand hunting lodge, with dark timber walls and a tiled roof painted to look like the striated gray-green leaves of an evergreen. Elaborate wooden carvings populated the eaves and window-sills with birds, squirrels, and even butterflies. Workers busied themselves around the grounds, widening stone archways, touching up bits of paint, and carrying building supplies in and out of every entrance.

I gaped. Rahad whistled.

"This is where you're staying?" I asked. I'd never realized Elaise's family made quite so much money selling wine.

Elaise laughed. "Where we live, actually. Well, in Lletra, anyway. Almost makes those years at the Library feel like a waste."

"Nonsense," came a voice from behind us. "The family needs a few scholars here and there. Helps remind people that we aren't just jumped-up grape farmers. Which is true, unfortunately."

We turned, and the voice's owner greeted us with an easy smile. He was tall, with Elaise's blond hair and delicate nose. His eyes wavered uneasily between the three of us, too polite to ask Elaise who her dangerous-looking friends were, too protective to leave us alone with her in case she needed help.

Elaise rescued the situation. "This is Daine," she said, "youngest of my three older brothers. The other two are probably out back somewhere. Daine, these are my friends from the Library, Jalina and Rahad. They've been on the road for a while and need a place to stay."

He nodded to each of us. "I think you've mentioned them before. Pleased to meet you both. You look, um—"

"The next time someone tells me I look like a wild animal," I warned, "I'm going to prove them right."

"Can we pretend I was going to say 'formidable'?" he said, smirking. I returned the smile.

"That's probably best."

"Well, our home is yours as long as you need it," he said seriously. "Dinner's at eight, but otherwise we all just grab food as we find it. You can have your pick of rooms, *especially* if you want either of the rooms in the back of the second floor. Elaise, feel free to evict anyone who needs the room less than your friends do."

"Hah. As if I needed your permission."

He shrugged. "It's nice when you humor me." He winked at us, then excused himself to run some errand. He turned and left toward the back of the house, his long legs carrying him out of sight in moments.

"He seems friendly," Rahad said.

"I thought you hated your brothers," I said.

"I hate the other two," Elaise explained. "Two guesses who took the rooms in the back of the second floor and left Daine and me the storage rooms beneath the attic."

"Ah."

The inside of the lodge looked just as busy as the outside, with workers doing renovations in nearly every room. Elaise explained that most of the bottom floor had been converted into a shipping operation that would pay for the house when they weren't living in it. By the time her father had his way, the house would hardly be fit to live in, but it would do for now. She led us up the main stairs, then around the hallway to the left, where a smaller staircase opened up to a small corridor on the third floor. She motioned to the second door on the right, and we all filed in.

"Now," Elaise said, closing the door behind us, "what's this about?"

It didn't take long to tell the story, having practiced it so recently with Reia. We left out a few details by silent agreement, but we included Aian's and Jurald's deaths and Andza's injury. Elaise nodded quietly through all of it, asking brief questions when something wasn't clear but otherwise letting us talk.

"Three questions," she said once we'd finished. "First, are you sure about giving Andza's book to King Sethric? It sounds like you want it preserved, not destroyed, and there's no reason to believe he wouldn't destroy it himself."

It was the question I expected: the same one Rahad had asked and the same one I asked myself every time my doubts found a voice. "True," I admitted. "I don't know him personally, of course, but from what I've heard, he's ruthlessly practical. He might see its existence as a threat and throw it into the nearest fireplace, but he might also see it as a weapon, something he can store in his quiver and use if needed. Sethric isn't the only guilty party mentioned in those pages.

"Besides, it's our least worst option. If we publish it, we risk civil war. If we keep it without publishing it, the king and the Order both have reason to fear us. But if we throw the prize between them, they'll be too busy dealing with each other to bother with us, and we'll still have Andza's other two copies if we need them. No one knows about those."

"When she says no one," Rahad corrected, "she means at least five people. The three of us, Andza, and Reia, plus whoever knows about the other copies."

"Right," I said. "But I trust the both of you, and if the others were going to talk, they'd have done so by now."

"Works for me," Elaise said. "Second question. This one's for you, Rahad. Why stay? You say that your debt with Andza is clear, and this was his task, not yours. Jalina has a stake in it for obvious reasons, and I guess that means I have a stake in it, too. But what's yours?"

My heart soared a little when Elaise said that she cared about something because I cared about it. It fell again when I realized I'd taken Rahad's help for granted. Was I starting to make the same mistakes as Andza? Assuming people would always be there for me just because they'd been there for me yesterday?

Rahad looked at me for a long moment before answering. When he did, his voice was clear and firm, his eyes determined.

"When that man stabbed me in Barste," he told Elaise, "Jalina ran toward the door, not away from it, and she didn't stand aside until he left. She called me an idiot afterward, and she was probably right, but she stood in front of me anyway. And again in the woods, when I was sure Andza was going to die, and I'd walked half a mile with him in the dark and didn't know which way to go, she rode toward us out of the darkness and helped me carry him into the woods." He shrugged. "How can I walk away from someone who's never walked away from me?"

I wanted to correct him, to say that it hadn't happened that way, that I wasn't trying to protect him either time, that he *was* an idiot for getting himself stabbed and for trying to attack a madman in the woods, but I didn't quite trust myself to speak just then or for a long moment after.

Elaise broke the silence for us. "About time the two of you started getting along," she said. "Okay, last question, and this is the big one. How can I help?"

It was all too much. Rahad's speech, Elaise's easy generosity, all the horrible things that had happened in the last two weeks. I hugged her instead of answering and wasn't the least bit ashamed when I started to cry.

"I think I'm starting to go slightly insane," Elaise said. "I've never had to think in this many languages at once."

"How much did you manage?" I asked.

"Just three chapters so far."

"Three *chapters*? It took me an hour and a half to do three paragraphs."

We sat in Elaise's room, clean and fed and happy for the first time in days. She'd insisted on seeing the book before going down to dinner and again as soon as we got back up to her room. As much as Elaise complained about her classes, she was an excellent linguist, and it had been too long since she'd been able to work those muscles. She leaned into the challenge of it, scribbling furiously.

"Want me to read what we have so far?" she asked.

I nodded to Rahad, and he opened the door to peer into the hallway. Seeing it empty, he pulled the door closed and motioned toward my feet. I took an old shawl from my pack and tossed it to him, and he stuffed it into the crack between the door and the floor mat, then came back to sit with us.

"Go ahead."

"Creepy," Elaise said, shaking her head. "A year ago, the two of you could barely stand each other, and now you have conversations no one else can hear. Okay, here goes."

We already knew part of the first chapter but didn't interrupt Elaise as she reread it. It started with Andza briefly introducing himself, then launched immediately into his claims, an outline of the evidence he'd gathered, and the steps that the Order had already taken to silence any witnesses. He kept his tone neutral and made clear distinctions between what he believed and what he could actually prove. Anyone who wanted to paint him as a madman would have a hard time of it.

The next section focused on a specific person that Andza never named but instead referred to as the carpenter: a middle-aged man, living with his wife and two children in a small village on the southern edge of Wryn's coast. He told the story of his involvement in the war, his specific role in several battles, and detailed accounts of what the survivors would have seen. Andza added brief annotations to every page: usually small references to eyewitness accounts, with references to other established works where he could give them.

"Are all the chapter headings like that?" I asked. "'The Carpenter' or something similar?"

"Seems that way," Elaise confirmed. "I only checked a few, but the others were similar. The farmer's story, the blacksmith's story, and so on. I wonder why."

"I thought it was obvious," Rahad said. "He needs to call them something, and he can't exactly use their names."

"It also proves they had a life afterward," I pointed out. "As important as it was at the time, this was just a part of their lives. They didn't just help influence a war. They also lived in the world that came after it."

"I guess that's true," Elaise said. "This way, they get the first say in how they're labeled. If people talk about the stories, they have to use the words Andza used. 'I was in the battle the fletcher talked about' or 'I saw the trick that the mason used.' Makes it harder to label them as something else."

"Hearing someone say all this out loud still makes me itch," I complained.

"Agreed," Elaise said. "It was bad enough translating

it. It's like I'm six years old again and I've done something I know I'm going to get in trouble for, and now I'm just waiting for one of my parents to find out."

A knock sounded at the door. All three of us jumped.

Elaise quickly hid the translated pages under the cushion of her chair, moved my shawl aside with her foot, and opened the door. "Oh," she said, "it's just you."

Elaise's brother Daine walked in carrying a platter with four mugs. Each one had a little wisp of steam floating above it. He arched an eyebrow at his sister. "Thought your friends might like something to drink after dinner, but if I'm not welcome . . ."

"Actually, we're a bit—wait, is that the six-year reserve?"

The aroma reached me, a wall of citrus, clove, and cinnamon that made my nostrils flare and my mouth water. "Whatever it is," I said, "it smells really good."

"Elaise and I are the black sheep of the family," he explained, passing out the mugs. He still wore the easy smile he'd had when we met him. I wondered if it was a permanent feature, the way some people always scowled regardless of their mood. "We like a little bit of wine with our mulling spice. Perfect thing for a cold night."

I took a sip. It tasted every bit as good as it smelled, and the hot mug warmed my hands and face. "It's good. Thank you."

"How did you manage to sneak a bottle past Ivram?" Elaise asked, taking a sip of her own.

"Oh, that was easy," Daine said. "Remember the unoaked Millstone Red from three years ago? I never told father where the last of it went. The way I figure it, Ivram owes me another six bottles of discretion, at least."

Elaise laughed. "Scandalous."

"I thought so, too." He turned to us. "Elaise mentioned

the two of you were from Sharme. What do you study there?"

"History and foreign languages," I answered.

"Art and literature," Rahad said. I almost choked on my next sip. Literature?

"History, eh? Shame you both missed the wedding," Daine said. "I assume that's why you were here? Not often a king marries an old woman and takes in her twenty adopted children."

"Maybe we'll catch the next one," I joked. I didn't want to lie to our host if I didn't have to, but I also didn't want to involve Elaise's family in what the three of us were doing. "The trip here took longer than we thought."

"Makes sense," he said. "The south road's been crowded the past few weeks. Not to mention the barricades at the south gate."

"There weren't any—" I stopped myself, but it was too late. I could tell I'd walked into a trap, even if I didn't know what it was yet. I saw Rahad's jaw tighten. We both tried to hide our expressions behind another sip of wine but failed spectacularly.

"What are you talking about?" Elaise asked, confused.

"Murders, dear sister." He let the silence drag on. The smile still lingered at the corners of his mouth, but his eyes had a hard cast to them now.

"The ones in the South Quarter? But those were a week ago. Why barricade the gate now?"

"Those," Daine said. "And the one on the road from Barste just last week. Bandits, apparently, though there haven't been bandits on that road in a decade. And then the two guards today. Killed in broad daylight at the south gate. They have a witness, but he's either a drunk or permanently deranged, and they can't get anything useful out of him."

"When was this?" I asked before I could stop myself.

"Just after sunrise," he said.

I swallowed. "Just after sunrise," I repeated. "Around the time we arrived, but I swear nothing like that happened while we were there."

"Must have just missed them," Daine said, shrugging. "I assume you 'just missed' the bandits on the south road, too?"

We were caught. I'd underestimated how news of Jurald's death would travel and hadn't anticipated that murders in Lletra would have already put people on edge. I didn't see how they could have anything to do with us, but in any case, Rahad and I had expected to keep to ourselves in Lletra, and we didn't even have a thin alibi for why we were really here.

"No," I said slowly. "That one we knew about. But I can't tell you what we know about it, or how it happened, or who was involved. And we can't tell you why we're in Lletra either. I understand if you want us to leave, but I promise you, if we thought there was trouble after us, we wouldn't have come here."

Daine looked at me for a long moment that seemed to stretch into forever. Then he did the same to Rahad, and even Elaise. Surprisingly, Elaise seemed the most uncomfortable. After several minutes of silence, he stood and walked to the window. A few flakes of snow drifted past the panes, too insubstantial to gather. They'd be gone by morning. Would we be gone with them?

"Whatever you're up to," he said, turning to face us, "you can't use our house as a base of operations, and you can't ask anyone to help you that hasn't already agreed to. If you need a place to sleep, that's fine. If you need a place to run a smuggling operation, or hide from the law, or whatever else you're plotting, look somewhere else."

"Fair," Rahad said.

"Agreed," I added. Elaise nodded, too.

"As for you," he said, looking pointedly at Elaise, "how much trouble are we talking about?"

"Remember that time we set Shadow free to see how fast he'd run?"

"That bad, huh?"

"Who's Shadow?" I asked.

"Father's old horse," Daine explained. "We set him loose one night. I think I was seven and Elaise was five. He ran for the fence as soon as we opened the barn door, and we didn't see him until the next morning. By that time, he'd gotten the neighbor's mare pregnant, kicked one of the stablehands, and ended the night by breaking his own leg in a ditch."

"Well," I said dryly, "I can promise not to get anyone pregnant."

"Same," Elaise laughed. We both looked at Rahad.

He shrugged. "I'll try not to break my leg."

Daine's smile came back, brighter than before. "Sounds like a plan. Let me know when it all goes sideways and you need someone to pull you out of it. Better yet, let me know before it goes sideways so I can find you somewhere else to stay. I hear the coast is beautiful, even in winter." He tipped his mug to us and made for the door.

"Oh," he said over his shoulder, "and could you bring the mugs down when you're done? My hands are full carrying around everyone else's secrets."

Elaise made a rude gesture at him. He grinned at her, then left.

"Sorry about that," Elaise said after he'd gone.

"Don't worry about it. We weren't counting on help in the first place. Everything that's happened in the last six hours has been a blessing. Truly."

"And if that trouble on the road is following us," Rahad said, "we probably don't want to stay here for very long, anyway."

"True. Just do me a favor before tomorrow?" I asked.

"Your mother's chapter? I skimmed ahead. Chapter seventeen, I think. I'll do that one next."

"Thank you."

"Return favor?" she asked.

"Name it."

"Stop smiling back every time my brother smiles at you. If he knows you like him, he'll walk all over you."

I opened my mouth to argue but couldn't think of anything to say. I hadn't smiled back at him! Had I? Judging by the truly despicable grins Elaise and Rahad shared, I must have looked like an idiot. I closed my mouth and turned away. My face felt hot, and I didn't think I could get away with blaming the wine.

CHAPTER THIRTY

"Stop slouching," Elaise whispered. "You look like a thief."

"I'm trying to look like a servant," Rahad whispered back. "I thought I was supposed to look bored and lazy."

"First," Elaise whispered, "if you think servants are lazy, you've never met one. Second, you're not a servant. You're an employee. Employees are supposed to look busy and industrious."

"Stop whispering," I whispered. "You both look suspicious." I set down my crate and straightened, pushing my knuckles into my back. "How many more of these do we need to unload?"

Elaise scanned the stacks we'd made so far, eyes resting briefly on the crate with the charcoal smudge on the bottom corner, the one that held Andza's book. We had no idea how we were going to get it into the king's hands. Getting it into the palace had already been an ordeal. It seemed like all three of Elaise's brothers were watching for signs that we were up to something. Any time the three of us sat together, they found some excuse to be in the room, either to look for something that took half an hour to find or to get something they'd forgotten to grab ten minutes ago.

It helped that they didn't know what to look for. No doubt they found it suspicious when we offered to help with today's delivery, but they'd agreed in the end. If nothing else, it would let them keep an eye on us.

"Another round and we'll be halfway done," she said. "We can rest for a minute as long as we're in sight of the door."

Truthfully, no one but Elaise's family seemed to care that we were here. The palace kitchens employed at least four dozen people, all of whom had better things to do than supervise the three of us. That might change if we spent too long wandering around with nothing to do, though. I sighed and went back to the wagon for another crate of wine.

I had to admit that most of my frustration came from being so close to the finish line but unable to cross it. Left alone for a few minutes, any one of us could walk up to the king, hand him the book, explain the key, maybe throw in a few anecdotes about the journey here, and we'd be on our way home by nightfall. We just had to persuade the guards to let us walk freely about the castle, then persuade the king that we weren't insane, then . . .

I sighed. Andza had spent fifteen years on this quest. I could hardly expect to finish it within a week of him handing it to me.

Still, frustrating.

Elaise directed us as we carried in the last few boxes. "Ten-minute break," she announced, slightly louder than she needed to, "then we'll carry in the rest. Don't go too far," she warned. That was a clever touch. If people assumed she was keeping an eye on us, they were less likely to do it themselves.

Rahad and I meandered toward a trestle table covered with the kitchen's throwaways: bruised fruit, burned bread, leftover cheese wedges. All perfectly edible but too unsightly to serve anywhere upstairs. We stood close together as we filled our plates and spoke low.

"So far, so good," he said.

"Considering we're making this up as we go along, I agree."

"Any idea what to do next?"

"No," I admitted. "But keep your eyes open. And maybe pray for a miracle while you're at it."

Kyrede watched the palace's main entrance, disguised as a guard he'd killed three hours ago. As far as he knew, no one had found the man yet, but they wouldn't recognize him once they did. Until then, he walked the man's patrol route, always with one eye toward the palace, occasionally nodding to the citizens of Lletra to let them know that they were safe with him walking the streets.

He turned a corner, and his view shifted. Now he walked along the bridge, wearing the face of a woman he'd met a lifetime ago. A wheelwright, he thought, but he couldn't be sure. He remembered her posture, though, and the way she walked, and settled into them without thinking. The street narrowed on the other side of the bridge but eventually opened out into a park that would give him a good view of the palace's southeast wall.

Another shift, and he stood on the third-floor balcony of an elegant manor. He drummed his fingers along the rail, watching the street below with disapproval, through eyes that had once belonged to a minor country noble.

He no longer knew which face belonged to him, and he didn't care. He only knew that he needed a distraction, something to pull attention toward one part of the palace and send the false king running to safety in the other direction.

His vision blurred again. When it cleared, his surroundings had shifted, and the sun had moved a small fraction of its path across the sky. He looked down at his hands but didn't recognize them. That no longer worried him, nor did the loss of time and distance. He trusted that he was where he needed to be, when he needed to be there. He believed that with absolute certainty.

But where was he?

Outside the servant's entrance, on the northern side of the palace. A wagon stood parked in the grand courtyard, drawn by two horses who shifted impatiently under their bridles. Only one person in sight: a tall blond man that whistled as he worked, checking the remaining contents of the wagon against his list, marking off whichever boxes had already been unloaded.

Kyrede crept close, shortsword drawn.

The man turned at the last second, and the thrust meant for his kidney glanced off his hip. He fell anyway, too stunned from the pain to even cry out. A hard kick to his stomach knocked the air out of him, and he curled in on himself, running from the pain.

Kyrede surveyed the wagon. Wooden crates filled with glass bottles. A fortune in wine, with dry straw packed between the bottles to keep them from rattling against each other.

Perfect.

Jaeri took the stairs two at a time, not even pretending to walk gracefully.

There had been two more murders at the south gate yesterday morning. Both victims belonged to the city watch, with another watchman still missing. And it had been an entire day before anyone told her! She hadn't bothered to ask why. She already knew the reason they would give her: murder was the city watch's responsibility, even if they were the ones being killed—maybe especially if they were the ones being killed. A princess's job was to stay safe inside the castle.

The worst part was that she knew it was true. She couldn't help with that, and trying to help would only put her in everyone else's way. Truth be told, she couldn't help most people with most things. But surely she could help someone with something.

Which is why she didn't come downstairs to bother Niklas early in the morning, or bring her bow down to the archery yard after breakfast for practice with the soldiers, or walk around the castle hoping for another duel with Swordmaster Yara. They all had more important business to handle today. Instead, she went to the one place in the castle where she knew she could help without bothering anyone. There were *always* dishes to do.

Familiar sounds greeted her as she reached the bottom of the stairs: crackling fires, simmering pots, clanking utensils, the noisy bustle of a small army of cooks weaving in between one another, calling out for ingredients or reminding each other of dishes that needed to be checked, stirred, seasoned, or plated. It felt good to be in the middle of so much noise, to float around the edges of this buzzing swarm of activity. She saw the pile of dishes at the end of a row of sinks and walked toward it, pushing up her sleeves.

Halfway across the room, another sound joined the din. One she didn't recognize at first, and even when she did recognize it, it still didn't make any sense. Why would someone be galloping horses out in the courtyard?

The sound of screaming filled the kitchens, and Rahad grabbed my shoulder and pulled me to the ground. We ducked beneath the table we'd been standing in front of a moment before and looked around to see what was happening. I heard glass shatter and another wild scream but couldn't see who was screaming. I looked at the nearest cook, a stout older man holding a paring knife, and followed his gaze to the other side of the room.

"Absent gods," I whispered.

Both of Elaise's horses were trying desperately to shoulder their way into the servant's entrance. The door might have allowed one of them at a time, but not yoked together as they were. Each one surged forward, only stopping to kick or bite when the other horse got in their way.

When I looked past them, I realized why they were so desperate to get inside. The wagon they pulled had caught fire, and they'd both run in different directions, straining against their bridles. Instead of getting away, they'd only succeeded in crashing into the wall in front of them, pinned against the stone by the inferno they were still attached to. Another few dozen bottles exploded in the heat, and the horses whinnied in stark terror.

Elaise ran forward, trying to calm them, but she couldn't get close enough to help and was only going to hurt herself trying. Someone else ran forward with a bucket of water, but between Elaise and the two horses blocking the doorway, they didn't accomplish much. One of the horses snapped, and Elaise pulled her hand back, screaming.

We rushed to her side and caught her just as she collapsed. She immediately tried to roll to her side and curl around her injured hand, but two others joined us. One sat behind her, supporting her shoulders, and the other put her weight on Elaise's feet to stop her from kicking.

"Elaise," I said, trying to sound calm, "we need to see your hand."

She shook her head, sobbing.

"Shh, it's okay," I said. I laid one hand on the side of her face. With the other, I pulled gently at her injured arm. Beside us, one of the horses went down with a broken leg and the other tried to drag it through the door and into the kitchen. I smelled cooking meat and fought the urge to throw up. "Will someone please do something about those horses!"

One of the cooks stepped forward with a meat cleaver. Twenty brutal seconds later, the screaming stopped.

Now that it had quieted down, it was easier to calm Elaise. It still took a measure of coaxing to get her to extend her arm, and she looked away as she held it toward us. Three of the fingers on her left hand were missing, and judging by the state of her clothes, she'd already lost a lot of blood.

I wasn't an expert on taking care of wounds, but after a week of looking after Andza, I had some idea what to do. I asked for a clean washcloth and got one. I wrapped it loosely around Elaise's hand, then reinforced the makeshift bandage with a cloth table runner. Elaise twitched violently with every bit of pressure, but once it was wrapped, she was able to breathe without sobbing.

"Hold your hand up in the air like this," I said, demonstrating. "Good. We're going to get you some help, okay? Just wait here. You're going to be all right." I had no idea if that was true but didn't want to think of the alternatives. Besides, what else could I have said?

I stood and motioned for Rahad to follow me. One of the kitchen staff immediately took my place and started fussing over Elaise. Instead of going for help, I walked over to the crate with the charcoal smudge and handed Andza's book to Rahad.

"What are you doing?" he asked.

"This amount of noise is going to draw guards from all over the palace. Our best chance of reaching the king is to join the crowds of people running *away* from the kitchens. I'm going to wait here with Elaise and make sure her family's all right. Take this and try to find the king."

He shook his head and pushed Andza's book back toward me. "I'll stay. You go."

I opened my mouth to argue, but he forestalled me. "You weigh a hundred pounds and look like you've been crying. Anyone who sees me stalking through the halls is going to arrest me. The worst they'll do to you is sit you down and give you something hot to drink. You should be the one to go."

It broke my heart to think of abandoning Elaise, but Rahad was right.

"Wait here," I said. "And keep her safe."

"Keep yourself safe," he said. "I don't think any of this happened by accident."

"I don't think so either. Wish me luck."

"*Fly true,*" he said in Jhendi.

I reached the top of the kitchen stairs as the first of the palace guards rushed down it, their scabbards and mail clattering as they passed. They didn't stop me when they saw me. In fact, they barely saw me at all. Rahad was right. I must not have looked like much of a threat.

Above, the stairwell opened into a narrow corridor, with four doors on either side and a larger one at the end. I ran for the larger door. It opened into the main entrance, with a grand staircase off to my right. At the top of the stairs, a walkway ran north to south, and each end disappeared into at least two other hallways.

"Damn. Which way . . . ?" I wondered aloud.

"What are you looking for?"

I nearly jumped through the doorway in shock. I whirled around, hiding Andza's book behind my back without thinking. The girl who'd spoken looked at me curiously, dark eyes narrowed. She looked eleven, maybe twelve. Old enough to have most of her height, though she crouched slightly as if trying to move quietly.

"Who are you?" I asked.

"*I* live here," she said. "Who are you?"

"My name is Jalina," I said. "I . . . I'm looking for the king."

"What's that behind your back?" she asked.

"Just a book."

I showed her the book, but pulled it back when she tried to take it. She glared at me and folded her arms. "I could call for guards, you know."

I looked around. The hall was quiet. The whole palace was quiet. I'd expected more . . . I don't know, shouting? Alarm? Where *were* the guards? I'd only seen the two on the stairway and no other souls since I came upstairs. I remembered what Rahad said about the disaster in the kitchens not being an accident.

"I don't think they'd come," I said. "I'm going upstairs. Follow me if you like, or hide somewhere until it's safe. I think . . . I think something else is going on, but I don't know what. I just know what I have to do." I turned and walked into the hall, toward the staircase. She trailed after me a few seconds later.

Once we reached the top of the stairs, I turned right onto the main walkway, then took the first left into a hallway. Dead end. I doubled back and went the other way, toward the southern edge of the palace. The girl followed me like a shadow and made about as much noise.

"Where is everyone?" I asked.

"I don't know," she said. "Where are we going?"

"You tell me."

Silence. Then, "Take the next right. There's a big room at the end of the hall. We can take the stairs up to the third floor from there."

I went where she directed. "I assume this means you trust me now?"

"If you're an assassin," she said, "you're not a very good one."

"I'm not a—"

I stopped. We'd made it to the end of the hall, which opened into a kind of reception area. Normally, petitioners would file in from the larger door on the right and line up to make their case to the person seated atop the dais. It stood empty now—or would have, if not for the dead.

There were six of them, all dressed in the same armor I'd seen on the guards earlier. Whoever killed them had either dragged their own dead away or hadn't suffered any casualties in the first place. The dead soldiers faced random directions, backs to one another, as if the attack had come from all sides.

I no longer wondered what happened to all the other guards in the palace. The two I saw earlier must have started running downstairs before . . . before whatever happened here. As far as I knew, they might be the only two soldiers left alive.

I felt the girl brush past me and held out a hand to stop her, but she pulled free. She walked toward one of the soldiers who lay face down. I don't know whether or not she recognized him or even wanted to. She didn't look at his face, which was turned away from her. Instead, she pulled his sword free from his scabbard and held it in front of her.

"Do you know how to use that?" I asked.

"Yes," she said. "But the one I practice with isn't this heavy."

I looked at her again—really looked this time. She wasn't crouching anymore, except in the way a cat might. She reminded me of Rahad at his most dangerous, thin and desperate, almost feral; of Elaise when she ran into something that stumped her and gritted her teeth against the challenge of it; of Andza, who had so many layers that it felt like he couldn't possibly be one person. How did a twelve-year-old manage to fit all that into a look?

"Who *are* you?" I asked again.

She looked back at me. "My name is Jaeri," she said, voice cold even as her eyes filled with tears. "I'm a princess. And I'm going to find whoever did this."

Kyrede knew he was running out of time.

His distraction in the kitchens hadn't drawn a fraction of the forces he'd hoped. Even with his gifts, he'd been hard pressed to make it this far into the palace. How many soldiers had he cut down so far? Twenty? Thirty? He could handle two or three at once, but four or more proved a challenge. They lived long enough to know that the attacks could come from any direction and swung at the air in desperation. He had a narrow cut across his right shoulder from such an attack and was lucky not to have worse.

He stepped back, and the soldier he'd just killed fell to the ground, hands covering a wound that traced a narrow path through her abdomen. He stood there for a moment, trying to catch his breath. Which way next?

"Up the stairs."

"Back the way we came."

"The next room, he must be in there."

Kyrede turned to face the voices and found an army standing behind him. Faces that he recognized and more than a few that he'd forgotten: everyone he'd ever been, everyone he'd ever killed. Row after row of the dead, packed shoulder to shoulder, stretching down the hall and out of sight. They whispered to him in his own voice, multiplied a hundred times, urging him on. The woman he'd just killed stood up from the floor and took her place among the ranks. She didn't even look down at her own corpse as she did.

He wasn't surprised to see them. If he was being honest with himself, they'd been following him for years. But if they were going to show up now, the least they could do was make themselves useful.

With a thought, he scattered them in every direction. They moved with inhuman speed, carrying the tools or weapons they'd carried in life: swords, hammers, and spears; scythes and shears and long-handled axes. A few ran with their arms stretched wide, their hands curled into long claws, mouths open in wordless screams. They crawled along walls and ceilings, clambered over furniture, and disappeared through doors. Within moments, he heard screams in every part of the castle.

Kyrede ran forward to meet those screams, a single shade among many. The last doomed remnant of Kerra's past, come back to avenge itself.

We reached the fourth floor just as the screaming started.

Jaeri froze, caught halfway between running away from the danger and running back downstairs toward it. I saw her moment of indecision stretch into something longer, that near-paralysis that comes from not knowing what to do, or from knowing what to do, but not knowing whether you're brave enough to do it.

Fortunately, I didn't have the same problem.

"Whatever it is," I said, "it's happening below us, which means it isn't in our way. Let's keep moving."

"There are people downstairs who can't fight," she said.

"And we can? We have no idea what's down there or what we would do when we got there. But if we find your parents, we have a better chance of figuring that out."

"You're right. Sorry." She lowered her sword. "This way. There's a trapdoor that leads to a guard tower on the roof. It's easy to defend, and you can see the whole city from there. If anyone's still alive, that's probably where they are." She didn't sound very hopeful.

"Even if it's empty, people might still be alive." The screaming downstairs proved that, but I thought better of mentioning it. "And we can signal for help from up there."

We heard boots coming up the stairwell behind us: at least a dozen people, moving at a dead run. Reinforcements? Or had the attack that swept through the lower floors already made it upstairs?

A moment later, the mouth of the stairwell darkened. People spilled into the hallway like a flood, clambering over each other, their faces a chorus of wordless fury. Some carried weapons, but most carried simple tools or nothing at all. A few had wounds that should have been fatal, but more than that, they looked . . . wrong. Their limbs were too jerky, their eyes wide and unblinking even as their mouths opened in silent screams.

We ran, but not fast enough.

They caught up to us in seconds. Just before they reached us, I looked over my shoulder and saw a middle-aged farmer raise a scythe over his head. I screamed and tripped, landing hard on my forearm. Jaeri stopped to fight, lashing out with her sword, but if she managed to hit any of them, they didn't seem to care.

I tried to crawl away, but my arm gave out underneath me with a loud crack, and I fell face first into the stone floor. I rolled onto my back, half blind with pain, and saw the wild-eyed farmer above me, scythe raised in a two-handed grip. He brought it down with a flash, and I raised my arm to stop it . . .

. . . and watched as it passed through my hand without hurting me.

As soon as the blade "struck" me, the farmer straightened and ran past me as if I wasn't there. Two soldiers in uniforms I didn't recognize sliced through Jaeri with swords that left no wounds. They, too, ignored her after dealing harmless blows. A few others swung as they rushed past, but none of them hurt us, and none stayed to finish us off. With a shock, I realized what was happening. None of those people existed. They were a feint, an illusion sent to flush us out and keep us distracted.

More importantly, I knew who had sent them.

"Jaeri, listen to me. Jaeri, stop!"

She lowered her sword, surprised to see that she was still alive. "Jalina, what . . . ?"

"None of this is real," I said, using my good arm to push me into a sitting position. A handful of illusory attackers ran by without reacting to us. Jaeri flinched, even as she saw me ignore them. "There's someone in the castle who can make us see and hear things that aren't there."

"Who?" she asked, uncomprehending.

"Me."

Up until he spoke, we wouldn't have thought the man next to us was any more real than the dozens who had just passed. We should have known better. This one walked, instead of running, and came after the others had cleared the way. Before we could react, he knocked the sword from Jaeri's grip with his own shortsword and threw her against the wall with his free hand. I stood to help, but as soon as I found my feet, he kicked me hard in the ribs, and I went down again.

He bent to pick something up off the floor, and I realized that I'd dropped Andza's book. I tried to say something, some lie that would throw him off track, but I could barely breathe except to cough. Jaeri wasn't much better off. She clutched her shoulder where she'd collided with the wall, and her eyes didn't seem to focus on anything.

"Kyrede," I managed. I needed to buy time, but speaking hurt. Everything hurt. "That's your name, isn't it? Andza told us about you."

"And what does Andza know about me?"

"The scholar doesn't know as much as he thinks he does."

"I should've killed that heretic years ago."

I gaped in shock. All three voices had come from the same man, but all of them sounded different. The first sounded like a kindly old woman, the second like an amused lover. The third sounded almost rabid; I could practically see the foam-flecked snarl that delivered those words. They spoke on top of each other, as if each speaker was unaware of the others.

I gathered my courage. One arm against the wall, I managed to stand again. My other arm was definitely broken, and my ribs screamed at me if I took more than half a breath. "He said you were insane, for one thing."

He smiled at me, and I felt the panic start to claw its way up through my stomach and into my throat. I was buying seconds at this point, not minutes, but it kept him from looking at the book—or at Jaeri, who was starting to stir. If she could manage to slip away and find help . . .

"Stand up, Jaeri."

This time the speaker came from our left, in the direction

the shadows had fled. A tall, slim woman with a sword walked toward us gracefully, eyes fixed on Kyrede. Sword-master Yara, personal guard to the king. Who else could it be? Jaeri stirred at the sound of her voice and started to crawl toward her on hands and knees. Too slowly.

"The king's bodyguard."

"Sent to stop us."

"Sent to test us."

"Actually, I was sent to look for her," she said. If the multiple voices bothered her, she didn't show it. "You're just a bonus."

This time, the voices responded as one. "He should have sent you sooner."

Kyrede moved as three different people, a layered collection of shadows that raised their weapons to strike. Yara dashed forward, but not quickly enough. No one could run twenty feet in half a second. Jaeri kept on crawling, unaware of the danger she was in.

Without thinking, I ran forward and wrapped my arms around Kyrede's waist. He threw me away easily, and I felt my broken bones twist beneath the muscle, but I managed to distract him for long enough. Furious, he swung at me, but the tip of his sword missed my throat and traced an inch-deep cut above the length of my collarbone. Then Yara was on him, and he couldn't afford to worry about anything else.

As Yara kept Kyrede occupied, Jaeri crawled around the edges of the fight and made her way to me. Seeing my blood, she pulled off her shirt and pressed it into my cut. I screamed.

"Shh, it's okay. You're going to be all right," she said, echoing what I'd told Elaise earlier. It didn't calm me any more than it had calmed her.

Behind Jaeri, the two fighters danced around each other. Yara was much faster, but she needed every bit of that speed to keep the fight even. Kyrede moved as four separate people, then five, then six, with a crowd of illusions that moved independently of the man who summoned them. With no way to tell which attacker was real, Yara had to account for all of them.

Even so, she managed to slip counterattacks between the whirlwind of blades that threatened her. Most of them hit shadows, but one opened a cut above Kyrede's knee and forced him to back away. The shadows around him danced wildly as they settled into different defensive stances, but Yara didn't look concerned, only kept the tip of her sword even with where her opponent's eyes must be. As far as I could tell, she wasn't even breathing heavily.

"The prior told me I might have to face you one day," Yara said. "I've always wondered how my gifts would measure up against yours."

The prior? Her gifts?

"She's an Architect," I realized. "She can feel him move."

"Don't talk," Jaeri said. "Save your energy." But she spared a reverent glance at the swordmaster even so.

"You can sense me," Kyrede confirmed, in a voice that sounded more delighted than afraid.

"Even so, it's hard to ignore your own eyes," a second voice added.

"I can help with that," said a third.

The room grew several shades darker. A band of sickeningly bright violet light appeared in front of the swordmaster's face. She stumbled back from it, and it followed as if tethered to a point just in front of her nose. Even with my eyes closed, I could see the bright line of it against my eyelids. At the same time, a cacophony of noise echoed throughout the hallway, as if we'd been dropped into the center of a pitched battle.

All of that noise and light centered on the swordmaster, who struggled to orient herself with two of her senses screaming at her. Kyrede lunged forward, feet barely touching the ground. Yara managed a lucky parry, but her counterattack missed wide, earning her a shallow cut across the forearm. She stepped back, swinging wildly, and Kyrede dodged before scoring another cut against her midsection.

He pressed the attack, and she took one wound after another, accepting minor scratches to avoid killing blows. Blood flowed from both ears as the relentless sound shattered her eardrums. Still she kept her feet, reading his movements from the weight of his feet against the floor, letting instinct and experience fill in the rest.

A minute passed with Yara on the defensive. Two minutes. Three minutes, when every second she survived felt like a miracle. Suddenly the noise stopped, and the band of violet light disappeared. I blinked but couldn't clear my eyes of the glowing lines that lay crisscrossed on top of everything. The ringing in my ears felt like it would go on forever.

Even half dead, Yara managed to raise her sword and square herself against that writhing mass of shadows, though her hands shook from the pain. She stared forward, eyes unfocused, and didn't shake her head to clear her battered senses the way the rest of us did. Likely she was already deaf, blind, or both, and didn't know the illusions had stopped.

"Time to end this," the chorus of voices said in unison.

And beneath them, a smaller voice, one I could barely hear.

"Please," Kyrede whispered. "Let me fail."

He jumped forward, his feet completely off the ground, sword held high to slash down at the swordmaster's head. Yara closed the distance to meet him, advancing into a lunge that caught him in the air.

Kyrede landed with his throat against the hilt of Yara's sword.

The illusions surrounding him faded, and he fell to the side, twisting the swordmaster's blade out of her grip. Yara dropped to her knees next to him and vomited, again and again until nothing came out. Jaeri crept toward her cautiously, struggling to hold back tears. I fought to stay awake, but I was still losing blood, and I suspected I would lose that fight soon.

There was something I had to do before I passed out, but I could hardly think through the fog of pain. Andza's book! I looked around and saw it lying six feet from me, our translated chapters scattered around it. Kyrede must have thrown it aside when Yara rushed him. I crawled over to it and tried not to bleed on everything as I shoved the papers together.

I felt someone tug against my shoulder: Jaeri, asking if I was okay. I twisted away from her. I would be okay, as long as I could get Andza's book to the king. I had to explain it to him, before someone else found us, before I passed out, before I died . . .

She pulled again, and the pain disappeared, replaced with a sudden cold. That was a bad sign, I knew. With my last moments of consciousness, I pushed the book into Jaeri's hands.

"For the king," I mumbled. "Tell him that it's a gift from Jalina, from Casmhe. No, from Sharme. Tell him that my mother's name is Serine. Tell him . . . tell him that I know what happened in Puhrsa and that I trust him."

She clutched the book and nodded. She couldn't know how important it was, couldn't possibly remember my half-slurred message for the king in the face of so much death and chaos and emotional terror.

"Couldn't possibly . . ." I mumbled softly, drifting into unconsciousness.

And yet.

"I still can't believe you abandoned me," Elaise said.

"Abandoned us," Daine corrected. "I was just outside, remember?"

"Us," Elaise agreed. "That's right. And nearly got yourself killed running around alone."

The three of us rested side by side in identical beds on the second floor of Elaise's family home. The bottom had been given over as a makeshift infirmary, and we'd forced Elaise's brothers upstairs so that the nurses wouldn't have to walk all the way to the top floor to treat us. A fact that delighted Daine and Elaise immensely.

"I wasn't alone," I reminded them. "I had a princess to protect me."

"Romantic," Daine said.

"She's twelve."

"Much less romantic," he admitted. "She mention any older sisters?"

Elaise threw a pillow at him. He grinned and made a show of placing it behind his head.

"Not that I need any details . . ." Daine began. Elaise and I traded a look. Daine always said that when he was about to ask something intrusive. "But was it worth it? Running around and almost dying? Because I distinctly remember suggesting a vacation to the coast, and I would hate to think that we gave that up for something . . . less than worthwhile."

"I'm not sure," I said. "I think so, but we probably won't find out for a long time. If we ever find out."

"That's . . . unsatisfying to hear."

"Imagine how we feel," I said.

Rahad came upstairs at that moment with a tray of almond-crusted pastries from the bakery down the road. As the only uninjured member of the group, Rahad served as our envoy to the outside world. He left once a day to gather rumors from around the city and bring them back to us, along with whatever treats we asked for. He passed out his latest haul—keeping, as always, two for himself—and gave us the latest news around a mouthful of flaky bread.

"They're calling it an assassination attempt," Rahad said. "Which is true enough, but they won't say who did it. Most witnesses agree on the details, as crazy as they sound. Ghosts running through the palace attacking people, with at least a hundred dead. Everyone knows *something* happened, but the king won't say what, and neither will the Order, so everyone's inventing their own stories."

"Not that I need every last specific individual detail," Daine began.

Elaise sighed and started looking for another pillow.

"But is anyone going to find it suspicious that all this happened the day after you two arrived in the city? Or, say, an hour after you walked into the palace?"

"They might," I admitted. "But it doesn't sound like the people who matter are in the mood to confirm or deny anything, so I wouldn't worry about it."

"So we're just . . . waiting to see what happens next?"

"That's right," I said, smiling. After the year we'd had, sitting around and waiting for something to happen sounded like the two most delightful things in the world.

Two weeks went by with no word from the castle, and no one from the Order came by to check on us either. Our injuries had mostly healed, and though I wouldn't be self-sufficient for a while yet, I was well enough to travel with a group. Winter hadn't yet set in, but it would be here any day now. If I was going to spend my time waiting, I wanted to do it somewhere else while I had the chance.

Elaise and Rahad offered to come with me, but Elaise's family forbade it outright, and I reminded Rahad that he had more important things to do. There were still two copies of Andza's book somewhere in the world, and I wanted to make sure they were exactly where we expected them to be. Besides that, I wanted some time alone to process everything that had happened.

I found a caravan headed for Sharme and bought passage aboard a merchant's wagon. I'm sure his family thought I was quite insane. The task, I think, had kept me afloat. It had taken everything from me, but the enormity of it had given me something to lean on. Now that it was gone, I had nothing to sustain me. I was just a stupid child far from home, crying in the back of a covered wagon. Crying for Elaise, for Aian, for Andza. For my own incomplete childhood, or Rahad's, or even Jaeri's. For the parents we would never know. I cried for the cruel, pointless waste that the world seemed to make of everyone and everything.

The caravan dropped me off at the Library at sunset on the first day of winter. I'd gotten so thin that I needed two coats to stay warm. I stopped at my favorite café halfway up the hill to rest and get something hot to drink, but the proprietor didn't recognize me. Glancing at my reflection in the window, I hardly recognized myself.

My room had been kept for me, though not kept clean. The smell of dust greeted me when I walked in. I took in the familiar sights: my bed, my window, my bookshelves, the desk in the corner with its rows of pencils and inks. There, atop the desk, sat a small parcel wrapped in brown parchment. I crossed the room and lifted it. A small mark in the top corner bore the symbol of a royal courier.

I opened it reverently. I hadn't expected to feel its weight ever again. It was Andza's book, whole and undamaged. A slip of paper fell out of it and onto the floor. Though I'd never seen the handwriting, it was clear who wrote it.

Give me seven years.

We spent our time well, I think.

Elaise used her background in languages to become an ambassador, and her family's reputation as high-end wine producers gave her a second means of access to some of Kerra's most influential families. Most of the descriptions of Kyrede's "miracles" in Lletra come from eyewitness accounts she collected. She also began writing her most famous work, *On Two Battlefields*, which covers the second half of Ferrec's life, and her transition from soldier to ruler to widow. Many of the point-of-view chapters in Lletra are based on excerpts from that work.

Rahad, meanwhile, tried to trace Kyrede's steps.

Beginning in Lletra and working his way south, his methods were almost too insidious to mention. He started by "solving" the mystery of Jurald's death, which had completely stumped the local constables. Given his understanding of the events of the murder, his unique knowledge of Jurald's true identity, and a description of Kyrede that I'd given him, he was able to fabricate a connection between the heretic that attempted to assassinate the king and this seemingly unrelated victim, who turned out to be the Prior of Whitethrush Monastery.

The Order politely denied the possibility, until Rahad mentioned Kyrede's name. Then their denials became heated. When they threatened charges of heresy and possible damnation in response to a continued investigation, that only impressed the local officials more.

Over time, Rahad was given more unsolvable cases to tackle. Many of these cases stretched back several years and involved the deaths of one or more unidentified victims, usually alongside other mysterious disappearances. Comparing those to the stories in Andza's book, we were able to paint a picture of Kyrede's life, his unhealthy fanaticism, and his eventual decline into insanity.

The character of Jurald, unfortunately, is mostly a product of my imagination.

We know that there was a man named Jurald who served as the Prior of Whitethrush Monastery. We also know that he had a connection to Kyrede and that he was present for the events I described in and north of Barste. We know almost nothing else.

Given the lack of detail surrounding his life, I've tried to treat him kindly.

As for Andza and Reia, those two remain a mystery, even to me. I haven't spoken to either of them since the day we walked away from Puhrsa, but I wish them peace in whatever quiet lives they've chosen for themselves.

King Sethric, as we know, did not go peacefully.

Seven years after the events in Lletra, copies of Andza's book appeared in bookstores and libraries throughout the capital. Over six hundred copies in total, printed and distributed in secret for years before being released on the same day.

The effect was devastating. In his prime, Sethric might have survived the book's publication, but years of scandal and misrule had ruined him. Ministers held power in Traste by then, and they had little cause to support an unpopular figurehead. The Kerran Order of Goodly Works, still in an awkward position after Kyrede's attack in Lletra, saw an opportunity to even the power imbalance and ordered his arrest.

From there, the story gets complicated.

Many of Queen Ferrec's children spent their royal allowances on what you'd expect: food, wine, gambling, and other vices. But a few were wise enough to consolidate their power early. Though law and custom limited the size of their households to five hundred people, these households operated as miniature kingdoms in their own right, traveling from place to place to uphold the law, defend the innocent, and generally serve the public good.

Even among these few, Princess Jaeri distinguished herself. Some point to her innate grasp of leadership, of her ability to command hardened soldiers and veteran bureaucrats with equal skill. Other historians commend her for her political foresight, her boundless charisma, or her unflagging determination in the face of obstacles. Whatever the case, she seemed a natural choice for the crown, and many waited eagerly for the day when she would wear it.

When news of Sethric's arrest reached her, she immediately broke camp and marched for Traste. On the way, she gathered any allies that lay in her path. Though she sent messengers ahead to assure everyone that she only intended to keep peace in the city, the idea of thousands of armed soldiers marching on the capital made the ministers uneasy.

Some insisted on executing the king straightaway and barring the gates against a siege. Others argued for allowing Jaeri to speak at her father's trial, but only on the condition that her followers camped twenty miles outside the city. All of them feared a return to the old ways, with half a dozen warlords vying for a renewed throne and a new crop of ministers raised from the ranks of mercenaries and war criminals.

King Sethric settled the debate for them. The day Jaeri arrived, he attempted to escape from his rooms in the castle. The attempt failed miserably and ended with him being hacked apart by the very guards he'd bribed to release him. Instead of speaking at his trial, Jaeri arrived at the capital with a force of six thousand troops just in time for her father's funeral.

And her own coronation, of course.

On her first day as queen, Jaeri took the stage in front of thousands. She promised a peaceful rule, an end to war, and support for the decentralized government the people had created, one where the crown acted as a servant to the realm, not the beginning and end of it. She spoke of the responsibilities held by those in power and the orphans they made when they abandoned those responsibilities—pointed reminders that she'd lived on both sides of that line.

She didn't mention her parents. She didn't have to. At age nineteen, she'd outlived three of them, along with a host of brothers, sisters, dear friends, and comrades in arms. They stood at her side every time she spoke of the losses we'd endured or asked us to consider the world our loved ones would have wanted us to live in. They followed her as she descended from the stage and walked the lonely path back to the castle, memories trailing behind her like a cloak.

Did they plan it between them? That's the question I find myself coming back to, years later.

Sethric knew the day his rule would end. He knew which guards would be there to arrest him, which players would move to support him or speak against him when the news broke. He spent seven years building the system that would replace him, surrendering power and influence with each staged scandal. Did he choose his successor as well? And if so, how many details did he share with her while he had the chance?

It's possible that Jaeri just happened to be in the right place at the right time. Close enough to reach the capital before her father's trial, but far enough to gather allies along the way. It's an odd coincidence that Sethric's failed escape happened an hour before Jaeri reached the city, that she appeared at the gates the very minute the bells announced his death, but stranger things have happened. And if her public image rose as her father's fell, isn't that always the way of things? The young replace the old, and the future always shines brighter than the past.

I can only speculate, but I will say this. Her coronation speech sounded remarkably well-rehearsed.

Other historians will have to answer these questions. All I can offer you are the few details I remember and my apologies for not paying better attention at the time. But it's hard to know what to look for and impossible to guess which details will matter decades later.

Besides, I had my own affairs to settle at the time.

EPILOGUE

I boarded a ship to Jhendi on the first day of spring, six months after the events in Lletra, a little over three years since the day Andza walked into our shop and changed my life forever.

I'd exchanged a few letters with my father since he left Casmhe but had never been to see him, and since I'd already decided to put off my studies for the spring, it seemed like the perfect time for a visit. He wasn't expecting me, so I had no one to collect me once we made port, but the idea of finding my way through a strange city based on a hand-sketched map and a vague description of his neighborhood didn't scare me as much as it would have a year ago.

We docked on the west side of the north island, so I had to take a short ferry south to reach the part of town where my father lived. As we glided slowly across the bay, I could see the jumbled stacks of buildings that formed the city itself, and behind those, the endless rows of low mountains and patches of dense jungle that formed Jhendi's sparsely populated mainland.

My father's new shop sat at the end of a wide alley, not far from the pier. Some part of me expected everything to look the same, so I was shocked to see how much had changed. The window display held toy sailboats and paper kites instead of colored glassware, the counter stood on the opposite side of the room, and the entire back half of the shop had been given over to a small indoor restaurant, with an open kitchen and a scattered handful of two-person tables.

A woman stood behind the counter. My height, perhaps a little shorter, with brown eyes and long black hair that she'd tied back with a colorful bit of cloth. She flinched when she saw me, but that was understandable. I'd had a chance to brace for this. She hadn't.

"We're closing soon," she said, eyeing me but pretending not to. "And the restaurant won't be open for another hour."

"That's fine," I said, idly browsing the shelves. "I don't have anywhere else to be."

I made my way to the back of the store and sat down at one of the tables. She didn't follow, and I didn't mind. We were going to have to face each other sooner or later, and it felt good to have a chance to rest my feet after walking all day. Two more people came in to look at one of the sailboats, paid, and left. The sun dipped another half hour toward the sea. Eventually I heard someone walking toward me.

She'd changed her face. Only slightly, but the effect made her look younger. Thirty, rather than forty. Too young to be the person I knew she was. She'd lightened her skin as well. It sat a shade closer to native Jhendi, and I suspected it would shift again every time I looked away for more than a minute.

"Can I get you something to drink?" she asked. Even her accent sounded different.

"Anything you like," I said simply. "But bring two glasses. We have a few things to talk about."

She stood still for a heartbeat. Then she nodded. I waited as she walked to the front of the shop and turned the lock, then walked back behind the kitchen counter to grab two glasses and a bottle of wine. She set them between us and poured a generous serving into each. Then she sat across from me, hands in her lap, eyes down. The doomed prisoner, awaiting judgment.

"The truth is," I began, "I've rehearsed this conversation so many times that I no longer have any words for it. None. And I don't suppose you do either."

She shook her head. "How much do you already know?"

"I have all the facts and dates," I said. "I just want to understand why."

"Then you know about the cave," she began. "Our mother sheltered us from the worst of it, but she had two daughters to protect, and the horror of it broke her. She never said anything, but I knew she resented us for what she had to do to protect us. I saw the love turn to hatred in her eyes." She looked at me, tears falling. "I knew someone would come for me one day, and I never wanted to be in a position where I had to choose between my safety and yours. I couldn't trust myself with that. Your father argued, of course, but I was determined."

"So why stay?"

"Because I wanted to see you grow up. I wanted to see you live in the world I fought for." She wiped a line of tears away with the back of her hand. "I'm sorry. I know it's far too late for that, but there it is."

"There it is," I agreed.

But what was I supposed to do with it, now that I'd heard it?

Five years ago, if she'd walked into our shop and told the same story, I'd have forgiven her on the spot. I'd have rushed into her arms and placed all my trust in someone who had left me before. Thanks to Andza, I had a sense of how much the past weighed, and I knew it was too heavy to fit into a single apology. But I also knew what it meant to be haunted by the past, to wake up every day next to a ghost of your own making.

I didn't want that future for either of us. I had to believe we were all strong enough to face the truth.

"Whatever your reasons," I said, "they don't change what's going to happen next. From now on, I'm not going to hide anything from my father, and I'm not going to let him hide anything from me. So you can just . . . be whoever you need to be. If you want to go back to being Miss Talia, or invent some entirely new person, you can. I survived seventeen years without a mother. I can survive a few more."

She flinched as if I'd hit her, and I let my words sink in for a long moment.

"Or," I said, taking a breath, "you can go back to being Serine. I don't know what will happen if you do. I have no idea what that world looks like. But if you want to try living in it, then so do I."

She didn't speak for a long time. Then she nodded. "Okay," she whispered. "More than fair."

We finished our drinks in silence. Then, because my father still wasn't back, we stood and started readying the restaurant for the evening meal. We didn't talk as we worked, even when she showed me where to find the tablecloths or how to cut the stems for the flowers on the tables. Whatever hung between us, it was a delicate thing, too new to sustain the weight of anything we might say. Like a newly opened seed, offering its first roots to the soil.

Who could say what might grow?

THE END

ACKNOWLEDGMENTS

This story took a long time to write, and I couldn't have done it without support along the way.

Many thanks to my friend and fellow writer Sam Wappel. Sam and I met at a writing group over a decade ago, and we've been sharing work with one another ever since. Here's to another hundred years in the trenches, man.

Sam also deserves a share of the credit for introducing me to Tricia Aurand, whose thorough analysis of theme and plot added some much-needed focus to the later drafts. I spent long hours poring over Tricia's notes, and I'm a better writer for doing so.

Speaking of thorough, Valerie Gwynn of Pen Gwynn Editing has an attention to detail that's nothing short of incredible. Her careful eye prevented a (frankly embarrassing) number of mistakes from making it into the final draft, and her kind words and encouragement were just as valuable.

Thanks to Bruce Brenneise for the best cover art a guy could ask for, and for letting me nerd out about Dutch landscape painters.

Thanks to Liz Mrofka at What If? Publishing for answering my endless list of questions and guiding me through the dark and forbidding landscape of-self publishing.

Finally, and most of all, thanks to my wife and best friend Sarah. For reading my stuff before there was anything worth reading. For the life we've built together. For twenty years of love and support in this and everything else.

ABOUT THE AUTHOR

 J. Kyle Turner lives in Northern Colorado with his wife and a very handsome cat. Check out more of his writing at: jkyleturner.com.